Prologue

Four Years Ago

Perry pared the gloves after sparring class, each still hot and heavy. But he'd grown immune to the clawing stench of sweat over the years. Liked it, even.

Thursday nights were his favourite – the special kids. But these kids really were different – different to all the other cocky little sods who came for a quick-fix lesson on how to *spark someone out*. See, boxing was about control, respect, discipline – the exact opposite if truth be told. And although the Thursday night kids struggled with the moves, each had more heart than all the other wee shites put together.

'Night, night Perry.' Josh patted Perry on the back, shifting from one rigid leg to the other as if he had no knee joints.

'Night buddy. Same time next week?' Perry began using the mismatched gloves to rain a flurry of blows around Josh's stomach, none of which landed.

Dodging each of them a second or two too late, Josh smiled, his big green eyes fixed on the gloves, awaiting the next jab he wouldn't be able to catch. 'You watching *Raw* tonight Perry? Braun Strowman is fighting.' A set of puny arms almost twanged when they flexed. 'Rooooaaaarrrr!'

'Dude! What did I tell you?' Perry messed Josh's shower-damp shock of dirty blond curls. 'It's all fake. All girly hitting! Boxing's where it's at. Now, that's a *real* sport.'

'No! It is real, Perry! You're just saying that because you're jealous you're not a wrestler.'

Perry freed a deep booming laugh, just like he did every week when they had the same conversation. 'Oh, they couldn't handle me, Josh. I'd take big Braun and I'd give him a one, a one-two, a one-two-three…' Shadow-boxing a circle around the boy, Perry's chin-length dreads whipped with every snap of his wrist. 'Uppercut. Knockout!'

Two over-sized trainers scuffed arcs in the concrete as Josh tried to catch-up. 'No! No! You couldn't. He's too big!'

'Right! Come on trouble!' Josh's mum called from the door. 'I think you've annoyed Perry enough for one week.'

'Oh, he's fine Jill. Always a joy.' He laid a heavy hand on Josh's shoulder, all sinew and bone. 'See you next week, mate.' *I hope.*

Josh skipped away before turning to give one last flappy wave. Then, he was gone. Perry continued to stare as the door squeaked painfully on its hinges, his smile dying with every sway. Although he'd been expecting nothing else, the buzz of the phone caused his heart to lodge in his throat.

10PM SAME PLACE

He felt the moisture in his mouth congeal to a chalky paste. As expected, the instruction was brutally simple, but he read it a few more times regardless. Only the car alarm wailing somewhere nearby broke his glare from the screen, his breath resuming when he realized it wasn't his. Still, Perry quickly snatched his keys from the counter and turned to give the gym one last long look. He flicked the lights, stealing the shine from the brass bell and wall of trophies.

Jailbird

JD Horner

For you.

Fly high.

Some birds are not meant to be caged, that's all. Their feathers are too bright, their songs too sweet and wild. So you let them go, or when you open the cage to feed them they somehow fly out past you. And the part of you that knows it was wrong to imprison them in the first place rejoices, but still, the place where you live is that much more drab and empty for their departure.

Stephen King – *The Shawshank Redemption.*

Jailbird

If only she'd told him sooner, he thought as he bolted the last padlock. He could have played it differently, worked out a plan, a *legit* plan. A little snigger ran away from him when he recalled how he thought Mel was having an affair. When she finally confessed why she had been working double shifts at the restaurant, he only wished she was. But it was debt. A big debt. The bailiff kind of debt.

Perry left the old life years ago. Didn't want to end up like the old man – banged up to rot the rest of his life away. And Mel, she was the one who turned his world around, or rather, she was the one who made him want to. So, he got himself sorted. Got a job coaching at his brother's gym and a lovely flat on the South Side. Just one-bedroomed mind you, but it was enough. Life was good (obviously, the *don't speak too soon* kind of good).

Simple, he'd thought. One quick job. In and out. And it had been easy, *too* easy, to make that phone call. But there wasn't just him to consider, not now Mel was seven months pregnant. This would be a one-time thing.

Like he used to, he'd picked up the load in the early hours from a derelict shipbuilding warehouse in Leith. Funnily enough, he never saw a soul - you never did on the higher end of the production line. Yet he could feel the eyes stalk his every move (and not those of the colony of pigeons cooing from the shit-covered girders). As always, the batch was on the third rust-riveted tank on the top floor gallery. That part, at least, went smoothly.

Part two was to hold it for twenty hours before transporting the haul to the Unit for dispatch. The riskiest part. The nervous breakdown part.

But so far so good he thought as he checked the boot, lifting the felt base where five large cellophane wrapped packages lay wedged where the spare wheel should have been. Sighing, he covered them again and slammed the boot shut. Mel would bloody kill him if she ever found out. *But she won't find out, will she?*

3

Unlike his thoughts, the late-evening roads were eerily quiet, and he was vigilant to keep his twitchy foot to a credulous 33mph. Perry glanced in the rear-view mirror again. Only the smiley face of the number 9 bus ignited the blackness behind him. He pinched his lips between his fingers and reassured himself. *Nearly there, son. Nearly there.*

The car began winding through deserted industrial blocks, their metal grille eyes gawping, their roller-shutter mouths screaming, *God, what are you doing back here, Perry? Are you insane?* 'Yeah, I bloody must be,' he muttered as he turned off the radio.

It wasn't long before Perry spotted the familiar sign indicating the last turn to the unit – DOLAN'S WHEELER DEALERS. Even now, he scoffed at the irony of it. Dolan may as well have hung a neon arrow sign flashing *Get Your Smack Here!* Perry didn't know how he got away with it. Perry didn't *want* to know how he got away with it. He indicated and turned left.

The garages bordering the courtyard were locked and barred. All was dark save a single light which flared over a red shutter, the number 2 emblazoned across its ridges in stark white. Suddenly, the light flashed off and on, then once again as Perry coasted so close, his bumper almost kissed the corrugated steel. He killed the engine and felt the adrenaline burn through his veins. Someone walked over his grave, again and again, as he craned his neck to check out every window. *To think I used to love this feeling…*

After a few more steadying breaths, he cracked the door and took three loping strides to the boot. *The quicker this is over with the better,* he thought as he began to pile the bundles into the army-green holdall, the hydraulic clatter of winding metal somewhere in front. That sound was reassuringly familiar – the final hurdle, the handover. *Might even make it back in time for Game of Thrones* and he smiled when he thought of Mel waiting for him, curled up on the settee - a cup of tea in one hand, a gherkin sandwich

4

in the other. Back to his ordinary, boring, bloody wonderful life. Smiling at the thought, he slung the holdall over his shoulder. But just as his fingertips grazed the gaping boot door, a stampede of heavy boots began to shrink towards him from every direction.

'DO NOT FUCKING MOVE! DO *NOT* FUCKING MOVE! DROP THE BAG AND PLACE YOUR HANDS ON YOUR HEAD! *NOW!*

Ah, fuck!

Chapter One

Now

Charlotte rapped on the rippled glass, tugging her ponytail taught before straightening the bottom of her shirt in a series of sharp, irritated jerks.

Comicon! Can I go to bloody Comicon? She huffed for the umpteenth time, now positive that was to blame for her light-headedness. *So much for trying. So much for prioritizing. So much for acting like a bloody adult!* She really should have learnt by now – DO NOT SPEAK TOO SOON! Charlotte sucked at her cheeks till they collapsed when she recalled telling Greg he was a star for taking on some extra shifts at the housing department. That she was proud! Ha! To think, she had thought it might even be for that weekend in Paris to visit the museums. Or dare she say, a bit extra towards the deposit for a business premises? Maybe, even, to begin the baby fund? But no! It was to go to fucking Comicon…in fucking Birmingham!

A reply came in the form of a distant yet cheery, 'Come in!'

Charlotte let out her last grumpy huff then entered. She made her way to the information wall opposite, letting the familiar fusty aroma of the past neutralize.

'Evening boss,' she said as she checked the whiteboard, smudged with swirly grey layers of erased days. Charlotte really liked her Custodial Manager, Mr Miller. Although he was old-school, he treated the prisoners with respect. Had it back in abundance too (unlike her Supervising Officer Kevin Riggs). No, Kev was a whole other kettle of fish.

'Hi, Charlotte. How're things with you?' he asked, pushing his half-moon glasses up the crooked nose still partially buried in a pile of papers.

'Good Boss, thanks. Just checking how our newbie got on today.' Charlotte's eyes skimmed the board. No red writing. No double under-scoring. No starring of names. For the first time that day, her shoulders dropped an inch or two.

Mr Miller griped as he freed himself from behind the desk propped steady with an old broadsheet and hobbled over to meet her. He'd told her a long while back that his right knee was nothing more than a crumbly chunk of Lancashire cheese after a decade in the Parachute Regiment. It was a powerful image and she tried not to imagine it…or smell it.

'Well,' he sighed as he rested his hands on the back of the chair beside her, 'he's been very quiet. Stuck to Amos' side all day. The wing is on lock-down. Powell and Morrison called in sick…*again*.' He raised an eyebrow of unspoken understanding which Charlotte mirrored: the regular duvet-day takers. 'When the night shift starts, we'll let the inmates out for an hour or two before bed. You can check for yourself then.'

'Oh, good. I'm sure he'll find his feet soon enough.' She turned to him and folded her arms as the idea struck. 'You know, if you're short staffed, just give me a shout. If I've got nothing on, I could do a double shift?' There was far too much fervour in her voice for someone offering to do a double shift. But anything, even spending her days with a load of category A prisoners, seemed better than watching Greg lose himself in his virtual world instead of living with her in the real one.

Mr Miller's muted blue eyes creased at the corners as he folded back into his seat. 'Everything okay Charlotte?'

'Oh, yeah! I'm good. Just saving up the pennies for Christmas, you know…'

'Hm,' was the unconvinced reply, especially since it was over 3 months till then. He signed the last page of the booklet before grabbing another. 'I'll keep that in mind. Thanks, Charlotte.'

'No probs. I'm gonna grab a cuppa before shift starts. Do you want one?'

'Oh, I could murder a strong coffee, if you excuse the pun,' he drawled as his eyes screwed over the contents.

The staff room already looked like some sort of penguin colony even though it was still half an hour before the start of shift. Charlotte was smacked with a whiff of Maureen's famous mince and tatties. *Ah…That explains it then*, she thought, feeling her mouth water and wishing she hadn't brought a tuna sandwich for dinner. 'Excuse, Dom,' she said, dipping her knees to slide under the bulbous stomach blocking half the doorway.

'Sorry Charlotte,' he whined, his voice oscillating as if thrown back to adolescence. He stepped back, wiping a tear from his cheek.

'Somebody's giddy,' she tittered over her shoulder, a tad confused. From the corner of her eye, she spotted the hand Pete brandished at her. Jim followed it up with a beckoning nudge of the head. As she squeezed and shimmied between the obstacle course of occupied chairs and tables, Charlotte noticed that everyone was sniggering and laughing. Even Big Tina's puckered cat's arse of a mouth was slack for once. A smile began to tug at the corner of hers.

Charlotte fixed her hands on the table and leaned low. 'Right you two. What've you done?' Half chastising, half amused, her eyes ping-ponged from one to the other.

'Us? Oh, it's no doon tae us this time!' Jim flattened the thick grey moustache which buried everything snugly from his nostrils to his bottom lip. He fanned his hand of cards.

'*What's* not down to you?'

After years of working with the pair, she knew only too well what mischief they were capable of. Poor Simon Degning had been off for a fortnight with nervous exhaustion after he was asked to accompany Pete in wheeling a dead body to the morgue. Simon was the one who nearly died when the 'body' sat up and wailed. No matter how many times Jim apologized, he couldn't stop the screaming.

'Don't…suppose…you've seen…Kev yet?' Pete managed between spurts, a Celtic mug held close to his mouth but never quite reaching it.

'No. Why?'

'Well, between last night's shift and tonight's,' Jim faltered into a fit of wheezy laughs as he put down two cards and picked up another, 'he looks like he's hid a fortnight in Marbella!'

Pete's hand finally gave the wobble it had been threatening, sloshing his steaming tea over the edge. 'Ah! Ya bastard!' he cried, shaking his hand dry. He sucked his lips to his teeth as he checked the scald.

'What? Noooo! He's not had a fake tan, has he?' Charlotte paused, the knot of her tie only half-way to her throat.

'A don't know if a wid call it a *tan*…' Jim oozed, twirling the side of his moustache now. And it was a very handsome moustache. Very *Magnum PI*. He had eyebrows to match.

Between blowing his bright pink fingers, Pete laughed. 'His…His face is the same colour as his hair! Know whit a mean?' He regularly finished his speech off with that question. Charlotte thought it a sort of speech impediment given he was quite a nervous soul. He lifted his cool nerdy glasses to mop his cheeks with his cuff. 'He could be Morph's ginger twin. Know whit a mean?'

Charlotte whizzed the knot to her neck, tucked the tail into her trousers and grinned widely. 'Oh, I just need to make the boss a coffee then I'll come right back for the briefing. This I cannot miss!'

It wasn't long before Kevin entered with his head angled down, paying more attention than usual to the clipboard in his blotchy orange fingers (chocolate brown where they fused with the hand). A series of soft coughs and clearing throats hushed the room and Charlotte gnawed harder at the knobbly bit at the side of her mouth.

At last, lifting his whiter than normal eyeballs, he cautiously surveyed the room. When they were met with the usual apathy, his back straightened. There followed a self-assured kick of his brows before he smiled to himself and got down to the business of the changeover. 'Right, it seems like it has been a relatively quiet day shift. Main issue – McGregor has been having a dirty protest in seg. It's been cleaned but, Rogers, Ambrose, I'll need you to keep checking that the glass is clear.' Kevin eyed them carefully, but the officers merely gave the grumbled protest expected to marry with such a task. *Clatty bastard.*

Instantly, his pathetically narrow shoulders levelled. 'Andrews is beginning to display more agitated behaviours. He's due for release next week. As you all know, he's been here a long time and feels more secure on this side of the bars. Just keep it in mind that he might try to escalate things in order to stay.' An understanding mutter trickled across the room.

Kevin finished his briefing standing a little taller, his voice a little deeper, feeling a lot cooler with the *Saint Tropez* his little sister had practised on him for her *Hair and Beauty* finals. 'Any other AOB's before we begin?'

Charlotte held her breath and felt her joints seize as Jim raised his hand.

'Aye, Kev. We aw jist wanted tae say,' and his hand swept around to show how he spoke for everyone, 'the loss of Dale Winton has affected us greatly and we all genuinely admire your tribute. The man was a born entertainer and true gent.' He raised his can of *Irn-Bru* and kept his voice sombre. 'To Dale.'

As Pete's mouthful of tea spurted across the table, Jim looked evidently pleased with his efforts as his shoulders bounced and eyes disappeared.

Kevin's eyes, on the other hand, were cartoon wide and, although no-one thought it possible, his cheeks even fierier. 'Fuck you, Jim,' he snarled, the clipboard lowering along with his dignity.

A gruff voice heckled from the pool table, 'Anyone fur a can a Tango?' The white ball cannoned into the triangle of dots and stripes with a loud clack. 'Heard they're cheap as chips in the canteen.'

The roaring laughter swelled, boisterous but good-humoured.

Suddenly, minus his cane for once, Mr Miller burst through the doors. His forehead and eyes crumpled as he jabbed a pair of glasses at them. 'Right you lot! Keep it bloody doon! You can hear you on the wing. The men are already pacing their cells like caged lions never mind you lot adding to it!'

Mr Miller's eyes flicked left, saving an extra chastising glare for Kevin. Her own cheeks now burning, Charlotte watched through her fingers as Mr Miller's face froze. Almost comedically, he did a double take and stepped back on his good leg. 'Whit the...?'

Puffs of air exploded in random bursts around the room. Tables were slapped, feet stamped on the insipid grey lino, and Mr Miller's eyes began to twinkle with amusement rather than chagrin. He dropped and shook his head as he turned for the door, whistling a jolly tune as he limped his way back down the corridor. Charlotte was sure it was the Oompa Loompa song.

The cells improved with the term of their inhabitants. Located nearer the staffroom and offices, the short-termers' cells were stark and clinical, the off-white brick embellished with only graffitied furniture and the odd topless pin-up. But the further down the cells unfurled, the more time there was to invest. Lamps, televisions and family pictures began to add a bit of life until you reached the far end of the strip – where the cells were a more permanent kind of home. Considering the length of his sentence, Amos' cell was more welcoming than most. It was her first port of call.

He lazed on the bottom bunk, the bendy desk light bestowing him a halo and spotlighting the book in his hand. With one eye closed, he read his copy of *The Lost Symbol*, his other double the size through the magnifying glass. His new roommate, Gary, lay slumped across the top bunk, just a pair of shell-shocked eyes engrossed in the TV.

'Evening gents.' Charlotte turned down the radio crackling interference in her ear.

'Miss Croft!' Amos boomed, followed by three deep troughs of a laugh. The magnifying glass dropped to the book. 'How are you this beautiful evening?'

'Wonderful as always, Amos. You okay?' It was a much more enthusiastic welcome than she was used to at home where all she'd receive was a perfunctory, 'Hi,' as Greg kept his eyes on the screen and focused on killing the enemy.

'Just fine, Miss Croft. Just fine.' He finished with a dazzling smile, sounding like he had just left the sunshine of the Caribbean last week instead of 40 years ago.

'You all right Gary? How'd the first night go?' She kept her tone ignorantly bright as if she wasn't the one who'd spent the whole night watching him cry under the scratchy grey blanket.

He pulled the shrivelled thumb from his mouth but kept his eyes on the screen, still wide and unblinking. 'Aye, no too bad, miss. Ta.' Gary's natural lankiness made him seem even more scrawny than most of the druggies who came to stay, the grey sweats extra baggy about his bones. *At least he'll have a chance to fatten up while he is here*, she thought.

'Good. First night, worst night.'

The small room became suddenly murkier. 'Evening. All well, Miss Croft?' His *evening* was spoken very differently from hers. Through the nose and suspicious. Always suspicious.

All three of them glared at the doorway where Kev stood: his hands behind his back, his chin high, his face scrubbed so hard it looked like it might bleed.

She was highly tempted to point out he'd missed his ears but why spoil what was sure to be a more entertaining shift? 'Fine, Riggs.' A brow raised to question what he wanted. Behind her, four startled eyes popped, trying to work out what the hell was amiss with his face.

'Good…Good,' he said like he didn't quite believe her. His eyes darted one more time around the room before his long legs scissored off to the next cell.

Arsehole. Charlotte shook her head at the empty space before turning back to the others.

Amos' legs slowly eased out on to the floor, his joints cracking him straight. 'Don't suppose there have been any hospital letters, Miss Croft?'

Charlotte hated giving him the bad news…again. 'Not today, Amos.' Her eyes wrinkled an apology. 'Tell you what, I'll chase it up in the morning again before I leave.'

'Oh, that would be great, Miss Croft. Thank you so much.' His head bobbed cheerfully as he set up two cups but used only one teabag.

Although the cell was in good spirits, she left silently cursing a few choice words under her breath. How long did Amos have to wait for his bloody op? Since she'd known him, he'd always had his nose buried in a

13

book. It was his escapism, his link to the outside world he would never get to see again (and not just because of the cataracts). Now, he was struggling to read the large print books she had brought, even with the use of a magnifying glass?

Whilst she mentally rehearsed the tongue lashing some poor sod was going to get in the morning, Charlotte leant over the metal rail and peered into the different levels of prison life. The night was unusually quiet: no sobbing newbies, no bust-ups at the pool table, no alarm sirens blaring from the shower block. More importantly, no signs of the Spice which had blighted the wings of every prison of late. And of all the drugs she had seen abused behind bars, she just didn't get this one.

You only had to follow the key phrases to find it: oot yer face, aff yer tits, mad wae it, buzzin'. And God only knew what you would find when you did. It could be anything from the terror in Ronny Pool's eyes as he screamed that his wall was crawling with tarantulas to the foam flowing from Big Jerry's mouth as his pin-sized pupils stared unblinking into a hellish abyss, a golden stain seeping through the grey marl of his sweatpants. But, by far, the most common was *The Zombie. Why would anyone on God's green Earth desire that privilege?*

Yeah, it had all been very quiet of late…

'Miss Croft!'

Charlotte's gaze slipped to the upper level to find Doug's big brown eyes gawping at her, his knuckles bleached around the mop handle.

'You better come quick. It's Davey. Aff his tits. Pish everywhere. A canny wake him.'

'Bollocks!' she growled as her heavy boots clanged up the metal stairs, two at a time. *I really am developing a bit of an unfortunate knack for this speaking too soon malarkey.*

Chapter Two

Muffling a yawn, Charlotte stood in the shadows and watched as the early morning sunlight made a start on chasing away the nightmares and demons. And like she did with most things in life, Charlotte saw the beauty in how the beams sifted through the skylights like someone reaching in from heaven, a sign of hope or a reminder there was a meaning to it all. It was the artist in her. Or rather, it's what drove the artist in her.

Only when the prisoners spilled out on to the landing with the tenors of an orchestra tuning, and only when each soul was accounted for (that part always brought a sigh of relief or despair), did Charlotte turn for the office. But even after the call was finished, she sat glaring at the receiver in her hand after chasing things up with a guy who sounded as cheery as Ross from *Friends* after his second divorce. He'd made the huge mistake of informing her, 'We've no got a referral fur an Amos Gladstone.'

'What a twa…' she sniped just as a gust of air grazed her face.

'Morning Charlotte. You not left yet?'

Jolting straight, Charlotte looked up to find a freshly shaven Mr Miller, his salt and pepper hair combed slickly back. She lay the phone back on its cradle and watched him limp to the filing cabinet. He unlocked the top drawer and began to sprint his fingers along the packed rows of green cardboard sleeves.

Charlotte forced the lid on top of her pen before it found another job to delay home time. 'Not yet, Mr Miller. Was just chasing up the hospital for Amos. He's really struggling. But they've booked him in next week so at least that's something.' She began removing her radio before it asked her to stay behind and help in some way too.

Snatching out a leaf, Mr Miller's eyes scanned the contents more closely as he mumbled, 'You're a good soul, Charlotte Croft.'

Her pale skin blushed as she tried several times to slot the pen into the top pocket of her shirt. 'Erm, Mr Miller, is it okay if I accompany him along with Jim? We're both back on days next week. I would just like to see it through…'

'Of course, yeah. Just make sure it's marked in the diary…and let Kevin know! Don't want him being so stressed that he ends up getting a tattoo or his knob pierced.' Mr Miller shook his head and grunted, 'Bloody fake tan. What was he thinking?'

For once, Charlotte didn't bother checking the kitchen or lounge when she got back to the flat (purely to avoid being pissed-off into alertness by the bowled over beer cans, coiled socks and mountain of pizza crusts sure to be awaiting her). Instead, she left a trail of bags and boots all the way to the bedroom where she fell into bed and pulled the quilt over her with a gratified shiver.

'What the…?' she grunted after only a few seconds, lifting her left butt-cheek to fumble for the rumpled clump of something bulging beneath her. Her hand surfaced clutching a pair of Greg's dirty boxers. 'Ew! Fuck's sake!' She ogled them for a second before tossing them towards the laundry basket. She missed. *I will not get pissed off. I will not get pissed off.* Shaking her head, she turned to set the radio alarm only to find a hastily written note on the torn corner of a manila envelope.

'Oh, what the hell now?'

Greg rarely left notes, but when he did, they were usually bad news: *Your Auntie Liz has had a stroke; The toilet's blocked and I can't fix it; I can't make the exhibit today. We're short staffed.*

I will __not__ get pissed-off. I'm really going to try not to get pissed off. Taking a deep breath, she began to read it:

Adam called. He says he's going to be staying in London on business soon. Asked if you wanted to come for a visit. Said for you to give him a call when you're up.
Love you. See you tonight. G x

Five hours later, she sprung up, stuffed her feet into her well-worn slippers and headed for the kitchen, throwing Greg's dirty boxers and odd socks in the washing basket as she passed. It was hard to ignore the burnt pot steeping in the sink and the acrid smell of burnt beans which hung in the air, but she gave it a go anyway. Instead, Charlotte made herself a coffee, totted up the time difference with her fingers and began to dial when she realized Adam would be up and about.

'All right, Wee Yin? How's it going?' His words were so bouncy and bright, she could tell he was grinning as much as her.

Although she heard him loud and clear, the mere distance and rank of the call caused Charlotte to plug a finger into her ear. 'Hiya! I'm good! How are you?'

'All good here. You still on nights then?' She could tell he wasn't smiling anymore.

'Yeah. Last one tonight though, thank the Lord! So, you're coming to London?'

'Sure am! There might be some scope for me to join the practice on your side of the Atlantic for a while.'

'Really? Oh, Adam! That would be amazing!'

'But don't get your hopes up just yet Charlotte!'

Too late! Charlotte had already leapt to her feet and was pacing parallel to the worktop. She lifted each of the six teaspoons Greg had used to make each of his six cups of tea in her absence. Laying them in the Belfast sink like they were made of the most fragile crystal, she slid the sash up gently, unable to bear the smell any longer.

'It's only a possibility. The firm needs someone experienced in Scottish criminal law to help with a particularly complex case in Glasgow. But that's a *might* Charlotte!'

Oh, but it was so much more than that. 'I know, I know,' she whined, her heart already set. 'So, when are you here?'

'The 18th to the 20th. I've got a meeting with one of the partners in London. I've booked a room at the Tower Bridge hotel. Had an idea you might want to come?'

Charlotte's slippers quickly scuffed across the tiles to the Prince calendar on the cork noticeboard, skimming her finger across the numbered squares until it landed on the weekend highlighted in bright green. 'Yes! It's my weekend off!'

'I know. I already checked with Dickhead.'

'Adam!' Her nose wrinkled.

'Sorry.' She knew he wasn't. Not when *Dickhead* was Adam's reference of choice when it came to Greg. 'Anyway, I'll book you a flight early Saturday morning and a return late on Sunday if that's okay?'

'A flight?' Her words sored an octave or two, her head already shaking in refusal. 'It's too expensive. Just book me a train.'

'*No* Charlotte! The flight is far quicker…and safer. By the time you got here by train, most of the day would be wasted.' When she said nothing, he tried to make that option sound even more appealing. 'Don't worry Charlotte! You'll arrive in style and the plane is always more reliable than the train service.'

'God sssake, Adam! Fine!' she snapped before trying to forget that small, extremely horrendous part.

Charlotte stopped dancing for a second to taste a bit of the curry sauce. 'Mmmm.' She closed her eyes to savour it as a buzz of excitement kept her mood buoyant. *Adam. London. Adam in London. With me!* The front door slammed closed and she tried to ignore the first sinking niggle as Greg's bag crashed to the floor instead of being hooked on the BAG peg. *It's fine. Relax. Put it on his 'things to do' list.*

'Hey,' Greg smiled, pecking her on the cheek. 'Smells great Charlotte. I'm famished.'

See, he does appreciate you! She tried to clasp the crest of the wave again. 'Won't be too much longer.'

From the corner of her eye, she recognized the familiar shaft of light ignite Greg's face as he pulled his first can of *Stella* from the fridge. All before he'd even taken his jacket off. This time, Charlotte couldn't ignore the second niggle as the other woman in their relationship made herself present. What's more, she had a funny feeling it was Stella who had an edge on her when it came to who Greg would choose to save in a fire.

Instead of dancing, she began to shuffle from one foot to the other, suddenly realizing why she wore holes in her slippers so quickly. 'Good day?' she asked, placing the lid back on to the pot with a thump. She let her nostril flare perish before turning to him.

'Same old, same old,' he replied over the hiss of the ring-pull. He took a large gulp and gave a long, satisfied gasp as he slumped on to a chair. 'Did you speak to Adam?'

'Yeah. I'm going to stay with him in London next weekend. I hope you don't mind?' She already knew the answer. She doubted he would even notice.

'Of course! It'll be good for you to catch up with him. I might ask

Bob over then. Get a bit of a battle going with some of the boys on the old *Call of Duty.*' Accompanying a rolling burp, he rubbed his hands together like he'd just come in from a blizzard. And instantly, like the lid which had begun to rattle at her back, Charlotte felt everything boil to the surface, everything she tried not to feel when they spent more than 5 minutes together.

Swallowing her lips, she lifted the lid, popping the simmering bubbles in rather aggressive loops of the wooden spoon. *What the hell's happened to you, Greg?* When they first met, he had as much ambition to be an artist as her. Now, he was contented with the life which was only supposed to be a temporary measure until they could get some finances behind them for *The Dream*. And in that one moment, even that one thing which made her hold on more than any other – the thought of a tiny set of fingers wrapping around one of hers – wasn't enough anymore. Not at the sacrifice of her own sanity.

The wooden spoon slammed hard against the worktop, spraying a deep mustard splattering of spicy sauce up the white-tiled splashback. 'Greg, sometimes I think you only walk vertically through fuckin' habit!'

Chapter Three

'Bloody…pain…in the…*arse*!' Charlotte growled as she fought with the jammed locker door. It released under a final, forceful yank, causing her to fall back a step. A few deep breaths later, she hung her jacket and checked her reflection in the mirror. 'Shit,' she gasped, lunging towards the pale face and raw eyes staring back at her. Her finger dabbed around the sockets as if it would magically erase the redness and frustration. *Pointless* she realized just as the black and gold flyer caught her eye. *An Evening with Eva White – Abstract Natural Wonders.* The bright yellow post-it note attached read:

Gone home. Banging migraine but wanted to give you this while I remembered. Let me know if you want tickets. My brother is a curator at the Burrell. Pete. X

Erm, I'll pass thanks! Another low growl was killed quickly with a Polo Mint. After twisting the top of the packet to a lethal foil spike, she slammed the door shut. Although, Pete's offer was *slightly* more tempting after her conversation with Greg. For once, Greg sat quietly and listened. Perhaps something in her monotony let him know she meant it this time (or at least, she was dangerously close to not giving a shit).

It was his reaction which caught her off guard. He *agreed* with her. They were in a rut of contentment. His term, not hers. He told her how much he loved her and that, when she was off the following day, they would sit down and start making plans to move forward. Yet, that's what had broken her. Here he was, at last, offering her the future they had worked so hard towards, but she found no solace in it. Because, what niggled her most, was the thought that she didn't want to move forward with *him* anymore.

Scraping her red curls back into a ponytail, Charlotte polished her eyes one last time and made her way to the staffroom.

'Hey, Charlotte!' Audrey called, a real tan glowing against her starched white shirt after a fortnight in Alicante. Her bronzed skin was enhanced by the baby pink lippy and (as always) matching baby pink nail varnish. Charlotte wondered what colour she would choose tomorrow. No two days were ever the same.

'Hiya,' Charlotte grinned but it felt odd like she was lifting 20kg dumbbells with a set of particularly flaccid muscles. Nevertheless, she was more than glad to see Audrey's pretty little face. Her partner in crime. Or rather, her partner in anti-crime.

They had worked the same rota for years after completing training together (of which Charlotte had only missed a couple of shifts after a bad case of gastroenteritis). Audrey, on the other hand, had much more time off due to the fact she was more accident prone than Mr Bump. To date, the list included: a fractured ankle from a stair fall, two black eyes and a nose realignment after a minor car crash, three cracked ribs from her bathroom slip in some ludicrous heels and a broken wrist from a pissed-up hen night at the roller disco.

'How was Spain? You look fab. Your tan is almost as good as Kev's,' Charlotte sniggered as she took a seat but kept her gaze trained on the murky, barred windows.

'Oh, it was great. The villa was beautiful.' Audrey stretched both golden arms out in front of her as if the sun was beaming above instead of a clinking fluorescent tube. 'Just long, hot days spent by the pool reading…and drinking cocktails. All a distant memory now though,' she finished with a grumble as she went over the list of duties in her hand. It broke the daydream, and when she gazed at Charlotte again, it was like she was only seeing her for the first time. Her eyes pinched, she tapped Charlotte's arm. 'You okay?'

'Oh, yeah. Fine. Didn't get much sleep though. They're still doing the roadworks right outside the bleedin' flat.' Charlotte couldn't share, not now when she was a feather's touch away from breaking. She pinned up her smile and tried to divert the focus from her. 'How's lover boy?'

It worked a treat. 'Oh, he's great.' Audrey's tan topped up in front of her eyes. She tutted when she noticed one of her acrylics were lifting at the cuticle. 'He's amazing. I mean, I'm beginning to believe he's…*The One*.'

His arms folded, Ben leant on the wall beside the dog racing sweepstakes and sponsor forms. With one foot planted on it like he was sunbathing vertically, he looked so slick, Charlotte hoped he might slide down it at any moment. In between speedy, open-mouthed chews of his gum, he mumbled something out the side of his mouth to Jim, setting both sets of shoulders joggling. Then, his smarmy smile grew. He winked at Audrey and her face blushed more. And Charlotte wanted to vomit.

A dull ache, surprisingly like period cramp, gnawed at the pit of her gut. There was just something about golden boy which didn't feel right. Ben started on the wing 6 months beforehand. He was perfectly charming and seemed like a great asset…at first. Gradually, Charlotte noticed him get friendlier with the prisoners, a bit too friendly. Particularly with the wrong type of inmates: the kingpins, the murderers, the drug dealers and gang leaders who were top in the hierarchy of power. Those prisoners Charlotte kept extra vigilant with. The ones she visited out of necessity, not choice.

'Wow!' Charlotte's eyes distended as she blew away the billow of clouds swirling from her mug. 'Never thought I'd hear you utter those words!'

Audrey had never been the settling down type. Fussy didn't touch the sides of it. So much so, she earned the reputation, and name, of *The Duchess*. But it turns out Charlotte was wrong. Ben appeared to have seduced Audrey as well as the inmates…and now Jim by the looks of it. Strangely, that was what irked her most given Jim was usually on the same wavelength as her.

'Me neither,' Audrey whispered, eddying the foamy coffee as she tried to lift the bubbles welded to the sides. 'I thought he would get on my tits after so much time alone together. But if anything…' She stopped for a moment, almost like she was checking her own logic before adding, 'I like him more. He's just so attentive and confident, you know, like he can hold his own. And the sex…'

Charlotte quickly bumped a shoulder against Audrey's to halt any elaboration. 'It's nice to see you so happy.' That part, at least, she meant.

'Aw, cheers Charlotte,' Audrey gushed, readjusting a Kirby at the side of her neat bun, a flush of rose adding more warmth to her cheeks.

Just then, Mr Miller's appearance silenced the room. He leant heavily on his cane, his knee appearing to give him more jip than usual. 'Right listen up, you lot! No Kevin tonight. So, Charlotte, you'll be in charge. Anything major, I'll be burning the midnight oil in the office, so just knock.' He peered at her over his glasses. She quickly nodded her agreement. 'Nothing interesting to report from the day shift. Our old friend Spice is worryingly quiet at the moment so keep on your toes. I've got a funny feeling it will make a reappearance soon enough. Let's make it a nice quiet one tonight, eh?' and with that, he left as abruptly as he entered.

Charlotte downed her coffee, feeling the familiar knot knit her intestines. It wasn't that the role was any harder than her own. In fact, she'd stepped in so many times, it was second nature. But it was the responsibility which weighed heavily, the fear that something would go wrong on her watch. Up till now, she'd been lucky, perhaps because things were a bit calmer and more organized when *she* was in charge.

A dull buzzer signalled the start of shift, the drone of which caused her teeth to rattle in her skull.

Firstly, she popped her head into cell 201 to check for the herby perfume of weed. 'Stephen, Mr Miller was wondering if you could move to kitchen duty tomorrow? Robbie sliced his finger earlier, so he won't be able to do it.'

Stephen ran his white-furred tongue along the Rizla and rolled it neatly to make a super-thin cigarette. 'Aye. Nae bother, Miss Croft.' He lit his rollup, wincing an eye shut as the smoke stung. 'Ad rether that than the laundry any day.'

When she was hit with the creamy fumes of plain, old *Golden Virginia*, she gave the metal door frame a spritely tap. 'Brilliant. Cheers Stephen. Much appreciated.' With a quick parting smile, she was on her way again.

This time, Amos was alone, watching (or at least listening) to an old re-run of *Only Fools and Horses*. As if it would help, he swivelled the metal loop on top to get rid of the snow.

'Hi, Amos. How's it goin'?' Charlotte slid her hands into her pockets and smiled. Always a smile for Amos.

'Ah. Miss Croft. Good. I'm good!' He nipped his cig out (as he did every time she came into his cell).

Old-school manners, she thought, *a rare commodity these days*. 'I've got some good news for you,' Charlotte said, stepping further into the room. Her hips pivoted from side to side, the surprise impatient and eager like a puppy on a short lead.

'I always like a bit of good news, Miss Croft!' Amos gestured to the plastic seat next to his.

Charlotte lifted the gardening magazine and laid it on her lap as she took its place. 'Well, I phoned the hospital this morning. You've got an appointment next Tuesday! Me and Jim will come with you.'

It wasn't exactly the response she'd been expecting when his smile faded, and his milky irises glazed to opal. 'Oh, Miss Croft. I can't even tell you…' He faltered, picking up and lighting his cigarette again. After a few wobbly-lipped puffs, he managed, 'You've made an old man very happy.'

'Oh, shush!' she chided gently, scratching a short nail along the face of Alan Titchmarsh who was grinning like he was glad for Amos too.

Amos eyed her for a moment. 'You know,' he said before dragging deeply on the cigarette till it sizzled, 'you're not meant for this place.'

Charlotte's hand stilled, her head sloping to the side as she tried to read his words. 'What do you mean?'

He looked at the picture of Perry pinned to the wall and straightened it a little. 'Doves aren't meant to be caged, Charlotte. This place,' he sighed, shaking his long, greying dreadlocks as he tapped his cigarette in the wonky ashtray made in pottery class, 'it's only getting worse. It wears on the *soul*. If you're not careful, you'll end up trapped here. You're meant for so much more than this.' His cigarette swept through the air, a lazy tail of smoke flowing behind it.

Amazing, she thought, how even this man appeared to know her better than Greg. 'I'm working on it, Amos. I'm working on it,' she semi-lied quietly. If she were being honest, she would have said, 'I've been thinking about it a lot lately.' But, even to her, it sounded pathetic. And now that her bottom lip was feeling rickety too, she got to her feet and turned to leave.

'Oh, and again Miss Croft, thank you.'

'No problem, Amos.' She left with her head down. Outside, her hands hooked over the rail and Charlotte tried to steady her breathing so it was safe to move on without the fat tears spilling.

But it caught her eye then, the unmistakable loping gate and shiny, shaved head of Ben across the landing. Unremarkable on its own but paired with the fact he was scurrying out of John Noble's cell followed by Gary, looking around shiftier than Fagin himself – Charlotte felt her hackles bristle as she straightened. Her tears quickly evaporated as she edged back from the barrier as the two split – Ben pacing towards the staff room, Gary downstairs to the pool table.

Charlotte picked up her pace as she by-passed the cells at the end of the strip. Ignoring the blazing argument in cell 229 over whether Nicola Sturgeon was *shagging material*, she looped straight round to John's cell instead. Another lifer who had certainly made himself at home in HMP Broadhurst, he had a cell to himself with every luxury anyone could wish for: PlayStation 4, flat screen TV, Sky, a somehow never-ending supply of teabags and cigarettes. With an awful stammer which had been known to worsen greatly in front of a jury, he was quite simply a nasty bastard.

'All right John?' There was no smile this time.

'Evening MMMiss Croft. How are y-y-yeh? Hear y-y-y-yer in charge t-t-tonight?' He completed another clue in the crossword, a restfulness about him as if he had been doing it all night.

'Oh, you know me, John. I get all the good jobs,' she breezed as her eyes scanned what looked like a 5-star rated *Airbnb* booking. It only took a few seconds for her to realize there was nothing to rouse her suspicions. She was immediately more suspicious.

Charlotte curled her fingers around the rail of the top bunk. 'All quiet tonight?'

His stubby digits scratched over the hemp leaf tattoo on his neck. 'A-A-All's quiet on the W-W-Western Front,' he said, followed by a gap-toothed smile which caused something with too many legs to scuttle over every inch of her skin.

'Great stuff. I'll bid you goodnight then,' she replied flippantly, her finger skimming across the desk like she was checking for dust. 'Harum-scarum.'

'Eh?' John blew, his foxlike eyes tapering.

'15 down. Cheerfully irresponsible. Harum-scarum.' After another slow glance around the cell, she headed out the door.

But she lingered on the landing outside, her narrowed eyes sweeping up the wing as Charlotte tried to calculate what she already knew didn't add up. Because she felt it in the air - an unspoken warning, an electric charge which made her skin prickle and her ears buzz much like the stimulated silence before the lightning strike. Something was coming. She had just begun praying that it wasn't on her watch when the emergency lockdown alarm wailed, and all hell broke loose.

Chapter Four

Through a swarm of bodies, literally ducking and diving for a change, Charlotte spotted the red light shrieking outside Amos' cell. 'Shit!' she gasped, breaking into a sprint. Her heart hammering in her ears, she burst through the audience blocking the doorway and froze. Amos was on the floor, his eyes fixed and still, the gardening magazine splayed at his side, Jim pumping at his chest.

'Jesus!' Her knees thudded on the concrete and on Jim's orders, she blew two breaths then kept going. When Jim tired, they swapped, and Charlotte tried to remember the song to her rhythm (*Nelly the Elephant? Staying alive? Another one bites the dust? Christ Almighty! Surely not!*) as a few more officers stole the light to spectate in a sombre silence from the doorway.

The only thing to break it was Jim's growls as they became more frantic in nature. 'Come on, Amos! Come *on*!'

Just as Jim was about to take over the compressions, two medics laden with bags and cases made their way into the cell with such a bizarre serenity, Charlotte couldn't make her mind up if it calmed or unsettled her more. Jim, panting hard and red in the face, held out a hand and hauled Charlotte to her feet. 'Come on, hen,' he said, resting his hand on her shoulder and steering her to the door.

With a strange sense of detachment, Charlotte's eyes flinched with every shock of the defibrillator. If there was such a thing as an out of body experience, she was having it as the very link between life and death itself became a tangible, zigzagging rope of light that she watched from a few miles above the roof. Only her eyes moved, willing the blink of his, the twitch of his finger. But after 20 minutes, the medics sat back on their heels and quietly agreed (with a resigned shake of the head and downwards smile) to call time. The wave of life levelled and bawled across the screen. Her shoulder sagged under Jim's hand as she glared at Amos just as the finishing credits of his program rolled. *Hookey Street…Hookey Street…Hookey Street…Dead? Dead. Dead!*

Surrounded by a chorus of sighs, Charlotte remained gawking until she felt a hand gently wrap around her arm, towing her back down to Earth. It took a second or two for her to recognize Mr Miller.

'All of you in the staffroom for a brew. Charlotte, Jim – you come with me.'

Mr Miller pointed wordlessly for them to sit before him, his face sober. 'Now, I need you both to tell me *exactly* what happened tonight.' Perching on his elbows, he entwined his fingers and bumped the white-knuckled fist repeatedly against his lips.

Jim rubbed two fingers firmly against his temple and Charlotte knew he was trying to keep his brain inside because hers was trying to escape too. 'It was Gary. He caught me in the corridor, aw peely-wally. A knew it wis somethin' bad, but a never for a second thought it would be Amos.' He flipped his head back and stared at the explosion of flaking paint shards on the roof. 'Fuck!'

'Something's not right,' Charlotte whispered to her knees, her voice not sounding like her own. It was gloopy like she'd swallowed a whole slab of *Galaxy*. 'I was only talking to Amos five minutes beforehand. I told him about his hospital appointment. He was…fine.' Her glower slipped from one to the other, her forehead cramped. 'We've all seen it a thousand times before. That was Spice. He was sober as a judge when I spoke to him and I

30

know he didn't touch the stuff!'

'Hm.' Mr Miller jarred a finger in the deep cleft on his chin. 'What happened when you spoke to him?'

'Nothing really.' Charlotte stared past him to the cock-eyed yearly planner on the wall as she replayed it. 'When I went in, he was having a cig but put it out. I told him about his appointment. I could see he was a bit emotional as he lit his fag right back up again. He said thank you, and I left.' She shrugged lightly, unable to make sense of it.

'Or maybe it wisnae his fag he lit back up?' Jim raked his hands through his coarse grey hair as if just toying with the notion.

'Gary! Gary fucking Hobbs!' Mr Miller blasted, crashing his palm to the desk with such force, everything jumped: stapler, the silver-framed photo of his wife and daughters, whole-punch, a golf mug, Charlotte. 'I bet the stupid wee *prick* has left a butt laced with Spice in the ashtray and poor Amos has lit it by accident!' Charlotte jumped again – she'd never heard him use the word *prick* before. It made it all the more brutal. 'Get him in here now, Jim. God help me keep my hands from wringing the wee bastard's neck!' He slammed the frame back in place as Charlotte watched the vein protruding from his forehead thicken and throb.

Jim marched from the office, his laughter lines now deeper with something dark, his stubby teeth partially bared. When the door thudded closed behind him, Charlotte turned back to Mr Miller and rubbed her lips together as she debated whether to release her suspicions or not. 'Mr Miller, there's more,' she added tentatively. 'When I left Amos, I spotted Ben leaving John Noble's cell followed closely by Gary. It all looked a bit…sus.'

Mr Miller's pen stopped writing the report mid-word.

It was too difficult to tell if he was shocked or pissed off, but Charlotte could tell she was expected to elaborate.

'It might be nothing, I don't know,' her last words dipped as she began to question her intuition. 'I went straight to John's cell to see if anything was going on, but he was just sitting there doing a crossword.' Charlotte's head wobbled from side to side. 'It just didn't feel right.'

Closing his eyes, Mr Miller drew a long breath. 'You're right, Charlotte,' he confirmed as his pen timbred to the pink form like a tossed caber. He slumped back in his chair and began to swivel from side to side, keeping the rusty squeaks in time with every heightened inhale and exhale of breath. He stopped abruptly and leant forward. 'What I tell you remains between you and me. Agreed?' Although wide, his eyes were blunt and colder than she'd ever seen them.

Charlotte swallowed some more sawdust. 'Of course, Sir.'

Two fingers jogged on his bottom lip, deciding if this was a good idea. They stalled and he sucked in a breath which seemed far too air-filled for his lungs. 'Ben Stokes is working undercover, sent in by Titan to investigate how drugs are getting into the prison as well as how they are being distributed. He's been ordered to befriend those most likely candidates to see if once he gains their trust, they will attempt to bribe him to turn a blind eye. But it's not really the inmates he's focusing on Charlotte...It's the staff.'

Chapter Five

By 2am, the story was pretty much clear. A tragic mistake. *A bloody mistake!* Gary had snivelled and sobbed when he admitted how he'd left a Spice-laced cigarette in the ashtray, but there were no pats of comfort for his back. And surprise, surprise - he refused to say how he got his hands on it. He was put straight into segregation. Charlotte rightly suspected she would not be the one on his suicide watch this time, not when she would have gladly handed him a nice, strong leather belt to take with him.

When the statements were given, and the forms filled in, Mr Miller told her to go home. For once, she agreed given she was as much use as a chocolate fireguard.

Navigating the smothering dark of the deserted motorway (where her only companion was the eyes of the cats lassoing her into the gloom), Amos' last words played on loop in her head. 'Doves aren't meant to be caged.' They wound round and round until Charlotte was sure she could hear his message in the hypnotic whir of the gusting fans. Gasping straight, she turned up the stereo and rubbed her eyes.

Outside the flat, Charlotte began to tidy away the clutter in her car – the empty *McDonald's* cup Greg had left in the drinks holder, a *Babybel* wrapper partially moulded to the passenger seat *(really Greg?),* the paperwork in the passenger footwell from the training she had attended on de-escalation techniques. And when there was nothing else to tidy, she began to polish the dash and buff the inside windows with a dehydrated shammy. Anything rather than go inside. Because it wasn't just the prison keeping her caged. It was Greg. The realization made her shudder, and she remained there, her car gleaming, until the coldness seeping in forced her out. Okay, that and Mr Hobbs from 1A who was now sliding down the lamppost instead of just hugging it.

Given the hour, Charlotte clenched her teeth to silence the key as it threaded into the lock. But she needed have bothered considering the din coming from the lounge. For the second time that evening, her hackles prickled; Greg wasn't alone.

Her face puckered as she lowered the rucksack to the floor, rumpling more with each careful step which edged her towards the living room door, ajar to what sounded like a world of heady pleasure. At first, Charlotte presumed Greg was watching his not-very-secret, secret porn DVD (the very one she hoovered round twice a week where he planked it under the sofa cushion along with 3 very tatty magazines). But her breathing hastened as she spied through the slender gap just as a sharp, shrill cackle pierced the air. It was the kind of grating laugh teenage girls held when they loitered at the bus stop trying to impress the boys. Like most people, Charlotte had often imagined what she would do in such a situation – probably shout, yell, cause a fuss, kick over the table, kick his balls. Yet, her body remained obediently still, observing the scene with a chilled indifference and allowing Greg another length of rope to hang himself with.

Edging closer until she felt her own warm breath on her face, the one eye striped with a band of gold sharpened as he smothered the girl's mouth with his like he was giving her mouth to mouth. Charlotte freed a shudder given she'd only did it herself a few hours beforehand. Perhaps that's why she felt numb, felt no jealousy as his hands slipped to a breast and she groaned her permission. In fact, the thing which irked her most was that Greg was using what used to be her favourite Paisley silk throw (a birthday gift from her friend Hayley) as his shag mat. *Bastard!* That's what propelled her forward instead of backwards in small, cautious steps until she stood over them, watching for a moment as they continued to paw and probe. 'Evening.'

A very quiet grenade of a word, she soon realized.

'Shit!' Greg yelled as he sprang upright, his messy mousy hair shaking from side to side as he gasped like a fish on land to find some sort of explanation.

Charlotte was almost tempted to laugh as he tried to force his head through the sleeve of his t-shirt. Modesty suddenly a priority, he frantically tried to cover his moobs and beer paunch. He thrashed to find the right hole. 'W…Wait Charlotte. It's not what you think!'

Charlotte turned to the terrified girl with her tattooed sleeves, pierced lip and kohl-lined eyes. She paused for a moment, simpering in the irony that the girl reminded her of a younger version of herself. 'I think you better go home. Your mum will be worried.'

Clenching her black blouse shut to hide her own (rather well-endowed Charlotte couldn't help but notice) pair of modesties, the girl's wide eyes wavered uncertainly to Greg. His head now free, he nodded and turned away (and tried to hide his dying erection under an antique bolster cushion). The girl grasped her boots and biker's jacket before her socks swished her away to the door.

Charlotte waited until she heard it click closed before she turned for the kitchen, still unable to lay her eyes on him as the hunt for his boxer shorts began. *Need to put more fat balls in the bird feeder,* she thought as she gazed out the window and filled the kettle, perhaps the sight of Greg's acting as a subliminal reminder. A chair scraped at the table and she could feel his eyes heavy on her back, silently reading for any clues of the reaction to come.

Let's make this fun! she seethed, deciding to prolong his agony a bit longer. She rinsed several plates, a cereal bowl with a scattering of dehydrated *Rice Crispies* welded to the side (that added an extra minute alone) and wiped around the sink too. *Then*, she joined him at the table, placing a strong builder's tea in front of him.

'Charlotte,' he leant forward and reached for her hand. She allowed him to have it. 'She means nothing. *Nothing*. I love you so much, but…well…you know how things have been…' He lifted his best puppy dog eyes to Charlotte's (whose weren't judgemental or brimming with virtue, not self-righteous or damning, not angry even. But they were empty).

He floundered to fill the gap when her mouth remained straight. Licking his lips, he inched his chair forward again and again until the table inched with him. 'A…After our talk earlier, I called her to finish it. She turned up here and…she was begging! Throwing herself at me! And I tried…'

'Greg,' Charlotte uttered in the same monotone timbre which had become the norm of late, 'it's fine.'

His mouth so wide she could see the gold crown at the back, he jumped on the pardon. 'Oh, Charlotte!' he wailed as he slumped against the back of the chair and pushed his fuck-messed hair back from his wide hazel eyes. 'I swear, it's over. You're who I want to be with.' Blowing his cheeks, he latched on to her again.

She glared at it, his hand around hers. It felt uncomfortable and mildly repulsive, like when her Auntie Liz used to lick a hanky to clean a smudge of dirt from her cheek. Gently, yet firmly, Charlotte began to prise her hand from his.

'What?'

She gazed at him and his inside out t-shirt and his clown lips and such a stupidly large plug in his ear, it acted as a porthole to the toaster, and

Charlotte smiled a tiny smile. Because despite what had just happened, it was him she felt sorry for.

'Greg, if we were meant to spend the rest of our lives together, then why am I so unhappy and why are you shagging someone who looks barely legal?'

His brows plunged like he was trying to translate a rare dialect of Yiddish. 'But…I love you. I said I was sorry, Charlotte. This can't be it.' It sounded more like a question.

Charlotte patted his hand, then took a sip from her tea. 'Of course, it can.'

Chapter Six

Charlotte was immediately hit by *The Fear* as the taxi pulled up outside the terminal, her fingers shaking so much it took 4 attempts to pluck £20 from her purse. The daunting glass entrance was littered by smokers puffing frantically for their last nicotine hit. *Possibly their last ever,* she truly believed in her irrationality. In fact, she was almost tempted to ask for one even though she'd never smoked. Well, apart from that one time she was trying to piss off Adam when he said she had to stay in and study for her Higher Maths exam. To show she was now an actual woman, a *grown-up* thank you very much, she had lit up one of his. The look was topped-off with a smoke ring…aimed at his face. It certainly did the job. He was so pissed off he let her finish the whole thing before supplying her with another and another, back to back. Stubborn as ever, she smoked every one of them to the butt, making *Mmmm* sounds like she was eating a Black Forest gateau. Charlotte never realized it was possible to feel like a colour, but she surely did, and that colour was green. Not a rich forest-green or a zingy lime. It was more a *Kermit the Frog* colour of pea-green…and she never touched a cigarette again.

As she crossed the hazy threshold, she just about stopped herself from crashing into several sets of armed police: biceps bulging, arms folded, faces stern. No doubt, their attendance was intended to be reassuring. Probably was to most travellers. Not Charlotte. *What the hell? Why is there so many of them? Is there a security alert?* she questioned as she made her way towards the *British Airways* sign, gawking back over her shoulder at them…repeatedly.

On the plus side, she was early. *Very* early, so there was virtually no queue as she hiked a mile of empty zigzagging rows to reach the check-in desk (only 20 metres from the entrance as the crow flies, she'd already calculated with a hyper vigilance). Bobbing like her bladder was suddenly bursting as the one customer in front of her handed over a case, her inner monologue began its argument. *Get a grip! It is safe. People do this like getting a taxi. The pilots have families, you idiot! Do it every day. But what about that flight which disappeared into thin air or the pilot who went mental and took everyone with him when he flew into a mountain? The worst can happen.*

A prod in the back jolted her out of the debate, the woman at the desk in front calling, 'Madam?' and from her low ridged brow, obviously not for the first time.

'Oh!' Charlotte harried forward and handed over her boarding pass (which was tucked neatly in the picture page of her passport to save causing any inconvenience). She couldn't help but admire the assistant's impeccable make-up, just like Audrey's, except with the addition of a debonair blue scarf knotted around her neck. Charlotte's twitchy smile was not returned.

The woman's eyes remained glued to the screen, her false nails clicking against the keys, when she asked in a thick Eastern European accent, 'Do you have any luggage for hold?'

'Oh, no. Just hand luggage.' Charlotte, on the other hand, had a smile nailed up, and began fiddling the zipper of her leather jacket, trying so hard to look innocent that she immediately looked suspicious.

Another flurry of clicks. 'And can I ask, did you pick your case?'

Eh? Placing a finger on her lips, Charlotte's eyes creased as she looked down at the small case at her feet - a tatty, beige hand-me-down from her dad. 'Hm. I have no idea who picked it.'

At last, the girl's eyes, wide and questioning, flicked up. Her thick eyelashes fluttered under what looked like four strong coats of jet mascara.

'Pardon?'

An audible gulp crackled in her ears as she looked down at her case again as if the answer to her question might be written on it somewhere. 'I have no idea who picked it.' Her finger found her lips again as she gazed at the Union Jack logo above them and tried to think. 'I…I mean, it belonged to my dad and I'm sure he must have had it while my mum was still alive. Maybe she was the one who picked it? I can't say.' She finished with an apologetic shrug and an even drier mouth.

Something in the way the check-in girl's pupils constricted caused Charlotte's tongue to glue to the fleshy ridges on the roof of her mouth. *Holy shit!* she cried inwardly, almost hearing the snap of a rubber glove around a hairy wrist, actually smelling the artificialness of latex.

From the corner of her water-glazed vision, a man with a well-lacquered quiff manning the check-in desk to the right sloped forward. He flagged the sheet in his hand to gain Charlotte's attention. 'She said *packed*, madam. Who *packed* your case?'

Placing a shaky hand on the cool metal of the desk, Charlotte let the dizzy spell pass as the blood whooshed through her ears on its rush back to her head. The check-in girl cracked what might have been an actual smile, but it was too difficult to tell on a face which wouldn't have been out of place in *Madame Tussauds*. And just to add a little more to the humiliation of the whole debacle, the passenger at the other desk laughed loudly and shook his head.

Arsehole! What an arsehole! she repeated inwardly - affronted, aghast, wishing the ground would open up and swallow her if truth be told. If looks could kill, she saved him an extra hard one. He resembled some sort of well-groomed Viking: a dirty long blond mane streaked with gold tied back neatly from his chiselled features in one of those man-bun things she so detested. *Oh, he's one of them all right* - goes to the gym 40 times a week, has a protein-only diet, probably gets his sack and crack waxed too. *Urgh!* A full trendy beard, neatly clipped, and piercing blue eyes finished off the look. *No wait*, she peered closer – one piercing green eye and one piercing blue eye? *Amazing*, Charlotte thought as she stared for longer than necessary. *Still a total fucking poser though.*

With a sharp huff, Charlotte drew her daggers back to the woman in front of her. 'Me,' Charlotte corrected, a quivery hand on her chest. 'I picked, I mean, *packed* it! Oh, for the love of God!' She trundled her eyes to the heavens accordingly.

Tucking his passport and boarding pass inside his designer jacket (so expensive it didn't need a label or name emblazoned across it), the Viking laughed heartily again before strolling off with so much poise, it was quite he had taken all hers with him too.

All her liquids were bagged and organized before she got anywhere near security. In fact, Charlotte had spent most of the previous evening with the *Do's and Don'ts* list concertinaed on the kitchen table. It was regularly referred to as she packed, dog-eared and coffee stained when she'd finished. Amazing what a dose of nerves could make you do; today, she'd even ironed her travel outfit (when the only thing she usually ironed was her uniform and that was only for the first-time wear). The rest of the time, she folded it neatly over the drier suspended from the hall roof for the following day. Most of her other clothes stretched. But even her bra and knickers matched today (although she drew the line at ironing those). *Why would anyone iron their knickers?* she mused as she was beckoned forward with a severe hand flick. *Precious minutes of your life you'll never get back.*

After what felt like a prison riot training exercise, she was spat out at the other end, a dishevelled version of 20 minutes ago. 'Never again,' Charlotte grunted when she found a shelf and began to toss everything from each of the three grey trays back in her bag. This time, she didn't give a shit where the liquids landed. Feeling like her feet had suddenly swollen to a size 8, she fought to squeeze on a black Chelsea boot. And there he was again, with his wolf eyes, striding towards the sanity of Duty Free. Not a hair out of place on his head, not a bead of sweat on his brow, probably a seam ironed down the front of his *Calvin's*. *I hope your plane has an emergency landing or…or your oxygen mask falls down mid-flight.* Charlotte screwed her eyes to throw a hex after him as she hopped unsteadily, pulling on her other boot. But even in her current state of mind, she couldn't wish for the crash.

The Cuban cigars and single malts held no allure as she zoomed by, wanting nothing more than a quiet seat in a quiet corner where she could rock back and forth, curl a finger in her hair and maybe even suck her thumb. But after everything which had happened lately?

The bottle which caught her eye was purple and jagged, and looked quite exotic by her standards. 'Oooohhh!' Her pupils dilated as she held the nozzle to her nose. It was heady and intense, and very different from her usual safe, light scent. But Charlotte decided different was good (until she looked at the base of the bottle). *£105! Not a chance!* Looking around, she popped the tip of her tongue out and sprayed it liberally around her neck and wrists. Then, rubbing her chin like she was still considering it, Charlotte inched slowly along the aisle to the bargain stand with its eclectic mix of lidless wonders nearer the back of the shop.

Eventually, she settled for a bottle of *Rihanna RiRi Crush. Better than nothing,* she thought. Very chuffed she was too at the idea of paying only £15. Besides, who would know the difference really?

Just as Charlotte handed it over to the cashier, she spotted the Viking again. He was being served along the wall from her, where the perfumes were so exclusive, they were housed behind the counter on gleaming, spotlighted glass shelves. From the pink box which the over-smiley assistant placed carefully in the black and white bag tied with a silk ribbon, Charlotte could tell it was *Chanel*.

'Yer change,' the cashier grunted, interrupting her observation before dumping a receipt and too many coins in her palm.

'Oh, thank you.'

She merely looked past Charlotte and yelped, 'Next!'

'You're welcome,' Charlotte sniped as she snatched the plastic bag from the counter and stumbled to the side to make way for the customer practically dry humping her backside. Another two hexes were thrown.

'I'm getting the bloody bus next time,' Charlotte chuntered to no-one in particular as she began the hunt for a coffee. She glanced around the neon signs and familiar logos for a quiet spot to unwind for a couple of hours. But it was slim pickings; the generic public choice for a coffee had its striped seats already filled, its queues already stretched. Not ideal, but better than nothing, she settled for a vending machine latte and a packet of *Munchies* from *WH Smith*. Emergency survival kit now sorted, Charlotte made a beeline for the empty bench at the calmer end of the concourse. Her sponge earphones in place, she pulled out her CD of *Sign O' the Times* and slotted it into her Walkman. 'Who picked you, indeed?' She patted her bag along to the stark rhythm and snorted quietly as she chomped down on her first chocolate.

Every ten minutes, she checked her watch to find only one had passed, and every time she checked, the sweat misting her brow and top lip grew colder. Clock watching no longer an option without passing out, Charlotte reached across to her bag, undid the tarnished brass buckle and sought her sketchbook and art pencil: her number one go-to therapy choice. And Charlotte certainly needed it now if she stood any chance of boarding that plane.

Somewhat ironically, it was these exact types of situation Charlotte loved to capture. Although for some, the airport was no more than a glamourized bus stop, for most, there was an extra charge of emotion about the whole experience: the terrified passenger such as herself - teacup rattling, teeth chattering; the over-whelmed lady flying for the first time to make it to her only grandchild's christening; the student taking a gap-year to find themselves; the tired businessman flying home to his wife after the deal fell through.

The pencil thrumming against the pad, her eyes began their hunt for a subject. As always, there was a never-ending list of muses to choose from. The first person who caught her attention was the waitress in the café cordoned off with thick red ropes across from where she sat. Fresh as a daisy, dewy skinned with pale green eyes, Charlotte was immediately captured by her Polish accent but more so, her story. *Why was she here? Who had she left behind? A lover? A mother? Did her heart ache to be with them or was she escaping? Was she relieved?* But whatever her tale was, Charlotte couldn't read it in her face. *Too flawless.* So, the quest continued.

All the while, she chose to ignore the Viking who was seated alone at a table for four within the red ropes as a tired young couple queued - dad frantically choogling a gurney baby and mum thrusting a buggy back and forth like a Dyson as she tried to quell a toddler's screams. A VIP right enough. But no matter how she tried to find inspiration in the masses, it was him she kept going back to. And it wasn't because he was beautiful with the most amazing eyes she'd ever seen. Such banalities were inconsequential to Charlotte. It was how he utilized his table. There was a laptop, a phone, several sleek grey files and in front of them all, the bottle of perfume. She questioned then, was this how he prioritized his life? Who was the perfume for? Why the hell was everything parallel and perpendicular? Why did the file in his hand make his forehead pucker and furrow, make his eyes lose their crinkling amusement of earlier? And as the

44

shower of questions became a downpour, she knew she'd found her subject. *Oh, crap.*

Chapter Seven

Knotting her hair at the nape of her neck, Charlotte took the pencil from her mouth and put it to paper. And the more she sketched, the more captivated she was. Questions, questions, questions she tried to answer in soft, spontaneous strokes of graphite. And as the questions continued to teem, Charlotte slid out of her leather and hunched over the pad, more absorbed in a piece than she had been in a while. Instead of one sketch, she had seven:

1. The one with the arrogant, self-assured smirk when he didn't bother to look up as he handed the waitress his card.
2. The one with the troughs and lines which pulled at his forehead when he read the file in his hand.
3. The one with the fizzle of love in his eyes when he looked at the bottle in front of him.
4. The one with the contradictory flaring of the nose and clenching of his jaw as he checked his phone before dropping it back to the table.
5. The one as he typed, such an intensity in his eyes – passionate and serious and deadly important.
6. The one when his face cleared as he checked his watch and listened for his plane to be called.
7. The one where, every now and then, a small smile pulled at his mouth, softening his hard features like she had used her blending brush directly on his face.

The Seven Deadly Sins, she titled it cynically, a sneer twisting her lips.

The only thing to break her concentration was the pinched order requesting, 'Could all passengers for BA flight 2745 please make their way to Gate 14 for boarding.'

'Our Father, who art in Heaven…' Charlotte blew a corkscrew of hair from her face. She finished her prayer as she packed away her equipment, an urgency about her as if it was the last call instead of the first. An arm missed the sleeve of her jacket a second time and she noticed her subject put on his with far more grace. When she got to her feet, so did he.

Double Crap! More than keen to keep a distance now he had served his purpose, Charlotte hovered for a moment and sat back down, mumbling to herself and pointing as she confirmed she had everything, and everything was where she needed it. 'Passport and boarding pass in front zip of bag (check). Mobile switched off and placed in back pocket (check). Heart under ribcage instead of throat (still working on it).' The Viking was gone by the time she ran through it all again.

But as she scuttled passed his table, Charlotte noticed a single slip in his impeccability – his mobile. Her pace slowed but she didn't stop. *Leave it. Leave it,* she ordered herself, looking away as if it would merit her innocence. But she only made it as far as the *Please Wait to be Seated* sign before she heard her dad's words. *'Remember, kindness costs nothing, lass! You might need someone's kindness one day.'*

And right there was the badgering voice of her conscience and her shoulders slumped. *Ah, shite!* With little more thought, Charlotte reversed, sloped over the rope and grabbed it. Her eyes surfed the bobbing sea of heads, quickly spotting his man-bun thing on the horizon (not hard since he was a clear head above everyone around him). She broke into a jog along the runway of marble. By the time she could smell his rich cologne, her heart was thrashing, her breathing sharp.

'Excuse…me,' she panted, a hand reaching for him when he didn't stop. 'Excuse me,' she said louder, now lightly touching his arm. 'You…'

He turned abruptly, like he'd been expecting her, his face distorted and ugly, a million miles away from anything she had just drawn (or from what she was expecting in reply to her act of kindness). 'Look,' he started in a clear London accent (neither Chelsea nor Peckham, somewhere in the middle but firm nonetheless), 'I don't know who you are, or who you are working for. But whatever it is, I'm not interested. And maybe in future, you should ask permission before you sketch people!'

The force of his words thrust her back until she buffered unsteadily against a bin, her words wedged in her throat. She shrunk back further as he towered above her with a snarl, one eye emerald, the other sapphire. Her flailing hand landed on a hot, gooey lump of what she presumed was gum (possibly a full packet of *Hubba Bubba* by the sheer size of the mound). Yet Charlotte couldn't look, couldn't move. But he did, his face smoothing slightly, like he suddenly remembered where or who he was. And just as abruptly as he spun to her, he whipped around and loped away, and she felt a humiliation akin to being dumped by her first high-school boyfriend - Davie Munro. He'd been just as angry when she wouldn't let him get his hands up her top or her knickers around her ankles.

The phone burned in her hand. She looked at it, then to him, deliberating if her aim would be good enough to knock his bun off. But he was moving too quick, had too many people near. So instead, she swigged a mouthful of nothing, pulled her hand from the rubbery, pink sludge and watched in a quiet mortification as he was consumed by the swarming crowd.

Chapter Eight

Vinny unbuckled his belt a split second before the ping told him he could, setting the MacBook Pro up on the desk of his private pod in business class. All the way up to cruising altitude, he'd been dwelling on his encounter with the strange girl who had obviously been following him. But the question which really baked his noodle, was why? A spy from the competition? The press? One of *his* lackeys bribing for a deal?

Tommy Dolan's case was becoming more problematic by the second. Sure, there was a mountain of evidence to get him sent down for a very long time, but Vinny knew how easy it was to get off on a technicality, especially with a smart enough QC. Tommy's defence lawyer, the particularly fierce Kate Norton, was the best that money could buy. This case had to be watertight. But no matter how he tautened his arguments, there was something missing – he just couldn't quite put his finger on what it was yet.

Again, he began to scroll down the files on the screen, checking for a flaw in chronology or an inconsistency in fact. Yet the weird encounter drew his eyes away just as the plane banked sharply, his head swivelling slowly between a view of nothing but bright blue sky on his left, the leaden green hills of the *Campsies* on his right. *Who is she?* he thought, and his knee began to bob in the usual way it did every time he got worked up. He didn't like it one little bit.

'Excuse me sir, I don't suppose you left your phone in the terminal?' the young, blonde flight attendant sang as she straightened her stupidly small apron. As he looked up, Vinny snapped the laptop closed.

A scowl already swimming across his forehead, he quickly dismissed the notion. 'No, I have it right…' He paused, discovering an empty pocket where his phone should have been. Giving a sigh of inconvenience, he quickly patted and scrunched his other pockets before reaching for his briefcase. Nothing.

Already smiling over him, her heavily rouged cheeks bulged as she waved the phone in her hand. 'Someone handed it in at the gate and described you. Said you left it in the café?'

Raking his bottom lip with his advert-white teeth, the pieces clanged painfully into place. 'Right…Right. Thank you.' He smiled tightly as he took his phone back, a cringe clipping at his features. *Bloody hell!* The poor girl was only trying to help, to do a good deed…and the way he had dismissed her…*Shit!* He groaned a little as his head fell back to the creamy leather headrest. Unusually, this particular case was getting to him, but until now, he hadn't realized how much. Vinny would be the first to admit, he was a lot of things, but rude and paranoid he wasn't. He felt the immediate need to atone, to tell the girl that he had made a terrible mistake. He winced again when he thought of her palm planted in a pile of gum. Tapping the mobile against his lips, he racked his brain for a few seconds then asked, 'I don't suppose you have her details, so I can thank her personally?'

The stewardess sloped her toothy smile and shook her head. 'Sorry, sir. I don't. But perhaps you can check with the airport staff when you land. Maybe she left her details at the terminal?' Although her final word sored with optimism, he knew it was doubtful, especially given the nature of their brief encounter.

Opting to leave her seatbelt on, Charlotte finally opened her eyes when she felt the plane level, only wishing her stomach would do the same. Rigid to the point she was almost in pain, her hands seized the armrests with a vice-like grip, the scruffy Bill Oddie type at her side standing no chance in the silent claim for who the shared one belonged to. *Deserves him right*, she thought, considering his discourteous choice of snack. *Really? BBQ beef Pringles?* Her jutting neck tendons slowly drew her face away from the pungent odour and accompanying chomping noises. Another mechanical clunk and weighty drone from somewhere below caused her knees to spring wide.

'Madam? Would you like a drink?'

How can she be smiling? Doesn't she realize we're 30,000 feet in the air? 'A diet coke, please,' she warbled and swallowed, her knuckles resisting as she tried to peel her hands to accept the drink. The stewardess gave Charlotte a fleeting sympathetic smile before straightening her hat and rolling her trolley of goodies to the row behind.

Charlotte slid on her earphones and crushed her eyes, cursing the fact that of all the flights he could have been on, it just so happened to be hers. There he was waiting, bold as brass, standing in the priority boarding line for *her* flight. And the nerve of the man as he casually smoothed his beard and flicked through a magazine like he hadn't just verbally assaulted someone! Charlotte had hidden behind a pillar then a copy of *The Times* which had been conveniently folded on the seat at her side. Peeking over the top from time to time until he had boarded, she handed the phone in at the gate when it was her turn.

'Are you sure you don't want to give it to him yourself, madam?'

'Absolutely not! In fact, could you *not* mention I am on the flight. Don't want a fuss or anything.'

In the dark, she rehearsed, again and again, what she should have said to him instead. If it had happened in prison, she'd have been a bit more prepared, would have told him where to go with that scary authoritative voice which could even get Greg moving like he had a rocket up his arse. It became a bit of a game, when she tried to find a profanity using every letter of the alphabet, and she was on her 3rd round of J (her effort of jobby particularly lame compared to some of the examples from A – H) when the tyres screeched on tarmac.

Charlotte sucked in a huge lungful of the wonderful, polluted air of the capital as she made her way towards the taxi rank. *I survived! I'm alive!* But just as her hand touched a shiny black handle, she saw *him* across the road exiting the terminal. And he saw her, his face becoming strangely distorted again as he raised his arm to gain her attention. Much to her horror, he began to wave it. 'Fuck!' she gasped, her eyes near rupturing as she snapped her neck round to check if it was meant for someone behind her. There was no-one.

'Shit!' Charlotte ducked into the cab. 'The Tower Bridge Hotel, please!' It was cried in the squealy yelp of a piglet. Open-mouthed, she continued to watch his long legs dodge through the traffic to the central reservation, his head pivoting from side to side, his body edging back and forth in preparation of finding a gap big enough to make it across to her side of the road. 'Jesus Christ!' Charlotte screamed quietly as the tip of her nose smudged the glass, her hand gripping tighter on the bright yellow arm rail. Like Jesus had indeed heard her, the Viking got trapped in the middle of the junction. The acceleration of the taxi (and the fact she hadn't quite found her strength yet) thrust her to the tartan blanket at her back, but knowing she was safe, just like she had rehearsed, Charlotte made a fist and waved her wrist loosely at him like she was shaking an invisible tube of *Smarties*. The gesture was accompanied with a smarmy one-sided smile and an exaggerated mouthing of, 'Prick'. Much like Mr Miller, she rarely used the word. But just like he did when Amos died, and like the prisoners too, she rolled the *r,* nice and long. This time it was his arms which fell flaccidly to his sides, his hairy chin which smacked the concrete.

Chapter Nine

The super-rich pile of the striped carpet carried her silently along the never-ending corridor, ship-like and stylish. '403, 405, 407, 409,' she counted along, checking the reservation printout before knocking on 411. A *Do Not Disturb* sign hung askew on the door opposite. On the floor, two empty green bottles of something expensive, a pile of plates which resembled something Greg might leave in his wake and a half-eaten burger – now cold and waxy. *Someone's had a good night,* Charlotte flaunted her eyes as she brushed her curls neat with her fingers. She felt (and probably looked) like she had been on the road for four days instead of four hours. There was a shuffling behind her closely followed by a beam of natural light which obliterated the artificial, subdued glow.

'Hi Wee Yin. Ma wee stinky sister,' Adam's husky voice teased. Sliding his tortoise shell reading glasses so they nuzzled securely in the nest of curls at the top of his head, he took a closer look. His brown eyes folded into a smile as he yanked her into a bear hug, playfully messing her hair and all her efforts.

'That description may be more accurate than you think after that flight. I seriously might have to go and check my knickers!' Charlotte laughed into his shoulder, his familiar smell of musk mingled with a pleasant back note of smoke instantly calming her. At last, his grip slackened so she could breathe, and he shooed her in, lobbing her case and bag on to what she presumed was her bed. It only took one quick glimpse around the suite to see how well Adam was doing. Two king-sized beds and a lounge? *Not bad, brother. Not bad.*

'So…how was the flight?' Adam tried his best to sound flippant as he poured the coffee. Yet he observed her cautiously as he added an imperfect lump of caramel coloured sugar to each mug.

It released in a rant. '*Oh*, just fantastic! Even better since some psycho arsehole gave me a load of grief beforehand. AND, he was on the same flight!' Charlotte collapsed on the sofa, so soft and sumptuous, it gobbled her up.

The spoon no longer clinked around the inside of the mug as his lips screwed tight. 'Why? What did he do?'

Plucking an over-sized cushion from her back, Charlotte tossed it on the bed and almost laughed as she watched him regress 18 years in a second. 'Well, I was a bit bored, so I just started sketching to fill the time. Unfortunately for me, *his* was the most interesting face I could find.'

The jangling of the spoon recommenced, finishing with two sharp dinks on the lip of each mug. 'Oh, aye? Interesting face?' He winked playfully, handing her what could have easily been mistaken as a dog's water bowl.

Like she had suddenly regressed to a teen too, Charlotte spun her eyes. 'Shut up! He had the most *expressive* face! Anyway, when I left, I noticed he had left his phone. *So*, being the good Samaritan that I am, I chased after him to return it. But rather than the thanks I was expecting, I got a right earful! He thought I was stalking him, for fuck's sake!' Using both hands, she lifted the mug to her lips and sipped gingerly at the piping hot foam. 'I think he may have been a paranoid schizophrenic.'

'Sounds like a mentalist to me,' Adam agreed, thrumming his fingers on the arm of the sofa, his beat brisk and impatient.

'Oh, that's not even the worst part!' Carefully placing the mug on the table, Charlotte needed both hands to elaborate. 'He saw me getting into the taxi and gave chase to start round 2! But the taxi drove off just in time and I managed to let him know he was a wanker and a prick at the same time!' A single nod of her head declared, *I showed him!*

The jumpy hand now pinned to the back of his head, he gazed at her, his grin beaming with pride. 'I've always admired your multi-tasking skills.'

'Thank you!' she returned unapologetically and shrugged, removing the flimsy earphones from around her neck. 'So,' Charlotte perked up and put her Walkman beside her coffee, wanting to forget every part of the last 4 hours, 'tell me about the job.'

'Well, I don't know much myself. The details were sketchy. I have a meeting at 5 with one of the partners. It should only take an hour or so then we can go for dinner. I'll be able to tell you more then.'

'Okay. Cool.'

He put on his glasses and held his phone at arm's length to check the meeting details again. 'Ready to hit the town for some lunch and a bit of shopping?'

'Yes! I'm starving after so much trauma!' Charlotte leant back and pulled her t-shirt over the waistband of her jeans which were adorned with a shiny new black button (a spare from the inside of her work pants). 'But, just not somewhere filled with the *beautiful* people.'

'You are beautiful!' Adam slurred and slobbered, his glasses somehow now awry as he crossed his eyes and pulled his best Quasi Modo face.

'Cheeky sod!' Her punch jolted his specs straight. God, it felt great, being able to punch him.

'Ow!' Laughing gruffly, Adam rubbed the top of his arm. 'That's for tonight. I've booked us a table at The Westwood in Covent Garden.' Expecting another thump, he dodged to the side when her eyes amplified with only slightly less panic than when she boarded the plane earlier.

'But I've not brought anything fancy to wear!'

'Well, that's why we're going shopping today!' he repeated in the exact upwards jaunt of hers. 'I think you've forgotten how to treat yourself, Charlotte. I mean,' he hauled up his shoulders and splayed his fingers, 'when was the last time you even got dressed up and taken out for a nice meal?' A hand still stiff in the air, his shoulders pinned at his ears, he awaited her reply.

Charlotte licked a finger and began to flick through the black leather guest book. *Hm. Nice pool! Room service? Yum.*

'God, Charlotte!' Everything dropped – shoulders, hand, stomach. 'You're too good for him and you know it,' he snapped.

'I know, I know,' she sighed, quietly closing the book over, a finger tracing gently over the gilded bird motif on the front. 'That's why it's over.'

'What? Oh, thank *God* for that!' he cried, throwing his head back.

Not sharing his obvious delight at the news, Charlotte kept her eyes down and Adam realized he was being an insensitive arsehole. 'Shit,' he closed his eyes and whipped back his curls. 'Sorry Char. Are you okay?'

'Yeah.' As her gaze stretched out at the bascule bridge which was raised to permit a frigate up the Thames, she took a second to consider how she really felt. Her mind quickly raced around her body, checking for weighty lumps and knots. But all there was, was a lightness. 'I really am.'

'So, what happened? I mean…do you want to talk about it?' Adam ventured, pulling lightly at a lock of her hair.

Surely, he must be ADHD? Charlotte realized he was the only person she knew who could watch a film, complete a paper, have a phone call and make dinner at the same time. A nose wrinkle mixed with a smile. 'Not today.'

Just for Charlotte, they headed for Camden where she could peruse the art shops and vintage record stores. She loved the bohemian vibe of the place, how the creativity flowed in every brick, tile and paving stone. It was abundant with everything she loved about life: from the tantalising, exotic spices of the street food stalls (turmeric perhaps, a pinch of cinnamon with a heady twist of allspice), to the reggae music booming in the independent record store with its window plastered in vinyl and neon signs. Above all, the people there were like-minded in their openness, priding their individuality rather than conforming to the norm. There were no trends here, just unique ways of expressing yourself. Charlotte felt right at home.

A rainbow of bulbs swayed above them as Adam filled her in on what had been happening in New York where, even though he earned a fortune as a prosecution lawyer, he still shared a shoe box with a computer geek called Norm. If he stood on his windowsill and tilted his head 50 degrees anti-clockwise and held his breath and balanced on the tippy toes of his right foot, he could see the broccoli treetops of Central Park. But he loved it, cramped bedroom and all: work was good, girls (plural) were good, life was good.

'So, what will you do now? Will you sell the flat?' Adam asked before professionally using the chopsticks to inch the noodles into his mouth.

Oh, for goodness sake! Charlotte, on the other hand, slurped noisily on the slippery strands snaking from hers. When she had drank in the last of them, she wiped the spicy red broth from her chin before swirling her chopsticks round her noodles, searching for a suitable clump to manage in a oner. 'Well, I'm glad you asked actually.'

An unusual tentativeness in her voice caused Adam to stop shovelling and look up. 'Why?'

'I've put the flat on the market. Greg can buy me out if he wants, or we can both leave but I don't want it and I'm not going to give it away either. So, if he wants it, he'll have to pay the market value.' *Slurp. Slurp. Slurp. Ssslllluuurrrppp.*

Flinching sharply, Adam wiped his stinging eye before giving the head dip which was slow but approving. 'Good. I have a few contacts in the property law sector if you need any help. Will you buy somewhere else?'

After nearly blinding herself too, Charlotte gave up on the sticks and took a sip from her beer instead. 'No, well, not exactly.'

Adam's brow arched, a prawn suspended halfway to his mouth.

'I…I want to move to Gran's croft.'

There followed a long pause. 'Really? It's been years since we've been there never mind since anyone has lived there. And it's in the bloody middle of nowhere.'

'Adam, I've been thinking a lot lately.' She leaned forward and began to pull at the soggy paper at the neck of her bottle. 'Things at work are getting difficult. One of the inmates I was close to died recently. Accidentally smoked a cig laced with Spice.' Using her other hand to hold the base, she sighed and pulled the label off entirely. 'It's everywhere. And now they're talking about staff corruption. To be honest, there is never enough of us to cover the shifts. The prisoners are on lockdown to deal with that. They're pissed off. We're pissed off. It's just getting worse.' By the time she'd vented, the label was rolled into a tiny, tight cigar.

'Charlotte,' Adam sagged, and the prawn plopped back in the bowl. He rested a hand over the port wine mark which flowed from his left ear to his shoulder and exhaled softly. 'I wish to God I'd never suggested you join in the first place. I only wanted you to have a stop gap while you set up house with *knob* features.'

It was barely audible when she spoke, partly because a steel band had begun their set on the pub terrace above them. 'Well, that's not going to happen now,' and she didn't just mean the house.

Adam began frisking for a *Marlboro Gold* and shook his head. This was getting way too heavy a conversation for a flying visit. 'So,' he sparked the cig a few times, blowing a plummet of smoke up in the air when it caught, 'what are your plans for the croft?'

Biting her tongue, Charlotte shuffled her backside on the bench and began drawing her ideas on the table. 'Initially, I'll still commute to work till the sale goes through. It's just over an hour. And I can't face sharing the flat until that sale goes through. I need to get away now. When I take the proceeds from the sale, and with my other savings, I should have enough to renovate the croft and set up my own studio. Go back to my art.' One eye tensed in preparation of the 'be sensible' chat.

But Adam just necked the last of his bottle, his gentle brown eyes glinting gold in the cool Autumn sun. 'Charlotte…if you're looking for my approval, then don't. You've already got it. I think it's an amazing idea, as long as it is what you want?'

Charlotte nodded so vehemently, he immediately saw the young, brilliant girl he had been left to bring up and parent: eager and keen and wide eyed and always wanting to please him. It made his heart melt all over again.

Charlotte posed in semi-circles as she continued to assess herself in the deep scarlet dress Adam had bought her earlier when they eventually made it to his favourite shopping district – Bond Street and Mayfair. She had picked it up in a fleeting moment of admiration when Adam had dragged her into *Browns*. Charlotte was only pretending to be an actual customer while Adam went off to try on another rack of labels. He threw the bag at her when they got back to the room, when it was too late to return it like he knew she would try to.

It was nice to feel sophisticated for once, especially when she slipped on the slick black heels she kept for special occasions (such as Hayley and Rami's wedding and Greg's Auntie Yvonne's funeral) – the black covering all basis. Double bonus. After a few wobbly practice steps, she finished the look with a sweep of rich matt red lipstick and her favourite big silver hoop earrings. 'Bring…on…The…Westwood,' she told her reflection with a final tottering turn.

Her phone pinged.

Come on Charlotte. Get a bloody move on! Got you a wine.

Butterflies? She rested a hand on her stomach to make sure. *Yip!* Actual butterflies whipped round her tummy. Happy, excited ones for a change.

Calm down, dear. On my way!

From the doorway, Charlotte scanned the high tables and booths. Adam was easy enough to spot, his chestnut mop of curls tumbling over his face, his glasses back on, his eyes inclined towards some papers in his hand. *Surely not his work face? Not now,* she thought, the disappointment of it instantly snuffing any fluttering wings as she remembered the distracted conversations and half-hearted replies of his uni days. All she'd wanted was a few moments of his undivided attention. Hell, just someone to watch *Home and Away* with even! Not that she blamed him, not with how he worked so hard for them both. *Just, well…not tonight,* she wished as she scooted in across from him.

'Evening,' Charlotte drawled like she was visiting the inmates on D wing.

Adam's head jerked up. He smiled approvingly and slowly removed his specs. 'Glad you could make it!' It was quickly followed by, 'You look lovely, Wee Yin,' to take the edge off the dig.

'Thank you!' Pointing at the two full pints in front of him, she jeered, 'How did your meeting go? Hopefully, not so bad it drove you to drown your sorrows?'

Her heart sored when he put his glasses back in their case and snapped it and the file closed. 'It went really well actually. In fact, I hope you don't mind but I've invited my boss to join us for dinner. I promise we won't talk shop all night. He's a good mate and we've not met up for a while.'

Pulling her mother's golden engraved compact from her favourite bag, Charlotte shrugged as she applied another coat of ruby to her lips. The *no shop talk* suited her just fine. 'No, I don't mind. The more the merrier.'

No longer were the words out when the light from the brass pendulum light (which illuminated the table in quite an unflattering manner, Charlotte thought, as she squinted to see if her wrinkles really were that bad) was eclipsed by something substantial. As her eyes slid to see what it was, the lipstick stuttered to a standstill on her bottom lip, her mouth, open wide and gaping like her compact. Thee fucking,,,Viking.

Chapter Ten

He looked as aghast as her.

What the…? Charlotte's bulging eyes swung to Adam. 'Adam,' she choked, nudging her head towards *him*, her eyes frantically trying to narrate her thoughts as she snapped the compact closed and wound her lippy away in sharp twists.

As Adam's pint lowered to the table, he glared from one to the other, his face resembling someone trying to pass wind discretely. 'Charlotte?' He shuffled over to make room. 'This is Vinny. Have you two met?'

Vinny glided in, his spine straight against the back of the booth and his hands flat on the table, looking like he was entering a negotiation with the Mexican Cartel. Somehow, that prospect felt easier. 'I'm afraid we have, although, I was a total dick.'

The familiar tingle on her lips and spiky prickles at the tips of her fingers reminded Charlotte to slow her breathing. 'Y…Yes! Yes, you were!' she stammered, keeping her stony eyes firmly on Adam, her pointed toe tapping at speed, her arms crossed tightly.

'What's going on?' Adam demanded now, his eyes batting between them.

'A…misunderstanding,' Vinny added gently.

With zero gentleness, Charlotte's reply was the most unladylike snort. She took a swig of her Bordeaux before pretending to study the poor attempt at Surrealism suspended on the wall above the booth.

'I thought your sister was tracking me in some way. I mean, the case is very high profile and she was beside me at check-in, then across from me at the café...and *drawing* me. So, when she started following me...'

Charlotte's cheeks flushed to the same colour as her dress.

As the penny dropped at last, Adam's tongue swept across his top lip before he cried, 'Shit!' He elbowed Vinny. 'You're the airport dickhead?'

A smile slinking along his mouth, Vinny opened his hands wide. 'The very same!'

Pivoting her head to the resonance of their amusement, Charlotte's eyes hexed Vinny for the umpteenth time as her glass smacked down on the table. 'I was bored...and you have a nice bone structure, *so*...' Her eyes flashed wide before they veered back to the painting.

'Thank you,' he replied casually and took a sup from his pint.

Charlotte could swear a puff of steam had just left her ears. 'Lots of people have nice bone structures you know! I mean,' she began waving her hand and pointing to prove it, 'even the glass collector over there. She has wonderful cheekbones! Or...or the porter in the foyer. He had very interesting eyes too, really like...crossed. It's nothing *personal*.' As a flustering humiliation rendered her a nudge closer to volatility, she restrained her arms across her stomach again and kicked Adam on the shin (partly to still his shoulders, partly because she just needed to kick something).

Vinny flung another dazed gawp at Adam, who just shrugged and probed his new bruise. A smirk threatened. 'I meant, thank you for returning the phone.'

Charlotte lifted her chin an inch. 'Oh...Right,' she croaked before clearing her throat to lubricate a passage for the words which appeared to be stuck. 'You're welcome,' she mumbled and quickly looked away.

His beard angled to his chest, his eyes wide, Vinny gave his best attempt at contriteness. 'And I really am sorry. It was my mistake. I tried to get you at the airport…but I could see you already had the wrong idea and weren't in the mood for a chat.' Mischievously, he swirled his tongue against his cheek and waited for what she would do next.

Did he just wiggle his eyebrows? Charlotte shrieked silently as Adam guffawed, the opposite of silently. *Surely, in this day and age, it should be possible to teleport back to the bedroom, or better still, back in time?* 'Yes, well…' She cleared her throat again and blew an annoying spiral of red away from her eyes. 'I thought you were chasing me, and after your *rant*…well, I wasn't going to just do nothing was I? But…I'm sorry about that too.' The final words merged and sunk.

'I *was going* to do *something*,' he corrected, plucking a few invisible specs from the front of his black *Tom Ford* V-neck pullover.

'Huh?' Her nose wrinkled.

Vinny's heart began to race from the thrill. 'You've used a double negative term. *Not* going to do *nothing*.'

'Oh.' A hand grazed her cheek where it felt like she'd been slapped. Not the first time he'd made her feel like that, but it certainly would be the last. 'Oh…well…I *do* apologize. No! In fact, I'd like to say, I *don't not* apologize!' A finger jabbing the table, she tilted her head sharply with each accentuation. 'If I realized I was going to have a grammar lesson over dinner, I would of …'

'Have,' Vinny interrupted, a finger pointing in the air. 'Would *have*.'

'Oh dear,' Adam sang quietly before sliding back in his seat, taking his pint with him while he debated if Vinny had a death wish.

'Oh!' Her laugh was low, her eyes a glazed shade of manic, a clear warning in her tenor. 'I would *have* dug out my copy of *Eats, shoots and leaves*.'

Whoa! And who the fuck are you? For the first time in months, his attention was captivated by something other than the case. He shook his head slowly and offered a genuine, if a tad bewildered, smile. 'Truce?' he said, and ventured a hand towards her, half expecting her to smack it away.

Charlotte looked directly at him, her eyes blazing along with her cheeks. *Arrogant arsehole. Totally beautiful arrogant arsehole.* Like the whole issue was a nothing to her, she pulled a sweaty hand from under her armpit and held it out. 'Truce,' she agreed, like she was obviously the bigger person. As he slipped his hand into hers, he held her gaze with that colour of blue and green she knew her mixing pallet could never concoct, and she felt butterflies flutter, only this time, in her chest. Charlotte gasped when she realized it was a lot more than intimidation she was feeling, quickly snatching back her hand like he had scabies. 'Right! Should we go and eat?'

The Westwood was smart and slick, a mixture of old-world luxury but with all the trimmings of new world class: original artwork hung on the oak-panelled walls, plush peacock velvet chairs seated plusher customers and already Charlotte noticed too many pieces of cutlery for her to understand. A smartly suited maître d (somehow the fact he wasn't wearing a tie made him seem even more sophisticated, like he already owned it) conducted them to their candle-lit table. Another squirm curled her lip as, from the corner of her eye, she watched Vinny hold out a chair…for her! *Puke!* Opening her bag, she angled her ear to its mouth, to check if the phone (which was switched off) had suddenly peeled. Closing it again, she glided right past to the seat at Adam's side, saving her brother a glare, which stated quite clearly, *I know how to sit myself at a table, for crying out loud.*

The chair remained poised in his hands as Vinny watched her shuffle herself comfortable and drop her huge bag (which looked like it had been assembled from an assortment of carpet remnants and broken mirrors) to the floor. Without looking up, she hid behind the menu and Vinny shrugged, taking the seat himself.

A waiter took their order and Charlotte glared with a quiet loathing as Vinny put on his boss hat, ordering an overly expensive bottle of Burgundy. It caused her head to pucker, and not just because it cost her week's wage. More, it was the fact she'd not been given a choice, yet she didn't have enough knowledge to contradict. As Vinny snapped the wine menu closed and handed it back with another dismissive avoidance of the eyes, Charlotte noted the young man's almost undetectable shoulder sag. She also noted her blood begin to boil…again.

'Oh, excuse me, sir,' she called after him, a tentative finger in the air. 'I was wondering if you could give me some advice. You see, I'm no wine expert and I would like to know what would go well with what *I've* ordered.' Several fingers raked down her neck which she could feel had begun to blotch. It always did when she felt any emotion other than normal.

The waiter's shoulders slid back up into place and his face warmed in admiration of the honest girl who just put the guy who was so up his own arse firmly in his place. 'Absolutely madam. What did you order?'

The two began a passionate exchange, Charlotte jogging her head along with the young man's recommendations of how a light, young red would ideally work with both her chosen courses. Something with a good crisp acidity to cut through the meatiness of the scallop and offset the fattiness of the duck.

'Wow! I would never have thought about having red with seafood! Thank you so much for that. Can we order a bottle for the table?'

'Of course, madam.' The waiter's smile dropped as he addressed Vinny, a professional blankness taking its place. 'Will you still be requiring a bottle of the *Chambolle-Musigny*, sir?'

'Erm, *no*.' Vinny elongated his last word and sloped his head to the side as he looked only at Charlotte. 'We'll go with the young lady's suggestion. Sounds far more suitable than mine.'

'Very well, sir,' he clipped before he minced towards the kitchen.

Dumbfounded. Again. When was the last time someone had put him in his place, never mind repeatedly in one day? He considered her for a moment as she exchanged some details with Adam over 'The Croft' – whatever that was. Her natural red curls, her porcelain skin, those plump red lips. Charlotte certainly wasn't his usual type. She wasn't tall, her skin wasn't golden, her frame wasn't athletic. But there was just something about her and her smart mouth and her quick temper never mind those curves – soft and gentle, not a defined muscle in sight, ample breasts unlike the *Maltesers* stuck to a piece of cardboard he was used to. Feminine…*No Vinny*, he warned himself and quickly dismissed the notion with a brush of a hand over his eyes. *Not with all the mess that is Nadia.*

'God, that was amazing!' Charlotte sighed, her napkin tumbling to the table as if it was too heavy to lay anywhere near her stomach. There was an unadulterated appreciation in her eyes which closed to savour the last few chews.

How Vinny wished he could sup on whatever it was she had – long since had he lost that appreciation of a good meal. How did she hold on to it, that feeling like it was something extraordinary rather than just dinner? But she did, and he could see it in the warm glow of her cheeks and how it made her slouch against the back of her chair like she had just came.

'Right,' Adam barked, his serviette collapsing next to Charlotte's. 'I'm gonna jump out for a fag.' Easing on his coat, his eyes dodged around the room to escape Charlotte's glower.

'Aw, don't Adam! You need tae pack it in!' Charlotte, on the other hand, kept hers zoned on him as she rested her hand on the gold and white packet in front of her.

The itch to scorn tickled his lips as he heard her accent slip and broaden – another side effect of HMP Broadhurst. But it was only a few words, only every now and then, and only when she was worked up over something. Since it was him this time, he let it go. 'Yes boss!' he grunted, prizing the packet from her grip.

'Idiot,' Charlotte tutted as she followed his saunter to the exit, an unlit cigarette already hanging loosely in his lips, his thumb sparking the lighter to life at his side. *Hope your flint runs out!* When he made it to the other side of the glass, she felt a prickle of awkwardness over her body, causing her bare arms to goose bump, not unlike the skin of the duck she had just devoured. She rubbed the tiny peaks warm and flat then sipped on *her* wine, all the while smiling tightly.

'So,' Vinny exhaled, 'looks like you're close – you and Adam?' He began pulling at his beard, feeling a nervous tingle in his stomach, much like when you ask out the hottest girl in high school when you are a member of the chess club.

You think, Sherlock?

Mind your manners, lass, Dad scorned.

'Yeah, very,' she said quietly, watching the candle flames sputter, nudging the pepper grinder shoulder to shoulder with the salt mill, folding her napkin into a neat, long pipe – anything except look at him. *His* type was a regular in the prison and in the courtroom – the pompous lawyer: vain, overly-confident, thinking they had the ability to walk on water. The worst type. But the least she could do was be polite, for Adam's sake at least.

Vinny nodded, his eyes stalking her every move, measuring her scepticism towards him. He didn't know what it was, but he was gripped by a desperation to win her over, to gain her approval. Strange since he never usually gave a shit what people thought about him, especially in his line of business. But he decided she was like a little bird – beautiful and delicate and fiercely independent and the more you went to it, the more you wanted it to sit on your finger, the more it hopped in the opposite direction. And he liked a challenge. 'Do you see each other often?'

'Not as often as I'd like.' *Elaborate a bit, Charlotte!* 'Only when he comes over here.'

'You've not been over to New York?'

Charlotte finally slithered her eyes to his. 'Funnily enough,' she sat forward and wiped her lipstick from the rim of her glass, 'you've seen first-hand my aversion to flying.'

'Oh, yes. I forgot about that.' He fought another smile as he skated his glass in tight circles over the cloth. 'But you flew here?'

'Under duress.' Her face pulled long. 'I can just about manage a short flight. But only because I'm stubborn and won't let it completely conquer me. I don't think I could bare a long-haul flight though.' Her forehead crinkled, and her dinner repeated at the very thought. 'I'm already having palpitations just thinking about flying back.'

'Just make sure you tell them you packed your case this time. You don't want to spark a full-scale security alert into the bargain.'

Now it was Charlotte who fought the smile which snatched at her lips. 'Ha, ha,' she drawled facetiously.

When Adam returned, windswept and reeking, they went over the position being offered. Vinny was heading the prosecution team involved in securing the conviction of one of the most notorious drug lords in Scotland. But the case was complex, and given its nature, Vinny wasn't exactly brimming with witnesses. He was confident there was enough evidence for a conviction, just not confident enough. That's where he needed Adam's tenacious legal eagle eyes, to go over the whole thing with him, to make sure there were zero gaps or loopholes which Ms Norton would undoubtedly find.

'I don't know what it is, but I have a bad feeling about this one...' His head shook gently as he tried to work out again what it was.

It seemed to load him down in some way, make him more human, a real person. Perhaps his honesty made him *slightly* more endearing. Charlotte's teeth lightly clawed her lip as she tried to weigh him up - maybe he wasn't as bad as she thought after all. It would certainly go a long way in explaining his reaction, or rather, over-reaction at the airport.

'And he's an evil fucker. If we can get him put away, I'm sure we will see a huge impact on the drugs supply chain.'

'Amen to that,' Charlotte mumbled as she dug around her bag for a pen and the battered notepad she used for her shopping and Greg's *things to do* list. She began to total up her share of the tab.

Her gaze flicked up when the table was silent, and she realized they were awaiting her input.

'Oh!' Charlotte lowered her pen. 'I'm a prison officer. I can't tell you what it's like. No matter what we do, the drugs always find a way in. It's like,' she paused as she totted up the unit's column and mumbled *carry the one*, 'a disease. People used to get clean when they went to prison. Now the drug situation is so bad, they are becoming addicted on the *inside*. And don't even get me started on Spice.' She shuddered and finished her sum. *Lord above!* She rechecked the prices on the menu. *And that's before I add on the wine!*

Smiling a nod of acknowledgement this time, Vinny took his credit card back from the long, burgundy wallet and slid it into his own. 'Well, coincidentally, Tommy Dolan is thought to be the key manufacturer and supplier of Spice in Scotland.' He pulled out a couple of twenties, placing them between the sleeves and handing it back to the waiter.

'Right Adam!' she ordered, her voice plummeting into her bag as she searched for her purse. 'Make sure you help Vinny get that scum put away! I shall look forward to tending to his needs behind bars.'

Although Adam laughed, it was clouded with the guilt that it was a very real possibility. 'Yes, Charlotte. Anything you say, Charlotte.'

'When is the case?' She brought her head out and stuck a hand in, swooping it in circles.

Vinny could feel a grin taking hold again. 'It starts at the beginning of January, so we've got a few months to make sure our case is watertight.'

'How long will it take?' Now her tongue popped out the side of her mouth as she dug deeper.

'Complex cases like this?' Vinny shrugged and pulled down his mouth. 'It usually goes on for weeks, if not months.'

Charlotte grinned with a hint of satisfaction and not just because her hand was wrapped around the familiar canvas bulge of her purse. Not bulging with money, mind you. Bulging with the last 6 months-worth of receipts, supermarket club cards and magazine discount vouchers. She smiled simply because Adam would be staying for a while. And, although it didn't make much sense to him, Vinny smiled when he realized he had the opportunity to be in her life for a while too.

Chapter Eleven

'You should have let me pay for my share!' Charlotte chuntered breathlessly as they made their way to a cocktail bar around the corner, trotting five steps to their every two yet still never catching up.

Vinny peeked at Adam like, for once in his life, he wasn't sure how to solve something. Adam took a long drag of his cigarette and shrugged as he stumped it out on the shiny ashtray on the wall outside. Blowing the residual cloud of smoke out the side of his mouth, he chuckled with a knowing sympathy. 'Sometimes, it's easier just to give in if she has a bee in her bonnet. You have to pick your battles with that one!'

He nodded wordlessly as he took in the instructions on how to work her. 'Right Charlotte,' Vinny turned to her as she caught up. 'First round on you?' He imagined if he had ever uttered such a suggestion to Nadia, she would have ground a very sharp stiletto on his big toe. He tucked his hands in the pockets of his matching *Tom Ford* jeans and watched in complete dismay.

'Yes…right…Yeah! Brilliant!' she puffed and grinned and pulled her tasselled bag strap over her shoulder. It merely fell again. Vinny began to think he was going to have to attend a course to re-learn his ideas on the reasoning of women, because everything he had learnt up till now seemed to be wrong when it came to Charlotte Croft. *Do I even hold the bloody door open for her?* he debated. Thankfully, a bulky, thick-necked doorman did it for him.

Charlotte decided to buy two of everything, just to make a point.

'How much?' she cried at the barman as he shook the silver cocktail shaker and looked a tad scared. *That's more than the bloody food bill!*

Vinny watched her face scrunch and the twenty-pound notes flag in her hand as she continued to give the barman what looked like a lecture of some sort. Scornfully shaking her head, her eyes fleeted across to him, her face immediately levelling to a smile which tried to say, 'Everything is just fine.' It kind of missed the mark...and he was smiling again.

The third spiced rhubarb concoction slid down her throat with far too much ease and Charlotte felt her reservations melt. A warm, fuzzy loveliness (aided more than a little by the potency of the cocktails) seemed to blur the last few weeks and a whole-hearted contentment filled the cold spots, purely because she had her Adam back for a bit. Her mum. Her dad. Her brother. Her everything. Vinny was off the hook for the evening too; she was just too damn happy (and tipsy) to be irked anymore. Besides, after a *very* rocky start, he'd been the perfect gent all night. *Yeah*, she admitted somewhat reluctantly to herself, *he really had*. Her face slumped on her fist swayed gently from side to side as she watched him chat to Adam about *the Committal for further examination*...Something about that beard and those amazing wolf eyes and the nose which was slightly hooked like a Roman emperor...All that hair. *I wonder what it looks like when it is all loose and free around his chin?*

Charlotte gasped quietly, a sense of guilt snapping her spine straight. Strangely, it felt like she was being unfaithful to Greg in some way. *Too soon for any of that nonsense*, she thought as she felt part of herself still lie with the man she had done so for the best part of a decade. No doubt, the lingering connection to him would pass in time yet she couldn't even imagine being with someone else, never mind someone like Mr Perfect Pants beside her. *Hell no!* Not with her untamed bikini line which she suspected made her knickers seem like they were adorned with a fancy red fringe. Judging by the lack of hair poking from his V-neck, his legs were probably more cleanly shaved than hers. Besides, he was sure to have a stunning other half – sleek and elegant and perfectly poised. Someone who rode the horses every morning and 'lunched' with the ladies at *The Ivy* before making her way back to work in a sleek glass tower where she ruled with an iron fist. A hiccup caught Charlotte off-guard as she shook her head. *Different worlds.*

'Just popping to the loo,' she announced with another *Hic!* before carefully dismounting the stool which she quietly grunted was impractical to have in any sort of drinking establishment.

'Charlotte, do you want another?' Vinny dared as she got to her feet, already learning to check first.

Charlotte looked over her shoulder to them, ready to dismiss the idea; the few unsteady steps she had just taken were warning enough that she'd probably had too much. But seeing Adam's face light up as he waved her martini glass in the air and with everything that had happened lately... 'Go on then, sack it!' She threw her hands up and ambled off to the ladies' room.

Vinny chortled as he watched her go, a perky strut to her gait. He shook his head. 'She's some woman, your sister.'

Adam's smile was shadowed. 'You've no idea. She's been through a lot. I worry about her.'

'Oh?' Vinny said, trying not to sound over-interested.

Adam ogled the brunette waitress with the tiny waist and feline eyes who collected the empties, but, for once, he wasn't in the mood. Pursing his lips, he turned his attention to Vinny but not his eyes. 'Yeah, we lost Mum to cancer when we were young. I was 11 and Charlotte was only 7. Dad did a great job by himself but then *he* developed lung cancer after years of working with asbestos...and smoking.' His eyes flashed wider at the bottle of beer in his hand as if to say *I know, I know. I should know better. Save your breath.* 'I had just started uni when he passed but Charlotte was only 14 and still at school.'

Vinny sat motionless.

'I fought to keep her. And we did it. It wasn't easy, being at law school and being a full-time dad! But Charlotte did her bit and had to grow up very quickly. She cooked most nights, cleaned the house, did the laundry instead of hanging out with her mates. I mean…she never complained – not once.' He took a guzzle from his bottle, and gasped as he put it down. His eyes became murky as he sniggered without humour, 'In fact, I think she did a much better job of looking after me than I did looking after her.'

'Shit…Mate. I…I had no idea!' Vinny blinked hard between his words. How long had he known Adam? And yet, not this. Being the boss, he was used to the sob stories: my dog is depressed; I've developed chronic fatigue syndrome after a migraine; my husband is having an affair with another man. Yet from Adam, the person who did have a valid reason to do so, nothing. Vinny felt his admiration for the Croft siblings reach new heights.

'It made her a bit more isolated in a way, dealing with all the responsibilities and burdens a 14-year-old should never have to. But she chose art as her outlet…and she is an *amazing* artist, Vinny.' Adam's eyes flared to Vinny to show him just how amazing, his face sparking to life as the sadness was superseded by a heart-swelling pride. 'She went to the Glasgow School of Art. She's so talented.'

Vinny frowned, trying to get the facts straight like he was piecing together a case. 'But I thought she was a prison officer?' Regardless, it made more sense – it suited her better somehow, being an artist. It certainly explained the bag.

'She is. And it's my fault.' The bottle still in his hand, a finger sprung free to jab at his own chest as he claimed full responsibility. 'I took the job in New York not long after Charlotte finished university. By that time, she had met Greg who was another 'aspiring' artist.' He air quoted his frustration. 'Money was tight, but they wanted to get a flat and Charlotte was desperate to have kids.' He tutted and shook his head at the thought. 'I think to have the life that she missed out on growing up…what I alone couldn't give her. A proper family.'

There was a stretched silence as Adam read his label with far too much diligence. 'It was me…I suggested joining the prison service for a few years. One of my mates dropped out of law school and joined. Said they always needed staff and the pay was good. I only meant for her to use it as a stop gap till they got on their feet.'

His elbows scaffolding him closer, Vinny's brows fell as he whispered, 'So, what happened?'

'Well,' Adam pointed a finger to the air, 'turns out Greg was a lazy fucker. Eventually he got a job, but again, Charlotte bore the brunt of all the responsibility. To keep everything going, she stayed in the prison service and she's still there. Well, for now.'

'But what about her art?' The words exploded from him like he was in the courtroom fighting against his most pure case of injustice.

Sliding from his stool, Adam began groping his pockets. 'Thankfully, she's now making plans to get back to it. Seems to have seen the light. They've split up.' A hand stuck in his pocket, he swayed a little and tugged it free.

'You must be happy about that?' Vinny questioned, sensing Adam wasn't completely on board with the idea.

'Oh, yeah. Absolutely. But I still worry. She'll be on her own, which I know Charlotte is comfortable with, especially as she was so used to it growing up. I just didn't see it for her. Funny how things work out.' Adam raised his eyebrows before taking another swig from his bottle.

Vinny didn't know whether to laugh or cry at the irony.

A flash of red zigzagged through the crowd towards them, abruptly halting when a well-oiled suit stumbled back into her, emptying half his pint down the front of her dress. Just as he would have done if it was Nadia (who would require Vinny to sort out any such situation promptly), Vinny was already on his feet and about to go over until Adam grabbed his arm. They both stared forward and saw how she gasped at the shock of the cold, then how her gasp turned to a laugh as she helped the drunk, with both hands, to where he had been standing. Wobbling like he was on a ship in a storm, he anchored his hand on her shoulder and apologized again and again, as she shook her head and shook her dripping hands that it was nothing. He leant over to the barman who handed over a towel. The piss head tried to blot it at her breast. Charlotte snapped it from his hand and looked like she said something very like *nice try* before drying herself and handing it back.

Speechless, Vinny leaned back into his stool.

Still staring forward, Adam smiled. 'Charlotte's low maintenance, if you catch my drift. She knows how to look after herself.'

I'm sure they do night classes at the Met, Vinny thought as his feet peddled backwards to find the footrest.

As Charlotte clambered back on top of her stool, she grabbed a pack of tissues from her bag and began swiping down her cleavage. 'Are you two okay?' Her eyes darted uneasily from one astonished face to the other, grinning from ear to ear.

'Yip,' Adam sang, tapping a corner of a coaster on the table. 'Just hammering out some ideas about the case.'

'Well stop!' Her hand dove back into her bag, fishing out some cleansing wipes now that her cleavage was more sticky than wet. 'I've only got you for one night so no more shop talk – the both of you.' One eye screwed shut as the wipe plunged deeper.

'Do you want to head back to the hotel and get changed?' Vinny asked, hitching a thumb over his shoulder and having no bloody idea what her response would be.

'Nah! It'll dry,' Charlotte dismissed, packing away all her cleaning paraphernalia. 'Ya beauty!' she cried suddenly, her hand shooting back in and pulling out her bottle of *RiRi. I knew you would come in handy!* After squirting it liberally around her neck and once down her cleavage, she finally dropped her bag to the floor with a heavy clunk.

Vinny recoiled slightly as he was smacked with a mighty pong of what he thought smelt like *Pledge* but at least he got that bit right – having no bloody idea.

'Right, fag time!' Adam yelped, finally remembering why he was standing. This time, he was off before Charlotte had a chance to nag.

Adam sat alone at one of the many empty tables which littered the cobbled street, his collar jerked high against the insistent drizzle and biting wind. He plucked a *Marlboro* from the pack, tapped the butt several times on the bubbled glass table-top and watched as it became dappled with grey, transparent blobs. After a few tries (and only when he lifted his coat as a windbreaker), he managed to light the cigarette and took two deep, sizzling drags for a good hit. Oh, how he missed the good old days when you could smoke in a pub instead of getting piss wet through like a social leper. But sitting there, soggy and alone, he gazed at his cigarette and began to consider that maybe it was just time to quit.

'Excuse me mate. Dae yae hiv a light?' the familiar accent but foreign voice asked.

'For a fellow Scotsman, of course.' Adam stood to meet the

stranger who had just been passing in the rain.

'Which part a Scotland are yae fae?' the man asked, straightening the dark baseball cap which shadowed his face. He hunched his shoulders against the downpour as he battled to get a flame.

'Glasgow originally. I've been away for years now,' Adam said as he took back the lighter.

'I don't blame you mate,' he laughed wheezily as he took a drag. But as he exhaled, his wit seemed to go up in smoke too. 'And ma advice fur yae would be to stay away.'

'Sorry?' The shift in sentiment caused Adam's fingers to curl into a fist.

'You heard.'

Adam felt his shoulders square and his feet plant themselves firm. 'And who the fuck are you?'

'A friend of a friend...Adam.'

Adam felt no pain as the blade slid between his ribs, only an overwhelming coldness like he was suddenly naked to the elements. Staggering back as if he was a lot drunker than he was, he placed his hands on his side, praying it had just been a punch. Perplexed, he looked down at his bloodied hand, the site of which brought him to his knees.

Chapter Twelve

'Oh, he's multi-talented! I remember even in primary school, he entered a competition because he thought he was amazing at robotics dancing. I've never been more embarrassed - he took to the assembly stage…and began to dance! He was playing an invisible fiddle…' Charlotte choked and spluttered, a hot pink trickle of cocktail running down her chin, sending her reaching for the tissues again. 'Then…opening an invisible can of coke!' She acted out the mime with more than a little bit of artistic license.

Vinny let out a long groan from his lungs. 'God, today you've made me laugh more than I can remember. I'm so going to take the piss out of him for that one. Hey Adam, you fancy hitting the Electric Boogaloo club in Soho later?' He became a robot too.

'Oh no,' she begged between nervous spurts of giggles, popping an olive in her mouth. 'You can't! He'll bloody kill me!'

'Well,' Vinny said, shaking his pint till it was flat, yet feeling like, at last, he was making progress, 'you'll need to think of something so that I don't.' The words were already out before Vinny felt a croak draw his vocal cords shut. The olive bulging squirrel-like in her cheek, Charlotte's chin remained wedged open.

'Shit.' His eyes fluttered quickly as he jerked straight. 'I…I just realized how that sounded!' He pulled at the neck of his jumper and wriggled in is seat, his own face flushing a little. Another rarity. 'I meant…tell me an embarrassing story about something you did as a kid and I'll call it quits.'

He tracked her features carefully until they softened. Breaking into what he hoped was a smile, she began to slowly chew on the olive, and he began to breathe again. 'Sorry,' he murmured. 'But you make me…nervous.' He bit on his bottom lip in just such a manner and Charlotte felt the sudden urge to bite his bottom lip too.

But the blood-curdling scream shattered the moment.

The young woman's hands lay limp at her sides, rich with a glossy red coating, her face ashen, her eyes gawping. Charlotte had seen that look too many times at Broadhurst – disbelief, shock, fear, the searching for an answer. Glaring at her hands, the woman screamed again, this time persuading the customers to put down their glasses, to dismount their stools. Charlotte was already past them and bolting out the door, Vinny at her back.

Her knees pounded dully against the unforgiving stone where Adam lay in a dark, sticky pool of his own blood, his eyes unblinking as the raindrops continued to pitter-patter down on him. A scream began to build in her throat, as did the temptation to lose herself in the terror. It took everything, but she guzzled it back and became Miss Croft.

'Adam? Adam? Can you hear me?' she cried, her hand cupping and briskly shaking his chin. *So cold.* She saw it then, the expanding poppy-red stain balloon across the new white shirt he'd bought earlier that day. Just a few hours earlier that day…It still felt reachable enough to step back to it. Surely? Charlotte let out a small whimper as she placed both hands firmly on the oozing red puncture, feeling the warm patch squelch beneath her fingers.

At last, Adam's eyes trundled to her, sluggish and scared and dull. 'Sorry, Wee Yin,' he whispered.

Charlotte scowled and shook her head vigorously. 'Why?' She tried to make it sound like a sneer, the very same one she used when he tried to persuade her to eat cauliflower.

'You're not goin' anywhere, ya tit. Don't move Adam. You're goin' to be fine. Vinny.' Her words were brusque and her eyes frantic as he remained dazed at her side. 'VINNY!'

It was enough to rouse him.

'Call an ambulance!'

'I've already done it, love. They're on their way,' the young barman she'd given a tongue-lashing to earlier said quietly leaning over them, one hand glued to his head, a wine glass wilted in the other.

'Right Vinny,' she barked, and he dunked his head with her every syllable, 'I need you to listen really carefully. I want you to take over me and put your hand firmly on the wound. Got it?'

All he got was that her mascara had slipped an inch. 'Yes.'

She eyeballed the wound and cried what he thought might have been the word *now*. Vinny placed his hands over Charlotte's. When she slid her hands from beneath his, he pressed down as hard as he could, feeling every part of the responsibility to stop his friend's life from escaping to the cold cobbles below.

'You! Get me some clean bar towels!'

The barman was back in less than 10 seconds with a fresh stack.

'Vinny, on the count of 3, lift your hand,' she ordered, rolling a fresh towel into a tight ball. 'Okay?' She nodded for him and he followed suit, his lips pressed too tightly together to talk.

Vinny mouthed each digit a milli-second behind her. When they reached 1, he lifted his hands and Charlotte packed the towel tightly against the wound. But during the changeover, she already noted the scarlet of Vinny's hands, already saw it was going to be like trying to plug a hole in the Hoover Dam with your finger. On her knees now, she put another two towels on top and pressed with everything she had. Keeping her eyes locked on Adam's, she felt Vinny place his hand on top of hers and push harder.

'Coats!' she screamed to the gawping eyes and mouths hovering somewhere above them. 'I need coats to keep him warm. Now!' Her command impelled the shuffling of nylon and the metallic whiz of zips before they were parachuting in from every direction.

'Adam, you're going to be okay,' Charlotte assured him as she tried to wipe a tear on her shoulder. 'You hear that? It's the ambulance. But you need to try to stay awake so I'm going to keep talking to you and you're going to keep answering. Right?' Her voice was strong, the only thing about her which was strong.

'Right,' he whispered, and despite everything, she could spot the tiniest of smiles on his blue-tinged lips.

'See? I told you. You need to give up smoking!' It was somewhere between a sob and scorn.

'Not now, Charlotte,' he groaned, his eyes becoming heavier under the warmth and weight of the coats.

As his eyelids struggled, her voice became more forceful. 'Who did it Adam? Who stabbed you?'

'Scottish. He was Scottish. Asked for a light. He warned me to stay…away. He…knew my name.' The words fractured, his breath stuttered.

Charlotte's head whipped to Vinny, her eyes slits. A targeted hit? A warning? Emitting what sounded very like an actual growl, she turned back and, although his hand remained sturdy on top of hers, Vinny's body sagged at her side.

'Well, don't you worry about that,' she snapped sharply as the flashing blue lights flaunted urgently on the lengthy windows bursting with the faces of stunned punters who watched on in horror. Charlotte suddenly knew what it felt like to be the silverback in the zoo who kept his back to the crowd. 'We'll get him.' And she shot to Vinny a glare of utter conviction. Nodding once, he was in.

But Adam didn't catch that part, no matter how many times Charlotte screamed his name.

Chapter Thirteen

The only colour Charlotte could see was the red which marred their hands, smeared their cheeks, gave a dappled, flowery pattern to her red dress. Her eyes furrowed to the two porters who had just barged through the double doors, each at the end of a bed cradling an old lady with candy floss hair and tissue paper skin. She lay so still, and was such a candle wax shade of pale, Charlotte thought she might have already passed until an incoherent moan made the sight even more haunting.

'Oh man! Did you see that last goal? It was a screamer!' the shorter porter with a mouthful of braces shouted over the poor old dear, robbing her of even more dignity. And no matter how Charlotte tried to comprehend it, no matter how she tried to grasp a hint of his ordinary day, she couldn't. How could the world go about its business whilst hers could end at any moment?

Although the waiting room was busy, everyone sat motionless and spoke in hushed, taught whispers – and only when necessary. Every other sound caused a flinch; the whoosh of the sliding door to reception, the beeps of the coffee machine and the far too infrequent call of a name. The air was crammed with heartache and fear, each worried thought making the oxygen heavy and pungent, almost too thick to breathe in.

Charlotte hadn't realized she was trembling until she felt Vinny shift and pull off his jumper, revealing a matching V-neck t-shirt.

'Here,' he whispered, rolling it up to slip over her head.

Numb to the core, Charlotte tilted her head towards him, allowing him to thread it over her and seek her hands through the sleeves, just like her mum used to when she was a little girl. She watched mutely as he folded the black wool to her wrists, and knew it was his way of showing he cared, that he was there for her without being able to use the words either. Perhaps he too was afraid to fracture the silence in case it had a cataclysmic consequence on what was going on behind the blue screens.

She could feel the friction of his knee bounce against hers, could see his hand polishing it till it burned. Charlotte looked up to him, his face lined like it had suddenly aged 10 years, as if he was responsible. But the words of consolation were too chaotic to be formed into something which resembled sense. So, she'd just need to show him. To let him know he wasn't to blame, to say thank you for being there, she gently curled her fingers in his, feeling the platinum band, cold and solid, on his wedding finger. He replied with a soft squeeze and didn't let go, not even when a lofty doctor in green scrubs called her name.

They were led through to a side room, where two CID officers were already waiting. There were no consoling smiles, no shimmers of empathy. But their scepticism barely registered.

'Please have a seat, Charlotte, Vinny' the doctor requested, his face equally stoic with a touch of *I've seen it all before.*

Her hand became more vice-like around Vinny's as her eyes pleaded for the news her mouth was too terrified to ask for.

The doctor began with a long, low exhale as he pulled the thin cloth hat from his head and leant his elbows on his knees, the surgical mask hanging loosely from his neck. Charlotte was strangely transfixed by the fact he wore *Crocs.*

'Adam is now out of surgery. Thankfully, all his main arteries were missed but his spleen was punctured so it had to be removed. He has lost a lot of blood, but he must have a strong heart, as it kept going until we transfused. But I have to say, if it wasn't for the fact you managed to stem the flow so quickly, I think we would be having a very different conversation.'

Her words were hoarse, rasping. 'Is…he out of…danger?' Charlotte was still staring at his *Crocs*. They were white. Brilliant white. *Not the best colour for a surgeon.*

He moved his head slowly from side to side, his eyes detached yet with an adopted benevolence. 'No, Charlotte. He is not out of danger. He is very ill, but the fact that he has got this far is a really good sign. The next 24 hours will be critical. After surgery, we put him in a drug induced coma to help his body rest and heal. If he makes it through that, his chances will dramatically improve.'

It must be me, must be my fault. There really wasn't any other explanation. She'd been there too many times, lost too many of the ones she was closest too. So naturally, it would happen to Adam at some point. It made her drop Vinny's hand just in case the curse extended to acquaintances too.

He slid it back to his thigh, as if wounded. Afraid eye contact was also a factor, Charlotte kept hers on the *Crocs*.

'In the meantime, I believe these officers would like to ask you some questions if you are up to it?'

Charlotte nodded at his *Crocs*.

Thankfully, Vinny was able to fill in her gaps. Once he'd explained he was the lead lawyer in the drugs case, and they both clarified their suspicions that the stabbing was not a random act, the officers unstiffened but seemed quickened by the fact this was something more than the result of a drunken brawl on a Saturday night.

'If you can think of something in the meantime, please don't hesitate to give us a call,' the taller of the two (who seemed like the boss, given his advance in years and that he asked all the questions) smiled. Her dad had told her that a gap between your front teeth meant you were a good singer, but she seriously doubted it in this case – not when it sounded like he smoked 50 roll-ups a day. Her fingers traced the embossed letters on the card - DCI Aitkens.

His younger sidekick, who seemed like the eager new kid given that he was taking such furious notes, Charlotte began to imagine she could smell burning, at last looked up and spoke. 'Where will you be staying, Charlotte? Charlotte?'

It still felt like she was working a few seconds behind everyone else. 'I-I don't know,' she stammered, at last noticing she was missing a shoe. *How the hell?* she thought as she slid off the remaining heel and clasped it gently in her lap. 'Erm, I'm staying at The Tower Bridge Hotel but supposed to check out in the morning. I'll see if I can extend the booking.'

Minion began scribbling again.

'She will be staying with me.' Vinny reached into his back pocket for his wallet. 'Here are my details.'

Charlotte never got chance to disagree, partly (or mostly if she were being honest) because she did not want to.

The pungent smell of disinfectant and warm plastic hit hard and brought her right back to visiting her dad in the hospice, something she had tried hard to forget ever since. A sickly, sweet clawing of something undecipherable hung in the background and Charlotte suspected it may have been illness itself. But the lights were dimmed and the voices of the nurses working in their wide arcing station were optimistically subdued. It was strangely soothing.

'Five minutes only!' they were told (whispered firmly by the short, frowning nurse with the big arse), on the condition they remained behind the glass partition (given their current state of *God knows what* contamination). Charlotte didn't have the energy to tell her they were innocents. Innocent victims of an unprovoked attack. That there was no brawl, that her brother hadn't looked at anyone the wrong way, he hadn't chatted up anyone else's bird or spilled someone's pint. Not when she saw him through the window, streamers of wires and machines and tubes invading him.

After a moment or two's hesitation, she moved forward – one small shuffle at a time in the flimsy slippers they had given her in A and E. Mentally, she took the seat at Adam's side, ran her finger lightly over his, avoiding the painful looking canula embedded in the top of his hand. Instead, she listened to the reassuring rhythmical beeping of the heart monitor and the hiss of the bag as it inflated and deflated at his side like a giant piston, pumping the life into him.

'God, Adam, you don't do things by halves,' she whispered, her voice parched. 'Dad always said you were the attention seeking one.' Her throat bobbed painfully as she stumbled slightly, her tows clawing to keep purchase of the foam soles. 'You've got to get better. You can't leave me by myself.'

She'd almost forgot Vinny was hovering behind her (with her shoe) until she felt his warm hand softly touch her shoulder, steady her. A friend, it said.

'Charlotte. He's in good hands and you need some sleep. We will come back first thing in the morning.'

What an amazing word it was – we. They were a *we*. It gave her so much reassurance in that moment that she wasn't just a *me*. That she wasn't doing this all by herself. There was no doubt, she felt the solace of that word *we* comfort her as she just stared, trying to marry the beginning of the night to the end. They'd been having such a great time. What lay before her didn't make sense, no matter how many times she replayed it. 'Sleep tight,

Adam. I'll be back first thing…I love you.' Kissing a clover of fingers, she stuck them to the glass, leaving a smear of love for him to see if he ever opened his eyes.

Chapter Fourteen

The taxi driver's wary eyes fleeted to the rear-view mirror for the umpteenth time, accusing them like they had just committed murder. To be fair, they looked like they had. As she felt Vinny vibrate again in response, Charlotte gently tapped his arm and shook her head. It was enough. With a single nod, Vinny understood and uncurled his fists over his knees, and she returned to staring blankly at London in all its early morning drunken glory. The nightclubs were emptying onto the streets: relationships making or breaking, friends swaying arm in arm as they began the snaking walk home, hungry drunks bobbing eagerly in the queue at the burger van. How she envied each and every one of them!

Soon, the taxi started bumbling over cobbles instead of concrete. Vinny unclipped his seatbelt and reached for some cash. The taxi pulled up at the imposing slate-grey doorway, as wide as a garage entrance, which opened straight on to the street. Handing over two crisp twenties, he said, 'Keep the change.'

Charlotte braced herself and Vinny's features twisted when the reply came in the form of a snide snigger. 'Nah-ha-ha! You're all right mate!' A pinched hand mottled with liver spots snaked through a hole in the perspex, dropping into Vinny's hand every last penny and note owed to him.

Keen to avoid another stabbing, Charlotte shuffled against him. But Vinny didn't move, keeping what she could only presume was his best death stare on the mirror.

'Vinny,' she said softly, although wrought, her hand trembling against his.

Albeit reluctantly and with a hiss, he began to edge out of the cab. She watched him jerk his t-shirt down as he held the door open for her. But as soon as she stepped out, he swan-dived his head back inside. 'Have a good evening, dickhead,' he spat before tossing in the cash and slamming the door shut with both hands.

Charlotte didn't notice the opulence of 17a St Anne's Mews, Notting Hill as they entered the darkened hallway: not the sanded and waxed parquet, not the quirky frosted glass wall which bowed around the kitchen, not the Oriental vase filled with fresh orchids or the Japanese lacquered table it sat upon. Not the pair of sculptures, on their own pedestals, which may have been made from old driftwood or weathered bone. Not the expensive smell of jasmine and cherry blossom. Not even when Vinny flicked the light on (which only spot-lighted their bloodstained limbs and clothes). In fact, they were the only two priceless works of art she did notice.

Vinny took her carpet bag from her shoulder, which was every bit as heavy as he expected, and gazed at how small she seemed especially now his jumper was down to her thighs, the neck covering only one shoulder and both hands swamped by the sleeves. 'Come on,' he coaxed with his head. 'I'll show you where the shower is. You can borrow some of Nadia's clothes.' He looked back and measured her with his eyes. 'She's a bit taller but I'm sure they'll do.'

'Thanks,' Charlotte whispered, stepping out of the already worn slippers and straightening them before she followed him up the cast iron spiral staircase, the ornate metal pattern cold and pleasantly gouging against her bare soles.

It led them to the top floor which was taken over by one giant room (or rather suite), a far grander one than she had been staying in with

Adam. On one side of the room there was a lounge area with two low Parisienne chairs perfectly aligned on each side of a grand open fire, a huge TV set into the wall above. On the opposite wall, the biggest bed she'd ever seen. It was layered with soft luxurious fabrics and too many perfectly arranged cushions to count. An ornate golden chandelier suspended low from the ceiling and Charlotte suspected it wasn't a million miles away from the theatre lights Adam had just been under. Each fold of the silk drapes was perfectly pleated, and everything, *everything*, was soft taupe and warm grey.

As her head swivelled slowly to take it all in, Charlotte suspected it was intended to ooze comfort and luxury, yet it had the opposite effect on her. There was *nothing* personal. Where were the slippers, the hot water bottle, the favourite dressing gown with the ripped pocket you wrapped yourself up in on a cold morning or after a piping hot bath? Where was the jewellery box with your favourite silver rings and the silver framed picture of your loved ones at the late Summer BBQ, all laughing? Where was that ornament your granny left you which you kept on display, not because you liked it, but because it reminded you of her?

Afraid to touch anything, Charlotte hovered somewhere in the middle, her fingers fidgeting at her back as Vinny slid a door she never realized was there until it opened with an affluent whoosh. Inside, the clothes were hung with such anal precision that Charlotte was sure if she had a ruler, they would be *exactly* equally spaced in 10cm intervals. Charlotte's antique wardrobe (with its dodgy shelf and background smell of mothballs) didn't even have space, not an inch of it – each piece of clothing vying for a slither of view. Some pieces even fell behind to an abyss, never to be seen again. Somehow, she had a good idea that there was no room for *Florence and Fred*, or *George* for that matter, in the arrangement. And maybe it was just her imagination, but it seemed to be colour coded? A perfect spectrum of outfits from red to violet?

'Right, let me see…' he muttered as if he was thinking allowed rather than addressing her. Vinny trawled through drawer after drawer until his hand settled on something fawn and silk. He held it up for Charlotte but seeing way too much white in her eyes, spun back quickly and placed the offending article back in the drawer.

As she watched him hunt, Charlotte began to feel sorry for him…and she was exhausted. *So exhausted.* Her eyelids drooped as she spoke slowly. 'Vinny? Do you just have an old t-shirt and maybe leggings?'

He turned to her and milked his beard, his eyes scanning the architraves of the ceiling like it was the inside of his head. 'Not sure about the leggings. Nadia doesn't *do* leggings. But I've got plenty of t-shirts.' Closing one secret door, he uncovered another. As Charlotte expected, it was equally anal. He pulled a perfectly folded plain back t-shirt from a shelf which topped 9 other perfectly folded black t-shirts. From a lower shelf, he picked out a matching pair of sweatpants. Holding them up for approval, his eyes crumpled as he awaited her verdict.

This time, she answered with a smile. 'Better.'

They felt lovely against her skin too, still a tingling red raw after she scoured away the dried blood in a shower which could have fit four people comfortably. All the more difficult to rinse out the pink water and flakes of red from though. And that was only the Jill bathroom. Vinny was using his Jack version on the other side of the room. When the marble shower was mostly back to white, Charlotte realized the one thing she couldn't wash away was her horror, the sickness of it recycling the cocktails and meal she had so enjoyed on the way in. Not so much on the way out.

There was a gentle rap at the door after her final heave. 'Charlotte? Are you okay?'

Oh, fucking dandy! 'Yeah…' she squawked, the acid still charring her throat and a cold sweat making her swoon as she perched on her knees and flushed the toilet. 'I'll be out in a minute. Don't suppose you have a spare toothbrush?'

'Top right-hand cabinet. Do you want something to drink?'

Clambering to her feet, Charlotte gripped on to the sink and opened the cabinet door where 5 toothbrushes remained hygienically sealed and standing to attention, just like Nadia's clothes. *Good God! Who has the time…and the money for this?* 'A cup of tea would be lovely…if you're making one?' Frowning, she poked each of the brushes over from their parade and immediately felt it was easier to breathe.

'Sure. How do you have it?' His voice ebbed as he was already on his way to the stairs.

'Black. No sugar,' she called, the toothbrush hanging out of her mouth muffling her words.

Charlotte balled her bloodied clothes in her arms, turning to inspect the imposing piece of art which hung above the super-king bed watching her. Ah, at last the 'personal' touch. Who she presumed was Nadia with Vinny, his arms wrapped around her from behind. His cheek next to hers, a supposedly natural laughter capturing their faces as if the photograph was taken in the spur of the moment. Photography wasn't Charlotte's strong point, but she did wonder how many times they had to rehearse the moment before getting that one shot. Somehow, Charlotte knew, quite a few. But it was like an act, a pretence – all black and white and staged. For her, it defied the logic of what art was. Art was meant to capture that fleeting moment of emotion in its most natural and sincerest form – to make you feel that emotion when you connected with it. It made you ask questions like: Who are they? What happened to her? Why does he look sad? That portrait didn't prompt any questions in her mind. Zero. She didn't feel love or laughter. If anything, Charlotte felt cheated. *But each to their own*, she shrugged as she made her way downstairs. But her feet halted a few steps from the bottom to eavesdrop in on Vinny's speakerphone conversation.

'Yeah, I brought her back here to stay. I hope that's okay. I couldn't leave her alone, not after that.'

'Of course not, darling. You did the right thing! I've got to go darling. Someone's on the other line. You take care.'

'Sure. Will do. Nadia…when are you coming home?'

'Vincent. Please. Not now…' She said it in one, long moan.

'Well, I think just now is as good a time as any to discuss it.'

'I need to get this finished Vincent. It's a really crucial time!' Nadia's voice became a sharp shade of soprano.

'This can't go on forever, Nadia. The situation needs resolving. *You* need to face it!' His became a low roar.

Charlotte moved back up a step.

'I will! Of course, I will…just not now. Darling, I really must go! It's Tom. It must be important.'

'Fine. Right. I'll speak to you next week.' Vinny clipped his last line, like he was cutting the conversation instead of the other way around. He strolled into view, staring at the mobile in his hand, his face fluttering between the multitude of emotions she had sketched what felt like an eon ago. Sighing heavily, he tossed it on a nearby chair.

'….27, 28, 29, 30,' she counted quietly before dropping down the final few steps. He had already made up the over-sized sofa into a bed and a steaming hot cup of tea was waiting beside each seat at the fire. *Is it a fire?* she thought, it's light so blue and uniform, it looked like there was no flame to it.

'Hi,' Charlotte whispered, hovering at the doorway, a set of toes tucked under like a fist on the wooden floor.

'Hey!' Vinny looked up, his face now blank. 'Those actually quite suit you,' he laughed gently eyeing his clothes on her body. Smiling, he took her ball of laundry through to the kitchen.

Charlotte looked herself up and down as she heard the beeping of buttons followed by a surge of water and a low hum. 'Yes, I am the Henry Ford of the pyjama world. Any colour as long as it's black.'

Back again, he held out a hand towards the fire. 'Please, make yourself at home. Are you hungry?'

Of course, he was trying to be helpful, but food? *Really?* Shaking her head, she perched on the edge of the chair, rigid and ridiculously expensive, and stared at the fixed blue flame which took up most of the wall at her side. Despite feeling the heat harshly against her skin, she wanted to move closer to thaw her insides.

Vinny watch her carefully as he took the chair opposite. 'Charlotte? Are you okay?'

Unable to break her gaze with the flame, her fingers coiled tightly around the mug, scalding to the touch. 'You know, I don't know what I will do if I lose him. He's all I have left.' The words were dead-like and far away.

'He'll make it. I'm sure he will. The doctors these days…they can work miracles and you heard what the doctor said – he has a strong heart.'

'Do you think it is anything to do with the case?' Unblinking, her eyes moved to Vinny, noticing how pale-skinned and white-lipped he was too.

His shoulders hunched an inch then fell. 'It does seem a very big coincidence.'

'I agree. So, what does it mean? Are you in danger too?'

He eased back in the chair and smoothed his beard. 'I have no idea.'

They both sat lost in their own thoughts, letting the events of the evening become a reality instead of a bad dream. With each vision of blood, each vision of her own hands pressed against the wound, the blood pooling over her fingers, Charlotte felt her eyelids become more cumbersome, each flashback sapping her. Her gaze slid to where he sat – the beautiful Viking. *So much for first opinions* she thought as she marvelled at how much hers had changed dramatically in just one day. 'Vinny, thank you for everything. I don't know what I would have done if you weren't there.'

'I would never have left you.' His words were soft, his eyes serious.

'I know.'

Vinny noticed her speech become elastic. 'You're shattered Charlotte. Go up to bed and get some shut eye. I'll take the sofa.'

Charlotte's words snapped back tight. 'No Vinny. I'm not taking your bed. *I'll* take the sofa.'

Ignoring her insistence, he stood and stretched a yawn, his t-shirt lifting enough to reveal the deep, toned v pointing to what was below his low-cut sweats. 'You're as pig-headed as Adam. I insist. Plus, I'm going to do a bit of bedtime research. See if anything springs to mind which might help with what happened tonight.'

Too tired to argue for once, she put her cup down without having had as much as a sip. 'All right. Thank you. I'll try not to waken you in the morning. I need to get to the hotel and then to the hospital.'

'I'm an early riser.' His finger circled the pad on the laptop. 'I'm coming with you.'

'Oh. Are you sure?' Charlotte asked as she floated to the stairs.

'Positive.' He raised an eyebrow, daring her to argue.

Nope, still can't. Instead, she smiled wearily and began climbing up the staircase, her legs heavy and resistant. 'Night Vinny.'

'Night Charlotte.'

He waited until the pale bare feet had padded out of sight before he slumped into the chair and buried everything his face had been masking into his palms. In all his privileged years, he'd never seen anything so horrifying. Sure, he'd heard it often enough in the courtroom, the grotesque side of humanity. Perhaps he'd even built up a professional detachment to it having heard it every day for the last 10 years. But never involving someone he knew, never a friend. Well, except once…

Trying again to shake away the thought, his hands ironed his face before he strode to the decanter and poured himself a 3-finger whiskey. Because, above all, he wanted to go up and hold her. Jeeze, he wanted her to hold him after that! He thought of how nice it would feel after all this time. His arms wrapped around her, the warmth of her. Hers around his back, stroking and comforting, his neck crooked in hers. When his thoughts of comfort took another course of action, he huffed it away and got down to business. Switching on the desk lamp, he gulped down a burning mouthful of single malt and scrolled through the data on his laptop to go over the finer details…again.

Her eyes already familiar with the new gathering of shadows, the story played before her eyes again and again, no matter how hard she scrunched them closed. Not even when she placed her head under one of the six pillows she had to choose from. It wasn't just what she saw, it was what she heard which haunted her: that blood-curdling scream, the sirens, Adam's laboured breath. Adam's breathing…dying. Pushing the pillow away for some air, she gasped as if it was for him and forced herself up onto her elbows.

The light from the spiral staircase defused into the room and

Charlotte could hear Vinny typing and clearing his throat quietly every now and again. It was comforting but not comforting enough. She grabbed a pillow and made her way towards the light and tapping of keys.

Charlotte appeared so quietly, Vinny's hand smacked to his chest and he fell back in his leather swivel chair as if a spectre had manifested at his side. 'Shit!' He puffed his cheeks and laughed. 'Are you okay?'

'Sorry,' Charlotte giggled, holding a hand up in apology, the other clenching the pillow tighter to her chest. 'I…I can't sleep. Can I sit down here for a bit while you work? I keep…seeing…' She shifted from one bare foot to the other and twirled a finger at her temple.

Oh, how Vinny wanted to wrap her up in the quilt and swaddle her. 'Of course. Just chill down here. There are loads of books on the shelf.' He nudged his head to a wall which could have very well been a wing in the British Library. 'Help yourself.'

'Thanks.' Charlotte hugged the pillow and tiptoed to the bookshelf, picking the first thing with an interesting cover. But just as she was about to return to her seat, her eyes were drawn up to the silver frame on the top shelf. There was Vinny, still soft around the edges, long before the now manly angles of his thirties. His arm was slung over another lad who looked just as joyous. Now *that* photograph spoke a thousand words and emotions. And they were so happy. So happy in fact, Charlotte couldn't help but smile along wondering who the other young man was and what they had been doing at the time. *A brother? A friend? Camping? A festival?*

'All right?' Vinny asked brightly.

'Hm…yeah.' She smiled politely in apology for her nosiness as she turned for the chair.

Plumping the pillow a few times at her back, she then opened the book and Vinny turned his head back to the screen. After only the first three pages, the words began to snake and smudge, but Charlotte Croft wasn't a quitter! She polished her eyes then turned over to page 4. This time it was her turn to be startled to find Vinny at her side.

'Here,' he said, sliding the other armchair to her feet to make a bed, finished off nicely by a thick chenille throw to use as a cover.

'Oh!' Her eyes sprung double-espresso wide. 'Thank you.' She pretended to read a few more pages. *Don't want to sleep. Hospital might…call.* And her last thought before her eyes gave in was how glad she was that it was Vinny she chose to sketch at the airport.

The next time Vinny looked at her, her eyes were closed, the book face down on her chest, her breathing even. And just like her, he felt better to have her near. He lifted the quilt from the sofa and carefully swapped it with the throw.

Before he tried to sleep himself, he stood before the bookcase and reached for the photo. As Charlotte had done, he smiled warmly and shook his head when he thought back to that weekend at Glastonbury. But his smile died, and he nodded solemnly to the image. Placing the frame back on the shelf, he angled it correctly and quietly vowed to get whoever was responsible. Yeah, he'd make sure Tommy Dolan spent the rest of his days being shagged up the arse too.

Chapter Fifteen

'Oh. Oooh. Ow! Ah. Ts!' A different sore sound griped with each inch Charlotte raised her neck from its awkward angle as she listened to the clinking and clanking of crockery coming from the kitchen. A broad shadow floated around behind the wall of frosted glass, making a breakfast she wouldn't put near her lips. Not when the smell of savoury and sweet was already knocking her to the wrong side of nauseous.

Suddenly, she scrambled up more urgently and reached for her phone. One eye still to waken, she called the ward.

'Good morning. ICU.'

'Erm, hello.' The sharp cough only partially cleared the frog from her throat as she croaked, 'Can you tell me the condition of one of your patients – Adam Croft? I-I am his sister, Charlotte.'

'Hi Charlotte. I'll just get one of the nurses to come and speak with you. Hold the line please.'

Ping! The struggling eye sprung open. *What the hell does that mean?* Charlotte felt the words coagulate in her arteries, already over-analyzing the brief exchange. Non-committal. Frosty and factual. *Fuck!*

Vinny was already at her side, co-ordinated impeccably of course, an open jar of Nutella in his hand. Smelling of an expensive and thorough sort of cleanliness, he looked every bit as fraught as her.

A hand plonked on her shoulder. Her friend. Her *we*.

'Morning Charlotte. I'm glad to report Adam has had a comfortable night. His stats have remained steady so that's great news.'

Every tense muscle unravelled as her eyes rolled back in her head. 'Oh, thank you! Thank you so much.' She tried harder to budge the frog. 'When can I come and visit?'

'The doctors do the rounds at 10 so any time after that is fine, Charlotte. We'll see you then.'

As she hung up, she glared at the phone in her hand. 'He's…had…a good night.' The last word became a squeak, and Charlotte pressed the phone to her lips to squash it.

'Oh, Charlotte! That's great. Bloody great!'

She managed a nod and a sniff. Yes, it was. But it was also only the first triumph in an epic war.

'Breakfast?' Vinny held up the Nutella, his voice full of hope.

'Erm…' Charlotte began to gather up the quilt.

Undeterred, he counted a finger each time he rhymed something off. *Cereal? Toast? A banana? Poached egg, fried egg, scrambled egg, omelette?* He carried on till he had no fingers left.

The quilt and two pillows bundled high in her arms, she paused, her words stifled by the load. 'Vinny, I feel ill. I couldn't stomach a thing. Once I see Adam, I'm sure I'll want to eat. We could maybe go for lunch…but nothing too fancy,' she added just in case.

'All right but I'm definitely taking you for lunch then,' he grumbled. 'Oh!' he pointed a finger in the air and jogged to the fridge before shouting, 'Yoghurt?'

Turns out, Nadia did have a sportswear drawer – full of matching leggings and vests (in every colour of the rainbow and every pattern of the jungle). Charlotte popped on a set (Henry Ford style), insisting on buying replacements for everything she had borrowed. After a quick check on Vinny's laptop when he had gone to collect his car from the lock-up around the corner, she realized these were the only set she could borrow. *Lord above! Has the woman not heard of Primark?*

The car itself was low and wide, a dull, bulletproof black and roared like a big cat. Just the fact that it received open-mouthed stares made Charlotte glad of the tinted windows. Plus, there were so many luminous buttons, it looked like an apprenticeship at NASA would be required to master them. *Give me my geriatric Beetle any day*, she thought sinking lower in her seat, *with its wonky wipers and temperamental CD player.*

'Alexa, play some jazz.'

Who the fuck is Alexa?

After collecting their belongings from the hotel and spending the rest of the morning at Adam's side, Charlotte folded and let Vinny take her to the café at the end of his street – not quite a greasy spoon but certainly not The Ritz either. But she wasn't hungry, not even when her favourite (jacket potato with lashings of tuna mayo) was put down before her. Seeing Adam just lying there, only a flimsy cluster of wires tethering him to this world – how could she eat? But having promised Vinny she'd try, Charlotte forced down the first mouthful. It bulged its way painfully down her throat before she asked, 'Vinny, do you know any cheap hotels near the hospital?' Her eyes remained angled down, her fork trying to hide the food on her plate under other piles of food on her plate.

'No. Why?' His bright eyes crinkled as he mopped his lips with a napkin which was of the slidable rather than absorbent variety. He took another bite.

'Well, you've been so kind but I'm going to take the next week off, *at least*. I can't impose on you but please don't think I'm not grateful for everything.' She looked up and sucked some tuna mayo from her fork before adding, 'Because I truly am.'

His mouth still full, he shook his head. 'Charlotte,' he took down the food with one huge gulp, 'you can stay at mine. I really want to help. Besides, I've already notified the office about Adam and have told them I will be working from home for the next week, so you can keep me company.'

'But…I'll be intruding. It's too much! And what about Nadia? I'm sure she wouldn't be best pleased that I'm over-staying my welcome – wearing her clothes and running up her electricity bill!' Charlotte wriggled uncomfortably in the leggings which ruched at the ankles, stretched to bursting at the arse and began forking her jacket potato to mash.

Vinny lifted his burger then put it back down. 'It's nothing to do with Nadia, to be honest. We're having a trial separation. It's my house. Besides, she already knows and is fine with it.' The repressed words just freed so easily, the very words he had not shared with another living soul, not even his own mother.

Her eyes springing to his, he merely took another mouthful, so she forced in another too. 'I'm sorry to hear that, Vinny. But…?' It just didn't make sense, so the question just burst out. *Well, while we're being honest…*

'But what?'

Charlotte began separating bits of red onion from her salad. 'Who was the perfume for?'

'Oh!' This time, he washed down the contents of his mouthful with a swig of Coke and shook his head again. 'It was for my mum. It was her birthday on Friday. I forgot all about it to be honest so had to buy something quick at the airport to keep her sweet.'

'Ah, right. Sorry…for being nosey. And about you and Nadia.'

Shrugging, he added more salt to his chips. The cellar was banged a few times on the table, and he tried again. 'Well, things still might work out, but that's besides the point. You're staying, and I will be completely

106

offended if you suggest otherwise.' He scoffed a fat chip and chewed it with an open mouth, smugly victorious.

It was very difficult to win an argument with a prosecution lawyer, she realized. Charlotte laughed. 'Fine, but on one condition.' The laugh quickly died when she unthreaded the long *dark* hair smeared in tuna mayonnaise and held it in the air, her top lip curling.

'Which is?' he chuckled as Charlotte tried to flick it from her fingers, the mayonnaise an effective adhesive. Ogling Vinny like he himself had shed it there, Charlotte reached over for his napkin to wipe it on.

'Well, you did say nowhere fancy! At least it wasn't short and curly!'

Now almost wrenching, she screwed up the tissue and placed it near his plate, her face still warped with some residual disgust. It was enough to kill the smidgeon of appetite she did have. Pushing her near full plate away, she added, 'I do my bit around the house and pay my way, and, as soon as you're fed up having me there, you tell me straight away.'

'Deal,' he replied in an instant, already knowing that would never happen. Not when he wanted her to stay forever.

Chapter Sixteen

Oh, it felt *so* good to be in her own PJ's, which really were an old t-shirt (*Diamonds and Pearls* tour – circa 1990) and leggings (Primarni of course), all with more wrinkles than Mick Jagger's face. But you could eat bolognaise in them, have a glass of red wine whilst watching a documentary about finding new Egyptian tombs in them, could empty the recycling in them if necessary, even have a jog in the park if you were that way inclined (which she wasn't). All without having to worry about them. *Lush!* A contented sigh left her as she joined Vinny downstairs, spotting a stack of takeaway menus piled *very* neatly on the table.

Vinny peered up from checking his phone, wearing the same matching charcoal sweats and t-shirt as the night before. Yet she could smell the strong aroma of fabric softener which only went along with a first-time wear (no matter what the bottle said). Charlotte knew this fact as she often wore the same clothes twice, maybe thrice…four times at a push. And there were no baggy knees or stretched necklines in his apparel – or wrinkles for that matter.

After a second or two of pondering what the fuck she was wearing, his eyes furrowed, both with that and an apology. 'I'm bushed. Can't be arsed cooking. Is a take-away okay?'

He looked as exhausted as she felt, his perfectly ironed attire in sharp contrast to his eyes. *And where are his socks and slippers?* she thought as she stared at his bare feet. It made him look uncomfortable, neglected in a way or like some benign form of mortification. 'Of course, yeah. What do you fancy?' she asked, pulling up her favourite green slipper socks, already planning to buy him a pair. A nice purple pair.

They chose Lebanese. The only thing Charlotte knew about Lebanon was it was Middle Eastern, the capital was Beirut and that it had a troubled past. She was looking forward to finding out more, especially since she had no idea what she had ordered.

And they ate in front of the TV on the big sofa, and Charlotte was very careful to keep her plate under her chin. She wasn't usually precious about such things, especially after living with Greg for so long. You had to choose your battles. But watching how Vinny carefully laid a dishcloth over his lap, balanced his plate carefully on it and leant over to meet every bite halfway, she felt she should make the effort too.

'That…was…amazing, but I don't think I can move!' she griped as she bent forward to lay her empty plate on the table, praying the ripping stitch in her stomach would resolve itself in a non-embarrassing way.

'I'm just glad you've eaten something! Don't plan on moving anyway after that,' Vinny said as he edged forward to clear up.

At the same time, Charlotte began gathering the trays, wrapping some meats in foil, the bread in a separate batch.

Vinny pointed to her bundles. 'Oh, don't worry about that. I'm just going to chuck it all anyway.'

'No!' she cried as he went to lift the leftovers. It sounded more like *naw*. 'That's a total waste! It's freshly cooked. It can do for lunch or a snack or somethin',' Charlotte scolded, drawing the foil parcels back towards her.

Vinny grinned as her accent broadened along with her incense, his fingers rubbing lightly over his spice-tingling lips. 'But you might get food poisoning.'

'Yer backside! It's fresh as a daisy. Plus, that was an actual animal which was gambolling and baaing in the fields not so long ago. I mean, I'm not part of the veggie police…but I don't think any of it should be wasted either. Anyway, when was the last time you had a ready meal?' Charlotte scowled at him as she snatched up the silver parcels and trod through to the safety of the kitchen.

A lot more often now since he was cooking for one. 'Hm. Last week,' Vinny grunted at her back.

Charlotte made some space between a half-eaten jar of chicken parfait and a tub of artichoke hearts. 'And can you account for how the food was sourced and prepared?' She spoke into the fridge as she slid in the leftovers and had a nosey around the shelves. You could tell a lot about people from the contents of their fridge, she believed. Pickled bloody walnuts? A very stinky blue cheese which she couldn't determine was supposed to smell so bad or was seriously out of date. Several bottles of expensive fizziness of course. A small tub of tapenade. A smaller jar of caviar. Anchovies. *Where the hell is the real food?* The contents of Vinny's fridge added up to nothing more than a few canopies for a champagne reception. 'Plus, it's cooked, had loads of nasties and salt added to make it last for a couple of weeks.' Her head popped back around the stainless-steel door, her eyes popping too. 'That's all before you re-heat it!'

For once, Vinny knew how some of his witnesses felt when he grilled them on the stand. 'All right! All right!' he said as he placed the last plate in the dishwasher then raised both hands in surrender. 'We'll have kebab for breakfast!'

'Don't be facetious!' Charlotte scolded, as she stomped by, nibbling at an artichoke, her face screwing as she couldn't decide whether to bin it or eat it. She endeavoured, given her current stance on waste, and continued her tirade from the other room. 'There are plenty of people sleeping under a railway bridge tonight who'd be glad of that food! I hate seeing things going to waste.' With some difficulty, she swallowed the last of the grey/green lump of mush.

His shoulders bouncing, Vinny kept his laugh low as he pulled out the last two small tubs of ice-cream from the freezer. *What an unusual creature*, he thought, in how she savoured everything, including the food on her plate. Everything to be cherished and utilized – nothing to be wasted or disregarded. Odd, yet a refreshing change – Nadia would use disposable plates and cutlery if it meant less work than loading the dishwasher.

'You're right. We'll have it for lunch or dinner tomorrow,' he said when he joined her back in the lounge, weighing the options of *Belgian Chocolate* and *Strawberries and Cream* for her choice.

Charlotte tried not to notice his biceps swelling with each rep, keeping her eyes suspicious as she plucked the strawberry choice from his hand.

'What?' he cried a laugh as he flopped beside her and, knowing she would approve, licked the excess chocolate from the lid. 'I mean it!'

Still dubious, Charlotte drew her narrow eyes to the TV and began to struggle with a comfortable tiredness which made her eyes slip and her mouth muffle a quick succession of yawns.

'Bloody hell!' Vinny grunted as his phone chimed again. With a snappy tut, he grabbed it, expertly tapping and swiping the screen in one hand, his ice-cream melting in the other.

'Everything okay? You seem…*popular* tonight.'

'Just notifications,' Vinny sighed, seeing there were over thirty attempts to contact him in the last 24 hours, ranging from the ridiculous to the downright load of shit. When he reached the one asking him to confirm *his* attendance to *his* law firm's Christmas party (Norma had titled it *Law and Disorder* again this year), he rolled his eyes and slid the phone neatly back in line with Charlottes, an antique with a screen the size of a Christmas stamp. Vinny recalled owning something similar 20 years back.

'Notifications?' she queried, digging for another scoop of ice-cream.

Eventually making time for a mouthful, Vinny shrugged. 'Yeah. You know – Facebook, Snapchat, Instagram.'

Charlotte mimicked the gesture and turned her eyes back to the screen. 'No. I don't use social media. Well, I do text and email. I'm not quite at the stage where I need to communicate via smoke signals or carrier pigeon just yet!' She slowly sucked on the spoon until the ice-cream melted away.

Vinny's spoon remained imbedded in his tub. 'No social media? At all?' Each question mounted further in astonishment.

Slowly, she took the spoon from her mouth and turned her eyes to his. 'You mean anti-social media? People in their caves, seeking approval over every aspect of their life from their 'friends'?' Charlotte scoffed as she air-quoted then took another spoonful. 'Nope. I prefer living in the real world, thank you very much. Adam showed me his Facebook page once.' The spoon began waving with each point. 'Full of idiots photographing what they had for tea or what a wonderful holiday they were having in the very exclusive four star all-inclusive in Crete. All trying to outdo each other by painting some fake *perfect* version of their life. There was even someone planting the seed that they wouldn't be in work the next day. *Oh, I feel so awful. Been up all night with the runs.* What a crock of shite!' She sat up then, and was about to have another scoop, but began flapping the spoon about again instead. 'I mean, who gives a shit? Just eat your dinner and enjoy your holiday without trying to impress everyone else or caring what they think because of what is lacking in your life.' By the time she was finished, her voice was sharp, and her forehead shrivelled into a frown.

His stunned eyes dropping to the tub, Vinny's mouth twisted against his grin. God, this girl blew his head more by the second. Not for the first time when it came to Charlotte Croft, he was speechless.

Misinterpreting the silence for scepticism, she swivelled her body round to face him too. Charlotte lifted a leg to fold under her backside but, hesitating, put it back on the rug. 'Right, I went to a Lenny Kravitz gig last month. People were recording the whole bloody thing! Recording the whole gig on a phone rather than being present and *feeling* it. I wanted to scream at them to stop. Live it! Feel it! Stop bloody recording it!' Her arms pleaded with each exclamation before suddenly dropping. She shook her head. 'And the poor kids - becoming seriously depressed because their filtered Instagram image didn't get enough likes or it was too easy to leave a comment for the pretty girl with the sad blue eyes and no self-esteem that she was pathetic or because they failed to reach the heady heights of an ugly, contrived, duck-faced perfection.' Charlotte pulled such a duck face. 'Trading the very thing which made you unique to make you the same as every other flawless face. People on Facebook with 319 friends. Seriously? How can one person have room for that many people?' She scrunched an eye close and held an inch of air between her thumb and finger. 'Only able to spread a teeny-weeny smidge of your love instead of giving a chunk of you heart?'

This time, Charlotte never gave him a chance to reply, which was just as well, as he couldn't. 'No, I'll still dance and sing my heart out at the gigs.' The thought of Greg made her sigh. 'I prefer the feel of real grass between my toes, real rain on my face. And here's the irony of it all.' The plastic paddle pointed one last time. 'The beauty isn't in this *perfection* everyone seems to be striving for; it's in the *imperfection*. The larger lady jogging down the street has so much more meaning than the skinny blonde with her luminous pink Nikes.'

Vinny continued churning his ice-cream to cream.

'All right then. How many of those notifications are about anything important? Or are they all just bragging about something wonderful they've just done, or trying to be super humorous, or completely pointless? And how much time of your life have you wasted checking?'

His insides suddenly shrinking, Vinny already knew the answer. 'Most of them...and a lot.' He tried to save himself. 'But one is from my mate who's doing a charity run for MacMillan.'

'And he could just call and ask you to sponsor him or, you know, talk to you in person?' she suggested, scraping the last of her ice-cream from the bottom of the pot.

'Yeah. I suppose. I don't disagree with you.' *I wouldn't dare,* he thought. 'But it's the way the world is moving. If you want to get by, you need to keep up.'

Throwing her head back, Charlotte laughed loudly, a foot stamping on the rug. 'Or what? You'll get left behind? Fall off the face of the planet? I'll take my chances. I mean, how many Facebook *friends* do you have?'

Bollocks. 'I don't know,' Vinny admitted, picking up his phone to check. '403,' he garbled as he proved her point perfectly.

'Ha! Exactly! No-one has 403 friends! Load of waffle!' she giggled, hurling the plastic spoon in the tub victoriously.

'All right, all right,' he agreed, taking her empty pot in case she started waving that around too. Nadia would have a fit if a drop stained her prized Persian. 'But it *can* have its merits.'

'I'm sure it has but you can save that conversation for tomorrow. I'm going to head to bed. Are you sure you're okay with the sofa?'

'I insist.' His hands full, he thrust his head towards the stairs. 'Go on. I'll see you in the morning.'

'Night Vinny,' she giggled, saving a friendly slap for his knee before making off up the staircase in the ugliest green slipper sock things he'd ever seen. They reminded him of something a retired rambler might wear. Again, he shook his head in awe of the girl who had just served his ass to him on a platter. Perhaps he should suggest a career in law?

'Night Charlotte.'

As soon as she was out of earshot, he opened the laptop. There was CCTV footage putting Tommy Dolan's van around the location of the murder. There was a blood-stained hammer found in the boot of one of the cars in Tommy's front of a garage business - the blood belonged to the victim. Tommy's alibi was shoddy to say the least – he and his wife had supposedly been at home watching NCIS. Now that really was just taking the piss. Easily dismissive. Plus, the two had a notorious run in at a run-down pub in the East End of Glasgow where Tommy had threatened to cut Jason's throat if he didn't keep out of his business. Still, no-one spoke up, but they didn't need to as the pub cameras recorded the whole thing – sound and all. What's more, Tommy had a motive. The victim, Jason Carter, was an up and coming name in the drug dealing industry. The drug squad had been monitoring the situation for some time and were building a case against his gang too – especially as the friction grew with Jason undercutting Tommy to get a greater share of the market.

But what there was, was a lack of concrete witnesses. Someone to take the stand. Someone from his own inner circle who might speak up against him. Usually, there was always one who would spill their guts rather than get their own backside thrown in jail. Perhaps a disgruntled former lackey who was given a good once over before being dismissed from service. Or even on the rare occasion, someone with a bit of a conscience. This time, Vinny had no-one. Tommy's vice-like grip of the drug world secured his anonymity and silenced everyone in his circle. He knew Kate Norton well enough – the rottweiler of the courtroom – able to twist even the most innocent and unclouded of statements into something incriminating and to her advantage. Vinny needed more - he just didn't know how to get it. But he would, if it was the last thing he did.

Chapter Seventeen

Oh! Was it? Yeah…no? Maybe? No. For the umpteenth time, Charlotte questioned what *might* have been another flutter which quivered ever-so-briefly over Adam's eyes, but it had been so small, and she had been willing it to happen for the last hour, so like every other raised hope, it was put down to wishful thinking. Or the possibility she had developed some form of telekinesis. But when it happened again, more definite and followed by the faintest of hoarse whimpers, she threw her book on the bed and lurched forward.

'Adam?' she checked, leaning closer and grappling for the buzzer. 'Adam? It's me. Don't panic. You're in the hospital.' The alarm beeped with a sense of ambivalence as Charlotte lightly stroke his arm, her face rivetted in his as the twitches gather momentum.

They built to a definite wince and rasp of, 'Charlotte?' but his eyes remained bolted closed.

'Hey,' Charlotte deflated softly and finally took an in-breath. 'Don't move, Adam.'

The doctor (she presumed only because he wore a stethoscope with his casual slacks and lilac cheque shirt) strolled in with as much urgency as the *Cadbury's Caramel* bunny. Without as much as a reassuring nod in her direction, he clutched the file from the foot of the bed and made notes as he spoke. 'Hello Adam! My name is Doctor Forrester. Do you know where you are Adam?' His words were annoyingly loud and deliberate, as if trying to reach in and pull Adam out from the haze.

'Hospital.' The word was fragile.

'That's right! You're in the ICU in St Bart's. Can you remember what happened?' he chirped, shining a light in Adam's eyes which fought bravely in protest.

As two more nurses joined him, Charlotte edged out of their way to make room and took the chance to assess if Adam had lost any of himself in the trauma. Was his memory intact? Had the lack of blood affected his brain function? Would he have a limp or a lame hand? Would he have a stammer or have lost his astuteness? Most importantly, would he still be a pain in the arse?

'Stabbed. I was stabbed,' he managed, his insipid hands scrunching the starchy sheet beneath his fingers as the pain registered along with everything else.

'Great stuff, Adam. On a scale of 1 to 10, how bad is your pain (10 being the worst pain you've ever felt).'

'Seven.' The word was so clipped, Charlotte knew it was more like a 15. Wide-eyed, she nibbled at a ragged nail as they administered a dose of diamorphine and set the driver up in Adam's hand, her arse shrivelling as the top of the canula was flicked open and a tube screwed in. *Fuck's sake! Take it easy, ya stupid bitch!* Very tempted to say it out loud, she began gnawing harder on another nail instead.

'Adam, when you feel the pain increasing, just press the pump in your hand. Don't worry, you cannot overdose but it will really help you get moving quicker, and we like to get people moving quickly.'

The fat-arsed cantankerous nurse from the first night put a cuff around his arm and Adam finally opened his eyes. The pillows crinkled like plastic paper as he turned towards her, his face yellowed and sickly, the lids halfway down his sunken eyes. 'Hi Wee Yin,' he croaked.

The sight of it almost brought her to her knees again. *Those eyes. Not* *quite alive. Not quite dead. Just like Dad. Just like Dad before...*But she swallowed it back and had a word with herself because Adam wasn't leaving, he was on his way back. 'Hey yourself,' she whispered although she wasn't sure why as no-one else was. This time when she took his hand, she felt warmth instead of a heavy deadness. Giving herself a few seconds of composure, she twisted the plastic name tag around his wrist so his name was visible. *Adam McGregor Croft.* 'Silly question, but how do you feel?'

'Oh, like I could run a marathon,' he began with a snigger which quickly twisted to agony.

'Easy!' Charlotte yelped and squeezed his hand tighter. Her belly tossed like she was on some sort of emotional rollercoaster: plunging and soaring and rolling and spiralling. Not knowing what was around the corner. Knowing there was quite a long way to go until the brakes screeched. So, not having much choice, she inhaled deeply and went with it. 'I can't tell you what a relief it is to hear your voice.'

'Snap.' Pragmatic as always, he asked, 'Where are you staying? Do you have enough money?' His voice dried silent.

'Sshh!' Charlotte rubbed his arm briskly. The last thing she wanted was to provide *Fat Arse* with an even worse impression of them as she removed the thermometer from Adam's ear, her perma-scowl giving nothing away. 'I'm fine. I'm staying with Vinny.'

'Oh, good. He's a good one. The drugs...this case. Pro-bono. Pro bo...'

She watched the drip drop of steady clear globules flow into him and patted his hand. *Still high as a kite,* she smiled to herself.

'Have the police found out...?'

Watching as *Fat Arse* trudged back to the station, she sighed, 'No, not yet.' Now that the chaos around Adam had settled a bit, Charlotte dunked a clean tissue in some water and dabbed his flaky lips. 'But they are coming here tomorrow to speak to you. See if there is anything more you can tell them. Have a good think about it tonight.'

In slow motion, Adam pressed his lips together to spread the moisture. 'I will but it just happened so quickly. So quick…' he tapered off, his voice becoming listless.

'Don't worry about it now. Just rest.' But as she dabbed his mouth some more, his lips relaxed and parted. She leant closer. 'Adam?'

'Don't worry Charlotte. It's perfectly normal. He will be slipping in and out of sleep over the next day or two. He has been through a lot and there are still lots of drugs in his system.' At last, Dr Forrester acknowledged her with the reassuring smile Charlotte only wished she could believe. Because she'd seen that reassuring smile before.

Autumn hung in the air when the glass doors released her: a clear, crisp chill with a foggy hint of smoke (the kind which smelt comforting like her gran's real fire at the croft). The sun had deepened from the gold of Summer to a burnt orange, as if becoming more furnace-like to revive the waning temperature. As she gazed at the clear, blue sky, watching her breath become the only sign of a cloud, the flash of his lights caught her attention. Charlotte felt an unforced smile stretch across her face and burst into a jog.

'He's awake!' she blustered before she'd even laid her backside on the stupidly low seat, the freshness of the gusty breeze clinging to her even after she shut the door.

'Really? Oh, that's amazing!' Vinny cried, smacking his hand against the buttery soft leather of the steering wheel.

'How did you get on today?' Charlotte asked, pulling her seatbelt into place before offering him her genuine undivided attention: head slanted, ears pricked, big blue eyes waiting. He saw what she meant about social media in that very moment. When he picked up Nadia, she barely looked up from the phone never mind ask him how his day went.

'So, so…' He wobbled his head as the car began to purr and careen towards the exit. 'I spoke to the detective we met at the hospital. There's a CCTV image of the suspect which they believe to be a certain David Sullivan. And he is one of Tommy Dolan's associates.'

There was something about Vinny's expression which didn't seem to harmonize with the good news. 'But surely that's great?'

Vinny tutted, and not just because of the car which had braked suddenly in front of him. 'It is…but they are slippery bastards, the lot of them.' One hand steered, the other one flourished as he explained, 'One good alibi and he walks because there are no forensics. They only thing they have is the CCTV image, and it's not the best. I mean, afterwards, he just seemed to vanish into thin air! There was no trace of where he came from or where he went. It can easily be dismissed in court.'

Charlotte heard her back teeth crunch. 'But there's Adam! He'd be able to identify the man.'

'I know he would,' Vinny said, before shaking his head. 'But it was dark, or so the defence would argue. The guy had a baseball cap pulled over his face. Their interaction was brief. Adam was drinking. You can't find someone guilty of attempted murder because they have a Scottish accent and a bad reputation.' The sting of Charlotte's glare chafed at his face.

'Bloody hell! Are you tellin' me that this guy might not even get tae court?'

'No, I'm not saying that…but it is a possibility. The CPS will need more.' He sucked his lips against his teeth and beeped the cyclist who thought traffic light signals did not apply to him.

Lurking like the smell of Greg's burnt beans, the silence shadowed them into the house where, feeling the need to escape it, Charlotte stomped up every metal fan-like tread to the bedroom. Unable to restrain it any longer, it released in a small, fairly controlled explosion as she launched her bag at the fancy chair and flopped face first into the mountain of pillows before punching them – repeatedly. Then, she filled her lungs to capacity before releasing the contents into a pillow with a scream. When her face turned a concerning shade of purple, she took a deep breath and did it again. She only stopped when she felt a little faint and began to see lots of tiny specks of light swim in front of her eyes.

When the last star faded and the buzzing in her ears became less angry, Charlotte pushed herself up and pulled the mobile from her back pocket. Just as her home screen flashed to life, the phone pinged urgently with backed-up message after message. It almost felt exciting, like winning the jackpot on the penny falls. That was until she saw they were all from Greg.

Groaning to God, she sat up and crossed her legs, then began to scroll through them. They started reserved and supportive at least.

Hi Charlotte. Hope everything is okay. Give me a text when you can. X

Hi Charlotte. Any news on Adam yet? Thinking of you. X

But the further down she swiped, so did his mood:

Charlotte I'm so sorry I fucked everything up. Please give me another chance. I wish I could be there with you. I love you with all my heart. Xx

'Oh, for the love of God! Eejit!' she yelled, volleying the mobile on to the bed so hard, it catapulted to the floor and sent Vinny back down the steps, his lips drawn to a small circle like he was a bad whistler.

'Wait, Vinny! It's all right.' Charlotte already felt bad enough after giving him the silent treatment never mind giving him the impression she had lost the plot entirely.

'Sorry, I didn't mean to disturb. Just wanted to see if you fancied a cuppa?' Vinny loitered hesitantly, one foot at the top of the stairs, the other a few steps below, ready to make a quick exit if needed.

'Don't suppose you've got anything stronger?'

Chapter Eighteen

Before she joined him, she caught up with Mr Miller (who told her to hang on in there and not to worry about returning to Broadhurst until she was ready). Greg was saved for last now that her tolerance level of him was a few fathoms south of rock bottom.

The phone didn't even seem to ring. 'Charlotte! God, I've been worried sick!'

Gravitating to the light, she leant on the windowsill and sighed, her fingernail scraping at a single spec of paint on the glass. A boy in the neighbour's garden was using his sister's head as aiming practise for his *Nerf* gun. 'I'm fine Greg. Things are looking good for Adam too…so you needn't worry.'

'That's amazing news, Charlotte.' The short pause felt like an eon. 'Can we please talk when you get back? I…I'm struggling here, Charlotte.'

Charlotte massaged the stabbing pain above her eye and so did the boy's younger sister when he found his target, sending her little pink specs awry. 'Greg…there's nothin' to talk about. Please don't make this harder than it is,' she groaned, pulling a hand down her face, watching as the boy dropped his gun and ran to his sister when he realized it hurt. He put his hand round her shoulder and tried to sooth her, partly she thought because he was sorry but mostly to hush her tears before they alerted the big people. When she was 6, Adam had done the exact same to her with a sucker dart. Charlotte had cried so loud, it brought their granny running out from the croft who, seeing the dart stuck to her head, screamed as if it had impaled her skull. Charlotte's tears were quickly transformed to hysterics of laughter as she watched her wee granny chase Adam round the garden, him too scared to run but more scared not too. Every time she got close enough, she'd lift a chunky leg to try to kick his arse and yell, 'Jist you wait till a get ma hons on you, Adam Croft!'

'But I've done a lot of thinking since you've been away. God, I miss you…Marry me, Charlotte. Let's get married. Let's have a baby. I'm ready.'

'Oh, Greg! Yer havin' a laugh!' she cried, turning from the window, a splayed hand bouncing to the heavens. 'It's too late! And trust you to come out with all the marriage and baby promises now when I'm here dealing with all this…*shite*!' She kicked the only black heel she had left across the room. It bounced off the hidden wardrobe, a rubbery black streak now marring the perfect white gloss.

'I know!' he howled like a wounded dog. 'But I don't know what to do! I can't face losing you, Charlotte.'

'And I can't deal with this now Greg!' Charlotte cried, raking her fingers through her hair as she wondered how to get rid of the mark. *Nail varnish remover?*

'All right! I'm sorry Charlotte. I'll let you go but please…think about it. I hope Adam gets better soon.'

'Bye!' she barked, jabbing the red phone button many times after the call cut.

Wiping away an angry tear with the flick of her finger, she cursed under her breath and licked the thumb under her sleeve to buff the scuffmark. *Bloody marriage? Kids?* Her thumb slowed for a fleeting second as she considered it until she reminded herself there was always sperm donation. She buffed harder until the black mark was gone, but so was the shine of the gloss. *Shit.*

Vinny darted away from the bottom of the staircase but had already

125

heard enough. He lined up three green bottles on the console table, turning each so the labels faced forward.

Not long after, Charlotte plumped heavily down each step, her eyes puffy and her neck blotchy, her green socks at very different levels.

'You okay?' Holding a careful grimace, he stuffed his hands in his pockets and swayed gently from side to side.

'You heard?' she snuffled, wiping her nose with what looked like half a roll of toilet paper. Reshuffling the white bouquet for a dry spot, Charlotte slithered into the chair beside the fire. Although the flames remained an incandescent shade of blue, it seemed cosier somehow now that the lights were dimmed, and twilight had descended.

'A snippet,' he lied, bending down to grab a box of balsam softened tissues from the cabinet under the bookshelf. He pulled at the perforated cardboard and placed them on the table at her side. 'So…that's your ex?'

'Yeah,' she said quietly, snatching seven tissues and adding them to her soggy pom-pom.

'What do you want to drink?'

'Anything wet and strong,' she drawled, bringing her knees to her chin and pulling the throw from the back of the chair around her shoulders.

He felt an edginess creep, seeing the throw used in such a manner – for comfort instead of embellishment. An impulsive notion to take it from her and arrange it neatly in its naturally contrived form over the back of the chair bombed into his head. Vinny began lining up the bottle labels with more accuracy and breathed heavily through his nose. 'This is quite a nice red,' he blustered as he held it up under the overhead pendulum light and scanned the label. 'Full-bodied and smooth. I think you'll like it.'

'Sounds like me,' she chortled until she realized he was seriously trying to please her. 'Oh. Vinny, I don't really give a shit about wine. I was only making a point on Saturday because I thought you were a bit of an arrogant arse.' Sniff.

Chuckling, he opened the bottle and smelt the cork.

Charlottes scowl sunk further. *What the...?*

The bottle seemed to pass the quality control test with a prompt nod and an approving, 'Hm,' before he poured them a good measure in hefty glugs. As he handed her a glass, he added, 'I *am* an arrogant arse. I need to be. Got to convince juries that I'm right and put away the bad people. You need a certain amount of arrogance to pull that off. But I was very rude to you that day. Sorry.'

Taking the wine, her eyes followed him as he sat opposite. 'Only because you thought I was something to do with the case. After what happened to Adam, looks like your instincts to be wary were bang on.' Her voice still wobbly, she put the sodden lump up the sleeve of her cardigan and plucked 3 fresh sheets.

'Hm. Maybe. But let's not talk about it tonight. It's all I've thought about for too long. Let's have a night off.' He held up his glass.

'Count me in,' Charlotte added with a final extra big sniff, chinking her glass with his.

The urge to know everything made him uncharacteristically prying. Was it over? More importantly, was she over him? 'So, when did you break up?'

Docking her glass, Charlotte pulled a face akin to having indigestion. 'A couple of weeks ago but it was over long before that. I was just waiting for the right moment. He provided it nicely when I caught him getting jiggy on the sofa with a girl who looked like she was fresh out of sixth form! A great boost for the ego, that.' Her nostrils still swollen closed, Charlotte sniggered gruffly from her mouth like she had a bad cold.

'Whoa! Shit. I thought I had it bad. What did you do?'

'Nothing. I let him go on until there was no misunderstanding of what was going on. I wasn't giving him a chance to explain it away. I knew it was my escape route without having the guilt that I'd left him. So…' Charlotte circled the wine in her hand like she was challenging herself to see how close to the rim she could get without spilling it and Vinny's knee began to bounce as he thought about her doing exactly that in his bespoke Italian chair. 'I waited till he was on top of her, his hands roaming all over the place,' just like hers as she explained it, 'and his tongue jammed down her throat. Then I crept into the room and stood right beside them and said, 'Evening!''

He just about managed to swallow the wine rather than spit. 'Christ! Remind me never to get on the wrong side of you! You're a cool operator. That's proper freaky, Charlotte!' But he was reassured – reassured because no woman who was still in love with someone would ever have reacted in such a manner.

'Well,' the word distended with humour, 'there was no point in making a scene because I was actually relieved. And the poor girl, she looked terrified. But it wasn't her fault. I just told her to go home.' She crossed her feet on the matching Italian ottoman which bridged the gap between them.

Vinny realized that he and Nadia had never used the thing in such a manner – as it had been intended. Nodding, he couldn't help but admire how she still remembered her kind side in such a situation. In fact, he realized she was one of the kindest people he had ever met. Selfless. The way she tried to return his phone instead of putting it in her pocket. How she tried to help around the house as payment when he had taken her in. How she didn't give a shit that she had barely a set of clothes on her back when it came to looking after Adam. How she fought for the right of the animal when she saved the leftover kebab. Rarely, *very* rarely, he met someone with the capacity to humble him. 'I hope you don't mind me asking, but if you knew it was over long before then, why did you stay?' His phone buzzed with yet another interruption.

'I'm not sure,' she answered honestly, her shrug light under the throw. 'But I'd already invested so much that the thought of losing it seemed like a…waste. As you know, I don't like waste.'

Switching the phone off without as much as a peek, Vinny tittered, 'Yeah. I've noticed,' before placing it on the highest floating shelf he could reach without standing. He shoved it back further, completely out of sight.

'But then I realized…,' and her button nose rucked a little, 'it was my life I would be wasting, my future. And when I accepted that, there was no going back.'

Tentatively, like someone trying escargot for the first time, Vinny crossed his bare feet beside hers, his green light to fire away.

So, she did, coiling a finger in a spiral of hair and checking for split ends to ease the bearing of her question. 'So, how long have you and your wife been separated?' she asked breezily, noting she was well over-due for a cut, each end branching like a deciduous forest amid the bleakest of winters.

Vinny laced his fingers gently across his chest and drew a long breath. 'Nearly 6 months. She's in Paris setting up another office in her investment banking company.'

'Sounds important.' Finding a particularly frayed strand, she began to divorce the branches.

'Yeah. It's *thee* most important thing in her life,' he said, his words barbed. He sighed and reached for his glass 'Before she left, we had a showdown. I gave her an ultimatum. Not my smartest move.' One side of his mouth dragged down mockingly now that he was able to find some irrelevance in it.

Charlotte's eyes pinged up. 'How?'

Pursing his lips, he was almost tempted to correct her that it should
have been a *why*. Almost. 'Well, she'd been spending more and more time
on planning the new office in Paris and we were becoming more and more
distant. We would go one week to the next, barely seeing each other never
mind spending any time together. So…I lost my patience. It takes a lot for
me to lose my patience! But she was investing her whole life in the bank
and there was nothing left for me. I mean, I love my job, but I loved her
more.'

His eyes slid from the ceiling to Charlotte, the only one he wanted
to confess to: his shame, his failure - the girl who had listened to him more
in the last 10 minutes than his wife had in the last year.

'Go on,' she coaxed gently, her toes wriggling in encouragement.

And after everything they'd just been through together, he did.

'I pinned her down the night before she left. Not literally! She was
packing in the bedroom.' He rested a finger on his lips and frowned. 'Or
was she picking?'

Charlotte bumped his bare feet with her socks. 'Hey!'

It felt like a spark – a warm tingly one. He chuckled then went on.
'I told her I was unhappy. That if we stood a chance, things had to change
when she got back. Or what was the point? I mean, why were we even
together if we were never *together*?' Vinny left out the big part– the part
about him wanting to start a family at some point. None of them were
getting any younger. How he didn't want to put it off anymore. How she
had tutted and rolled her eyes at him. The queen of convenience had an
inconvenience.

Angling her head to the side, Charlotte could see that memory
stretch and draw at his features. Never more had she wished she had her
sketchbook to hand. 'What did she say?'

A hand sliding behind his head, he gave a series of long blinks as he recollected. 'She agreed. She couldn't split herself in two and she wasn't sure what she wanted anymore. She said she wanted a trial separation while she was in Paris. A clear head to get on with the job at hand (firstly of course),' he augmented his eyes, 'and time to figure out if we had a future anymore. I asked if she still loved me and she said she didn't know. But at least she was honest.'

Is she fricking mad? Charlotte snorted quietly and pulled the throw tighter round her arms as if it could warm Nadia's frostiness. 'She might benefit from a bit of perspective. See that she has a fantastic husband.' And she meant it, nudging her toe against his again.

And he felt the spark again, except this time, it ran all over his body, his heart melting a little more, Nadia a by-thought. 'Like Greg has with you?'

'Yeah, but my relationship is *over* – no matter what is being promised. Ours isn't a temporary parting. There's no way back for us, and to be honest, I don't want there to be. For the first time in years (well, before this weekend), I'm excited! I've put everything on hold for too long. It's like my world has opened up again…is moving forward again.'

Vinny spun his finger gently around the rim of his glass. 'I don't know…The longer she is away, the more I think she may be right.'

'In what way?'

'Well, as well as giving her time to reflect, it's given me time to reflect too. And the thing which keeps coming into my head, is what does she think of me? I've been a good husband. She was always at the forefront of my thoughts and decisions. Everything I did was with us and our future in mind. She was my priority, yet why wasn't I hers? I think when it just comes down to it, we want different things.'

Charlotte heard the words of acceptance dampen and spiral around

131

the room. Hers tried to lift it. 'Surely, there's some hope?'

'Honestly? I don't think there is. I called her at the weekend to tell her about Adam and how you were staying here. Maybe it was because of what happened, but I needed her. But…she was too busy!' He shook his head. 'I mean, I'm supposed to be her fucking husband!'

Now Charlotte's lips slid to the side. *Poor sod.* 'What will you do?'

'I'll give it till the end of the month then I will fly over there. See how the land lies. We can't live in limbo-land for the rest of our lives.'

Charlotte knew that feeling all too well.

'Anyway,' he perked up and shook off. Point mute. 'What will you do? What's the plan?'

Charlotte's face lit up. 'Well, my grandparents owned a bothy in a remote part of Loch Lomond. They left it to me and Adam, but it's been lying empty for years. When I go back, I'm moving there.'

'A what?' he laughed, the word a new one in his dictionary.

'A bothy. The croft – it's a wee cottage on a nice sized piece of land. Sits right on the banks of the loch and it's well away from all the tourist hotspots.'

Ah. Vinny nodded, just like Adam had when she had told him. 'What will you do about work?'

'I'll still be able to commute for a few months until the flat hopefully sells. In the meantime, I'll get it liveable. Then, when the money from the flat comes through, I'll resign and give the full-time artist thing a go. Risky I know, but if I don't do it, I'll regret it for the rest of my life.'

Lowering his glass, Vinny grinned and spoke with an unwavering certainty. 'You'll do it. I know I've not known you for very long, but I can see when you put your mind to something how *determined* you are. Adam says your very talented…and I believe him.'

Charlotte coughed daintily and crossed her feet the other way. 'I don't know about that…but…I can't think of anything better than doing the thing you love most for a living.'

Controlled yet curious, a finger lightly stroked his temple. 'Are you not scared? I mean, being alone and so isolated from everyone?'

'Nope!' She leant over to the rather sad looking spider plant on the shelve and breathed on it like she was fogging the window of a bus to write her initials or draw a love heart. When Vinny's eyes questioned, she explained, 'Just feeding it,' before shuffling back in place. 'You see, me and the modern world don't gel very well! It's all moving too fast for me. Plus, I'm more than happy in my own company. I have a few close friends and Adam. Those relationships give me more than having 403 friends on Facebook.' Two brows and ten toes wiggled at him now.

This time he nudged her foot, passing the spark back to her.

'I'm sure once I get settled, I'll have plenty of people coming to visit. And when I don't, I'm gonnae light the fire, snuggle up with a big blanket, look out to the loch with a big glass of wine and drink it all in – each and every beautiful second of it.' Charlotte stared somewhere beyond the flames, a sigh which sounded like the epitome of contentment leaving her.

Vinny had always been a city boy. He loved the fast pace of it – it gave him a buzz. The high-profile career, the Michelin star restaurants, the bright lights of Oxford Street, the personal tailor, cool bars and fast cars, the cushy pad in Notting Hill, the bustle. But he could see just how good an artist she was, as she'd just created the most perfect picture he had ever seen.

'Well,' he declared as he got up and fetched the bottle, 'I'll definitely come to the lock for a visit if I'm welcome. It sounds amazing.'

Her eyes shot to him. 'The lo*ccccchhhhh!* Charlotte made a sound like she was trying to dislodge a hair from the back of her throat. 'Of course, you're welcome! Although, I'm not sure you'd like it. It is very modest! Besides,' her tongue poked at her cheek, 'do you even own a pair of wellies?'

'Nope! But I can rough it with the best of them, so I'll invest in a nice pair of *Hunters*'!' he simpered as he poured another glass, pressing her buttons, desperate for her to become all self-righteous and disparaging again.

'Mine are from *Millets*! Only £10. Very good they are too!'

Bingo. 'Erm, that's just a step too far! I can tame my ostentatiousness, but I draw the line at shopping at *Millets*!'

'An extra £150 for a wee white label on the front?' Her top lip looked as if it was being tugged by a piece of string. The very thought of it had her genuinely perplexed.

'An extra £200 actually and worth every penny, that little white label,' he pushed as he sat down again. *Push. Push. Push. Heart-flutter, tummy-churn, bits-stirring.*

Charlotte giggled and shrieked simultaneously. 'Is it heck…poser!'

'Poser and proud!' Vinny concurred light-heartedly, planting each foot beside hers with every *p*. He thought for a moment. 'Can I see some of your work?'

'Oh. Erm, sure.' She slid up slowly and unwrapped the throw. 'Of course, but I…I don't have my portfolio with me. I do have my sketchbook though.'

Somewhat bemused, he watched her skate across the oak chevrons in her green socks, then skate back, excitedly handing him the book, her breathing quickened. A sudden flashback of Tom Cruise in *Risky Business* played in his mind. Except, his socks were a very sensible white.

Although Charlotte could be quite guarded over her work, a reflection of her very soul, she couldn't wait for Vinny to see. It seemed only fair after he had just bared his soul to her. But mostly, she was desperate, not for his approval, but for him to see the world through her eyes, to *feel* what she felt.

Carefully and taking his time, he began to flick through and she stared as his face became unreadable again, no matter how hard she tried to decode the lines and twitches which wavered across it. *Boy, he would be a good poker player,* Charlotte thought as she drew her feet up beside her on the chair and began nibbling at the side of her nail.

Funnily enough, now he didn't seem to notice that her questionably clean socks were on the furniture as his head dipped slowly, again and again. 'Charlotte…these are just…amazing.' His finger lightly traced the face of an older man, his eyes so alive with kindness and sadness, he couldn't resist a touch, almost expecting the warmth of flesh instead of the coarseness of paper. And the deeper Vinny looked, the melancholier he felt until he needed to know why. 'Who is this?'

Pleased that at least her work had evoked a question, Charlotte got up and perched lightly on the arm of Vinny's chair. 'Oh, that's Amos. A prisoner who died of an accidental drugs overdose. He was serving a life-sentence for a pub fight. A freak punch. Killed the other guy. But a kinder, meeker man you could never meet. I know I shouldn't have, but I had a soft spot for him. I found myself gravitating to his cell the most. Not because I had to, because I wanted to. It made my shifts more bearable. He was…my friend.'

Vinny continued to get lost in his bottomless eyes.

'He was a lovely man, touched my soul somehow. Told me I didn't belong there, in the prison. To be honest, I don't think he did either. It's like he knew I was stuck just like him, but he pointed out that I had a choice. And when he died…' and she swallowed and tried not to remember, 'it gave me the push I needed. This was completed a few weeks before his death. He needed cataract surgery. His eyesight was *terrible* and the thing he loved most was to read. I saw it in his eyes, his misery at the situation. His eyes were the most expressive I think I've ever seen and up till this point, they were radiant and happy. It was the change in them which hooked me.'

A waterfall of red curls grazed his arm as she explained the story, sending more tingles through his body. He looked up at her as she stared at the picture, her eyes brimming with sadness, wishing he could touch her locks, wishing he could coil a strand around his finger. 'I don't know how you've done it Charlotte, but you've captured it beautifully.'

Forcing down another rickety gulp, she changed the subject before she embarrassed herself. 'Have you seen the ones I've done of you yet?' she asked, her eyes now glinting with a touch of mischievousness.

'No…' Vinny said warily, uncrossing his legs and anchoring his feet to the floor. 'I'm not sure I want to. Did you give me horns and a pitchfork?' He scratched the side of his nose nervously and felt his right leg gain a mind of its own.

'Don't be daft,' she tutted, taking the pad from him and flipping to his page. Tilting her head slightly, Charlotte studied his features like he was carved by Rodin himself. 'You have a very interesting face Vinny. Very beautiful and well-defined but you like to keep things hidden, like to keep control. That's what drew me to you. As soon as you sat down and got lost in your thoughts, they all came to the surface like an unfurling rose bud. It was amazing to watch. Ready?' Smiling, she held the pad to her chest, adding more drama to the big reveal.

His lips parted and he could feel the fire nip his eyes as they ballooned. He knew his face wasn't hiding anything now as he continued to gaze at her, completely oblivious to the fact that she had just reached into his chest and stolen his heart.

'Vinny?'

'Yeah...yes,' he quickly blinked back to life. 'I'm ready,' he said before swallowing softly.

Taking the pad from her, Vinny's eyes swam around the images which somehow seemed more like him than him. Each face told a story – he knew exactly what he was thinking, what he was feeling. He gazed at the one of him smiling and recalled how he was thinking of her at the check-in desk. It rendered him silent, wondering how a stranger at an airport got him more than the person who he had been married to for the last 5 years.

'You're amazing, Charlotte.' And he didn't just mean the art.

She coughed lightly again. 'Can I ask you something?'

'Sure,' he replied, an unusual quiver to his voice.

'Can I draw you? I mean *really* draw you – a complete piece of work?'

'So, you're asking my permission this time?' he teased to hide his humility that she would even want to.

'Yes! But, there's just something about you Vinny which is like a walking work of art, and not the obvious stunning looks and imposing stature thing. To be honest, I never usually choose subjects who are a classic beauty such as yourself. They can be quite 2 dimensional.' Her voice dipped to a whisper as she pulled a face to elaborate, 'Not much going on beneath the surface.'

Never one to take offence, Vinny felt what he thought others might have described as...wounded?

Unawares, Charlotte stared off somewhere beyond him and continued. 'I usually find the real beauty in the mundane. Like...like the loneliness of the widower with the loose gold band on his haggard finger just in the queue for his pension or...or the joy in the random act of kindness, the appreciation of the homeless man for the conversation, the hatred for your lover when they break their promise to love you forever. *Real* life. *Real* people...really.' She shrugged a tiny shrug and turned her focus back to him, her eyes creasing – amused and flummoxed. 'But you're the exception somehow...you have both.'

You see, Charlotte Croft saw past the intimidation which would have most other women flush scarlet and send their heart into a near-fatal arrythmia. Because she saw the real him, what was under the surface (or at least, she wanted to). And just the fact she wasn't intimidated by him meant she got instantly closer than anyone else he had ever met. He saw the challenge then. The challenge that it would take more than good looks and a fat wallet to capture Charlotte Croft's heart. It was uncommon ground for him.

'Well...as long as you don't want me to strip and laze across the sofa like Kate Winslet in Titanic.'

Charlotte could see a glaze of panic varnish his eyes that it was a possibility. 'Nope, nothing as exotic or as X-rated as that!' she giggled. 'I don't need you to do anything different. Just sit as you are and talk to me. Forget I'm even drawing. And Vinny...' She held her hand out for the pad, sniggering again as he began to writhe in his seat.

'Yeah?' he froze, his eyes wide.

'You can even leave your clothes on.'

Chapter Nineteen

'…and I don't care what anyone says, there was enough room for two people on that door…'

'The Seven Deadly Sins!' Vinny shrieked, prodding the title at the bottom of the page.

Shit! Her laugh peeled louder the wider his eyes became. 'Well…' she blustered and tried to match his offense as she made to grab the pad from him, but he snatched it to his chest, 'I got the wrong impression, just like you did!'

'Bloody hell! The Seven Deadly Sins!' His fair eyebrows still somewhere on the ceiling, he pointed at the title again, this time sharing it with Charlotte to let her know *she* had written it. 'I thought you were working for Dolan, not Satan himself!'

'Vinny!' Still laughing, she launched again for the pad which he tweaked a few painful inches away every time.

'Vinny!'

Eventually, he held it still enough for her to latch on. Still keeping hold of one side, he teased, 'You can go off people, you know.'

As he let go, she sauntered back to her seat and turned to a fresh page, smoothing her hand over the virgin sheet. 'Not me! You think I'm amazing.'

Oh, if only she knew!

Like a protective shield or some sort of buffer, he grabbed his acoustic guitar from the basement before he got settled into position. Then, he began to strum. His hair tied loosely for a change, strands of gold fell before his eyes as he listened and tuned. It made him more mailable, less harsh somehow. Still, Charlotte couldn't help but have a laugh to herself. It seemed even the beautiful people got edgy; she never expected that of Vinny – not with him seeming so comfortable in his own skin.

'Sooo, as I was asking before I noticed your…less than flattering *observation*, what was your worst job?'

'I was a cleaner in the hospital. Had a lovely pink over-all, half a shade darker than my skin. I looked like a giant willy. And the supervisor told me I was a natural buffer! Cheeky cow!'

'Sounds like…fun. How long did you last?' Vinny twisted a peg on the headlock and plucked at a string until its lazy twang levelled to more of a ting. His fingers fumbled to the next peg.

'About 3 weeks. I got fired for refusing to remove my nose ring! I got told it was *unhygienic*. After all the time it took for the thing to settle, I wasn't giving up on it.' Charlotte looked up when the pinging stopped to see Vinny's mouth was curling.

'What?' she yelled, checking her top for any spillages as he continued to stare.

'Nothing.' He dropped his head back to the strings. 'I was trying to imagine you with a nose ring.'

'Oh, I loved it! Adam…not so much. Had to end up giving up and taking the bloody thing out. He said I would get blood poisoning and that it would travel up and give me a potentially life-threatening brain infection.' Clenching the end of the pencil between her teeth, Charlotte recalled how smart Adam was at getting her to toe the line. Pencil back on the page, she scoffed. 'Talk about gullible! So, what was your worst job?'

'Oh,' he began to strum some cords, 'nothing as exciting as you. Probably telesales for a dodgy insurance firm. But they used to pay us in cash every Friday night and the money was good. Most of the time, I just worked in a bar.'

Charlotte frowned, smudging some of the harsher lines with her finger. With a few brisk sweeps of her hand, she brushed away the loose particles of graphite then pulled her head sharply to the right to check her shading. 'I was hopeless at anything like that. That was Adam's talent. And he was a *complete* flirt, so it suited him down to the ground.'

Vinny gazed at the long line of her naked neck, from the fleshy, very biteable lobe of her ear to the teasing glimpse of a collar bone, the urge to run his lips along it becoming painful. 'And you weren't a flirt? A good-looking girl like you?' His tune became suggestive and bluesy.

Jerking her head straight, a burst of laughter erupted from her. 'Oh, you must be joking! A – I never classed myself as good looking. B - I can't flirt to save my life. I look like I'm having a stroke if I even try. No, I just seem to fall into relationships.' She lifted her pencil to allow the shudder to escape. 'Thankfully, that won't be happening for a while.' Her eyes amplified, and Vinny dropped a note.

'Why?' The guitar basking across his stomach, he seized the strings silent and began to study her more than she was studying him: that flash of her eyes when he provoked her, how she itched her nose every now and again when the conversation turned to her, how her brow creased, and her tongue rested lightly against her top lip as she concentrated.

'After Greg?' The sheer absurdness of the question rendered it rhetorical. 'But I can see you would have been a major flirt! Totally cocky. Bet you had all the girls running! Honestly, I was quite surprised to find out you were married.'

Defensively, his eyes constricted as he prepared to dismiss her prediction but who was he kidding? They relaxed in defeat. 'Yeah, I was. And, yes, I did. But that was then…I lived a bit, but it got…boring.' A finger curled around his top lip. He would be the first to admit, he'd had his fair share of beauties. All hot. All vain. All self-assured. All materialistic. Not one of them able to hold a light to her.

Charlotte stopped for a moment and stared past him. 'Is it nice?'

'What?'

'Being gorgeous. Getting what you want all the time.'

'I wouldn't describe myself as *that*, but believe it or not, it does have its drawbacks.'

Charlotte noticed his brows plummet. The pencil became more urgent.

How can I put it? 'If it's Christmas every day, then it doesn't feel like Christmas anymore. It loses its allure. You can have too much of a good thing.'

She'd never thought about it like that before. Like the opposite of her, he had nothing to saver or relish because he had it all. *He* was what happened when you wanted more and got it. To have everything he wanted at his fingertips without the thrill or appreciation because it was…normal. It gave her a horrible, hollow feeling inside and it was then she saw the shadows of vulnerability on his face, a veil of something lacking in his eyes.

Lost in the map of something deeper, Charlotte began to sketch harder. The creases at the edge of his eyes, his soft lips, relaxed and parted. And the more she sketched, the more life-like they became until she could almost imagine the touch of them. The softness or forcefulness of them on her mouth? Each option had its benefits. The sweet taste of his warm breath. The heat of him against her. *Whoa!* Charlotte gulped involuntarily and yanked her head back from the pipedream on the pad. And it hit her all at once – how much she wanted him to touch her. Fuck, how much she wanted to touch him! And for the first time in her life, she knew what it was like to have that hellish, desperate concept of wanting more. *Oh, holy Lord.* Gulp.

'When I met Nadia, I was ready to settle down. I was fed-up of being a player. Believe it or not, *I* was fed up being used.' The pointy end of the plectrum pricked his chest.

Charlotte clawed a finger across her eyebrow to hide her face as she spoke, her voice too high. 'You? Used?'

'*Yes*, Charlotte.' It was that presumption that his looks somehow meant he didn't have feelings which pissed him off the most. 'Most of the women I had relationships with, had certain…expectations. And it certainly wasn't *being gorgeous*, as you put it. It was money, status, who you knew, what connections you had. What bloody car you drove!'

'I'd be screwed then. I've had my banged-up Beetle for 9 years,' she grumbled, rubbing a rare mistake frantically with the top end of the pencil before giving 3 sharp blows like the big bad wolf himself.

His fingers bumped over the strings so lightly they made no sound. 'They all wanted keeping in a lifestyle their looks had made them accustomed to. I had to live up to the fantasy. It was tiring. But Nadia, she was a bit different. She was so independent and focused, had her own money, her own career. But she still wouldn't have looked at me twice if I was just plain old Vinny from South London who drove a *Ford Focus* and worked at *Tesco's*.' *Shallow,* he realized now.

Charlotte swallowed her lips and kept her head down. 'Mm, hm,' she agreed with a muffled mumble, her cheeks still kindling. She could feel Vinny stare, could feel his eyes pull to lift her face to meet his. Inhaling deeply, she sucked in as much nonchalance as possible and tried to re-set her eyes to neutral. She cleared her throat before she spoke. 'Funny how things change. When I met Greg in Art School, he was so different. He was an artist too. He wasn't caught up with material gain and the superficial. He saw things like me. The present, the real. What was already there. He didn't want more.' *Hypocrite!* she screamed to herself because now she did. Her

143

eyes dropped from the shame of it.

'What changed?' Vinny asked, a hand resting loosely on the back curve of the guitar, the shape of which reminded Charlotte of the body of a well-proportioned woman, and his hand was on her ass.

'It would be easier to ask what didn't!' she cried, still finding it difficult to regulate her volume. 'We both planned to open a gallery and studio in the West End. Perhaps with our own little art school attached where we could do lessons. But it was the time of the financial crisis. We couldn't get a business loan. So, we bought a small flat as an investment. Adam offered to help us, but he was just starting out in New York and I wanted to do it by myself. So, he suggested I join the prison service for just a few years to get some proper cash behind us. Greg got a proper 9 to 5 too. And we just got stuck on the hamster wheel I suppose. I never lost my dream. But Greg, he lost his, lost his way. I can't even remember the last time he picked up a paint brush. He just stopped…seeing.'

Much to her relief, Vinny began to strum again. 'I guess we're both pretty much a pair of sad cases?'

The ambiguous shade of his words caused Charlotte to look up only to see his eyes heavy with something she couldn't quite determine. But whatever it was, it made her mouth clam shut and her stomach gripe. Replying with a quick, nervous smile, she circled her hand around the page, the pencil failing to make contact. 'Well, I…I don't think so. I'm okay with things. And you…you may still have a chance to save your marriage.'

This time it was him who finished with a, 'Mm, hm.' A low agreement of contradiction. When she peeped up again to understand it, there was a defiance behind his eyes like he saw right through and was reading exactly what she was thinking.

Oh dear! 'Right!' she blustered loudly, snapping the pad shut. 'My eyes are almost crossed I'm so tired.' Charlotte thought she should yawn loudly. It seemed the best thing to do, to add some credibility but soon discovered it was really difficult to fake yawn with any sense of authenticity. 'I'm going to call it a night. We can pick up again tomorrow.'

'Oh, okay.' Vinny shifted up the chair, his eyes blinking in a burst of flutters. 'Can I see it?'

'See what?'

Vinny chuckled and scratched the end of his nose with the plectrum. 'The picture.'

'Oh!' Charlotte laughed, or rather, cackled. She leapt to her feet and tucked the sketchbook neatly under her arm. 'Nope. Not until it's finished. You'll just have to trust me.'

Eyes blazing, Vinny sat back and pulled his jaw to the side, his tongue resting on the roof of his mouth. 'I do.'

Oh my! Head down, Charlotte skied to the stairs. *Must...get...some...distance,* she repeated the mantra with each upwards tread. 'Night Vinny.'

'Night *Charlotte.*' He said her name like a breath.

Vinny watched her disappear up the stairs along with his hopes of more. Wanting nothing more than to be up there with her. He, the man who could get most things, didn't have her. And it was agony. Squaring up and grabbing tighter the one thing he had any control over, his guitar, he began playing a grungy number, something heavy with a little more angst. But only halfway through the first verse, he stopped abruptly and slapped his hand against the varnished board. *What a bloody mess!* he thought, sucking in a sharp intake of breath through his fingers. He had a wife. He had a bloody wife! He *did* have a wife. A wife who didn't want him. A girl upstairs who had captured his heart quicker than the bat of a butterfly wing. A girl who was different from any other person he had met – who didn't care about any of the things which magnetized the rest. A girl who didn't give a shit about any of it, saw past it all. But he was processing Nadia's rejection. Perhaps that was it. Perhaps that was the thing which made him want to give his heart to her on a silver platter. Made him want her to want him. Because his wife didn't.

Carping loudly, he stood the guitar at the side of the chair and took himself and his whirling head to the sofa where he wiggled his toes, testing out the appeal of it.

As soon as her foot hit the safety of the bedroom, she was immediately hit by the vulgar picture above the bed warning her to bury her thoughts of more. *Dangerous those*, she reminded herself before diving in.

Charlotte tucked the quilt tightly around her neck and tried counting sheep. Feeling her chest rise and fall quickly under the quilt, she tried to relax her body and remember her mindfulness exercises: breathe from the diaphragm (she placed a hand there to help her focus), in…and out….and in…and out. Repeat. But his face continued to flood her thoughts and her breath hastened against her will. *What was I thinking?* Abruptly, she flipped over to her belly and kicked the quilt loose around her feet. It was wrong. So wrong. He was still married! They lived in different universes. Plus, she knew the real reason for the connection – circumstance. The way they'd been thrown together after such a horrendous event, his marriage in tatters, her relationship over. *No wonder*. Still, it didn't make it any more acceptable. And she certainly did not want to become embroiled in Vinny's marital problems on top of everything else. So, Charlotte made herself a promise to forget the notion and to leave as soon as Adam was out of hospital and went to sleep trying not to think of all the things Vinny had done to Nadia in the very bed she lay in.

Chapter Twenty

Charlotte gripped her stomach to stifle its gurgles (not the hungry type) as she padded down the stairs. With each downwards step, she wrestled to subdue any signs of adoration, just like she'd been doing for the last 20 minutes in bed - practising her grumpy face every time she felt it twitch in the wrong direction. Yet, although she'd had plenty of practise with Greg lately, it was very, *very* difficult.

Her nausea doubled when she realized Vinny was gone: his makeshift bed neatly folded away on one side of the sofa, the early morning dust particles undisturbed and still. *Shit! He knows. Christ, he knows!* Charlotte whined and gingerly bit a fingertip – soaring straight to worst-case scenario, obviously. All the while, her eyes sprung around the lounge for a note, his mobile, some sort of clue to show he hadn't strayed too far. But there was nothing, so she shuffled aimlessly to the kitchen, one sock half off, one leg of her leggings concertinaed up to her shin.

But as the gushing spray from the tap split between squirting her and filling the kettle, her one open eye spotted the note sitting on the breakfast bar alongside a continental breakfast for one. Set out so regimentally, it had Vinny written all over it. Even the grapes seemed perfectly uniform like he'd binned the funny shaped, mottled ones (the very ones she bought from the *Wonky Food* section). Charlotte's hands fumbled to sit the kettle on its base as she eyed the arrangement, her chest pounding like she was about to receive her degree results all over again.

Pass – he knew nothing and simply had somewhere to be.

Fail – he knew she wanted to suck the tip of his finger when he had tested the piquancy of the velouté he had made to accompany last night's meal (which Charlotte thought tasted very similar to the canned *Campbell's* condensed cream of chicken soup she and Adam used to eke out with half a loaf of *Mother's Pride* to make a hearty lunch for two).

Morning Charlotte,
I couldn't sleep so headed to the office to catch up on a few things. Made you some breakfast to tide you over. I shouldn't be too long. I'll take you to the hospital when I'm back. In the meantime, make yourself at home and if you need anything, just give me a buzz.
Vinny.

Hm, inconclusive, she thought. *Borderline. Perhaps the chance of a resit to make things right?*

His handwriting was beautiful, like the kind practised in Victorian times – deliberate and without flaw. Giving an already exhausted sigh, she slouched onto the stool and gazed out at the quiet Notting Hill cobbled lane as it went about its business: a frazzled mum in skinny jeans and ballet pumps ushering her young children down the street, straightening caps and ties as she went; an elderly lady with arthritic joints and wiry white hair watering the deep purples and warm oranges of Autumn blossoming in her window box, talking to her beloved flowers as she did; the cycling business man, suit and helmet, simultaneously pushing pedals and phone digits. But for once, Charlotte saw none of it, her mind trying to answer the million questions it was asking itself instead.

Vinny ran to the office. He usually did when he had a lot on his mind. The computer screens were still cold and grey, the phones hushed and unblinking, the chairs neat and obedient under every desk except his own. Leaning forward, he closed one eye and took aim, lobbing a screwed-up piece of paper at the bin. Vinny cursed as it bounced off the rim. He never missed. He never *used* to miss.

There followed a frustrated kick back of his chair before he stooped to dispose of his failed attempt on the way to the wall of glass. With his hands resting on his hips, Vinny realized he never usually stopped to consider the view from his window, only ever seeing it as a symbol of his status, a reward for his achievements. Yet today, he looked and tried to see. To see the world through Charlotte Croft's eyes. To see past the worker ants, all unconnected yet somehow a collective, weaving obediently to their destination through the concrete garden below. Then he saw…well, nothing much different if he were being entirely honest. Until, that is, the two coffee-wielding, phone-swiping strangers veered an inch off course and crashed…into each other. Their hands flailed at the shock of the disturbance to routine, a crossness even, that their everyday humdrum had steered in a different direction. But when they stopped and took notice of each other instead of their coffee-stained selves, there followed a smile. A connection. A coming to life. And suddenly they were like two red roses in a blizzard and Vinny was really pissed off at himself for noticing it. He pulled back and marched towards his desk again, kicking the bin over as he went. 'Bollocks.'

As soon as he had woken from his sleep (although the odd powernap interspaced between long, restless hours hardly constituted the term *sleep*), the feelings from the previous evening were even stronger. But so was Vinny's sense of panic. So, in a bid to control it all, he separated himself from the girl who had steam-rollered him, with her red curls and shrewd mouth. Because he was afraid, afraid that if he didn't move then, he would never be able to get away, would lose all control. And where would that leave him? Yet as soon as he had his feet tucked under his ergonomic desk, he could feel the magnetic pull to get back to her. A jangling of sorts, what he supposed was a nervousness, made any sort of mental concentration impossible, not when all he could concentrate on was her bright blue eyes and splattering of freckles across her make-up-less face, her skin pale and perfect. Withdrawal symptoms, he presumed.

Slumping across his desk, his head dropped to his folded arms. 'Fuck,' he mumbled into the frosted glass top, watching a cloud condense beneath his mouth. He watched it for a while, appear and disappear with each inhale and exhale. It seemed to echo his thinking – tell her, don't tell her – like someone plucking the petals from an ox-eye daisy to decide if they are loved. Growling as the answer still eluded him, he sat up and opened the laptop, hoping to hide from her for a few more hours in his work. To think straight. *Control.* But before he even had chance to log on, the phone buzzed in his pocket. A stomach lurch accompanied the realization that it was from Charlotte. And it was the longest text message he'd ever received in his life:

Morning Vinny. I'm going to head out for a bit today. Do a bit of shopping. Don't worry about coming to the hospital with me today. I can get the bus. Get some work done and I'll see you when I'm back. C xx

PS – I fixed the hoover. The wheel was clogged with long brown and blond hair! It's running like a baby. I'm sure the burning hair smell will pass in a day or two.

PPS - Oh, and I unblocked the u-bend under the little sink in the kitchen. You're not supposed the put anything greasy down it, Vinny! The London sewage system is full of fatbergs as it is!

PPPS - I wasn't sure how to work the dishwasher so I just put in a little bit of washing up liquid and pressed the on *button. It seemed to be making a noise, so I think it is working!*

He exploded in a short, astounded laugh. His mouth still agape, it was still resonating as he re-read the message. Then once again, just to be sure. Smoothing back his already perfectly smooth hair, he toyed with the notion of cancelling the plumber he'd arranged to come that afternoon but held off; the place was probably flooded with soap suds by now. He also needed to let Charlotte know that a cleaner came around on Wednesdays and Fridays (who brought their own hoover too). But the main thing which caused his chin to remain slack was how she was able to do it. How did she just take his choice away? Because just the knowledge that if he did choose to go back home, she wouldn't be there caused an even greater panic to shrink his lungs. And then he admitted to himself what he already knew: he didn't have a choice when it came to Charlotte Croft because he was completely in love with her. Vinny checked the time and called Nadia.

Chapter Twenty-One

By the time Charlotte reached the hospital, her bag was bursting with goodies to cheer up Adam (or at least make his time there more bearable): a new set of pyjamas and toiletries (most definitely not to his usual high standard but beggars couldn't be choosers), a *Puzzler* magazine (more for her than him), the new *Stuart McBride* novel (Adam's favourite author), 2 packets of *Munchie's* (a mutual favourite which they used to share over some late-night study sessions), a pack of cards (probably a bit optimistic but still), a bottle of *Lucozade* (she wasn't sure why only that it seemed to be the poorly person's drink of choice), and a couple of broadsheets (definitely just for him and a great place to hide her latest copy of *Heat* magazine).

Charlotte found Adam sitting up and watching TV in a side room of his new ward, the light cheerier now that there was an actual window.

'Morning!'

'Hey, Wee Yin. What've you got me?' Grimacing a little, he pushed himself up, the mattress crunching beneath.

'Easy, Adam. Don't burst a stich! What makes you think I brought you anything?' she said, straightening the pillows at his back before easing him gently into place.

'Oh, because you're the best sister in the world,' and he smiled his usual, cheeky, adorable, amazing smile.

'Well, I may have a thing or two if you're a good boy.' Charlotte began unpacking her hoard and his groans of appreciation resounded with every reveal (until she pulled out the *Harry Potter* pyjamas).

'Charlotte, you're having a fucking laugh! I'm not wearing them!'

He griped but not in pain (at least, not physical pain).

'What? You love Harry Potter! And I need to take back and wash the ones Vinny gave you.' She knew fine well it would mortify Adam – it was why she chose them. Somehow the thought of a top shot lawyer who resided in New York wearing them tickled her greatly.

'God sake, Charlotte. You're a right pain in the arse sometimes.' He threw them on the bed and glowered till his eyebrows met in the middle.

'I know!' She smiled as if proud of the fact, thanking God that he at least left her a brother to annoy.

When his new doctor did her rounds, she was more than happy with Adam's progress. And his slinky grin showed he was more than happy too, but for a different reason. The beautiful Dr Quinn wanted him out of bed that day, and if he continued to mend at the same rate, she predicted he would be released by the end of the week. Adam was practically drooling as he nodded compliantly with her every order and Charlotte shook her head in disdain.

It was all a merry by-thought, watching on anxiously as the nurses grabbed Adam under each arm and hoisted him up, his face contorting and twisting. Easing his legs to the side, they caught him again as he pushed himself to his feet. Charlotte watched his face warp and lips leach any hint of pink. Only the knuckle jammed in her mouth prevented her crying out the word *stop*.

After a few tussled loops of the room, Adam was set in the wipeable high-backed chair, a mist of sweat covering his clammy face.

'Well done, Adam! Here, have some *Lucozade*.' Charlotte thrust the glass at him, her face tight, as she tried to at least do something helpful.

'Ta,' was all he could muster, sounding like he had sprinted 15 miles instead of shuffling 15 metres.

They spent hours filling in puzzles, watching telly (which seemed to be filled by judges and antiques and one particularly tenacious judge who *was* an antique), managing a few games of pontoon (Charlotte was ecstatic to find Adam back to his normal cheating self in having, literally, a couple of aces up his sleeve). When Adam had lunch, Charlotte went to the canteen and ate a grand total of three bites from a stale cheese baguette. She wrapped the rest up for later.

Following the film reel of staff photos which unspooled along the barren green corridor, Charlotte wondered just how long she could stall before she had to head back to Vinny's. The thought filled her in equal quantities of dread and joy as she paused to gaze at Staff Nurse Gordon McKenna's black and white portrait because his was by far the happiest she had seen. Every other one looked like the subject had groaned, 'Oh, why the hell is this necessary?' just as the camera clicked. But not Gordon. His smile made her smile too. *Good on yae, Gordon!* she thought as she ambled on to stuffy Sue Simpson, *Head Cook*. From what Adam had said about the hospital food, it was no wonder she wasn't too happy at having her face plastered on the wall.

But when she arrived back and began shuffling the cards again, Adam took the decision into his own hands. Sighing, he removed his glasses and placed them on the bedside cabinet. 'Charlotte, I love you to bits, but I'm exhausted. I need to sleep.'

'Sure…Of course…Sorry!' she blustered, her shuffles decelerating to a stop. Cupping the cards straight, she put them back in their box then sprang up to stuff a foot in a boot.

Adam suddenly sounded more awake. 'Charlotte? Are you okay? You seem a bit… jumpy.'

'Oh, yeah. I'm good.' Charlotte kept her eyes glued on the zip she briskly whisked up, then down, then up again before settling somewhere in the middle. Wrapping the scarf around her neck, she yanked her hair free and began to justify her rashness. 'Just probably tired. And relieved…that you're on the mend!'

Utterly unconvinced, Adam stroked his birthmark, like he always did when he was perplexed or worried. 'Are you sure? Is everything all right at Vinny's?'

Routing around her pockets for the gloves which were mingled amongst empty sweet wrappers, copper coins and shreds of tissue, Charlotte bought a few seconds. Keeping her head down, she pulled out a handful of *stuff* and *bits* and *fluff*, carefully separating the gloves as she spoke. 'Oh, absolutely!'

'Don't worry. I'm looking after your sister well,' a deep voice informed from somewhere behind her.

Everything which had been in her hand was now falling through the air. Charlotte dove quickly to rake the pile back up from Adam's blanket, thankful there was no heart monitor attached to her. A gust breezed by her, his expensive cologne smelling delicious – spicy and sweet. Then, like she'd suddenly picked up some of Vinny's tendencies, Charlotte shuffled and straightened the newspapers and magazines till it was difficult to determine if there was one in the stack or ten.

'All right mate? Bloody hell, you look a lot better. Nice pyjamas!' Vinny grinned as he planted a hand on Adam's shoulder.

Adam rolled his eyes and tutted as he brushed a hand over *Gryffindor's* rampant lion. 'Yeah, I'm good. Tired, but good.' It was his first thought. 'Any news from the police?'

Removing his leather gloves with a single swift tug of each finger, Vinny perched on the edge of the bed. 'Well, I spoke to the detective today. A warrant has been issued for David Sullivan's arrest and he appears to be keeping a low profile, which looks better for us. But forensics have nothing.'

'I'm sure something will turn up.' But Adam didn't sound very sure as he turned away and began groping between the jug and plastic tumblers for his specs, tomorrow's food menu suddenly a priority.

The last thing Vinny wanted to do was set him back. 'Of course, it will, bud. There's loads of CCTV footage to scroll through yet. It's nigh-on impossible to outrun it these days. And once we find out where he went, the chances of finding something concrete which links him to the case is inevitable.'

Adam said nothing and Charlotte noticed him tick the country vegetable casserole option for lunch and the vegetarian cottage pie for dinner.

That bad, eh? She made a mental note to bring him some tasty form of protein tomorrow. *A big, juicy gourmet burger, maybe?*

Adam swiftly changed the subject as he ran a pen up and down the list of desserts. 'Oh, Charlotte. Can you remember to bring my phone charger tomorrow? God knows what's waiting for me when I fire that thing back up.'

At last, she lowered the papers from her mouth. 'I've been looking but I can't find What kind is it?' Charlotte placed the heap on the bedside cabinet then opened the cupboard below to check.

'Erm, a Samsung Galaxy S9 plus,' but she didn't hear him.

'Adam?' she asked, her voice still echoing in the stale-smelling cupboard. Stale with what reminded her of her granny's lilac talc, Greg's soiled socks mixed with the vinegary residue of old newspapers. 'Did you not say that the guy who stabbed you asked for a light first?'

'Yeah. Why?'

She turned to them both, a clear, zip-lock bag in the air. Its contents: a mobile, a bunch of keys, half a packet of *Wrigley's Extra*, a 3-

pack of condoms (Charlotte didn't dare look to see if they were ribbed, or strawberry flavoured, large or small even) but most importantly, a fluorescent green lighter - bold and beautiful. 'Wouldn't happen to be this one by any chance, would it?'

Chapter Twenty-Two

The lidless cherry lip balm landed in her lap when Vinny finally broke the silence as he flicked the windscreen wipers to full. 'I still can't believe it.'

Leaving zero gap at the end of his sentence, Charlotte's words were the flood waters gushing over a collapsing dam. 'I know! I just pray to God he wasn't wearing gloves.'

'Well, Adam was pretty sure he wasn't, and he's got a good eye for detail. If there's a print on that lighter, Sullivan is finished. It'll help with Dolan's case too. Makes him look guilty as sin, the bastard, even if it is just circumstantial. The police seemed pretty hopeful.'

'Are you not worried?' She sure as hell was.

'About what?' Vinny asked coolly but she could still feel the car accelerate beneath her nonetheless.

For the first time that day, Charlotte turned to face him with his strong jaw and broad shoulders. The mere sight of him caused her heart to swell and shrink at the same time. Sure, he was much bigger than Adam but that made no difference when it came to knives and guns. 'That they'll try to get you.'

Vinny flipped through the playlist options displayed on the dash. 'Nope. After Adam, they'd only look even more guilty. The next time something like that happened, it couldn't be argued away as circumstantial, not even by bloody Kate Norton. It would be an open admission of guilt. Dolan's not that stupid.'

Charlotte ogled the nerve tic in the dip of his temple.

'Are you hungry?' Vinny turned up the heating and steered the conversation away.

Not in the slightest. 'Yeah, I could eat,' she lied sleepily as she watched the streetlights lengthen and fuse into a bright orange ribbon of light.

The sombre hue of her words lured his eyes from the glittery concrete nodules peppering the journey ahead. 'Good,' he laughed, 'because I cooked up a feast before I came to pick you up from hospital.'

Charlotte's neck twanged 90 degrees right. 'No, you never!'

'Erm, yes I did!' He gave another soft chuckle. 'I was home by twelve. I was a bit bored after popping an 8ft wall of soap suds.'

'A what?' she garbled, so twitchy now she found herself poking yet more buttons (this one inclining her until she was near horizontal). What's worse, she couldn't seem to detach her digit. Instead, she flicked the switch in the other direction.

Difficult as it was, Vinny managed to remain unsmiling as she droned upright. 'So, I went for a food shop and cooked you a nice meal. Thought you would be tired after being out for *soooo* long.'

The seatbelt now had the confines of a straitjacket (partly because the shock of his words had caused her to propel herself much further forward from her starting position, mostly because he was on to the fact she had been avoiding him). She yanked it several times before it gave. From the corner of her eye, Charlotte spotted what she hoped was the hint of a smirk as a beam of passing headlights spotlighted his face for a split second. But it vanished with a glance to his blind spot before he glided into the fast lane.

'Oooh, erm,' she squirmed, her arse now on fire as well as her face, and Charlotte realized she must have found the heated seat button. Flailing, she began fumbling for the right knob to depress. 'Vinny...you didn't have to do that. I…I was thinking more of beans on toast.'

'Well, it might have to be. It's been in the oven since 4!'

As Charlotte prised a boot off with the noise of a pained animal, Vinny loped towards the kitchen, a waft of garlic and herbs filling the air. 'It's fine!' he yelled, ducking away from the plummet of steam before it singed his beard and eyebrows off.

Perhaps it is just my imagination, she tried to rationalise what felt like a shift in the parameters. Okay, so he still walked the same, spoke the same, looked at her the same. Yet, it certainly didn't *feel* the same. Trying to work out precisely what had changed, Charlotte straightened her boots neatly, hung up her coat and followed the smell (all delicious but with something slightly stringent in the background). *Shower gel?* she guessed wrongly. Her stride became quickly sapped, like she was suddenly thigh deep in water, as she drifted towards the dining table which didn't look a million miles away from the indulgence of the Westwood. *What the…?*

'Erm, do you need a hand?' she asked, scratching the side of her head to make sense of it.

'Nope. All under control. But you can open the wine,' he said, carrying a volcanic tray to the counter.

Rather unsuccessfully, she pulled at the corkscrew, then screwed it deeper into the cork until it punctured the other side and snowed the wine with spongy bits. But she didn't notice as she continued to stare as he dished up, all confident and proud and bloody gorgeous and totally making her feel ill. And she knew why. Why she felt sick then hungry and then even more nauseous till eating was out of the question. This was way more than the effects of an odd, emotionally charged set of circumstances. Two fingers drove against her lips to wedge her mouth shut as he arranged the food, a tea towel slung over his shoulder, his head tilting every now and then until he was happy (much like her when she was composing a painting). It was *love. Holy Mary Mother of God! How can that even be possible?* Charlotte wilted into the chair and dabbed a finger into his wine to remove the debris.

And she ate his delicious food (although she had to force it), and she drank the rich, buttery wine (didn't have to force that as much, bits and all), and she answered his questions but struggled to come up with any of her own. It was all becoming dreadfully uncomfortable, until that is, inspiration struck when she recalled the photo.

'The picture,' she burst when the thought fell into her mind from out of nowhere. 'Who is it?'

'What picture?' Vinny asked, re-filling her glass with a sweet, smooth dessert wine which married particularly well with meringue, or so he said. Personally, she would have opted for a cup of tea.

Charlotte thumbed to the room behind her a few times before she spoke. 'The one on your bookshelf.'

Immediately, his face levelled...and opened. Opened so wide, she could see everything. More than in the airport. More than when he played his guitar. A pandora's box of every emotion under the sun, hope included.

Vinny sighed and smiled. 'Ah, that's me and Harry.'

Her spoon sunk to the bowl as she gazed at a smile which held more sadness than joy. 'You look close?'

Vinny tilted forward and nodded slowly, pushing his bowl away. 'We were. Very.'

The poignancy of his tone caused Charlotte to lean closer too, her frown deepening. 'Were?'

'Were, yeah. He died.'

Talk about sticking your bloody size 5's in it, Charlotte thought to herself as she fought the notion to slap herself...hard. 'Jesus...Vinny, I'm sorry…I didn't mean to…'

He pulled up a one-sided smile. 'No, it's fine, Charlotte.'

'What happened?'

'Cocaine. Cocaine's what happened.' Vinny sneered, the guilt of it still raw. 'And I had no bloody idea. I was supposed to be his best mate and I didn't have a clue until I found him. We shared a flat in Oxford. Went to nursery together, school together, uni too. Both wanted to study law. To be honest, I think we just wanted to be on the same course as each other! I knew he was partying hard, but so was everyone. That's what students did! Then, I went to waken him up for our rugby match. He was late…as usual! Or so I thought…'

Now he looked like the one who wanted to slap himself and Charlotte was tempted to reach for his hand until he began dabbing up crumbs with his fingers. 'He had a heart condition. One of those undetected one's which any of us could have. His heart just stopped…'

Somehow, Charlotte knew this huge contributing factor made no difference in Vinny's head, not when it was clear to see he put the blame firmly at his own feet. Her head slanted to the side as she tried to connect his eyes to hers. 'Vinny.,.,it wasn't your fault. If he had a heart defect, it could have happened at any time.'

'Or never if I had been a better mate, if I had spotted the signs.' He tensed his eyes closed for a second, allowing the regret and culpability to consume him once more. And he didn't fight it, not when he felt like it was deserved. 'So, for Harry, for the life he lost, I was determined to make a difference. It's why I take a special interest in the cases like that scum bag Dolan's.'

Ah! So, that's what Adam was droning on about when he woke up. But she couldn't utter a sound, not when she saw how it burdened him, like his calling was somehow his penance. A lifetime spent trying to make up for a crime he never even committed. But more than anything, for the first time, she could see he wasn't infallible. That he *was* flesh and blood after all. Just like everyone, he had baggage too.

He peaked up to gauge if she blamed him too.

Never more had she wanted to lead him by the hand upstairs. Then she wanted to open his wardrobe and pull out every perfectly ironed and piled and folded and hung set of clothes. She wanted to spill some wine on the carpet and mix up his socks into odd pairs and move the heavy metal rectangular base of the bedside lamp 18 degrees skewwhiff to show him he didn't have to fear losing someone so much that he had to be a control freak. That it wouldn't mean the loss of something precious if he took his eyes off the ball for a second. That was way too much responsibility for any one person to bare. How could she make him see, there were just some things he would never be able to control no matter how hard he tried, the death of Harry being one of them? But more than anything, he didn't have to worry about what she thought because her most prevalent thought was how much she wanted to straddle him on the chair he sat in and kiss him hard.

Eventually, when her flush subsided, she managed to put into words what she was thinking (the non-explicit summary anyway). 'I think you are the amazing one, Vinny.'

Well, I wasn't expecting that, he thought, his eyes grazing up to hers, acceptance ringing clear in them.

Hers fell as she continued plucking at the now crumb-free tablecloth. 'To go through all that, to achieve what you have, to work to stop it happening to others.' Charlotte shook her head. 'It's nice to know you're human, Vinny. And what a bloody amazing human you are.' If she was in any doubt that it was love, she wasn't now.

Stumped again, he watched the little bird get closer.

Chapter Twenty-Three

In a contemplative silence, she helped Vinny load the dishwasher and he quietly re-arranged everything so that it fit better. More than anything, all she could think about was that she loved him, *truly* loved him. That, and the promise she had made to herself (no matter how hard she tried to flick away the pesky angel perched on her shoulder). He was still forbidden fruit regardless and Charlotte suddenly had a greater empathy for Eve. The sheer frustration of it caused the last bowl to get forcefully wedged in beside another plate, the screech of china against china like nails down a blackboard.

She didn't look up to see what she could only imagine was Vinny's scorn as she flopped back down in her chair. One prostrate, very reluctant finger gently pushed the wine glass away. 'Vinny, that was gorgeous, but I'm shattered. I feel really rude but I'm going to have to call it a night.'

Instinctively, he opened his mouth to argue but closed it slowly, raking his top teeth against his bottom lip. 'Yeah…of course.' Suddenly forgetting how to work the damn machine, he jabbed every button. Finally, he found the big, flashing green one before slamming the door closed. He spoke to the knives magnetized to the stainless-steel bar: arranging them into size order (largest first), spacing them equally and adjusting them till they stood perfectly vertical. 'It's been a tough few days. I'm sure a good night's sleep is exactly what you need.' When he'd finished, he kept his distance, leaning on the worktop and folding his arms across what he hoped was the beginnings of heartburn.

Charlotte wanted to scream at him to stop being so amazing, to stop making it so bloody hard. Several fingers raked down her neck, the welds now raised and angry. 'Thanks. And thanks for the meal, and for picking me up…again.' She smiled, getting to her feet and slapping his shoulder, bold and platonic.

'Night Charlotte.' Vinny sighed, flattening a residual powdery white ball of bubbles which had been camouflaged by the pristine white kickboard.

'Night Vinny.' Charlotte didn't turn back.

Feeling the meal like a lump of stone in his stomach, he continued to scrutinize the light at the top of the stairs until it clicked to black. More regret mauled at his insides when he considered how many chances he'd missed to tell her, each wasted opportunity being re-written as he sat alone. In each new version of events, he told her how he had phoned Nadia to say he wanted a divorce. That it was over. That he wanted her. But it was the end part, her reaction, the part he couldn't predict which had held the words from his tongue.

When there was nothing left to tidy or straighten, Vinny sought his guitar, feeling the urge to at least do something with his hands, even if it wasn't exactly what he had been imagining. He cradled the neck and brought it back through to the kitchen and began to strum what he was feeling.

Charlotte listened to the melody, soft and soulful, yet so melancholy it made her eyes prickle and a lump wedge in her throat as her mind travelled around all the sad of late. Like what had happened to Adam and how she nearly lost him. How she still might, even. Like poor Amos, and how she wished she'd been able to do more. Like Greg's offer which made her grieve a little over what she was turning her back on. Like Harry, dying before he had even lived. But the most potent thought in her head was the man downstairs. For what could have been? For what would never be. It felt weird to cry so much. Sure, she could shed tears of frustration from time to time, but rarely a good, proper, snot dribbling, face crunchingly ugly, cry. Yet she'd done it so much lately. Not usually a crier, Charlotte thought perhaps her tears had all been spent on her mum and dad. In all honesty, she didn't really know why she was crying now but went with it anyway – it felt oddly good. A release. But the guitar quietened, and she tried to, pulling the quilt over her head and blowing her nose into the tissue in silent spurts.

'Charlotte?'

Shit! She quickly sniffed and swiped her eyes, but her voice was strangled and thick when she warbled, 'Yeah?'

His dark silhouette began to float up from the staircase and settled at the mouth of the room. 'Are you okay?'

Charlotte buried her face further under the quilt. 'Yeah.' She forced a raspy laugh. 'Just being a bit silly. It's been a strange few weeks and…it's just caught up with me tonight, that's all. I'll be fine.' *Please go away! Please go away. Please never go away.*

In the pitch black and balmy air of under the quilt, she listened carefully for his footsteps to plunge back down the stairs. Instead, she could hear them pad heavily towards her. 'Shove over,' was the order given.

Obediently, Charlotte shuffled to the cold patch and watched in something hovering between fear and ecstasy as he slid in beside her. With vast eyes, she slowly laid her head back on a pillow as he settled himself under the covers, kicking around his feet, patting the quilt around him, shimmying like he was breaking in a new mattress. 'Right,' he huffed, hooking an arm behind his head. 'That's better.'

They lay there, neither saying a word, neither moving, just like a postcoital Mr and Mrs Stickman – except there were no satiated smiles to accompany their huge eyes. At last, Vinny found the guts to break the impasse as his hand landed at her side, open and waiting. Without a second thought, she grasped it and he laced his fingers in hers. Charlotte could hear her own breathing as an electrical current passed through her body. How she wanted to turn to him, to arch her body against his. She wanted him to roll on top of her, to crash his mouth to hers. Every cell in her body was alert and ready till she ached, ached for him until it almost escaped her in a whimper. *Fuck, you could strike a match on my legs! And my bloody minge is like the front cover of The Joy of Sex! Bloody…big, bouncy 70's bush! Ginger bush! He might scream. Maybe he only thinks such things are of ancient legend and myth! And garlic. Why did he have to use so much bloody garlic?* There certainly wouldn't be any vampires hunting in Notting Hill tonight, that was for sure. Nothing like the lack of personal grooming (or just a razor for that matter) to enforce some sexual self-control. But the mere thought of him so close beside her made her swallow again, her mouth so dry, she was sure it must have sounded like someone scrunching up an empty bag of cheese and onion. *Shit! Can I taste onion too?*

How do you go about it? he asked himself, staring at the ceiling, her soft hand lost in his. Vinny could feel her scared stiff beside him. He had to admit, he was too. In the old days, you wouldn't be in bed with a girl unless it was going somewhere. Moreover, things had changed so much in recent years, the art of wooing another was a complete minefield. He only had to think of the cases he had overseen in the last year alone. And he *really* didn't want to do the wrong thing, to read too much into why she was crying, why she looked at him the way she did. And he certainly didn't want to be accused of being a perpetrator in the *Me Too* movement.

But he had hopped into bed with her! *Shit, Vinny, what a position to put yourself in!* It was instinct, a reaction. It was bloody stupid, especially when he thought of how he said it, how wide her eyes were. Startled bunny wide. But to be so close was torture. His thumb itched to sweep across her hand to read for a squeeze of approval that he could move it to the next level, to perhaps ask her permission for a kiss? Just then, Charlotte swallowed loudly again. Was she scared of him? *So, how do you go about it these days? Fucked if I know!* So, to be safe, he did nothing.

And they just lay there, terrified in the darkness. Mr and Mrs Stickman.

Chapter Twenty-Four

The morning sunshine bled stripes through the shutters, his arm heavy around her middle. The brightness was exactly how she felt – like she radiated from somewhere deep inside, the darkness, a stark reminder. Charlotte lay there, keeping her breathing steady and slow for as long as she could; there'd never be the chance to get this close to him again. More importantly, she wouldn't allow there to be.

'Mmmorning Charlotte,' he said huskily.

'Morning Vinny.' She morphed the words into another fake yawn (a bit better now with practise), awaiting the awkwardness to hit, the pulling back of stray body parts.

'Coffee?' he suggested brightly, his hands staying exactly in place.

Her eyes were ample now she realized how close her backside was to his ample bits. She was ashamed to admit it to even herself, but her eyes had wandered to his bits plenty recently. Definitely ample bits. 'Yes please,' she squawked.

Vinny lay there for a few seconds longer before he unwrapped himself and planted his feet. This morning, he devoted a few seconds to a toe wriggle – the luxurious nap of the shag-pile felt extra nice between them somehow. He perched on his toes to roar a huge yawn, his sweatpants hanging low enough to see the concave dips at the side of his butt cheeks before he tottered happily for the stairs.

Oh, Lord help me! Charlotte swallowed as she slid up the bed.

With the kettle under the tap, she leapt to the loo for a rapid emergency brush of her teeth and a swift de-crust of her eyes. 'Don't freak out! Stay calm! He's just being a good friend,' she whispered disparagingly to her reflection whilst pinching her cheeks rosy.

Diving back under the quilt, she tried to position herself in her best natural yet alluring pose – the one we all hope we will look like in the morning if we ever get the chance to waken up with a Vinny: hair splayed seductively like a mermaid under water, relaxed fingers resting just above her eyes, mouth closed instead of catching flies. In fact, just like Kate Winslet with *The Heart of the Ocean* dangling between her boobs. Somehow, Charlotte got the feeling she probably looked as desperate and lusty as Blanch Deveraux after a dry spell. The grim vision forced her upright and she crossed her legs and folded her arms just as Vinny appeared back up the staircase. A grin from ear to ear, he handed Charlotte a mug before settling beside her again (above the quilt this time), flicking the TV to the news channel. With another push of a button, the fire below it ignited.

'Oh!' She flinched, the coffee dangerously close to spilling.

'Did you sleep well?'

'Yeah, I did actually.' Charlotte tried to read the lips on the screen because all she could hear was *Blah! Blah! Blah!*

'Good. What do you fancy doing today?' he asked breezily as he turned to face her. Like this was *normal*.

'I don't mind.' Charlotte shrugged, trying to hide the beam that he was already planning to spend the day with her. *Grumpy face!* she reminded herself. 'What do you want to do?'

'Hm…nothing,' he said, his bright blue and green eyes melting her like butter on a hot day. 'Let's have a film day…here.' He patted the quilt. 'It's supposed to be pissing it down later. Let's watch loads of cheesy films and eat lots of crap and be bed potatoes for the whole day. I mean, when was the last time you did that?' *Perhaps if I download* You've Got Mail, *she might get the hint. Better still* – Notting Hill.

'Honestly? Years.' Somehow, Charlotte had a strong inkling this was not his usual pastime either, not with the way he normally looked like he was scared if she dropped as much as a *Jammie Dodger* crumb on the carpet.

'Well, let's go visit Adam this morning then come back here and do it.'

'Okay. Sounds good to me.' A day in bed with the man of her dreams, what wasn't there to like? *The fact that he is married.* Cursing the angel, she lightly scratched the bridge of her nose. 'But what about Nadia? I'm sure she won't be too pleased about her husband spending the day in bed with another woman, you know,' she sat up and smoothed the quilt across her legs, 'even… just a *friend.*'

As if he hadn't heard, Vinny scrolled through the channels before tutting and settling back on the news again. 'I'm sure you're right but it's really none of her business anymore. I told her yesterday I want a divorce.'

'Why?' Charlotte cried, pivoting her head to him, her wild curls springing.

Oh, God help me, that hair. It made his stomach throb so much he looked away again. 'Because I know *definitively* that it is over.' He slid a hand behind his head, pulled a knee up to hide the threatening erection and continued to stare at the smiley weather lady as she forecast a storm moving up from the south.

'How? *How?* I…I mean…' She tucked the quilt under her armpits and snapped her arms to her side, accusing, 'You were still swaying the other day.'

Releasing a happy-go-lucky yawn, Vinny picked up the remote and scrawled through more options and Charlotte noted the pink shiny indent where his wedding band used to be. 'I'm not swaying now, Charlotte. Let's just leave it there.'

Chapter Twenty-Five

What the hell is happening? What is going on? Is this normal for a friend thing? I've not got matching knickers on. Charlotte sang the jingle over and over again in her head as she sat on the cool bathroom tiles in just her full black undies and questionably white bra. Her legs were splayed in front of her as she fanned her freshly shaved bikini area with one of Nadia's old copies of *Vanity Fair*.

As soon as they'd returned from the hospital, she'd raced for the shower with the new pack of disposable razors and foam she'd manage to sneakily buy from the infirmary shop. (She'd requested Vinny wait outside so she could buy some *feminine* products. He didn't need telling twice). And although she tried to convince herself, it was just because it needed doing (especially now that she didn't have to use her downiness as some sort of Greg deterrent), she sat defeated. Because she knew exactly what she had been trying to do. She knew exactly what was coming, just from the way he'd curled his pinkie in hers when they were forced to the back of the elevator by the bed and two porters accompanying it.

'I like you,' he'd said ever-so-quietly.

'I like you too,' she'd replied, even quieter.

Without another word on the matter being uttered, she knew - they were at the next level. And she wanted nothing more. Yet...Yet, there was still Nadia. So, she couldn't...but she *really* wanted to...God! Did she want to! Charlotte groaned, her head gonging softly against the fancy flat bars of the shiny chrome radiator. Perhaps if she stayed there long enough, the whole debacle would disappear...

'Charlotte?' Vinny knocked gently, worried that she'd been gone for an hour, more so, that there'd been no noise at all now for the last 20 minutes.

'Yeah?' she drawled, mentally exhausted and resigned to the fact that of course, it was never going to go away.

'You all right?'

Vanity Fair slapped against the tiles. 'Nooooo.'

'Riiiggghhhtt. Do you want to talk about it?'

'No.' Charlotte tore tiny shreds of toilet roll, dabbing each on one of the many leg cuts left by the lethally sharp shitty blade.

Perplexed, Vinny began to edge away. 'Shall I...I'll give you some peace then...'

'Yes...No! No.'

'Okay...okay.' After a moment or two, Vinny hunkered on to his backside and stretched out his legs (the exact same position she was in on the other side of the door).

'Have I done something wrong?' The question sounded breathy.

'I don't know. *Maybe.*'

He recoiled a little, his brow furrowing as he raked his brain for a time he could have offended her. The only thing he could think of was that they'd shared the same bed, held hands, got closer. So, it must be the question of *them* which was troubling her. 'Have you done something?'

'Not yet.'

Right. So, we're playing The Mystic Meg game? 'Can you tell me?'

Silence.

'You know you can tell me, right?'

'Yes. But...' She dried up.

And he was desperate to keep his little bird singing. 'Okay...Let's talk about something else then. Maybe that will be easier.'

But it was the door, the *only* thing dividing them now, which made it easier to ask what she needed to know.

'Vinny, when you said you liked me…what did you mean?'

Ah, right. The question of *them.* His heart began to sprint in his chest. 'Well, it's pretty self-explanatory Charlotte.' Or was it because her silence didn't exactly fill him with confidence? He elaborated and hyperventilated at the same time. 'I meant I *like* you…like you.'

'Oh.'

She sounded crestfallen.

And now he felt crestfallen. *Shit.* His stomach slipped to his feet as he scrunched his eyes tight. *She doesn't feel the same.* He tried to salvage something, anything. 'Is that what you're worried about? Because, don't be. I shouldn't have said…'

'No! Yes! You should have.'

He smiled, scraping a nail lightly against a knot in the wood of the door. *Fuck it. In for a penny…* 'And when you said you liked me, did you mean *like* me…like me?'

Another eon passed.

'Mm hm.'

Now, his heart nearly exploded as his head fell back against the wall. 'Riiiggghhhttt. So, do you want to come out and we can talk about it?'

'No.'

'No?'

'No…I…I…'

I can't say it. I can't bloody make myself say it! More panic. When the words still wouldn't come, Charlotte sprang to her feet, her bare soles slapping against the marble on the way to the glass cabinet. *There must be something to write with surely?* she cried to herself as her hands groped up and down the shelves. Her panic soared when all she could lay her hands on was the 10 pack of razors and value shaving gel (which smelt oddly like the pungent background smell of last night). After yanking open every cupboard door and drawer, she found a rich burgundy *Dior* lip liner. She shrugged; it'd do.

Pulling a few squares of loo roll, she began to scribble:

I can't do this.

With very shaky fingers, she flattened and pushed the flimsy note under the door, in much the same way one gets change of a tenner from the machine at the amusement arcades. Only part way through, Charlotte jerked back as it was plucked through from the other side. Just like the machine too.

Charlotte heard a huge sigh, a shuffling of movement then his footsteps stomping away. Then, nothing. Sagging back to her bottom (now crisscrossed with the red-lined pattern of the tiles after sitting for so long), she wanted to cry again as her head fell in her hands. But less than a minute later, she heard him plod back and settle on the other side of the door again.

A crisp, *VK* embossed piece of stationary was delivered back to her. A *VK* monogramed pen too.

Why?

And so, the archaic pre-curser to texting began: the sending of notes exchange (just like high school).

Charlotte: *Because you're married.*

Vinny: *But I'm getting a divorce.*

Charlotte: *Still. It's a bit soon.*

Vinny: *Maybe but does that make it wrong?*

Charlotte: *You might change your mind. Nadia might change her mind!*

Vinny: *No, she won't.*

Charlotte: *How do you know?*

Vinny: *She said she wanted a divorce too. That it was the right thing. It is the*

175

right thing! And even if she did, I won't change mine.

Charlotte: *If you say so.*

He tutted and shook his head with that one.

Vinny: *Charlotte, I like you…A LOT.*

Charlotte: *I like you too…A LOT.*

Vinny: *Please come out.*

Charlotte: *I'm scared.*

Vinny: *Me too. I really am. But I'm more scared of being the guy who really, really liked this amazing, crazy girl once with these bloody God-awful green sock things and a bit of a temper but did nothing about it. Plus, I'd really like to kiss you now…*

That message was finished with a hand-drawn kissing emoji.

A laugh and a touch of a sob escaped as Charlotte read that note several times then checked her groin for any sign of shaving rash and Vinny tried to adjust his hard-on to somewhere less obvious and more comfortable.

Another minutes silence.

Then, the toilet sneck snapped open.

Chapter Twenty-Six

'Heterochromia iridium,' he repeated as he teased the long red curls twisting and twirling across his chest, a feeling of complete contentedness warming his bones (as well as other places). 'It's a rare genetic thing. My Dad has it too.'

Charlotte listened to the rain battering at the windows. The weather lady was right today, and she was glad. Could it be possible they were the only people in the world at that moment in time? It sure felt like it. 'Ah, right. It is very beautiful. I thought it might have been an accident, like David Bowie or Gordon Brown.'

Vinny laughed so hard, her head choogled on his chest until she felt dizzy. 'Gordon Brown only has one eye! The other is made of glass!'

All the weight of the last few weeks gone, Charlotte giggled too, all fluffy and floaty like a cloud. 'Perhaps they couldn't get it the exact shade as his other one.'

He'd done it. He'd tamed his little bird. And this one – she wanted him for him. Not his fast car, not his fat wallet, not because of his career choice or the house on the quiet cobbled street which cost a small fortune and caused Nadia's friends to weep with envy when they came for a bragging session. In fact, he knew Charlotte didn't give a damn about one little bit of it – only him. And now he had her, he never intended on letting her go.

'Vinny?' Her voice was suddenly serious from under the scarlet mass.

'Charlotte?' he mimicked.

She slithered up on an elbow to face him, her beautiful Viking. And he really did look like a Viking - his hair fanned on the pillow, the tribal tattoos she now knew ran the full length of his back (from the year he spent travelling through Polynesia). Not to mention the muscles – lots of muscles. And hair! A real man with hairy legs (thankfully hairier than hers now that she'd managed a sneaky shearing session) and a feathery line which darkened and thickened the further down it travelled from his belly button. *Definitely wilder between the sheets.* 'Vinny,' she repeated, closing her eyes for a second before asking what she was terrified to know. 'I just…don't want to get in the way of things or contribute to the break-up of your marriage.'

The worry of it etched shadowy lines on her face and he ran his fingers up and down her back as if trying to erase them. 'Charlotte, *this* is nothing to do with the end of my marriage. My marriage was already over. But I told Nadia when I did because I wanted to finish that officially before I started this. And I couldn't put that off any longer. Either of them.'

'I know,' she sighed, knowing she no more had it in her to stay away from him as he had it in him to stay away from her. Her eyes wrinkled for a moment as she curled her finger in a lock of his hair. 'What is…*this?*'

His hand cupped the side of her face, her cheeks flushed, her lips swollen, her hair like she'd been caught in a hurricane. '*This,*' he inhaled her delicate scent now inextricably mixed with his own as he studied her, 'is quite possibly the best thing that has ever happened to me, Charlotte Croft.'

'Me too, Vinny…' She gasped suddenly, her finger releasing the lock to plant her hand on his chest. 'Shit! I don't even know your surname!'

'Knight.' *And you better get used to it,* he thought, *because it's going to be yours one day too.*

'Me too, Vinny *Knight.*'

'Hm, well, now we have that sorted that,' he added huskily as his hands began to fumble to find a way under the quilt, 'let's just get on with

178

whatever *this* is.'

Chapter Twenty-Seven

It was a long, slow meander to the vending machine where she gave Adam enough coins for a *Snickers*. 'Honestly, Char, I'm going stir crazy. And don't even get me started on the food.'

'I know but it's not for much longer. Have they said when they are freeing you?' She counted what was left in her hand and frowned – there was only enough for a *Milky Way*.

'All being well, Friday.'

Charlotte reached in and pulled out what she felt was everyone's runners up version of a chocolate bar. 'Well then, that's not too much longer,' she mollified as she took his arm and headed back along the long glass link corridor.

'I know,' he huffed, then eyed the passing doctor with the blonde hair piled high on her head and larger than average bust. Tutting, Charlotte tugged his arm.

'What?' He smiled roguishly, evidently getting closer to his old, charming self by the second.

Although Charlotte scowled as she held open the door to an enclosed garden, she was over the moon really. 'We need to think about what we're going to do when you get out. I've packed up most of my stuff already, but it will take a few days to get the croft habitable.' *So much for smelling better out here*, she thought, nearly gagging as a stench of urine knocked her sideways. Not from a cat, not with the pile of crushed and buckled *Tennent's Super* cans littered under the nearby thorn bushes.

Adam stopped and held on to her arm for support as he pulled up the heel of one of his Harry Potter slippers. 'Charlotte, I won't be able to fly. And there's no way I can survive a train from London to Glasgow. When I get out, I'm sure Vinny won't mind if I crash with him for a couple of weeks till I can travel. If I still feel I need some recuperation time, I'll get the train up and come and stay at the croft for a few weeks.'

'But I can look after you. The train won't be that long,' she pouted, as she sat rather gingerly on a severe looking steel bench, *DONNY IS A DICK* and a very basic diagram of a penis scrawled across the surface in permanent, black marker.

'You all right?'

'Yeah. Oh, yeah. Just got a bit of a sore erm…' *Vagina! Vagina! Vagina!* 'Erm, back.'

'Charlotte, honestly, it's the only way.' Adam sat down beside her and pulled his thankfully non-branded grey dressing gown around his knees. 'You've got enough stuff of your own to sort out and…' He jabbed the fleshy top of her arm to get her to look at him instead of her shoes. 'I'm going to be okay, Wee Yin.'

But it was hard to let go of the fear of losing him, to trust that everything was going to be okay this time.

Charlotte sighed and picked up the chocolate bar at her side. 'Fine, but if you are struggling, I want you to promise to tell me Adam.' She bit a chunk, her eyes inflating a little when it wasn't as mundane as she remembered. Struggling with the mouthful (which had turned to gloop and stuck to her teeth), she continued, 'Then, you need to come home to me.'

'Of course, I will,' he breezed, popping another nicotine lozenge.

'You need a shave by the way,' she chipped in, determined to get the last word as usual. 'I've got some razors in my bag.'

As Charlotte waited at the empty bus stop outside the hospital, her belly heaved in a nauseating loveliness. When her mouth gave the watery warning that she might throw up, she pulled the flimsy headphones from her ears and called Vinny.

He answered after only one ring. 'Hello, Miss Croft. How are we today?'

Charlotte's face radiated pure happiness as she kicked her way through the pile of green and gold leaves which fringed a tall kerb behind the shelter. Flashbacks of his mouth on hers, his weight on her, her hands on his backside bombarded her thoughts…The ache became painful again. 'We are most fine, Mr Knight. Have you had a good day?'

'Productive…but I don't think I can cope without seeing you for much longer. How long are you going to be?'

'Not long,' she said, ducking into the shelter to check. 'The sign is flashing that the 117 is due in three minutes precisely so I'll be back in half an hour.'

'Good. Are you sure you don't want me to come and get you?'

'No,' she said, pulling her mohair scarf away from her mouth, suddenly feeling like she needed more air as the biting wind caused a scattering of leaves to eddy around her feet. 'I'd be back by the time you got here. You keep working. I'll be there soon.'

'Okay. What do you want to do when you get back?' he asked ever-so innocently, and she could just see him pursing his lips and stroking his beard. The memory of how that beard had tickled down her body that morning still so fresh, she gulped softly.

'Hm,' she moaned, untying the scarf altogether and sweeping her foot in wide arcs in front of her. 'I don't know. What do you suggest?'

'Oh, I'm sure I can suggest a thing or two. I don't suppose you're wearing those lovely black panties. You know, the ones which have a nice, sensible coverage for such a cold day?'

Charlotte gasped before folding into a laugh. How was she supposed to know she was going to meet the love of her life when she packed for the trip?

'Actually, I'm not wearing any knickers!'

'Excuse me love, can I just get in behind you to check the timetable?' the man (possibly a med student, she deduced, in that he was young and looked tired and wore a lanyard) said with a weird smile and amused eyes. It was clear, even if she hadn't succeeded in shocking Vinny, she'd certainly succeeded in shocking him.

Charlotte yelped, 'Sorry!' then scurried to the end of the shelter but it wasn't far enough. She edged outside, her face burning, Vinny howling in her ear, the stranger still gawking oddly at her.

'On second thoughts, I'm going to start walking.'

Although she scurried two full bus stops away to catch the bus, she wasn't late, and ran through the warren of cobbled streets, her trusty bag jogging behind her, just to make sure. And he kept up his side of the bargain too, suggesting more than a thing or two to blow her mind and make her emit guttural sounds she'd never made before. He made her eyes roll back in her head and her body buck against his and she wondered if she had known it was possible to feel like this if she would have left Greg much earlier. *Without…a…fucking…doubt,* her mind screamed with his last 4 thrusts.

When Charlotte woke alone, the late afternoon heavens had faded to a troubled mauve, rolling and wafting, swiftly changing. The foreground of tree silhouettes made it feel like she was spying through gnarled, black fingers to gain a glimpse of something ethereal. It was beautiful, she thought, the contrast between the two. So contrasting, they actually complimented each other like…like…lamb and mint sauce or turkey and cranberries or strawberries and cream. And now that her idea for a new composition on complimenting contrasts had taken on a total foody spin, Charlotte slid up on her elbows. *I'm famished.*

Vinny sat at his desk, his knee bouncing, his eyes razor sharp, lost in something undoubtedly important. With a slinky smile, she tiptoed silently towards him in just one of his shirts and gently massaged his shoulders to announce her arrival. And although they were at the beginning of their…*whatever* it was, it didn't feel weird to her, the sharing of an unreserved tactile intimacy she'd never had before, even after years with Greg.

'Hey baby,' he oozed, placing his hand on top of hers.

When he called her baby, it made her cramp in a nice way, in a come back to bed way. 'Hey you. Still working?' Her lips tickled against his ears.

'Yeah…Always looking for what I'm missing.' His voice faded as he spun his head and caught her mouth with his. *And now I've found her.*

She broke away to catch her breath. 'Can I help?'

'I wish you could but it's all confidential. I keep scrolling through these files looking for…I don't know what! It's doing my bloody box in! I know it's there, but I just can't see it.'

'I can cook tonight. You stick with that.' Charlotte let go to see what delights she could concoct from a fresh parsley plant, pasta shapes she'd never heard of before and a small jar of capers.

'Nope.' Reaching after her, he snapped her on to his lap. 'We're going out for dinner. I need to get away from this screen and take my beautiful woman out for something nice to eat.'

It took Charlotte a full 5 seconds to realize he was talking about her, all three of his words throwing her.

My – she was his already? Not just dating. Not just fucking. Not just seeing how things went.

Beautiful – more in the eye of the beholder, she thought.

Woman – technically she supposed but had always felt like more of a tom boy on the inside. Part and parcel of being brought up in a house full of men.

'Sounds wonderful. But remember, I've only got three outfits to my name soooo…' She spun her eyes and kept her lips screwed with the last word.

'Well, I'm sure you'll look amazing in anything. Plus, you can scold me for being a snob and cheer up the wine waiter!' He kissed her lips smooth and grinned.

Thankfully, the restaurant was nothing like The Westwood. On the contrary, it was a charming little place with snail shell swirly glass panes in the windows – a family run French Bistro called *La Maison*. It was cosily dark with only a handful of red check-covered tables, each with a candle burning in a bottle of wine, months of wax droplets rolling down the neck like lava flow. The rutted, whitewashed walls were disguised with photos in frames of every shape and size, some black and white, some colour but all with big smiles and warm hearts.

A loud voice with a strong French accent boomed, 'Vinny! Welcome! Welcome!' and Charlotte snatched back the hand she was just about to use to check if a string of onions strung from the ceiling was real. It belonged to a small man with floppy grey hair, smiling eyes and a cigarette hanging out of his mouth. Unlit and whole, he spoke like it wasn't there at all, or at least like he had forgotten it was.

He ogled Vinny like the actual prodigal son had returned before planting a kiss on each of Vinny's cheeks. His well-worked, callused hands remained clenched on Vinny's arms. 'Where 'ave you been? I was beginning to think you no like us no more!'

His arms pinned to his sides, Vinny could only shrug. 'Work, Gabriel. Always work.'

'Arh! You work too 'ard Vinny!' and he threw his hands in the air. 'Too 'ard. Come,' he said, looking back to them as he scuttled to a table at the window. 'I feed you well tonight. D'accord?'

'Oui, d'accord,' Vinny chortled as he sat on the tatty wooden bistro chair which looked like it wasn't built to hold his frame.

'Bonsior, belle,' Gabriel oozed as he turned to Charlotte. She jumped a little and laughed as he planted a kiss on each of her cheeks too before yanking the jacket off her back. When he held a chair out for her, she didn't dream of ignoring it this time, and Vinny flaunted a glower as he reached for the menu. Charlotte merely shrugged and reached for a menu too.

But Gabriel had different ideas. 'Oh, no mademoiselle!' The cigarette bobbed as he spoke. 'Tonight, we 'ave a feast for you.' Hands waving, he began to speak with them too. 'To start, we 'ave some fricassee of mushrooms, some garlic baguette. C'est *tres* bien! Tres bien! And for main, we have chasseur.' His eyes rolled to the ceiling as he kissed the clasped tips of his fingers 'Just like home! D'accord?'

'Oui! Cela semble fantastic, merci.' With a little flutter of her lashes, Charlotte laced her fingers lightly under her chin and smiled.

'Bon! I bring the wine,' and he dashed away in a whirlwind, pausing briefly to light a candle which had blown out before he whizzed off through the louvre doors.

Flumping back, Vinny was unsure whether to laugh or pout in a sulk. 'So, you'll let him order for you, will you? Take a seat from him? Let him choose the wine?'

'What can I say,' Charlotte rested a pinkie on her lips and let a hot drop of wax coat and set on the other, 'I'm a sucker for a French accent.'

'I'll need to remember that for later, mon Cherie.' He wiggled his brows and tucked his chair back into place, his knees slotting between hers. But Charlotte seemed far away, her lips and eyes tensing a little as she peeled the wax off.

'Are you okay?'

'Yeah. It's just…if you know this family, aren't you concerned that they're going to wonder who the hell I am?' Charlotte's eyes fleeted to each of the filled tables, to the pair of puffy white chef's hats floating around the gap above the louvre doors, to the pretty girl pulling a pint behind the bar, to Gabriel as he slapped the top of the dated sound system because the cliché accordion music had stopped.

Vinny took his folded napkin and snapped it loose, laying it across his lap with a frown. 'I'm more than happy for them to know who you are. We're doing nothing wrong!'

'I know.' Charlotte repeated the action with less vigour.

'And besides, I've never been here with Nadia. This wasn't her scene. She rarely visited somewhere with less than two Michelin stars never mind a family run bistro.' He bent forward and tilted her chin up. 'So, relax.'

'Okay, I will.'

Without even being asked, Gabriel poured them another after-dinner coffee as Charlotte unwrapped the foil from her mint chocolate. She began to nibble at a corner then placed it on her saucer before she released the thought which had been troubling her all night. 'Vinny…I need to go home on Saturday. It looks like Adam is getting out on Friday. He asked if it's all right if he crashed at your place for a few weeks till he is up on his feet.'

'Of course. I wouldn't have him anywhere else.' But he sounded as thrilled at the prospect of her leaving as she did. Although he knew it was coming, he still couldn't face the end of what had been the best few days of his life. *Reality certainly does bite.* He watched her closely as he took another sip of his espresso. 'Do you need to go so soon?'

Charlotte crushed the foil into a shiny, gold cube and flicked it at the green bottle, the candle now just a white stump. 'Yeah. I need to move my stuff this weekend before I start work again next week. And I *cannot* stay in that flat another night with Greg.'

He felt his throat tighten at the thought of her not being there, a loss in his cool, an imbalance in his usual level-headedness. Being vulnerable – he hated it. What was this girl doing to him? He glided his hand across to hers, trying to subdue the impulse to beg. 'But your boss said you can have as long as you need. Stay another week.'

Shaking her head against her will, she sighed, her hand going limp in his. 'Vinny, it would only be harder to go. I need to get back to work now Adam is going to be okay.'

He sloped forward and gripped tighter, very tempted to blurt out what he felt, what he *knew* – that he loved her. That he wanted to spend the rest of his life with her. Sure, it sounded crazy, but the main thing was, it didn't feel it. On the other hand, he didn't want to send her running out of the door without pausing for that leather jacket which had seen better days. *Note to self – take the girl shopping sometime soon!* Erring on the side of caution, he pitched it somewhere in the middle. 'Then don't go at all. Stay here.'

Her head still shaking, she peeked up to see he was being perfectly serious. 'Vinny, I can't,' she whispered. *But I really want to! Want! Want! Want! Argh!*

'But...But I've just found you.' His voice tautened.

It felt hellish, the thought of severance, because she would happily spend the rest of her life waking up beside him, under him, over him (she really didn't mind which as long as her limbs were wrangled in his).

Conscious of the fact she didn't want to sound like a bunny boiler, she sighed, 'Vinny, out of everything which has happened in my life lately, you are the one thing which has made it all okay. We have loads of time to figure things out so that this can work…if that's what you want?'

'Of course, that's what I want!' His voice intensified as did his eyes. 'More than anything.'

It felt easier to breathe already, now that there was a way forward, now that it wasn't the end of the best thing which had ever happened to her. She smiled and picked up her chocolate again. 'Then that's what will happen.'

They both bolted straight when what sounded like the *Allo! Allo!* theme song began with a blast.

An hour later, Charlotte picked up the sketch pad and set herself up at her usual place beside the fire. Even after such a small time, it was her spot now, her chair, right beside his. Vinny just wanted one quick last look at his work before he closed the laptop for the night. But she made the most of the opportunity to spend some more time on what she considered to be her finest piece of work, or at least, her most precious.

But her subject was becoming unreachable, his frustration masking everything else until it was all she could see. 'Fucking…Norma! I've got a fucking hearing then! Jeeze! Why the hell?' He pushed back his chair and escaped to the kitchen, brushing long blonde strands away from his tired face.

Charlotte sighed and massaged her own brow, his frustration becoming somewhat contagious. Laying the pad down quietly at her feet, she crooked her neck to make sure he was out of sight. She grabbed the bottle from the table and tiptoed speedily to his desk to fill his glass, hoping she could at least intoxicate him into relaxation. But when she saw the pictures in the open file in front of her, she froze, until the wine waterfall turned her green socks red.

Chapter Twenty-Eight

'Charlotte…are you sure?' Vinny tore another piece of kitchen roll and began mopping up again, silently thanking the heavens that the spillage was on the parquet and not the rug.

Peeling off her socks, she stared at the three pictures now splayed across his desk. Dolan in his *Range Rover* driving out of a *McDonald's* car park, his passenger side occupied by a woman. The tanned face was mostly obscured under a *Yankies* baseball cap – didn't hide the plump, glossy lips though. The three stud-filled piercings along the lobe of her left ear. The same purple Fitbit on her slender wrist. The Duchess. 'Yeah, I mean, I study people for a living Vinny. How they move, their stance, their features. But it's not just that.' Charlotte pointed to the picture. 'It's the tattoo. Audrey has that exact same tattoo of a dragon on her wrist.' She felt the wine sour and sting.

'If you are right,' he got to his feet and took the socks from her hand, his face suddenly alive, 'this is what I've been searching for. We've never been able to identify her.'

Sinking into his chair, Charlotte drew each picture towards her, propping her head with her palm. 'That's what I'm worried about. I don't want to be right. I can't believe it…but it does make sense.'

He began pacing at her back. 'How do you mean?'

'Vinny, please sit! I feel like I'm going to have a heart attack as it is!'

'Sorry, baby.' He dropped the socks and the soggy balls of claret kitchen roll in the wastepaper basket. 'Here.' He held out his hand and was about to lead her to the sofa. But she bent down to the bin, pulled her socks out and hung them on the rim to collect later. *Then* she took his hand.

'Go on,' he urged, handing her a refill.

Charlotte shut her eyes as if she could hide from the truth of the matter. 'Spice in the prison had been a bloody nightmare, especially over the last few months. But…she went on holiday a few weeks ago, and things really settled. I mean, it was just like it ceased to exist and normal service resumed. I never in a million years would have made the connection, at least, not to her anyway. She'd been seeing another prison officer called Ben who was on holiday with her. The night they returned to duty, the night Amos died, I thought he was acting a bit dodgy beforehand. Caught him sneaking out of one of our more higher category prisoner's cells. It didn't look right. So, I told Mr Miller when we met afterwards. He told me Ben was working undercover to investigate the staff. It was the only way to explain how, after all our measures, it was still getting into the jail so easily. But…it was Audrey – right under his nose.' By the time she had finished, Charlotte felt her teeth begin to chatter. She turned to Vinny, her eyes glazed with a shiny new fear. 'What are we going to do?'

He lightly traced his fingers over his beard, back and forth and back and forth. 'Not panic. We're going to have to think very carefully about our next move because we cannot say you have had access to those photos.'

Charlotte began tapping a finger to her lips, her face lost in thought. Her finger halted suddenly, and she looked up at him. Vinny could almost see the flash of a lightbulb above her head. 'But we could say you have had access to mine.' Thrusting her glass at him, she jumped from his side and grasped her mobile from the arm of the chair. The lines on her forehead deepened with each manic swipe of the screen until they ironed out when she found the photo of their last Christmas night out. 'Here!' Charlotte flashed the screen at Vinny. It clearly showed Audrey, merrily toasting with her glass of bubbles, her tattoo clear and unmistakably the same, the three piercings, each with a twinkling Christmas tree dangling from them.

A glass of wine in each hand, he eased forward, his eyes fleeting from the phone to Charlotte. He continued to repeat the action as he spoke. 'You're a bloody genius, Charlotte Croft! A bloody genius!'

However, she really didn't feel like one. 'Ooooohhhhhh shit!' She sagged back down to his side and let her face fall to her hands.

'Oh…Charlotte!' He looked around for somewhere to put the glasses and opted for the table by the fire to be on the safe side. As far away from any of the evidence as possible seemed best, especially with the way Charlotte's limbs and fingers thrashed when she was worked up. 'I'm sorry. That was very insensitive of me.' He kissed the top of her head.

'She's ma fucking friend! And you're tellin' me she's Dolan's side kick? I mean, I've worked with this girl for years. Her!' Charlotte prodded towards the desk of pictures. 'She's the one whose been smuggling that shite!' Now she brandished her finger at the desk in between poking her phone screen. 'SHE killed Amos. I was there when he smoked the bloody thing. I was the one pumping his chest. That will haunt me forever!'

'Charlotte! Charlotte!' Vinny cried, clasping the phone from her hand before she accidentally deleted the only usable piece of evidence. He put it on the armrest and gently grasped her wrists. 'Charlotte. There was nothing you could have done to save Amos. But there is plenty you can do now to make sure his death wasn't in vain.'

'What?'

Vinny tethered her hands to his thigh. 'I think the first port of call is to speak to our detective friends and join the dots. Then, they can meet with your Mr Miller and those who are carrying out the probe into your prison staff. Perhaps, if this Ben is really on the case, he will be able to get close enough to monitor her movements. Then, when they know she is loaded with a new batch, they swoop and catch her red-handed.'

Charlotte tried to flap a hand. Vinny held tighter. 'Right. Then what?' she huffed, trying to itch her nose with her shoulder. 'She goes down but what about Dolan?'

He spoke low and soft, towing her towards the calm. 'We offer her a deal – become a witness against him or face a much longer stretch behind bars. Plus, if she has any feelings for this *Ben*, he may be able to sway her more easily.'

'But I don't understand! Why is she with Ben if she is with Dolan too?' Charlotte cried, almost searching for her own loophole to merit Audrey's innocence.

Vinny shrugged. 'What better way to keep an eye on the investigation by getting close to the investigating officer.'

'But how did she know?'

'Dolan. Or just a coincidence?'

Charlotte felt like her brain was imploding.

Chapter Twenty-Nine

Her brain was still imploding days later when they went to pick up Adam. For the moment, it seemed best to keep Adam in the dark over the change in their relationship status (although Charlotte had to warn Vinny not to change it on his Facebook page when he tutted that there wasn't a *married but getting a divorce and now in a new relationship* option). Things were complicated enough without adding that into the equation.

The car journey was too quiet. To remedy that, Charlotte flicked through the radio stations rather than talk about the fact she was leaving the following morning. But as soon as an advert blared, or a song came on that she didn't like, she tutted and began pushing and turning and twisting again. Vinny pressed a magic button on his steering wheel, his playlist taking over to still her fingers. Charlotte moved on to the air con. His eyes fixed on the road, Vinny reached over and took the twitching hand and set it on his thigh. It only made Charlotte pull down a sad smile, knowing they wouldn't be able to touch each other at all soon.

Vinny parked in a quiet corner, under a shedding silver birch but as Charlotte touched the door handle, he reached over her and pulled the door to.

'Not yet, Charlotte. Can we just have 5 more minutes before we go in?'

'Yeah.' She dropped her hand and turned to him. 'Of course.'

Vinny used his time wisely. She remembered kissing as a teen – how the focus was to perfect your technique rather than the intimacy of the act. God forbid you get a reputation as a bad kisser. Then with Greg, they never really kissed except for a quick pre-curser to even quicker sex. Yet, in that very moment, it was exactly what it should have been: intense, sensitive, intimate, mind-blowingly arousing.

Charlotte toyed with the idea of pulling him into the back seat as she did up the top button of her blouse and straightened her jacket, but they were already late. Feeling like a wound-up toy, she blew her cheeks and went to open the door, but again, Vinny reached over and stopped her.

'Charlotte, I need to wait a minute. If I go out now, I'll get arrested.'

'Oh,' Charlotte giggled. 'Right.'

As Vinny leaned back and thought of his secretary Norma (an absolute diamond but the hairy moles thing was enough to kill an erection every time), Charlotte re-applied her lip balm and fanned her face with the brochure for *Knight and Forbes Solicitors* she found in the car door. Though it blanched her cheeks, it seemed to stoke the flames singeing her chin.

She flicked down the mirror. 'Shit!' she squawked, brushing her fingers across what was a red-raw abrasion. 'What will I say to Adam when he asks what's happened to my chin?'

'That you got your chin stuck in a glass trying to lick the last drop of wine from the bottom?' Vinny laughed loudly, recalling how she almost did exactly that last night – she really did hate waste – wine especially. 'Or, you got a bit heavy handed with your new *JML Finishing Touch Flawless*?' He was still thinking of Norma and how he gave her one as her secret Santa gift last Christmas. She still hadn't used the bloody thing, at least, not on her face.

Charlotte spun to him half laughing, half squealing, 'Vinny!'

'Oh,' he howled now that her chin looked like she had been hoovering the rug with her mouth. 'Oh!' Wiping another tear from the corner of his eye, he groaned, 'I love you, Charlotte Croft!'

Her raw chin fell further.

Then came the silence.

'I'm sorry.' Vinny broke it, his laughter dying as he quickly looked out of the window. As he seemed to instantly change his mind, Charlotte closed her mouth and fluttered her eyes away to the crafty traffic warden encircling the car in front of them.

'But it's true.' He turned back to her. 'I've never met anyone like you, Charlotte.'

Charlotte and Greg had been together for nearly a year before he said it. There were lots of: I like you, I like you a lot, I really like you, I really, *really* like you until a half bottle of vodka and two snakebites helped him eventually manage to drop the L bomb. And even now, she was sure it was only because she was wiping vomit from his face.

'I love you too, Vinny. Do you have a pound?' There was no doubt in her voice, no reservation at being imprudent. Because, at the end of the day, it was true. She loved him, every last square inch of him. Wholeheartedly. He dropped the coin in her hand, his face questioning. Without answering it, she leapt out, dashed to the meter and bought a ticket. Before she reached Vinny's Audi, she placed it under the windscreen wiper of the battered *Ford Mondeo* before the gobsmacked warden had chance to type in the rest of the details or take his incriminating photographs. Vinny laughed aloud and shook his head slowly from side to side as she strolled back, dusting her hands like a gymnast about to own the parallel bars.

Charlotte suspected she closely resembled the ginger kid in *The Snowman* cartoon as Vinny clasped her hand and led the way to the entrance. He loved her! And she loved him! More than she loved another living soul.

As the elevator opened at floor 1 to let out the poor porter in charge of wheeling an old dear (who silenced the whole lift when she declared with the gruff rasps of a heavy smoker that she didn't want a vaginal probe scan because nothing had been up there since 1974), Vinny was already plotting how to get his hands on Charlotte again. Perhaps Adam would still be exhausted and would need a long afternoon nap. In that *perhaps* moment, he would take her to the sofa like a pair of lusty teenagers with that extra spark of excitement at maybe getting caught.

Charlotte nudged his arm, knocking the strange far-away smile from his face. 'Vinny?'

'Huh?' His eyes flew open.

'Come on. We're here.'

Like an impatient meerkat, Adam was sat in his chair, his belongings already placed on the bed for packing. 'Thank God! I don't think I could have stood another second in this place. The woman in the next room has been wailing for her husband all night. The nurse told me he passed away 20 years ago. Then she was asking for him to come and take her 'cause she was ready to go. I mean, no harm to the old dear, but I was kinda praying that he would.'

Charlotte snickered as she packed his toiletries into the case. 'Well, you'll sleep better tonight. Here.' She handed him a set of Vinny's clothes. 'Get changed and we'll spring you from your cell.'

'Je-Sus Charlotte! What the fuck has happened to your chin?' he cried, flinching slightly as he slowly stood, his foot chasing an evasive Harry Potter slipper.

'Oh…eh…' She fumbled her fingers against the bottom of her face, her eyes protuberant.

Vinny's eyes looked watery as his finger circled around his own face, his nose crinkled. 'Yeah, I didn't want to say anything but it's really red. Looks a bit angry like it's been rubbed really hard?'

'I tried one of those…' Her finger tapped her hot chin, trying to buy a few seconds. 'Erm, I tried one of those bloody charcoal face mask things but I think I had a bit of a reaction to it. It felt like it was welded to my chin. Think I removed a layer a skin by the time I got it off!' Her voice trill, she zipped the bag closed.

Thankfully, Adam seemed to have bought it. He tutted as he spread the clothes across the white waffle blanket. 'You're dangerous with your DIY beauty skills. I remember sitting in A and E when you burnt your leg after using some hot wax thing! Leave it to the professionals next time.'

'Will do! Right, we'll step out and let you get changed. Give us a shout when you're done,' she sang brightly, already pushing Vinny out the door. As soon as the door was closed, she slapped his arm.

'Ow!' he protested, half laughing.

'You're evil!' she scowled.

'Sorry,' he oozed, cupping her face.

'No, you're not.'

'You're right, Charlotte Croft.' Vinny's voice turned to honey. 'I'm not sorry one little bit.'

Adam closed his eyes as he let the breeze wash away the stale hospital odour. 'Ah, civilization!' he groaned as he inhaled it through his nostrils like it was roast Sunday lunch flavoured.

Charlotte leant in to zip up his coat.

'My arms work, you know,' he protested but Charlotte ignored him and did it anyway. Linking her arm in his, the three ambled slowly back to the car.

'So,' Adam fastened his seatbelt and began to rummage through his white paper bag of assorted pill boxes. 'What's the sleeping arrangements?'

Vinny threaded the Audi slowly through a beaded necklace of

199

roundabouts towards the exit. 'You take the bedroom. There's a TV up there and it's en-suite. Once you're more mobile, I'll set the basement up as a spare room.'

Abruptly, the rustling of paper ceased. 'Are you sure, mate? I hate being a nuisance. I know you've been put out enough already.'

Vinny smiled, tapping his finger along to the *Childish Gambino* album Charlotte had asked him to add to his 'thing' earlier (which he explained was called *Spotify*). 'Adam, you're not putting me out at all. I'm just glad I can help.'

'Where will you two sleep?' Although he addressed Charlotte, his eyes bumped along every black and white strip of the zebra crossing along with the yummy mummy pushing a pram.

Charlotte felt her face flush as she looked at Vinny in the rear-view mirror, her eyes warning his to keep his mouth shut.

Vinny winked. 'I'll take the sofa. Charlotte can crash with me in the lounge or on the bedroom floor on the air bed. Might be best to be in the lounge, Charlotte, because we need to be up at 4 to get you to the airport. I don't snore, honestly.'

This time, she smirked and mouthed the word liar to his reflection. 'I'm easy,' she yawned and looked out of the window. *I'm getting good at this fake yawning now!*

'Charlotte, is there any chance you could stick it out a couple of weeks with Greg until I can come up and help you with the move? It's going to be a fucking nightmare doing it on your own with a *Beetle*.' As Adam turned around to face her, she noticed how much paler he seemed in the real light of day.

'I'll be fine. My mate Rami has a van. Him and his wife Hayley are going to help me move everything tomorrow afternoon. To be honest, there's not that much stuff to move until the flat sells. I'll only need my clothes and stuff for cooking. Once the croft is aired and dusted down, it's perfectly suitable.'

His tired eyes wrinkled for a moment before losing the energy to fight. 'All right,' he muttered. 'When are you back to work?'

'Monday morning.' Her tummy gurgled.

'And when are you talking to the suits?'

'I don't know,' she sighed, running her hand up and down her seatbelt. Her tummy was a bubbling cauldron of nerves now. 'Vinny's spoken to a Detective Coleman. He's in charge of the Dolan case in Scotland. I'm sure he'll want to speak to me as soon as I'm back.'

'I spoke to Coleman again last night. He has arranged to meet with you and Mr Miller on Monday after your shift but not at the prison obviously. He'd prefer you go to somewhere neutral so has arranged a meeting room at the Buchanan business centre. Do you know it?'

Her nose wrinkled. 'Yes. Why? What about internal investigations? Surely they need to be there too?'

'The problem is, we don't know how far up this thing goes. When Coleman called Mr Miller to tell him about the meeting, Frank said he had doubts about the Titan team. He knows some of them from years ago. He's definitely not sure about Ben or whether he is involved. I've asked for Coleman to keep you as far out of this thing as possible. The less it seems you know, the better.'

From where she sat, she saw his jaw grind and flex as things got a lot closer to real.

His reflection eyed her, all the fun of earlier vanished. 'I could switch my schedule around a bit. Come with you?'

She gazed out the window as a young woman, her shoulders curved, her face wishy-washy, laid a bouquet of pastel blooms and a pink balloon in the remembrance garden for the children who never quite made it. Charlotte wanted to cry for her loss, so tangible, she had to look away. She was almost tempted to ask Vinny to stop the car so she could just go over and lay a hand on her shoulder, just like Vinny had with her when Adam was stabbed. To give her a *we* instead of just *me*. But it was a private moment, she could see that. And in that glimpse into her anguish, Charlotte realized how lucky she was to have lost her parents rather than her parents lose her or Adam; what created you rather than what you created. God was so smart, she thought, the way he appeared to have given us an innate, predisposition to cope when it was that way around. Children always felt distinct. Sure, there was the need of a parent but with their own separate identity. From the woman who stood there, it was clear to see it was a huge part of her buried in the ground. The best part. It felt unbearable. She gulped and gulped again. 'No. Someone needs to be close for Adam.'

'I'll be fine! All I'll be doing is watching telly and playing with myself. They wouldn't have let me out if I wasn't ready,' Adam protested. 'I'd feel better if you had Vinny there.'

Charlotte shook her head firmly, her patience now tested by such trivialities. 'No, Adam, and that's final!' She cracked the window an inch and closed her eyes, hoping the nausea would pass. 'I'll be stressed enough without worrying about you collapsing in the shower or at the bottom of those ridiculous stairs. Besides, Mr Miller will be with me. And once I show them the photo, ma bit's finished.'

Vinny shared an exasperated glance with Adam, both knowing there was no way she would change her mind. They drove home silently, each worrying about the other in equal measure.

The heavy atmosphere evaporated as soon as they escaped the suffocating confines of the car.

Vinny slung the rucksack over his shoulder as he stooped slightly to fit the key in the lock. 'I bet your dying for a proper cuppa, mate.'

'You've no idea,' Adam moaned as he stepped inside. He turned back to Vinny and began twisting invisible levers in the air. 'Do you still have that coffee machine which looks like it has been stolen from *Costa*?'

'I do,' Vinny said with an air of smugness as he booted the door shut behind him. 'A coffee of your choice coming right up.'

They made straight for the kitchen. As they parked themselves at the table, Charlotte reddened a little at the thought of what she and Vinny been doing on it that very morning. Reaching across, she put a bamboo mat at Adam's place, keen to separate him from the memory.

'Right!' Vinny barked, all business. He smacked his hands together then rubbed them vigorously. 'What are we all having?'

'A double espresso,' Adam requested, and Vinny became slightly worried about the chances of Adam having a nap after that. Wordlessly, he raised an eyebrow to Charlotte.

'My usual,' she smiled. She doubted that Greg even knew she had a usual, but Vinny, he had it perfected. A decaf cappuccino with a light dusting of cocoa powder (which he always formed into the shape of a heart). 'Thank you.'

'My pleasure,' and his smile made her heart nearly explode with what a lucky girl she was.

They all froze and looked up when they heard it. Three pairs of confused eyes tracked the footsteps crossing the floor above and the pair of feet which dropped slowly yet very purposefully down each step of the spiral staircase. Charlotte wasn't sure if she was more terrified or relieved when she saw they were in very high black stilettoes. Each watched open-mouthed as the long legs and stunning body they were attached to uncoiled to reveal itself in all its glory.

'Hello Vincent,' she purred.

'Nadia?'

Chapter Thirty

Fuck!

'Nadia?' he repeated, the cup now swinging from his finger.

'Oh, Vincent,' she sighed with a kind of longing which caused Charlotte's toes to curl, especially when it was paired with such a look of adulation as she sashayed her way to him, her silky raven hair swishing over her perfectly poised shoulders, her heels clip-clopping pure class across the parquet. When she halted in front of him, her saucer-like chocolate eyes stared into his until Charlotte felt her nails cut her palms. Nadia wrapped her well-manicured hands tightly around his neck just like she had in the car before they picked up Adam. Vinny's body gradually thawed, and he conceded with a wary hand to her hip. Their bodies seemed to fit so well together, Charlotte thought, Nadia's eyes reaching his chin instead of his chest. The convex and concave at just the right levels. Two corresponding pieces of a jigsaw. *Double fuck!*

A few painful seconds later, Vinny placed his other hand on her side and peeled her back, his face confused but his tone polite. 'What are you doing here? You never said you were coming.'

'I was homesick.' Nadia shrugged lightly and spoke with the intonations of a toddler. 'Besides,' she added, turning away to settle her chiding glare on Adam, 'I heard someone was in town causing lots of problems as usual! Thought I'd come and check it out for myself.' She held for Adam a reprimanding flare of her eyes before kissing him firmly on the cheek, the kind of kiss you only held for a fond friend. Family even.

'Hey Nadia,' Adam's cheeky grin was genuine and oblivious.

'Lovely to see you.'

'Oh, Adam!' Her hand rested on his cheek. 'How are you, my love?'

'Ah, you know me, Nadia. Can't keep a good man down.'

Charlotte's cartoon eyes soared to Vinny. They were reassuringly as horrified as hers. Open-mouthed, his shoulders shot to his ears just as Charlotte became her focus.

'And you must be the lovely Charlotte?' Nadia guessed, slanting her head to the side to assess her with a quick yo-yo of the eyes.

Charlotte gulped softly and stammered, 'Y…Yes. Lovely to meet you, Nadia,' her hair feeling suddenly limp and dull, her skin naked and full of flaws.

'Oh, the pleasure is all mine,' and she bent down to sting Charlotte's cheek with a kiss. It smacked hard, the stench of Chanel which accompanied it. *Chanel Chance* to be precise. Audrey wore it all the time. The inference caught her breath – the perfume, at the airport, it was for her. *FFFFFUUUUUCCCCCCKKKKK!*

'I'm so sorry about what has happened. You've all been through such a terrible ordeal. I'm just so glad you're going to be okay Adam.'

Charlotte shifted from side to side and sat on her hands, her nostrils beginning to flare, and not just because of the fragrance she'd copped a mouthful of.

'Thanks Nadia. I'm going to be fine. More fire in the belly to get the bastards sent down though,' he said, tapping the bamboo mat rapidly against the table.

The noise began to grate on Charlotte's nerves, like she was being counted down to explosion.

Nadia quickly spun to Vinny, a prima-ballerina, smiling as if their marriage was akin to Ma and Pa Walton's itself. 'Darling, can I have a coffee too? I'm just going to finish unpacking my things first then I'll join you all.'

Unpacking? Her things? She's bloody staying? Charlotte just about held on to her scream.

The cup remained loose at his side. 'S-Sure, yeah.'

After a painfully natural kiss, she fluttered lightly up the stairs like the red soles of her heels were spring loaded. As Charlotte admired the sheer grace of the woman, she just knew - knew that woman did not seem like someone who had walked out of her marriage, who didn't give a shit, who was bored of her husband, who wanted something different. Not to mention the Chanel. Charlotte had got it wrong. She'd got *him* wrong.

Fuck! Fuck!

Feeling winded, she slid a hand across her stomach where it felt like she had just been clouted with a heavy boot.

'Nadia looks brilliant, Vinny. I can't believe it's been over a year since I last saw her,' Adam added, and Charlotte leant on her knees and struggled for breath.

'Well,' Vinny growled lowly for their ears only, 'I don't know what she's doing here. We're getting a divorce.'

'What?' Adam shouted a whisper, halfway out his coat. 'You guys seemed solid.'

The pain of it caused her to slouch further down the chair.

'No.' He rubbed a hand over the back of his neck. 'No, it's been over for ages. I have no clue what she's up to. I'm really sorry to get you guys caught in the middle of this.' His eyes stayed with Charlotte. Hers stayed on her boots. Her very scruffy boots.

Adam put the dangling half of his jacket back on. 'God! Don't worry about us, mate. We'll get out of your way. There's that café at the end of the street. Let's go there for lunch Charlotte. I'm dying for some proper grub. Give these two a bit of privacy.' When he turned to her, he was startled to see she was already on her feet.

'Sure,' she said, the word sounding dead.

'No wait!' At last getting his arms to work, Vinny plonked the cup beside the coffee machine before waving his fingers wide. 'Stay here, *please*. Go into the lounge and I'll go talk to Nadia to see what she wants. Probably only here to get started on the divorce settlement. We've not really had a chance to discuss it yet.'

Or at all, Charlotte's mind filled in the gaps with a cautious cynicism. She yanked up her zip. 'Naw! We don't want to be in the way. You two need some privacy. We'll only be down the road.' When she at last lifted her head, her eyes held an agonized look of *don't even bother*. 'Come on, Adam. Lunch is on you.' This time, she let him zip up his own jacket as she waited outside for him to catch-up.

The rich red tomato soup tipped from her spoon and she watched as it trickled through the air and back into her bowl. Ladling another spoonful, she did it again.

'What's up, Wee Yin?' Adam asked, his burger cleanly demolished, a slice of gherkin and a few breadcrumbs the only sign that it had ever existed. That, and the splodge of mustard at the corner of his mouth.

'Huh?' Her face cast up like she had been interrupted in her attempt to solve the problem of third world hunger. Then her fingers fumbled some curls behind an ear. 'Oh, nothing. There's just so much going on…My brain is hurting.' The spoon clanked loudly against the side of the bowl as she gave up altogether.

Adam repeatedly twanged the ring pull of his coke, his head

slanting slightly. 'Are you sure?'

'Of course, I'm sure!' She sunk her teeth into a mouthful of baguette just to prove it but found there wasn't enough moisture in her mouth as it became a doughy clump. Although she helped it along the way with several gulps of water, it still felt like she was swallowing a tennis ball. 'Just thinking about the move tomorrow, then work on Monday.'

It was very tempting to break down into another ugly, noisy, wet, flurry of tears and tell Adam everything. But Charlotte felt the shame of it gag her. The shame that she had been fucking around with someone else's husband. The shame that she had been foolish enough to trust this so-called husband like no other. The shame that she had got it wrong and had done wrong. And from Adam's reaction to Nadia, it seemed he was as close to her as he was to Vinny. What she feared most was not her own shame, but his. That he would be ashamed and disappointed in her. So, she held her strange, unnatural smile along with her nerve. Putting all her heartache to the side, she decided this wasn't for Adam's ears, not yet. Not when he was just getting back on his feet. Plus, they had a case to work on together. Nothing, not even her broken heart, could come in the way of that.

A hand resting on the purple stain on his neck, he considered her closely, his eyes narrowing as his tongue tried to dislodge a piece of meat wedged between his back teeth. He'd seen that look before – when it seemed she had the world on her shoulders but clammed up. And no matter how much he asked, he knew she wouldn't crack. Not until she was ready. Just like the time she'd lost his beloved iPod (which she begged for and promised to guard with her life when she was studying for her finals at the Mitchell Library). Charlotte didn't speak at all that night, pale and distracted and guilt-ridden. Just like now. Back then, Charlotte had broken the following morning over breakfast. Adam told her she'd left it on the worktop and hadn't even taken it in the first place. From then on, she only stuck to her trusty portable CD player just in case.

'Hm. All right. But you know I'm always here for you.' He laid a hand on her arm. 'No matter what.'

'I know.' Charlotte took another tender swallow and pushed her soup bowl to the side. She swallowed again and spoke before the next wave of agony sucked the words from her. 'Anyway, you need to find yourself a lovely woman who will look after you when I can't. I mean, you can't be a bachelor forever, Adam.' She ignored the stout waitress (the very one who served her the hairy jacket potato a few days beforehand) and how her very pronounced eyebrows sunk as she collected another load of leftovers.

'Err…yes I can! Or at least, until my good looks start to betray me, and I'm forced into the conventional,' Adam snorted, and she looked at those big brown eyes and shaggy brown curls and felt the next wave hit.

Siobhan, the bitch, Charlotte thought, keen to find an outlet for her pain. Siobhan had dated Adam all through uni. Even helped with Charlotte – taking her to get her hair done, cooking sometimes when Adam was doing his finals, giving her boy advice. And Charlotte had liked her too – a lot. She just seemed to complement their unconventional set-up, that is, until she started fucking around with Adam's best mate. It broke him, and Charlotte had tried to piece him back together the best she could, but he didn't quite fit together as one – gaps and holes where they'd once been solid. From then on, Adam had never been in another relationship. He had, however, been in plenty of beds.

'Hm…one day,' she exhaled slowly, tapping the side of her mouth to let him know he had something at the corner of his.

Wiping away the yellow blob, he sneered, 'Don't hold your breath, Barbra Cartland.'

Not for the first time recently, the world still turned as hers stuttered and stalled. But she put on a good show, reading the papers (or at least turning the pages), playing games of dots on a napkin (Adam won every time), predicting the lives of the customers like, 'I think she was rich and beautiful once until she killed her lover,' kind of nonsense or, 'He's definitely a stalker and has a wall full of newspaper clippings of Judy Finnegan.' Each of Charlotte's premonitions were equally sinister. After their third coffee, she blamed her shakes on the caffeine hit.

'Do you think it's safe?' Adam yawned, his eyelids half shut, his fist propping up his stubbly chin.

Scribbling her pen impatiently over their last game of noughts and crosses, she snapped, and not because Adam had whooped her ass again. 'Oh, this is bloody ridiculous! You need tae rest! If their havin' a spat, we'll go to a hotel for the night. I can't be doin' with even more drama, especially when it isn't ours.'

'Yeah, I think you're right.' He sat up, his hands brushing over his face. 'I'm bushed.'

'Come on,' Charlotte said firmly, throwing a fiver tip on the table and getting to her feet. 'I've got a spare key from when Vinny had to go to work and I went to see you.'

They stood in the hall, ears angled up the staircase. Immediately, Charlotte could hear the hums of a conversation – calm and cordial. She felt sick again.

'At least they don't sound like their killing each other,' Adam muttered as he threw his coat on the newel post and headed for the lounge.

'No,' Charlotte said almost soundlessly, feeling the pain of that cause the contents of her stomach to churn even more. 'No, they don't.'

Adam seemed to drift off in an instant, soft snores catching at the back of his throat every now and then. Tucking the quilt round his back like she used to on the rare occasions he got a night out when she was younger, she stroked her hand softly through the chestnut curls he had inherited from their mother, the colour she had envied terribly instead of the striking shade of red she had her father to thank for. Carefully, she lowered to the chair at the fire where she sat, prostrate, her hands tucked between her knees.

Over the next half an hour, she stayed exactly like that, cramp in every muscle, listening to Adam breathe evenly at her side, listening to the fridge babble like it had an upset stomach too, listening to the conversation above her which, although she could not hear the words, she could certainly hear the sentiment - soft, loving, caring. It was all shattered by Vinny's bawling laugh.

Charlotte moved then but only to close her eyes as if that could dilute the agony of it. Of course, it didn't, not with that laugh telling her everything she already knew. How could he? The thought of him on top of her only that morning seemed a million years ago, those eyes blazing into hers in a way no-one else's ever had. Wasn't it only a few hours ago that he said he loved her? *All a lie! All a bloody lie!*

Before the sob escaped, Charlotte reached into her bag, yanked out her curled notepad and began to write (quite difficult considering how much her hands were shaking). When she was finished, she folded the note carefully with one perfect crease and left it tented on the table beside Adam's glass of water. She lifted his phone (the passcode, she knew, her date of birth) and checked Google to see there was a train leaving for Glasgow central at 5.30 from Euston. Even surprising herself, she managed to book a seat.

But her escape plan (which involved no fuss, no drama, more importantly, no suspicions) hit an iron wall; her case was still at the top of the stairs at the mouth the bedroom.

'Shit,' she cursed quietly, gazing up the steps in all their spiralling glory. Somehow, Mount Everest seemed a more appealing option at that moment in time. Her fingers cramped on the top of the newel post, she peered up and noticed even the hushed tones of the conversation were silent. Perhaps they were having a silent stand-off? Perhaps Nadia's red soled shoes were bobbing, and her arms were folded, and she was sitting with her bloody perfectly poised back to Vinny? Perhaps…Perhaps she didn't want to contemplate anything else. The mental torture of it aside, she needed her bag. Her hands started the climb first, her face screwed like she was trying to make herself a stone or two lighter until her feet synchronized.

In the most unsophisticated, bumbling fashion, she rounded the last spiral and spied it just at the side of the doorway, her faithful old bag which she had *packed* herself. The metal swirls of the top step chiselled her knees as she inched closer until her nails grazed the leather handle. So near yet so far, she made her fatal mistake then, unable to resist a sideways glance as she wrapped her fingers around it. As her lungs collapsed inwardly, she drooped to her backside and gagged her mouth, wondering how it was possible to feel like you were being beat up without anyone laying a finger on you. Because there, standing in the middle of the floor, was her Vinny (*her* Vinny?) with his tongue rammed down Nadia's throat, his hands hidden amongst the silk hair at the nape of her neck, Nadia completely lost and limp in the moment.

This time, she didn't stay long enough to watch the gory details. This time, she didn't wait until things really heated up to announce her presence. This time, she had no bleedin' right. Holding her breath and her sobs, she slid the bag ever-so-carefully towards her then descended even quieter than she had gone up.

Despite the fact she was already cutting it fine to make it to Euston, she unpacked her sketchbook and tore out the picture of Vinny. In the bottom left hand corner, she wrote in dark, scrawling jerks:

Thanks for everything!
I am sure you will spend many a happy hour gazing at yourself.
Charlotte.

'Prrrriiiicccckkkk!' she snarled, realizing her first impression was bang-on. Her face twisting ugly with hate, she hastily rolled it up like it was a wallpaper sample from *B & Q* rather than what she was calling her masterpiece a few hours beforehand. Nearly knocking over the glass, she tossed it beside the letter, and with a last check on Adam, dashed for the door, closing it silently behind her.

Chapter Thirty-One

Charlotte didn't cry. Not when the taxi driver dropped her a mile from Euston when the roads were gridlocked because of the tube strike. Not when she was running for the station and a rude businessman with a coffee in his hand painfully shoulder barged her and told her to stick to the left side of the road like the traffic. *What the fuck? The pavements have lanes now?* Not when she realized, due to the tube strike, no seats had been allocated on the train, and because she had made it by the skin of her teeth, she had to use her faithful leather bag as a seat in the breezy corridor between coaches C and D (thanking her lucky stars it wasn't one with a loo). Not when she realized she'd left her phone at Vinny's. Not even (but very, very close) when the elderly gent with the flat cap who sat across from her asked if she would watch his bags so he could go for a drink and brought her back a coffee, water and a packet of prawn cocktail.

The Roman numerals of the ornate Victorian clock tower suspended above the concourse informed her it was just after 10 when she arrived back in Glasgow. It was already swarming with the usual Friday night crowd, many of whom hovered underneath the clock itself, waiting. The anxious parents waiting to pick up their daughter after her trip to the cinema with the spotty boy they didn't like so much. The bald divorcee, checking his breath and checking the white rose in his lapel was straight, waiting for his first blind date ever as he tried to forget the wife who left him for the ice-cream van man. The best friend waiting for her best friend, feeling the excitement build at what a force to be reckoned with they made when they were together. Formidable.

She'd heard herself say it a hundred times before – 'I'll meet you under the clock.' But as she gravitated towards it, an emptiness she had never experienced before sat on her chest. No-one was waiting for her, and she was waiting for no-one.

At that very moment, she didn't belong anywhere or to anyone. Like when her dad died except this time, she had nowhere to go, no big brother to protect her. It would be too late to call Rami and Hayley, especially with a tiny tot in the house (never mind the fact she never knew their number off by heart anyway). Wasn't it funny how no-one remembered numbers these days except their own, she thought as she perched on a cold, metal seat (at the end of a row of cold metal seats, the one at her side covered in solid French fries and what she hoped was a chocolate milkshake puddle) and recalled a time, when landlines were the preferred choice of contact, and she could remember everyone's number like her own surname?

At first, she almost went with the notion when her mind conjured up Audrey's face, temporarily forgetting who she really was. Then, feeling like she was surely developing an ulcer, she realized the only person who had Adam's number was Greg. *Great.* She lugged the case back under her arm and made for the exit.

'Storie Street, please,' she said breathlessly as she slammed the door of the taxi behind her.

'No problem, darlin'. Busy day?'

Why the hell did it have to be super-smiley, chatty driver tonight of all nights? *Wish it was grumpy twat from last week.*

'Am sure this tunnel is just gonnae collapse wan day! A mean, dae yae see that? Water. Leaking in fae the Clyde. A mean, how kin that be right?'

On the upside, he liked the sound of his own voice more than hers and she got away with the odd *Yeah* and *Hm* every now and again, her ears no longer listening but her subconscious mind prompting her as to when the gaps needed filling.

Unsure whether to knock or not or what the break-up etiquette was, Charlotte loitered on her own doorstep realizing there was every chance what's-her-face was giving Greg a blowjob on *her* sofa. But it was still her flat. So as more of a warning than a pleasantry, she pressed the bell once and waited only a minute before letting herself in. Another strange noise halted her in the hallway, only this time, it made her smile because it wasn't the usual guns firing, bombs exploding of the Xbox, or shagging for that matter. It was the hoover.

Unwrapping her scarf slowly, she edged towards the lounge, more shocked than the night of Greg's indiscretion. Because there he was, with more headphones on, although these ones were of the plug-in, music variety. He hummed along as he pushed the hoover around, picking up the hose and frowning as he checked the suction against his hand. Charlotte folded her arms and grinned, wishing she had her phone to capture the occurrence being that it was so rare, it was almost worth creating a Facebook account for.

'*Black Hole Sun, won't you come, and wash away the pai…*' Greg's voice rocketed until it sounded like he had stood on a tac. It looked like it too, the way he nearly hit the ceiling and clasped his chest when he spotted her. His foot kicked the cylinder several times before it managed to land on the off button.

'Hi,' he panted, unplugging an earphone from each ear.

'Hi.' Charlotte smiled, impressed he had a sweat on. And for the first time in a long time, she was glad to see his face.

216

'Cuppa?' Greg lay the hose down on the arm of the sofa and wiped his brow with the bottom of his t-shirt.

Charlotte looked around the room. It was perfect. Not a dust particle or beer can ring stain or pizza crust to be found anywhere. 'I'd love one,' she sighed as she sagged to the arm of the sofa.

'Here.' He pulled out his phone and handed it to her. 'I think you'd better call Adam. He's already phoned four times to see if you were home yet.'

Rolling her eyes, Charlotte clutched the phone, but Greg didn't let go. So, in that awkward moment, she kept her eyes down on the Batman screen saver until he did. 'I'll just go put the kettle on,' he grumbled and plodded off towards the kitchen, his head down, the crack of his arse poking out the top of his ill-fitting jeans.

'Thanks, Greg,' Charlotte called after him, as grateful as she could manage given everything.

'Here we go then…' she mumbled quietly as she dialled.

'Charlotte?' *Pissed off Adam.*

Bloody hell! She recoiled, holding the phone at a safe distance as she rattled a finger in her ear to kill the insufferable tickle. 'Hi Adam,' she said, brushing her hair away from her face, preparing for the lecture. 'You all right?' Her words were obliviously breezy.

'Never mind me! Are you all right? Fuck's sake, Charlotte! I've been worried sick!' *Frightened Adam.*

What year is it? 2006? 'Sorry. I didn't mean to leave my phone. I was going tomorrow morning anyway so thought it'd be easier if I just went today instead. Plus, things were a bit *tense* at Vinny's.'

'Well, you could at least have waited until I was awake.' *Worried Adam.*

'Oh, and what time were you awake?' she asked lightly, pressing her finger into the soil of her favourite peace lily. Her eyebrows shot up when she felt it was damp. To make up for lost time, she blew on it a few times for good measure.

'Well…that's insignificant.' *Rumbled Adam.*

'Adam,' she slipped down on the sofa, then, giving a little, 'Ew!' scooted to the end when she remembered what had been happening on that very spot a few weeks ago. 'I'm tired. I'm sorry. I just wanted a fresh start in the morning and you're there now anyway. I'll give you a call on Monday night after the meeting. Let you know how it went.'

'A bit hard, Charlotte, since I've got your phone here.' *Condescending Adam.*

'Shit,' she spat. 'Can you send it please? Pretty please? I'm happy to live without it for a few days anyway.' More than happy.

'Where will I send it?'

'The croft, of course!' she snapped firmly, her nose wrinkled in a pissed-off kind of way in that he would even consider otherwise.

'Okay…Okay. I hope the move goes smoothly tomorrow. Wish I could be there to help.' *Lovely, squishy Adam.*

That was the one which made her eyes pool as she nodded silently and pushed her plant to its rightful place (covering the curry stain on the coffee table). God, she needed him now more than ever. Still…'It'll be fine, honestly. I'll give you a buzz on Monday.'

'Night Charlotte…Oh…Right! Wait! Vinny wants a word.'

'I can't! Someone's calling for Greg! Night Adam!' The words sprinted from her mouth in a shriek and she quickly jabbed the screen to cut the call. Charlotte shrivelled her lips into a ring and congratulated her quick-thinking skills before gathering what wits she had left to go join Greg in the kitchen.

He sat expectantly at the kitchen table, a steaming tea ready for her, a sandwich at its side. 'Thought you might be hungry too,' he smiled nervously. A small thoughtful gesture, but enough to break her nonetheless.

Everything sagged as she drooped onto the chair beside him and stared at the sandwich (tuna mayo, of course) until it blurred to an indiscriminate beige lump. Then, at long last, a huge, racking deep sob shrunk her lungs. It was followed by another and another.

'Sorry! I'm sorry! Do you want cheese instead?'

When she didn't answer, Greg realized it was more than the choice of sandwich filling which was at issue and pulled her to him where her tears were mopped up by his *Nirvana Nevermind* t-shirt. 'There, there,' he soothed and stroked her curls as she blew her nose into the dish towel he handed to her.

Then, when she could catch her breath, even after what they'd been through lately, she told him everything: how she had been feeling about them, Amos' death, Adam's stabbing, how they were linked. And then, she wasn't quite sure why, but she told him about Vinny.

Looping her hand quickly around the toilet roll (which Greg had fetched when she got to the Adam part), Charlotte waited for the thumping of his Star Wars mug on the table, waited for him to yell, 'Fucking hell!' and spit her name. But it never came. Instead, he listened: nodding for her to go on, holding her hand, pulling the face of her dad's watch around until it was facing the right way up. When she had spilled out the last of the gory details, she peeped up at him like she had just confessed to murder.

Holding his cards close to his chest, he shook his head and bit his bottom lip till it turned white. 'Charlotte,' he picked up her sandwich and chomped off a massive chunk, 'you don't do things by halves!' Flecks of wholegrain and granary fell on his t-shirt.

'No, you're right. I don't!' She snivelled some more tears into the tissue, and despite everything, chuckled a little as he patted her hand.

'So, what now?' he dared to ask, slowly placing the sandwich back on the plate.

'Greg,' she began, already softening the blow with a downwards slant to his name. 'I love you. I do. We've been through so much together, but just the fact that you were with…What's her name?'

'Gillian.'

'Gillian and I was with Vinny. You must know. Our problems started way before now.'

Conceding, he began to nod slowly and rubbed his thumb lightly over her hand. 'Is there nothing we can do to at least try?'

She placed her hand over his. 'No, Greg. I know after a while, things would slip and none of us were happy with how we ended up.'

He drew in a long, restrained breath and blinked his agreement.

'Anyway, what about you and Gillian? She seems like a nice ki…woman.' Charlotte cleared her throat and grimaced as she forced down a mouthful of the milky tea. She hadn't taken milk in her tea for over a decade after giving it up for lent. *Erh!*

'Yeah, she is but I'm not hitting a mid-life crisis just yet. I don't know. It's a wait and see. And what about you and…Vinny?'

Her laugh was laced with a hurtful spite. 'That's a been and gone – not even a wait and see. My own fault, really. But the whole situation was…crazy. It was like we were in our own little world for a while. Well, that was until his wife brought us all crashing back to reality.' Charlotte straightened her shoulders and folded the dishtowel into decreasingly smaller rectangles. 'And I may be many things, but a marriage wrecker, I am *not*.'

'No,' Greg agreed. 'You're not.'

Charlotte tilted her head, spotting a glimmer of the man she fell in love with back in the day. 'I think you need to get back to your art, Greg, instead of that bloody Xbox. It's my Prozac. I think it'd make you so much happier.'

Almost like she had read his mind, he grinned. 'I have. Come on, l want to show you something.'

Greg led her to the studio, in the middle of which, stood a huge canvas propped on an easel. An abstract of midnight blues and blacks, indigoes and violets. A swirling vortex of night. In the centre, a tiny ball of piercing white.

'My God,' she glided forward, stooping to scrutinize the work from various angles. 'Greg…it's amazing. It's one of the best things you've ever done.'

He shifted his weight from one foot to the other, a hand spread in ponder across his chin. 'Do you think so?'

'Yuh!' She huffed her approval like an American teen, planting her hands on her thighs to get a closer look.

'Well, it's a house-warming for the croft. A little something to say I'm always here…and that I'll always love you. And that I'm sorry for fucking things up.'

Pivoting her head to him, Charlotte slowly straightened. 'Greg…this isn't a blame game. We grew apart. Things change. It was my fault too. I'll always love you too, but we only live once. I want us both to be as happy as we can be. I of all people know, tomorrow isn't a given. I just don't think we can do that together anymore.'

He slung his hand over her shoulder. 'You're right, Charlotte Croft. I hate to admit it, but as bloody usual, you're right.'

Charlotte threaded her hand around his waist and continued to get lost in the work of art in front of her.

Chapter Thirty-Two

Rami drove (of sorts). Hayley and Charlotte squeezed, a bit more intimate than was comfortable, into the passenger side, a couple of boxes wedged awkwardly at their feet so all 4 knees wavered at different levels. Greg followed in the Beetle.

'See?' Rami bragged as the gear stick clunked back down to third gear. 'Told you we could get it all done in one trip!'

Charlotte and Hayley simultaneously threw him a glare. 'Yeah,' Hayley growled, pulling a teething ring from under her backside. 'You were bang on the money there.' She ogled the bright pink plastic hoop, then for somewhere to put it. 'Never mind the fact that I've not been able to feel my left leg for the last half an hour and I've practically got a gear stick rammed up my arse!' She tossed it on the dash.

'Now, now, children,' Charlotte said, adopting the manner of Miss Jean Brodie herself. She glowered at the Google Maps app on Hayley's phone, wondering why the dot was going in the opposite direction to them, no matter which way she turned it.

Charlotte loved Rami and Hayley. They were one of those couples who bickered like it was a dying art yet held an unrivalled mutual adoration which made the whole thing just work. One minute she'd be throwing a glass at his head. The next, she'd be straddling him on the sofa like a cowboy at the rodeo. And there was something magical in the way Rami still eyed her like she set his world on fire (baby belly and all), or the way she was ready to claw the eyes out of any woman who laid their eyes on *her* man. Charlotte was hoping she would eventually grow out of that stage at some point. Hoped that the birth of Sofie might help. But she was wrong. Just at the petrol station she was ready to have a go at the checkout girl because she stared too long at Rami's arm of tattoos. Thankfully, she just put her arms around his waist this time and gave her *the look*. It was more than enough to detract most.

Soon they began winding down a steep hill were the sheep weren't only in the fields, the road ahead now a cloudy obstacle course.

'Move, ya dim-witted baw a wool!' Rami yelled and thumped his horn, the sheep scarpering like they had seen a farmer with a set of sheers. From then on, he continued at a crawl just in case a fluffy surprise lay around one of the bendy corners, especially now that the visibility was non-existent as the wipers were losing the battle to keep up with the rain which thrashed against the windscreen.

'There!' Charlotte pointed as they passed a gated road which veered sharply to the right, recognizing the ancient yew tilted halfway between horizontal and vertical (and all the easier to climb in canary yellow wellies, she found). 'That's the entrance.' She tutted at the phone in her hand and handed it back to Hayley now they had found it by luck rather than with the help of the man with the 1950's newsreader accent. After crunching the gearstick of his brother's Kohli Builders Ltd van into reverse, Rami eased back a few metres and turned. When the nose of the van kissed the gate, Charlotte jumped out and was smacked with a vertical sheet of water and wind which stole her breath. Simultaneously drinking and breathing, she dipped her head and drove the wide metal gate open.

The van filed through first closely followed by Greg in the Beetle. At least he had the savvy to wait for her after she thrust the gate closed. She jumped in with him and they carried on down the bumpy track until the dirty white, rough cast walls and slate-tiled roof which sagged in the middle came into view – the croft. And when it did, she could almost hear her mother's peeling laughter which ended with a light snort, see her father call out joyfully that he'd caught a huge salmon (which looked more like an average seabass), smell the broth her granny had simmering on the stove, see the chess board her and Adam used to fight over until one or the other smacked it and all its pieces into the air, all before she set her eyes on the tiny black wooden front door (which, after getting into *Tolkien* when she was 10, had her believing the place was built by an actual *Hobbit*).

Deep down, Charlotte knew that's why she wanted to be there – to get a glimpse of that feeling one only gets as a child. Safe. She remembered waking as a youngster in her bed in the rafters, a storm howling painfully outside, rain battering at the tiny window as the skeletal fingers of the old oak tree clawed to get in. Yet, she wasn't scared. Exactly the opposite. She was toasty safe, under the same roof as everyone else in the whole world she loved. After her mum passed, Charlotte never had that feeling again. But the crumbs of it remained here at least.

Greg rolled the car to a standstill in front of the old galvanised coal bunker at the wonky gable end, eyes and string the only kind of spirit level back when the croft was built. Yanking her hood over her head, Charlotte watched her own sneakers dash up the grey chipped gravel. Under a rotten wooden canopy, she leaned back on her heels to roll the half cask planter to the side. Beneath it, the huge iron key lay where any self-respecting burglar would have found in a second, mossy and wet. The ancient lock was stiff, and she began to worry that it had seized altogether. But after a hefty clunk to the left, it gave way and Charlotte lifted the iron latch to her future.

The smell hit her first: stone and smoke and ash and dust, all shrouded in a heavy, clawing damp. Then, more subtly, the smell of her mother's sweet perfume and her grandmother's wild herbs mixed in with the residual creamy tobacco smoke of her Da's pipe.

Charlotte wanted to cry again, to tell them what had just happened to her. To sit on her Dad's knee as he told her she was his beautiful big girl and he'd kick anyone's arse who hurt her. She didn't know what made her want to cry more – the fact that they weren't there, or the fact that she could feel them so strongly, she almost expected them to be.

Before her eyes even had chance to adjust to the darkened room, the other's piled in behind her, gasping and shaking off the wet. 'Bloody hell, Charlotte! Look at that view!' Rami bellowed, striding across the cold flagstones and wiping a few cobwebs from the edges of the flaking wooden sashes to open the view.

Charlotte strolled to his side and rested her hands on her hips, proud and scared at the same time. 'I know. It's something, isn't it?' Her eyes traced the shingle path as it meandered to the jetty she and Adam used to dangle their bare feet from as they caught star fish, red crabs and even the odd lobster. Oddly, she noted the grass had not long since been mowed and the hedges were trimmed. *Strange.*

'Rami, Greg – you start unloading.' Hayley jabbed a pink talon towards the door. 'Oh, I suppose me and Charlotte will have to get started in here.' She had a knack of saying it like the boys had got the good side of the bargain. However, this time, the boys looked at each other in a way which said wordlessly that they were on to her. But Hayley being Hayley, she never gave them chance to air it. 'Today!' she yelped. Rami huffed and marched off with a grumble. Greg followed behind with less fuss. Nearly dislocating her neck as she craned to make sure they were out of earshot, Hayley dropped to the *Radley* bag at her feet and popped back up with a bottle of prosecco in the air. 'Too early?' she suggested, already unwrapping the foil from the cork and unwinding the wire.

'I guess not,' Charlotte shrugged before spotting some freshly filled firewood in the brass bucket at the side of the iron grate. 'What the…?'

'What…is…it?' Hayley squeaked, her face screwed to the side as the cork popped.

Charlotte pointed slowly to each, her brow furrowed. 'The garden's been tidied and there's fresh firewood in the basket. I've not been here for nearly a year.' Perplexed, she turned back to Hayley who was magically producing four flutes from the bag now. Even more puzzled at how she'd managed it, Charlotte felt the beginnings of head cramp.

'Does no-one else have the key?' Hayley handed Charlotte a glass.

'No. Well, Mrs Dickson in the farmstead up the hill pops her head in every now and again, but she would have no way of knowing I was arriving.' Shrugging, Charlotte slid her glass on the cast iron mantle and began piling the firewood in the grate. They were still there, the steel brush and shovel and poker hanging on a steel stand. As a girl, she used to sweep the ashes to help her gran (although she probably made more of a mess). Charlotte smiled at the thought.

The room got suddenly darker as a hooded figure filled the open doorway. 'Coo-wee! Anyone home?'

'Mrs Dickson?' Charlotte squinted over her shoulder into the gloom.

The shadow waved.

'Come in!'

'Oh Charlotte! Lovely to see you, dear. I hope you don't mind, but I gave the place a bit of a spruce up. Adam called a few days ago to say you were moving in. We were so excited to see this place have a bit of life in it again,' she garbled, pulling the waxy, green hood back to free her tight grey curls much like a bunch of flowers from a magician's hat.

'You didn't have to do that, Mrs Dickson but it is very much appreciated. Did you do the garden too?' she asked, handing Mrs Dickson a square of kitchen roll and noting she was still in a turtleneck. Charlotte never remembered her in anything else (albeit she had every colour of the rainbow), not even in the heatwave of 2001.

'No, dear,' she said, cleaning her glasses till they squeaked. 'That was Mr Dickson. He always did have a soft spot for you, you know! Couldn't wait to get the Flymo out when he heard you were coming back,' she blustered as she put her Deirdre Barlow-esk spectacles back in place, squinting her gaze around the room as if they were still streaked useless. 'Gosh, it's awfully dark in here. Let's get the lights on.'

'I need to switch on the electricity at the mains first, Mrs Dickson,' Charlotte said, stumbling towards the cupboard under the stairs but stubbing her toe in the process on a box which hadn't been there before. 'Ow! Shit!' she gasped before the place was suddenly flooded in light.

'Language Timothy! No need, dear. I did it earlier. Now, let's get a fire lit and you dear...' she motioned to Hayley.

'Hayley,' she announced, her first glass of prosecco demolished in her hand.

'Hayley. You can make the tea. Fresh milk in the fridge and sugar in the bowl.' Mrs Dickson waved a crooked finger towards the kitchen which could have easily been mistaken for a cupboard.

'Yes, Mrs Dickson,' she wobbled her stretched chin from side to side, her eyes bulging like a petulant teenager. She sauntered off, one hand on her hip, the other holding up the empty glass like she was expecting someone to run along aside her and fill it up. When Mrs Dickson kneeled at the grate and began stuffing scrunched-up balls of newspaper in the gaps between the firewood, Hayley turned back, stuck out her tongue, then marched towards the kitchen.

It wasn't too long before they all sat round a real, roaring fire, their teas untouched with a layer of wrinkled skin congealing on top. The first bottle of prosecco was finished and being used as a candle holder, another bottle opened and afloat in a bucket of icy water from the loch. Once Mrs Dickson made sure Charlotte had everything she needed, she bid them goodnight.

'God, she's a feisty old filly,' Hayley laughed with an irritated appreciation as she refilled her flute.

Her heels resting on the slate hearth, Charlotte wiggled her toes against the flames, swaying back and forth in the faded rose wing-backed *Parker Knoll* rocker. It smelt fusty, the very aroma of abandonment, but she loved it none-the-less. 'Yeah, she's a no-nonsense sort but a real treasure. I think I've seen her like…five times in the last ten years, yet she treats me like I've never been away. Don't feel so alone now,' she murmured as she rubbed her hands in front of the flames.

Greg sat nursing the same glass he had been holding for the past 20 minutes without putting it to his lips. 'You're not alone, Charlotte,' he said so quietly, it was ear-splitting.

Her hands stilled as she watched it all drag at his face. Boy, did she feel it too, and not only for him. 'I know, Greg. It's just… made all this a bit easier.'

Rami and Hayley exchanged a knowing glance like they were intruding, which they were. Not on an awkward moment, but a tender, poignant one.

Rami yawned and stretched way too obviously (just as badly as she had done with Vinny), eyeballing the watch on his wrist like he never knew he had one. 'God! We better start making tracks. Granny Morris will be climbing the walls. It's well past her gin time.'

'Shit! You're right! I never realized. It's half eight!' Hayley downed the rest of her glass, her acting skills only marginally better than Rami's. There was the start of a commotion as an assortment of limbs scrambled into coats and boots.

Greg rolled his eyes as he walked to Charlotte's side. 'Remember, if you need *anything...*'

Nodding, Charlotte said nothing as she fixed the snagged collar of his blue polo shirt. Even when there was nothing left to tuck under or straighten, she kept her hands there. 'Thank you.' *Not just for the move*, she thought, but for making this as easy as it could possibly be. *For letting me fly.*

He stared for a moment as if to say something before quickly pecking her cheek and spinning for the door. 'I'll get you in the van,' he said to the others without turning back, tucking his hands in the back pockets of his Levi's and disappearing into the rain.

Rami was quick to follow. 'Enjoy, Charlotte. See you soon.' He threw up a hand and was gone.

Hayley pulled down her smile as she gently took hold of Charlotte's arms (already mottled from sitting too close to the fire). 'I think this is going to be amazing for you, Charlotte. I know you'll smash it.'

It was exactly what she needed to hear, especially after the week she had just had. Nothing like a good old dose of heartache to shred your confidence to a million pieces and make you question your decision-making skills.

Charlotte nodded and nodded some more until it was safe to speak. 'Thanks Hayley. And thanks for today.'

'Anytime.' Another kiss on the cheek and she was off too, sprinting away towards the van.

'Wait!' Charlotte cried, her socks shuffling back when they hit the wet wall.

'What?' Hayley shouted over the roar, her coat now a tent over her head.

'Look after him, will you?' Her heart broke a little again as she watched Greg in the passenger seat of the van, staring blankly ahead.

'Of course, I will! He's going to be okay, Charlotte. I promise you. And so are you!' Marching backwards towards the van, she pointed and yelled, 'You wait and see!' A red coattail fell across her face. It was quickly snatched up. 'I'm always right. Just ask Rami!'

Charlotte closed the door when the rain began to pool on the wrong side of the doorstep. Her chin on her hands, she watched from windowsill as two red taillights bumped and rolled till they disappeared up into a kink in the hill. The melancholy moment was rudely interrupted as the spider (which must have been accidentally flown in on a banana crate from Latin America, and from its sheer magnitude, merited a name and pet status) from the web she had her elbow wedged in began to stomp up her arm. Not that she wished them any harm or anything, but spiders weren't exactly her favourite creepy crawly in the world, not when one had attached itself to her knee-high white socks when she was only 7. And no matter how she screamed, yelled, kicked her little knobbly knee, it didn't budge. Turns out, it was only the green leafy top from the tomato Adam had been munching on which had stuck, along with a new, life-long phobia. Wailing, she shook the cardigan off like it was on fire and kicked it to the corner of the room, her body shuddering as someone continually walked over her grave. Seemed she wasn't alone after all.

Chapter Thirty-Three

The unmistakable Victorian chimney stacks, grey brick and fortress-like, propped up the equally dreary sky as she indicated to get off junction 8. Just the view caused her insides to twist painfully, her hand slipping under the seatbelt to massage the tender bit under her rib. *How the hell and I going to get through this?* Facing Audrey again. Pretending she knew nothing. Walking by Amos' cell knowing it would be someone else reading on his bunk, someone else's calendar blue-tacked to the bricks like he never existed. The unrelenting questions she would face about Adam and if she was okay. And she never even had the option to tell anyone, 'No, I'm not actually. Because, as well as all this *shite*, I stupidly let myself fall in love and he broke my heart…and it's very, very painful.' Not even her favourite upbeat morning radio show could cheer her up, especially when the jingle for *Land of Leather* with the guy who sounded like the voice of the *X-factor*, painfully elongated every L (and there were a lot considering the showroom was in Lower Lowton, Lennoxtown). Groaning for too many reasons, she switched it off with a sharp prod.

Pottering – that's how Charlotte had spent the weekend. Pottering around to find a new home for each of her old belongings. Pottering from room to room, getting familiar with the old place again. Pottering in the search for something only to find she wasn't sure what. When everything had a place (which considering how much she had, only filled a few hours and a few shelves), Charlotte set the easel up at the window seat and began to take her mind off things in the form of a small watercolour of the appropriately watery day. But after only 20 minutes, the paint brushes were rinsed and dried, the mixing pallet was wiped back to blank – just like her creative side (rendered derelict by the unsettling coldness in her chest).

So, she began pottering again - hanging Greg's painting above the fireplace before doing the more menial tasks like going to the supermarket for supplies and cleaning the inside windows and emptying the bucket from the leaky roof in the bedroom for the fifth time.

But when she ran out of ways to potter, she ran out of places to hide from the truth. Because not even living the dream with the crackling fire, French wine and unrivalled view of the loch could erase the pain in her bones. The pain of his betrayal. The pain of his mouth on Nadia's. More than anything, although Charlotte couldn't admit that part yet, the pain of his absence. It felt like there was a gaping hole where her middle used to be, and if she were to wrap her hands around the pain, it would be like trying to grab a cloud.

Before the hole consumed her to nothingness, her brain recoiled from it, seeking solace (and other places to hide). This time, it was her granny's rocker with the same squeak of 20 years ago with every jaunt forward (and Gran reminding herself every night to look out the WD40 in the morning); it was her Da's fishing rod, still threaded with a line and hooked up over the window like he might grab it at any moment and trundle down the jetty; it was the picture of *The Sacred Heart* in the alcove at the front door which her Ma blessed herself in front of every time she went out or came in. That pain was on a different level - darker, deeper, chronic – and enough to remind her, she'd been through worse...and survived. Because, at least he was still alive...probably shagging his wife right enough, probably forgetting her like last week's next new fad.

Fucker, she thought with another mouthful of the Shiraz on offer at the *Co-op* in the village, ready to draw a nice, neat horizontal line (one Vinny would have been proud of) under the whole sordid, wonderful, amazing affair. But it caught her eye then, taunting her from the pine dresser at the other side of the spitting flames.

Charlotte slid it from the shelf and opened it to the raw, rich images of his face which she had captured so vibrantly at the airport. Each one smarted and the hole flourished. *Finish it*, she ordered herself, a hand poised on the sheet, willing herself to rip it out and throw it into the flames. But no matter how many times she urged her hand to act, to destroy the memory once and for all, it didn't budge.

Because, despite everything, she loved him. Otherwise, why would a single kiss of betrayal from a guy she'd known for barely a week hurt so much more than her partner of 8 years having a full-blown affair right under her nose? Knowing, no matter how much she tried to convince herself otherwise, she wasn't quite ready to obliterate the last tangible piece of evidence that he existed, she slammed the sketchbook closed with a snap and began rocking in her chair to the tedious ticks of the rickety old grandfather clock at the top of the stairs as they counted her down, ever-so-slowly yet most definitely, to the inevitability of facing the world again. Alone.

The whine of the door caused Mr Miller to look up from signing off another cell search request form. 'Charlotte love! Come in! Come in!' He waved his hand in erratic hoops. 'Close the door behind you.'

Just the shades of concern his face held was enough to set her lip to wibble-wobble mode. *Nope, not ready to do sympathy today.*

Inhaling deeply, he rolled a pen above his top lip like he was sampling a very good Cuban cigar. Charlotte stood before him, her arms crossed at her back, staring beyond the bars and barbed fences at the seagulls swooping and soaring in the distance, wallowing in their freedom.

'I'm not going to ask you any stupid questions about how you're doing.'

It took only those few words to cause her lip to tremble more, so she nipped it still.

'Come on, love. Sit yourself down.' Mr Miller nudged his head towards the sofa under the black and white picture of the prison in its Victorian heyday. The officers in those days seemed more severe and each sported a moustache which carefully swirled up at the ends. Jim would have fit in nicely.

Taking a deep breath, she sat with her head down and her fingers locked on her lap.

The spot beside her sagged and she could just make out the black cambers of his knees slant to hers. 'Charlotte, we don't have to do this today. Have more time.'

Strangely enough, her knee began to bob, which caused her throat to bob painfully too. Did she ever do that before him? 'No. It will look more suspicious and I want to get it over with.'

'Okay,' but the word was long and uncertain. 'Are you up to the meeting later?'

Pale hands which didn't feel like her own swept down the length of her thighs. 'Yeah. I'll follow you there after the shift if that's okay?'

'Of course, yeah.'

Her back straightened a little as did her voice. 'So how have things been here?'

'Oh,' a dismissive hand swiped through the air, 'we'll talk more later. Just remember to keep it as normal as you can. Tough ask, I know. But you're a wee trouper so I'm sure you'll manage.' He finished with a proud dad smile and an accompanying pat on the back. Another *we* moment. God, was everything going to be such a painful reminder? What else? Beards? Fucking kebabs? Heaven forbid, red wine!

Charlotte rested her hand on the finger-print smirched brass on the outside of the staff room door and counted down from 3. Bypassing zero, she began counting in minuses.

'Charlotte?' a familiar voice interrupted just as she reached -4.

Bollocks. Her face neutralized as she turned to him. 'Hi Ben.'

'Charlotte, I….' he broke off and smiled contritely, like he was being sincere. Trying to be sincere. Acting at being sincere?

'I am sorry to hear about your brother. It must have been awful.' A beefy shoulder buffered against the wall next to the fire hose reel as he chewed hard on his gum.

The first of many fake smiles dragged at her lips. 'Thanks Ben. He's on the mend, thank God. It's just facing this lot…and all their questions.' She threw in an eye-roll for good measure.

Abruptly, Ben pushed himself upright and thumbed towards the staffroom, his chews accelerating. 'I could go and tell them all to play it low key if you like?'

Despite warning herself not to, to keep control, that her every movement was being measured, her head shook with far too much vigour. 'No, it's fine. It'll only come up again at some point. Just want to get it over and done with.' Her hand groped back to the metal plate and she tried not to baulk or flinch when he laid a hand on her shoulder.

'Well, you know we're all here for you.' He gave that smile which she could not determine was friend or foe, but what she could sense, was it knew more than it was letting on.

'Thanks Ben,' she said, another forced smile rigid on her face as she finally thrust through the door, immediately dulling the hubbub. Audrey popped straight into her vision, waving urgently, her eyes heavy with mascara and concern. But who was it for? *Herself? Me?* Paranoia was exhausting Charlotte quickly realized. Filling her lungs to bursting point, she waved back before making her way to the table, consoling pats smacking her on the back as she went. *We. We. We. We.*

'Oh my God, Charlotte!' Audrey gasped and Charlotte noticed her nails were a deep purple today as they clutched at her arm. 'Are you okay? What the hell happened?' As usual, Charlotte's coffee was waiting although she wasn't so grateful for it this time, especially when there was a good chance it was laced with arsenic.

Everything seemed too loud – the clack of the balls ricocheting off each other at the pool table, the dull clunking of the bottle of coke being spat out by the vending machine, the rain which drove against the window, the silence of those at her table as they waited for her to elaborate. 'Probably some smack head. But Adam's okay. Lost his spleen but at least he's still here.' A hand clamped over her mouth to stop her yelling, *'No thanks to you and your boyfriend!'* Never a violent person, Charlotte had the uncommon sudden urge to rip Audrey's bun out by the roots. Then she thought of Vinny. *Buns too? God help me!*

Pete ogled her, his face looking as if it was in as much pain as hers. 'Oh, that's awful, man. Know whit a mean?'

'Jesus,' Jim added, his thick brows ploughing angrily. 'That's fuckin' heavy Charlotte. I'm glad he's okay.' His hairy hand patted her arm gently and Charlotte could at least sense the genuine in his concern. 'You awright, hen?'

'I will be. Thanks Jim,' she grumbled, pushing away her cup.

In the morning, she took Peter Murray for his routine heart check at *The Queen Elizabeth* before supervising the French lessons (with the quirky Mrs O'Shea who after every sentence said, *D'accord?* and she tried really hard not to think of Gabriel).

In the afternoon, Charlotte and Jim accompanied Raymond Woods for his court hearing in which he was accused of stabbing a neighbour after a long-running family feud. Charlotte almost felt seasick as she followed the key witness sway in the stand.

The prosecution lawyer stood confidently, with such an air of self-assurance, and she tried not to envision Vinny doing the same. 'So, Mrs Brooks, after Mr Woods left the tenement, you said you saw something shiny in his hand. Could it have been a knife?'

Mrs Brooks stumbled back and clasped on to the oak lip of the stand, licking her scarlet, smudged lipstick and flattening her badly highlighted blonde hair, her dark roots an inch or two too long. 'Am no sure Your...Highness. I think it might of been a chicken curry.'

As the gallery erupted, Jim's shoulder juddered next to hers. Despite picking up on the grammatical error, hers juddered too.

After another check of her mirrors, Charlotte sank lower in the Beetle and thrummed her nails rapidly on the shiny *VW* badge at the centre of her steering wheel as she glowered at Audrey's white *Mini* speed through the gate. 'Yer face wull stay like that if the wind changes, Charlotte Croft!' she heard her granny warn as she found herself hexing again. It quickly vanished, and she shimmied up when Mr Miller got into *the Nissan Qashqai* she had deliberately parked behind. When he was out the gate, she followed, the *Beetle* chugging in starts and bursts until she remembered to move up to 2nd gear.

They parked side by side in the dank underground car park (the pillars of which did not feel strong enough a buttress for the thirty floors above it, the ceiling low and suffocating) then took the elevator to the eighth floor, quietly ignoring the strong smell of piss saturating the small space. The office it released them in, however, was bright and modern albeit, eerily quiet.

'Evening. I'm Frank Miller. We have an appointment with Detective Coleman.' He patted the top of the counter like he was checking his back pocket for change.

The girl (although the noun is being used in the most loose of terms) pulled her head up from her copy of *Take-a-break* (her eyes a second or two later). Snapping the pale pink bubble ballooning from her mouth, she directed them with a single flick of her hand. 'Through the double doors. First right then left.' Her head fell again.

'Right!' Mr Miller nodded his thanks to the dandruff-flaked crown of her head before flaring his eyes at Charlotte. He wasted no time in following her instructions, Charlotte just his shadow, until they stood outside the door. 'Ready?'

Her heart galloped furiously in her chest. Tugging each cuff down, she nodded quickly before she changed her mind. There was a total of 4 Mississippis before a tall suited man opened the door. He looked from one to the other and smiled. 'Charlotte? Mr Miller? Please come in.'

'Ladies first.' Mr Miller held out an arm in an attempt to alleviate the seriousness.

Never been called that before, her eyes said as she stepped forward, only reaching as far as the mouth of the room before she peddled back into Mr Miller's chest.

Chapter Thirty-Four

The consummate professional, Vinny wore a straight face and a suit, grey and sharp (definitely not off the peg with it being so well tailored to his every limb). His long legs were crossed as were his arms. In that instant, she knew the pain she harboured was a lifetime kind of thing. Suddenly, he uncrossed everything and eased forward, his eyes moving in a predatory fashion, Charlotte his prey.

'Please have a seat,' the detective ushered, pointing to the two very different height chairs opposite them. Charlotte threw Mr Miller a beseeching look which he misunderstood with a reassuring nod and began to use his cane as a staff. Having little choice, she took the lower seat, then sank lower.

Detective Coleman sat on Vinny's side of the table, a slender shadow compared to the man at his side. He moved the plastic fern peppering his view with a frown, a bright smile replacing it when he could see them clearly. 'I'm glad you both came. As you already know I am Detective Rick Coleman and this is Vincent Knight, our lead prosecutor in the case.' Charlotte eyes didn't move with the direction of his hand; the stayed zoned on the very dark mole under Coleman's left eye. A certain malignancy about the pigment made her think he should have it checked.

Coleman laced his fingers and Charlotte wondered if he took his tarnished gold wedding ring as seriously as Vinny took his polished platinum band. 'Charlotte, I know you've had a heck of an ordeal lately and we really do appreciate how you have managed to move this case forward.

The reason we wanted to see you alone, is we're not 100% on who we can and cannot trust.'

Charlotte remained anaesthetized as Mr Miller cleared his throat and straightened the knot of his tie. 'Well, now we know that Audrey is responsible for smuggling Spice into the prison, what do we do now?'

At last, Vinny found his voice but did not address Mr Miller with it. 'Absolutely nothing.' His tone was low and measured, and Charlotte dropped her eyes and began to peel up little strips of skin at the side of her nail.

When she lifted her gaze, it was to Coleman. Like when she was painting, she began to really take notice of him then, to understand his far too easy to read story. Perhaps he would have been a heartbreaker in the 90's, but the job had certainly taken its toll: his sandy hair only an echo of the carrot red it probably once was, premature eye bags, slightly puffy features from too much self-medicating the pressures with the booze, deep lines gouging the sides of his mouth. His clothes were ill-fitting, the neck of his shirt an inch too wide, a world away from *Mr Saville Row* on his left. There was a dullness about him, a tiredness. Yeah, Rick Coleman had certainly had a tough paper round.

Vinny vied for her attention. He adjusted the stack of papers in front of him like a newsreader does to fill the awkward, dead-air moment at the end of a broadcast. He laid them so they sat perfectly parallel with the edge of the table as he spoke. 'The fewer people who know, the better. We're already tracking Audrey's every move. When we think she is about to drop a new batch, the police will be waiting. Until then, it is essential you carry on as normal. The less you're suspected to be connected to the case, the better. Thankfully, Audrey has not been to see Dolan for the past few weeks. We are sure she is unaware of the connection between Charlotte and the Adam incident or that one of the prosecution lawyers is Charlotte's brother. We believe that would have been a decision made higher up the chain. But we must make sure it stays that way, otherwise the connection to Charlotte will be made, and she will be in danger.'

Accompanying her exaggerated eye roll, Charlotte let out a single, hollow laugh, much to everyone's confusion except Vinny's. To avoid the confused glares, she kept her head down, counting the thuds of her heart which she determined were exactly double the speed of the soft ticks of the chrome wall clock. *As if you give a shit* she thought as she kept her eyes on what she hoped was a *Malteser* covered in fluff at her feet. She checked, bringing her foot down on it, feeling it crack to crumb under the tread of her boot. *Yip, a Malteser.* It felt satisfyingly good and more than a little of her wished it was Vinny's head.

A hand sprung free from across Vinny's chest as he began to explain. 'If we can make sure Audrey is caught before she sees Dolan, no connection can be made. We know you won't say anything Charlotte about the real circumstances, but if she goes to see him and says that her mate's Scottish brother Adam was stabbed in Covent Garden last Saturday in a random attack, it wouldn't take an Einstein to make the connection. And when he wants to turn the screw before court, he has another…screw. Charlotte. So, Audrey is the key to his prosecution. If we catch her in the act, we stand a good chance of getting her to give evidence against Dolan in exchange for a lighter sentence.'

He kept his voice controlled, like he had rehearsed the speech, but she could already feel his knee bobbing, a rhythmical beat pulsing across the cheap laminate.

'Silly, silly lassie,' Mr Miller muttered but Charlotte could hear it wasn't in anger – more, a frustration that he never saw the signs mixed with a bit of sympathy for the girl who had always lit up his wing. Tutting loudly, he reached in to silence the phone ringing in his pocket, pulling his glasses down an inch as he peered at the screen. 'Sorry. The wife.' He tucked it away again. 'So, what do we do in the meantime?'

Detective Coleman made a spider with his hand and bounced it rigidly on the rainbow blue table as he spoke. 'You just keep doing what you're doing. If you see anything which you think may be of interest, I would like you to report it to me - *directly*.' His hand stayed rigidly arachnid and unyielding on the last word.

Mr Miller shuffled forward and leant on his cane. 'What about Ben? Surely the fact that he is having a relationship with her indicates his involvement?'

Vinny folded his arms again. 'The jury is out on that one. That may be the case, or it may be the case she knows exactly who he is and it's a case of keeping her enemies closer. To be fair, he has an impeccable record up till now, but that doesn't mean shit as far as all this is concerned.'

Coleman bowed his head to Charlotte like she was 8, an obvious misinterpretation in the trauma she was exhibiting. 'Okay? So, do you have any more questions?'

Yeah, why the hell is he here? Almost tempted to scream the words, Charlotte sensibly opted to shake her head from side to side instead.

Mr Miller polished his bad knee some more, finishing with a light, sharp smack. 'Nope, not that I can think of,' he said brightly. 'But I'm sure I'll have a thousand of them running through my head all night!' Charlotte knew the feeling.

Coleman reached into his long beige trench coat, far more Columbo than Luther. 'If you do, here's my number.' He slid the card over the table but kept his finger on it and pulled up a very blonde brow. 'Just make sure you two act as naturally as you can. No whispering in corners, if you catch my drift.'

'No…No.' Frank took the card, then ran his eyes over Charlotte, who sat whitish and silent. 'Come on, lass.' He rested a hand on her shoulder. 'You need some rest and you've got a long drive ahead of you.'

Charlotte shot to her feet before his sentence finished.

'Wait!' Vinny mounted, a hand springing forward as he tried to control his tone. 'Wait. Can I have a moment to speak to Charlotte…alone please?' He slipped his hands into the restrictive safety of his pockets and glared unflinchingly at Rick.

Glancing up, Rick paused for a second before slowly getting to his feet. 'Yeah,' he said uncertainly before snatching each of the scattered papers in his haphazard pile from the table. 'Yeah, of course.'

Frank glowered at Charlotte.

'It's fine.' Another fake smile.

Then they were alone.

'Hi.' Vinny spoke gently, trying to tame his little bird again, sliding her phone across the table. 'Are you okay?'

Charlotte gnawed the side of her mouth as she snatched the mobile and tucked it into the top pocket of her shirt. She let the words build some energy before releasing them. 'Who's looking after Adam?'

'My sister, Lucy. Much to their mutual protest.' There was a weighty sigh. 'Charlotte…I don't understand.' Gone was the control of earlier as his voice became unusually shaky; this was the part he could not rehearse. 'Please, tell me. Why the hell did you go?'

Keeping her eyes down, Charlotte scraped her fingernail to lift a bit of blue tack bonded to the tabletop. 'Because yer wife had just walked in the door and I was shagging her husband. A bit of an awkward position to be put in really.'

He took a few stunted steps until he was right back to where he'd started. Careful, careful little bird. 'But…' He gave a little huff, a confused huff. 'It was over. I love *you*, Charlotte.'

Childish, she knew, but it didn't stop her vociferous jeer. 'Look, Vinny. We had some fun. Things were…intense and we were both feeling…vulnerable. But I'm home now…and I just want to get on with my life.' The blue blob between her fingers was being worked hard to make a perfect sphere.

'Charlotte?' His eyes crumpled, and his mouth gaped, his knee began to judder even though he was on his feet.

Charlotte was sure the syndrome had a name. Twitchy leg disease or something like that?

'Are you having a fucking laugh?' His voice suddenly flared. 'Is that all it was for you, a…bit of *fun*?'

Her fingers kneaded manically as she at last met his eyes. 'No, Vinny. It wasn't. But I think it was…for you.' With a swift bare of her teeth, she flicked the sphere and listened as it landed with a dull thwack on something hard – Vinny's forehead. *Oh, fuck!*

They both stood wide-eyed.

Her insides so jelly-like, a laugh threatened but Charlotte did not give it a chance to make light. She spun for the door.

'Don't you dare, Charlotte Croft!' he cried, his steps no longer curtailed. 'Don't you dare walk out on me! I…I fucking *love* you.' Hands began flailing now as well as his words. Drowning. 'I know, it was awful timing when Nadia turned up. But…'

The snap of her head sent her ponytail veering. 'But what, Vinny? It was clear to see, that it was *anything* but over between you two. Oh, and did she like her perfume by the way? You know, the bottle you picked up at the airport? *Chanel Chance*, I believe?' Her adrenaline buzzed all over now. If it were visible, she'd have looked like the *Ready Brek* man, especially since she'd done nothing but rehearse for this show-down since the moment she walked out his door. Granted, perhaps not quite so soon.

Falling back a step, his eyes dwindled. 'Huh? What the…? It was *Chanel No5*, I think you'll find. It's the only one my mum wears. Here.' He tapped and swiped his phone before propelling it across the table with far more force than he had done with hers.

THANKS FOR THE PERFUME SON.
I ALWAYS LOVE A BIT OF CHANEL!
LOVE YOU MORE THOUGH. MUM XXX

Charlotte took a fleeting glimpse, gave a sneer, then thrust it back. She checked her nails again for some reason. She wasn't sure why since they were always cut short and neat. Never fancy. Always practical. *Unlike Nadia's.* 'Well, either way, you left me and Adam downstairs for long enough while you two sounded like you were having a right laugh to yourselves!'

'Charlotte…I was ending my *marriage*. And I ended it the moment I knew I wanted to spend the rest of my life with *you*!' His eyes emphasized the final word.

But his lyrics just seemed to beat off her. 'Some way to end a marriage, Vinny,' she sniggered as she wrapped her fingers around the cool, brass handle.

'What do you mean?' he blurted and took a step forward.

When Charlotte turned back slowly, there was almost a smile on her face. But it was fused with so much spite, Vinny stopped dead and drank a mouthful of air.

'With a kiss like that.'

The colour leached from his face as he clenched his beautiful heterochromia iridium eyes closed. Vinny stood motionless for a moment before opening them slowly. 'No,' he croaked so low, the word jammed and broke on the way out. 'Oh, no Charlotte. You've…You've got it wrong.'

'Mm hm.' Charlotte swallowed her lips and rocked back and forth on her heels. He saw it clear as a bell, that flash in her eyes like the first night they met. Only this time, it was so intense they turned to dense cobalt; she was about to explode. Was it possible there might be more than a smidgeon of truth in the myth about red heads with short tempers?

'If it even ended there.'

What astounded him most was that it wasn't Charlotte who snapped, it was him. Not even 10 years in the courtroom and 5 years of marriage training with the high-maintenance Nadia could help. Slapping a hand to his head, he began to pace like a claustrophobe stuck in a lift. 'Jesus! You think I could have put part of myself in her after I had just put it inside you?' His face was contorted, his tenor too.

It only fuelled her more. 'Yer tongue certainly didn't have a problem with it.'

An unsettling silence ruptured as his voice climaxed. 'I had just told her about *you*! We were ending things amicably! We were talking about how it was sad but that it was right! Christ, she even wished us all the best.' His voice suddenly nosedived. 'And. then she asked for one last kiss.'

Charlotte began to wonder how many ways she could expel the air frustratedly from her body before she started sounding like Audrey from *Corrie* as she blew another sharp huff from her nose. 'And you certainly gave her that didn't you, Vinny? While I sat at the top of the stairs WATCHING!' Every time she thought of it, she felt the air exit her lungs. 'You know,' her index finger jabbed and accused with every personal pronoun, 'I had the exact same conversation with Greg. I told him about you. We talked about how sad it was but that it was the right thing to do. And after he *helped* me move, I gave him a hug goodbye. A FUCKING HUG! He *pecked*, PECKED me on the cheek.' There was nothing peck-like

246

in the way her finger poked the spot. 'And even then, after what *you* had done, I would *never* have kissed him the way you kissed her. Not...not with the same mouth I had kissed you on.'

Taking his punishment, Vinny stood prostrate and silent until she moved to the door again where upon he lunged. 'Charlotte, *please* don't do this.' Broken. Shattered. Dying on the inside. Wolf eyes which pooled like hers.

Her head dropped to the white-knuckled hand clinging to hers. 'I didn't,' she uttered with a quiet finality before slipping her hand free and walking out the door.

Chapter Thirty-Five

The harvest moon hung heavy and low, and although there was no wind, translucent clouds billowed furiously across it. But even in the silver-kissed darkness, there was too much light, so Charlotte cut it off quickly with a sharp tug of the curtain.

Sleep aloof, his face had plenty chance to haunt her every time her lids fell. Contrite magnificence, exquisite confusion. But it was the hurt in his eyes which left her empty. Wasn't it supposed to make her feel better? Seeing him squirm? Letting him know she knew everything, watching him get caught? The guilt? Then why was an iciness, so like grief, ebbing its way around her body until she was quivering despite the layers of blankets weighing her down?

Her brain, like giving up any addiction, tried to rationalise a way back to him, started to tell her it wasn't that much of a deal – it was just a kiss. But she only had to remember that kiss, the passion of it, the greedy, deep need in each swivel of his head, how it rendered Nadia floppy in his arms. *No. No!* She was right. That kiss was still far too weighty with love.

It *was* grief, she at last admitted to herself as she listened to the owl twit-twooing somewhere close by, hauntingly alone too. The purest, most sorrowful anguish like every other she had suffered. And she accepted it, knowing she would mourn him forever like the others who were gone and those who would never come, the children she would never cradle in her arms or nestle to her breast. She felt just like the woman in the hospital who had lost part of her very self. Perhaps the croft was meant to remain silent, stirred only by the echoes of the past.

Vinny sat alone in every way at the heavy oak table of the deserted hotel bar. Not even when the waiter asked him, 'Another *Chivas Regal*, sir?' did his glare break from the loch, as still as a mill pond, a stark paradox to his mind. His suit jacket had long been discarded to the back of his chair, his tie unknotted and his hand swirling its fourth neat single malt. A thumb and forefinger pinched and released his bottom lip, over and over and over.

Charlotte was right. He had become lost in the moment with Nadia. Perhaps it was because it was a final goodbye, perhaps it was laced with too much folly when he thought of the freedom it would bring? The end of a bitter deadlock. His new life with Charlotte. His teeth gritted as he thought of what he'd done, of how hurt she must have felt to watch. Most people, after a while, would have shrugged it off as a moment of nostalgia. Because for him, that's exactly what it was. But Charlotte Croft wasn't most people. Not with how she could see things, *feel* things. And how could he make her see - it was a snapshot of the past, an echo of what was, not what *is?*

Of course, he did love Nadia. But not like *that* anymore. He didn't wish her harm, he wanted her to be happy too. But more than anything, he wanted Charlotte. Forever. He'd never loved or wanted anything more in his life. How could one moment of madness erase a future of joy? After seeing her reaction to him tonight, he questioned whether he should persist. But when he contemplated giving up on the one person he would die for, that was never going to be an option. Ever. But what he would do, was step back. Give her time to reflect. Give him time to plan his next move very carefully. And Vinny was an expert in strategy and the long-term game. This was one case he could not afford to lose.

Draining his glass, he gazed one last time across the motionless waters, feeling some comfort in the fact that she might have been looking across them too. That he was in some way still connected with her. If he could, he would get a rope and lasso the moon to make her see how much he loved her. Heavy with exhaustion, Vinny scooped the coat from the back of his chair and slung it over his shoulder. As he slowly strolled towards the exit, he pressed the redial button on his phone.

'Adam? Are you all right mate? Good…Good. Listen, we need to have a talk.'

Chapter Thirty-Six

'You need to have a housewarming, Charlotte! We'll help you shake off the cobwebs of the old place,' Audrey garbled with a mouthful of her breakfast roll. It was another Maureen special – square sausage, smoky bacon and a fried egg topper. On top of everything, she seemed to be able to eat what she wanted yet remain a well-toned size 8. *Cow.*

'Yeah!' Jim exhaled the word long and slow. 'Whit a brilliant idea, Duchess!' Charlotte found it hard not to laugh when she spotted the familiar notion of mischief prop up his caterpillar brows. 'We could have a paintin' party. Freshen the place up while we're at it.' He painted the air with an invisible brush.

Pete nodded enthusiastically, and Charlotte already knew how much he would like to warm-up her place, especially since learning her and Greg had gone their separate ways. But Pete was a treasure. Only in his mid-20's, he was one of the more discreet, gentler types of screw – sometimes to his detriment, mostly to his gain. She liked working with him; he was reliable, like a loyal puppy. Recently, she'd begun to realize his loyalty had gone far further than the professional:

Another coffee, Charlotte?

Wait! I'll walk you out to the car.

Here, my favourite film – Life is beautiful. (It just so happened to be in his boot.) *Watch it the night. You'll love it, I promise.* (And she had, crying huge fat tears, even more than her now usual huge fat tears).

Charlotte, have you watched the film yet? If so, cin I hiv it back? It belongs to my ma and she'd already routed around my room twice hunting for the bloody thing. God will the wuman ever learn! I'm moving out soon. Know whit a mean?

They're showing it at the Grosvenor next month if you fancy going?

All that matched with that longing look when he thought she wasn't watching, the big brown dopey eyes and gawping mouth? Yeah, he had it bad.

'Erm, thanks, but knowing you lot, you'd get pissed and I'd end up having my living room looking like a homage to Jackson Pollok. Once I have the place right, I'll have a wee night. Maybe even New Year? It's amazing then, especially if it's snowing. Lots of little cruise boats on the loch watching the fireworks.'

Audrey gripped her arm, the dragon tattoo breathing fire on her skin. 'Oh, that sounds amazing. Let's do it! People pay a fortune to stay there at New Year! We tried to book a lodge last year. It was booked solidly for the next four years!'

Charlotte wondered what *we* she was referring to. It certainly wasn't Ben; he'd only started at the prison in March. *All this making inferences* here *and deductions* there *is bloody tiring,* she sighed to herself as she grabbed the paper Jim had just folded in front of him.

'Yeah. I've been lucky, really. The place has been in our family for generations since it was built. I certainly wouldn't be able to afford it if it went on the market today.'

'But I bet your brother could!' Audrey snickered, then looked like if she could have caught her words in put them back in her mouth, she would have - her cheeks reddening, her shiny eyes fluttering. Just in that exact way as when you send a dodgy text message to the wrong person, just like the one she'd sent Vinny the night before which had been meant for Adam. *How you doin' knob cheese?* Charlotte had deleted the reply without looking.

She felt an icy shiver goose bump her skin. How the hell did Audrey know he was well off? *Stay calm. Find out what she knows.* 'And why's that?' she asked, flicking the newspaper over to the gossip page and taking another sip from her can of *Irn-Bru*.

Audrey began rolling her long dark har into a bun at the nape of her neck before shaking it out again. 'Well…I mean, he must be due for a fair pay-out after the stabbing.'

'I've no idea.' Charlotte tried to stare at the subheading – I BEDDED MY SON'S BEST FRIEND – NOW I'M PREGNANT. WHAT SHALL I DO? Suddenly Vinny's indiscretion seemed like a random act of kindness. She glided her finger along each word and kept her eyes on it. But she wasn't reading, she was counting. Charlotte shrugged. 'Maybe but I'm more concerned about him getting on his feet at the moment.' Licking a finger, she turned over to the puzzle page.

Given her profession, Charlotte hadn't really talked about Adam except to refer to her brother who lived overseas studying (which was partially true). The last thing she wanted was for any of the inmates to know what her brother did for a living – partly because she didn't want to be seen as the enemy. Mostly because she didn't want the prisoners barraging her with legal questions about appeals and loopholes as well as quotes for mate's rates representation. And she made a point of not telling the staff, knowing many had lips which were so loose, they'd easily sink a million cruise-liners. Audrey knew everything. It was the only explanation.

Audrey suddenly seemed very eager to focus on Riggs who, thankfully back to his normal colour, gave the morning briefing. *Another first*, Charlotte noted, a feeling of dread settling in her bones. They shared a small, wary smile before Charlotte pretended to listen to his spiel too.

She needed to get to Mr Miller, but Charlotte felt the eyes stalking her. And the thing which freaked her out most was that she didn't know by who, or how many for that matter. There would need to be a reasonable excuse to get to the office. Charlotte ran through some possibilities during lunch duty:

Reporting who threw the potato which bounced off Kev's head? *Too snitchy.*

Filling out the handover sheet for the back shift? *Kev's job but she was sure he wouldn't be bothered. But someone else might notice?*

A migraine? *Too out of character.*

Pick up a holiday request form? *I could certainly do with one!*

As she picked up another roast potato (although the word roast was debatable) from under a table, the familiar click of a cane tapped towards her.

'Charlotte, can I see you for a moment please?' His face was vacant, his mood undistinguishable.

'Of course, Sir,' Charlotte griped as she got to her feet and lobbed the greasy, white lump in a nearby bin. Her stomach squeezed tighter with each step and clack of his cane, especially when they bypassed his office and carried straight through each of the four formidable security gates until they were at the main entrance of the building. Never uttering a word, Mr Miller took a sharp right towards the management offices and admin rooms.

They stopped outside family consultation room number 3 – the finest of all 4 family consultation rooms in that the furniture was whole and matching. Mr Miller dropped his voice and put her out of her misery. 'Charlotte, some of Amos' children have dropped by unannounced and asked for you. Just luck really, they caught you on shift. I know it's not exactly…' he gazed over her shoulder then dropped his eyes to her again, 'protocol but I told them I thought you'd be happy to chat?'

'Oh!' Her hand fumbled to the garland of keys hung on her waste. 'Of course. I'd be happy to.'

Charlotte licked her lips and began to tuck her shirt neatly into her trousers (although there were no ruffles or rucks). What if they were pissed off? Wanted to go to town with the prison? Were angry at the staff for not protecting Amos?

'Charlotte,' Mr Miller said, laying his hand on her shoulder and smiling broadly. Another *we*. 'They are lovely.'

Charlotte ran her teeth over her bottom lip and gently pushed the door open, all thoughts of telling him she needed to talk forgotten.

A petite woman sat sandwiched between two beefy men on the leather sofa which looked too small for them. Charlotte immediately made the connection. In fact, she'd spent so much time with Amos, she recognized each of them from his descriptions as well as the photos he had shared with her. But it was more than that – each of them had his kind, smiling eyes and looking from one set to another, she could see there was no grievance in them. Her shoulders dunked to normal as she closed the gap. 'Hi. Tyrone?' Charlotte pointed her finger nimbly as she predicted.

'Yes,' he smiled, mildly perplexed.

Her finger skimmed along the row. 'Simone? Arthur?' Their equally surprised affirmations told Charlotte she was right. The only one missing was Perry. Amos always looked sad whenever he showed her that photo. 'Such a good boy, Miss croft. Got his life sorted, had everything to look forward to.' He'd shake his head. 'Bloody stupid boy, just like his dad.'

'I'm Charlotte. It's lovely to meet you all in person. Amos has told me lots about you.' She shook each of their hands in turn and took the chair at their side.

Simone began, her brothers flanking her with a quiet strength, but she didn't seem the type who needed it. Her tight black curls spiralled confidently from her head, and not in a Mrs Dickson kind of way; there was too much intention. Charlotte thought her skin might be made from butterscotch and her eyes treacle. It was clear to see she worked in the fashion industry; she had that certain glow about her.

'Charlotte, we all just wanted to come by and thank you in person for what you did for Dad.'

'I…I was only doing my job,' she stumbled verbally, wishing she was sitting here discussing how she was better at it, how she had saved Amos.

'We're not just talking about what happened, Charlotte,' Tyrone clarified, lifting his arm from around Simone's back, his voice so bottomless, it immediately forgave her. 'You treated Dad with respect, treated him like he was a person. He was so grateful for that, I can't even tell you.' He could have been Amos' younger self if it weren't for the impeccable stubble, cut with a razor edge and his lighter skin tone.

Tyrone was a maths teacher, Amos had told her. 'Made principal of the department, Miss Croft! My boy!'

Charlotte clenched her eyes tight and switched the phone shrieking on her belt to silent. 'I'm so…sorry for what happened.' She shook away the image which still disturbed her every time she closed her eyes. 'I tried so hard…'

A set of knuckles, misshapen and swollen through years of boxing, reached across the table and sat over Charlotte's. Amos had told her that Arthur fought a few professional bouts before an injury to his eye cut his career short. But Amos had been so proud when he opened the gym, helping kids getting off the streets and probably turning around many more lives than HMP Broadhurst had. *So kind*, she thought, *just like his dad*.

'You've nothing to apologize for,' Simone chided, the gold bangles on her wrist jangling as she waved away the notion. 'Dad liked you…a lot!'

'I liked him a lot too.' She looked to each of them. 'I hope he knew that.'

'Oh, he did Charlotte. How you brought him those large print books and the magnifying glass, chasing up hospital appointments, the prison allotment you helped him set up.' Her bangles clashed as she rhymed off the list. Then they stilled. 'But it was the way you had time for him. Spent some time every shift checking up on him and asking about his life, his family. He saw you as a friend.'

Swallowing back the impending tears, Charlotte ran her fingers along each link of the chunky chain looped to her trousers. 'I saw him as a friend too. He shouldn't have been in this bloody place.'

'But he was, and you made that a lot more bearable for him. In fact, he would tell us all the time that it was *you* who shouldn't be in this place!' Tyrone gave the same low resounding laugh as his father and Charlotte grabbed the succour that Amos was living and breathing in the three souls in front of her.

'Really? He told me just before he...' Even now, she couldn't say it. 'In fact, it was the last thing he said to me...' Placing her fingers flat against her lips, Charlotte got the irony of it then, that he had almost predicted the moment he was to leave this world.

'Well, you might know what this means as we don't.' Simone delved into her handbag before pulling out the small green velvet jewellery box. She handed it to Charlotte who rolled it around in her hand.

'What is it?' she asked, dragging her brow low.

'Dad asked us to get it for you before he died. He was *very* insistent. Said he wanted to get you a Christmas present this year for everything you had done,' Tyrone added.

Speechless, Charlotte carefully handled the small silver dove on a chain, before letting it dangle and take flight.

It took a minute or two before she even tried to explain. 'Your dad...he said doves aren't meant to be caged when he told me I wasn't meant for the prison service. I could easily have said the same about him.'

'Well, he's free now. And you?' Simone slid her head to the side and smiled, her dimples deep.

'I'm working on it,' she sniffed, twirling the dangling bird into flight with her finger. 'I'm working on it.' And she smiled because she really was this time. Charlotte had a feeling Amos knew it too. Her grin faded along with the subtlety in her voice. 'I promise we'll get to the bottom of this, if it's the last thing I do.' A shiver ran down her spine as she realized how it very well might be.

Chapter Thirty-Seven

Charlotte's heart sank to her well-worn boots when Mr Miller left just before the end of her shift, his brown leather briefcase in one hand, his *North Face* windcheater clenched in the other. *Shit*, she thought, walking away in the opposite direction like she hadn't noticed.

As soon as the first boot of the next shift stepped on to the wing, Charlotte sped to the locker room, taming her stride to a casual stroll when she noticed Audrey was already there waiting for her.

'You okay? Jim said Amos' kids popped by.' Audrey reapplied the zingy peach gloss to her lips in the mirror of her locker.

Charlotte sighed and nodded, snatching her jacket off the coat hanger. 'Yeah. It was very sad. They were lovely, though.' *Like you give a shit.*

'You know, I'm just at the end of the phone if you need to chat.' Her smile was warm and heart-felt as she locked her door, and Charlotte didn't trust it one little bit.

'I know. Thanks Audrey. I'm just so tired.' Charlotte brushed her hands over her face, partly to smooth the snarl she could feel twisting her lips. She slipped her arms into the cool sleeves of her leather, not bothering to take off her tie or free her hair like she usually did.

'Come on, Mrs,' Audrey said breezily. 'I'll walk you to the car.' *Fan-bloody-tastic.*

The place stank of stale ale and reminded Vinny of a cross between a Victorian public house and a Wild West saloon – all aged green leather and polished mahogany, the globe gas lights now fitted with bulbs instead of wicks. Apart from a few regulars, mostly ex-police who spent their retirement lamenting the buzz, the bar was empty.

'I just hope to fuck we can pull this off.' Vinny pulled his hand down his beard, knowing their hopes were tentative at best and all the planets would have to be in perfect alinement for it to work.

Rick swapped the one foot resting on the low brass bar for the other. 'We have eyes on her 24/7. I'm sure it's only a matter of time before Dolan will be putting the pressure on to get another batch into the prison.'

'But surely that's not his biggest market though? I mean, are you focusing all your attention in the wrong place?'

'No, Vinny,' he laughed. 'But you're right, it's certainly not their biggest market. What it is, is a way to test out each new batch for its potency, for side effects. The prisoners are effectively guinea pigs. If we can cut that part of the process out, it will be a lot more difficult for Dolan to roll out his product. Normal punters are getting warier to try something untested, especially with all the press coverage on how stronger it is becoming, how much more lethal it is.'

Vinny shook his head as he watched the bubbles fizz in compliant lines to the head of his pint, his mind drawn to Harry. How Harry's bloods showed a much stronger reading than someone who just snorted a couple of lines. Was that what happened to him? It was too strong? Too much for his heart to cope with?

Rick, who was downing two pints to Vinny's one, slapped Vinny lightly on the back to break his stare. 'We're the lucky ones! The kids today, it's like the jilted generation. And it's only going to get worse. I mean, they do nothing. They're bored. They don't know how to play. And I swear, most of them lack a moral compass. They're all fucking stabbing each other because they think life is an Xbox game. All living for today. Unfortunately, you can't buy a second life in the real world. But the scary thing is they don't know any different. For them, it's normal. At least for us, we were brought up, you know, climbing trees and riding bikes and lighting bags of shite to put on doorsteps.'

Rick sighed heavily and downed another quarter pint. 'Every service in the country is stretched to the max – the police, the NHS, education, mental health services. God help us in another 20 years! I just pray to God I can find a way out before then.' Rick pointed to their pints to let the bar man know to keep them coming. 'Jen, she worries, you know. We've lost a few officers lately.'

Vinny thought of Charlotte. Not that he *never not* thought of her. Or should he say (thinking back to the first day they met and correcting himself this time), he *always* thought of her. All passionate, nose wrinkled, spoon swiping. Scooping up his pint, he tried to keep pace with Rick.

Rick's phone shuddered across the Tennent's bar towel. He planted both boots on the ground and stood erect when he saw the name blaze across the screen. 'Charlotte.' He flashed it to Vinny.

An alarm jerked Vinny sober; she wouldn't call unless something was wrong. 'Put it on loudspeaker and don't mention I'm here,' he ordered.

Parked on a dark side street near the prison (which she quickly realized wasn't her brightest idea considering the car which had been parked behind her had just pulled away after picking up the lady with the high heels and black eye), Charlotte spilled out everything, her voice urgent, the words running into each other. She knew. Audrey knew. Which meant so did Dolan.

'Charlotte. Charlotte! Listen Charlotte! Even if Audrey knows, you carry on as normal. There's been a lot of coming and going to her home, a lot of phone calls. We're sure a new batch will be arriving soon.'

'But what if they know where I live?' she cried.

Vinny tensed his eyes shut and whispered, 'Fucking hell,' under his breath.

'Have you given any specifics?'

'Not really. They know I'm staying somewhere on the shores of Loch Lomond. But so are a few thousand other people,' she tried to rationalise.

'Well, that's good,' although Rick flared his blood-shot eyes to Vinny to suggest otherwise. 'As long as you keep doing what you are doing, they won't be interested in you. You're *not* a witness to anything.'

'Okay…Okay,' they heard her try to calm herself, try to steady her breathing. 'Please, Detective Coleman. Get her soon.'

'We're doing our best, Charlotte.' He pinched the bridge of his nose and sighed. 'Where are you?'

'Foundry Street. Near work.'

'Right. Wait there. I'll do a drive by. I'm in a Black BMW 5 series – registration PF66 AFQ. I'll give you a flash. Pull out in front of me and I'll follow you home.'

Despite a personal loathing of drink drivers, Vinny couldn't give a damn tonight that Rick was over the limit, not if it meant getting to her quicker.

'Okay. Thanks Detective Coleman,' she whispered, her voice halfway between relief and nothingness.

'No probs, and Charlotte?'

'Yeah?'

'Call me Rick.'

She laughed, albeit nervously, and Vinny felt it split him in two and tried to quell his thirst to rip Rick's throat out by downing his fresh pint. If it weren't for the wife and four kids who he spoke about constantly and had already told Vinny he adored more than anything, he might have.

'Okay…*Rick*,' she said, a tad more life in her voice.

'See you in 10.' He smiled and hung up. 'Come on, gypo,' Rick sang cheerily, draining the dregs. 'Might as well drop you off at the caravan while I'm there.'

Grabbing his coat, Vinny managed to grunt a thanks.

When Charlotte's indicator winked to come off the main road, Rick's headlights flashed a goodbye before zooming past. Then, there came an unadulterated darkness, the kill of her engine wiping out even the most stubborn of lurking shadows so that she faced a sheet of black. With no more than the glare from the tiny screen of her mobile, she groped her way to the black of the door.

But if Charlotte thought she'd feel safer once the door was locked securely behind her, she was wrong. As the first, long match struck to get the fire going, the thudding knock at the door caused her heart to launch to her mouth. Quickly snuffing the flame, she remained perfectly still in the darkness: wishing her granny's rocker was bigger to hide behind, wishing they would vanish, wishing it was the wind.

Three more knocks were followed by a jolly, 'Coo-wee!' and Charlotte sagged back on to the soles of her bare feet, her hand where her heart should have been.

'Coming, Mrs Dickson!' she blustered, dusting her knees as she stumbled for the door. Oh, and what a wonderful sight Mrs Dickson was. 'Come in!' Charlotte said, keen for the company.

'No dear,' Mrs Dickson said, waving her hands. 'I just wanted to give you this parcel. Arrived earlier this afternoon. Adam's friend Vincent took it in for you then asked me to pass it on. Said he couldn't do it himself?' Gazing off dreamily into the darkness, she pushed the over-sized frames up her nose and leant against the doorway. 'Oh, he's a very handsome young man. Certainly made my life a bit more interesting, having someone so lovely to look at when I'm churning the butter!'

As Charlotte battled to fit the familiar name into the wrong place, Mrs Dickson's huge lenses began to mist.

'A refreshing change from Mr Dickson and the saggy arse of his cords and elbow patches!' A flirty girly giggle made Charlotte flinch, especially since it sounded a bit off coming from someone in their 70's. Mrs Dickson elbowed Charlotte in the arm. 'See you soon, dear,' she said as she walked off tittering to herself.

Charlotte glowered at the long box of new acrylic paints in her hand, her jaw slack, still trying to work out what the hell was going on. Ever so slowly, she closed the door and teetered towards the unlit fire, all the time ogling the package, trying to work out how the *Winsor and Wallace* logo tied with *his* name. She flopped on the rocker sending a puff of dusty specks shooting into the air. *What…the…actual…fuck? Bloody Adam!*

The parcel clattered to the floor as she lurched for her mobile, punching a shaky finger on each digit like it was Adam's chest.

'Hello!' he answered, his super-chirpiness immediately confirming his guilt.

'Adam! Whit the hell hiv you done?'

'What do you mean?' he feigned innocence…badly.

'Why the fuck is Vinny staying with Mrs Dickson?'

'He's not…He's staying in the caravan that belongs to her.'

If that wasn't a technicality then she didn't know what was. *Thee* caravan Charlotte was looking at on the field next to her house. She stomped to the window in question and pulled at the curtain so hard, the pole popped from the wall and bounced off the top of her head.

'Ow! FFFFUUUUCCKKKK!' she roared. 'Why?' Charlotte rubbed

her head where she could already feel a lump forming, quite a large one given the embroidered curtains were heavier than the wrought iron pole they were hung on.

'Because…he needed a place to stay to work on the case…and…' He sighed. 'Look Charlotte. He told me what happened between you two.'

'So?' She checked her fingers for blood.

'Charlotte, I think you're taking things too far.'

The hand smacked to her side. 'Oh. Oh, well!' She began to pace, the iciness of the flags on her bare feet splintering her already jagged tone. 'Well, thank fuck it's nothin' to do with you and what you think!'

Whoa! he thought. It rarely happened, but she was reaching that meltdown point which sent even him running for cover. He was suddenly glad to be stuck at Vinny's pad. 'Would you stop being so pig-headed and just listen?'

'I think you've said enough Adam! And who's looking after you?' she accused with a snap.

He huffed loudly. 'Vinny's sister. Don't worry, she's as much as a pain in the arse as you.'

'I highly doubt that because I'm just about to become a *gigantic pain in the arse*, Adam!'

'Bloody hell! Calm down, Charlotte!' He only said it because he was nearly 500 miles away.

'How dare you Adam!' Like she was suddenly 15, she stamped her foot, her soles frustratingly quiet against the robust stone. 'Tell him to leave!'

'No Charlotte. He's doing me a favour. I feel better knowing he's near.'

Best not fill him in on recent events then, she thought, knowing she wouldn't have a leg to stand on then. She palm-slapped her head. 'I'm fine!

Will you both just let me get on with my life!'

'Charlotte, the guy loves you, though I'm not sure why…And I know you love him too.' It was ever so tempting to add, 'Because otherwise you wouldn't be acting like such a psycho!' but Adam managed to stop himself – he liked Vinny too much. The least he could do was help return the favour by trying to save his life too.

Pinching the bridge of her nose, Charlotte sucked in long, hard breaths. 'I swear tae God,' she seethed through her teeth. 'Will you just butt out?'

'I will…I promise. It's up to you two now. But the last thing I'm going to say is…just give him a chance. He was gutted when I spoke to him a few days ago. *Really* gutted. I've never seen him like that. He managed to hide all the shit with Nadia. But he couldn't hide what happened with you.'

Her eyes rolled so far and hard into the back of her head, it felt like they might wedge there. 'And the last thing I'm going to say is *no*. Now piss off…and keep doing what Vinny's sister tells you. She seems like she's got you down to a tee…and I love you.' Although she barked the declaration, she meant every word and made sure she said it to him every time she said goodbye…just in case.

'I love you too,' he growled in exasperation. 'Call you tomorrow.'

Adam hung up and typed quickly.

The gleam from the mobile irradiated his face a sci-fi green in the dark as Vinny read the message again, his stomach traversing precariously between dread and relief.

Feral cat's out of the bag mate, sorry. Take cover!

Chapter Thirty-Eight

Now that he could, he switched on the light. A sore groan followed as it lit up his semi-derelict home for the near future, painfully highlighting each damp patch, broken hinge and questionable stain. What's more, the place suddenly seemed to smell worse. *Too harsh*, he mused and switched it back off. Charlotte was going to be irate as it was without the grating light adding to it. Vinny pulled a smoke-stained string above the misted window which gave off a less severe glow. *Better*, he thought as he fetched another plastic glass to join his own from the Formica cupboard above the compact sink. He poured two large measures without even knowing if Charlotte liked whiskey. Then, he planted his hands on the thoroughly stained, stainless-steel draining board and waited.

It wasn't long before he spotted her marching up the crest of the hill, her arms swinging resolutely at her side, her wild red curls bouncing and twirling behind her. Despite the make or break severity of the situation, he began to laugh (especially when she jolted abruptly to a stop, her foot lodged in something). After she wrenched it free, she advanced with even more conviction, her chin pointed higher in the silver moonlight.

Oh, how Charlotte was looking forward to battering the door to show she meant business - her fist clenched in preparation, her nails digging painful half-moons into her palms. But, much to her disappointment, the door was wide open.

'Come in, Charlotte,' Vinny called gently from somewhere inside and she battled the sudden urge to cry because of how much she loved that voice, that voice of a traitor.

'I can't,' she yelped, her arms hooked to her hips, looking over her shoulder to the croft as she considered giving up and turning back.

'Why?' He edged towards the blackness.

'Because…I think I've stood in cow shit!' she snapped before lifting her Millet's welly to do a smell-check.

Vinny's frame filled the doorway and she looked away before he could glamour her into submission.

'Take your wellies off…,' he looked her up and down, and covered his mouth with his hand to hide a grin, 'and come in Charlotte.'

Vinny didn't dare stay to watch, afraid his closeness would send her stomping back down the hill again. It took only two strides before he began to crouch and shuffle in at the table and waited. Several fingers pressed his mouth shut as he heard her curse under her breath mixed with lots of flapping and shaking and thudding sounds as well as the odd grunt of *Fucker!* and *Get aff!*

Then, there were a few seconds of silence whilst she smoothed her hands over her bobbly black long johns (HMP Broadhurst's finest) before wrapping her bobbly, long, grey Arran knit cardigan tightly around her body like thermal armour. Although it was an attempt at composure, no amount of preening and deep breaths seemed to help. With more than a little trepidation, Charlotte trod up two flimsy steps (which she couldn't decide were metal or plastic as they seemed to be a hybrid of the two), closing the door behind her and retracing his steps across the harsh felt in her green slipper socks.

Gliding in across from him, she took a large gulp from the glass, feeling the whiskey burn a hole to her stomach. *Uuurrgggghhh!* Charlotte hated whiskey but would have drunk mouth wash at that very moment if it took the edge off. 'Vinny,' she groused without looking up. 'What the hell are you doing here?'

Vinny sucked his lips against his teeth like he had just dipped his toe in scalding bathwater. 'I could lie,' he blew softly, his knee already jiggling, 'and say it was because Adam suggested it for work. But I won't.'

The ball landed back in her court with an ear-splitting *thwack!* and Charlotte slumped against the rigid foam at her back. He wasn't even going to try to justify it? She forced her eyes up to his, the most she'd been able to look at them since before the Nadia incident, and tried to keep her voice sturdy. Tried but not quite. Gone were the designer slacks and matching t-shirt ensemble she was used to when he was lounging. Instead, he wore an old *Oxford University* hoodie with a bomber on the second 'o', his hair loose around his shoulders...and never more beautiful. 'Vinny, this is pointless. I just want to get on with my life.'

He ran his tongue quickly over his lips and bobbed his knee faster. 'Well, you see Charlotte, that's where me and you differ. You see, I don't think it is pointless...even if you do.'

'I'm not going over old ground Vinny! I think I've made myself clear enough. But I don't have the energy for this, not after today.'

'I know. I was with Rick when you called. I was in the car with him.'

The proximity was painful. 'Vinny go home. This is hard enough as it is.' Charlotte made a zombie noise as she took another mouthful. *The Walking Dead* kind of zombie.

'Charlotte. Let me just be clear.' He leaned his elbows on the tiny table, his face getting too close. 'You may have given up on me, but I haven't on you. And you were wrong, by the way.' He retreated his spine to the sponginess at his back like his words were a lunge in a round of fencing.

'How?' Charlotte was never wrong. Her nose wrinkled, and not just from the smell of what she thought was a combination of wet dog mixed with a slice of the cheese she whiffed in Vinny's fridge not so long ago. Regardless of the source, it caused Vinny's heart to nearly explode into a million pieces because he missed watching her nose wrinkle like that. How could the wrinkle of a nose nearly cripple a man useless?

Feeling the need to move more than his knee, he began waving his whiskey in hoops in the air, his index finger erect and drawing attention to each point like he was in court. 'What you saw was a *snippet*. Yet you, with all your *artistic* observations of life, you took it and made it *forever*. That's not fair Charlotte.'

From the tongue flicking against the back of her teeth, he could see he was really pressing her buttons now. But it was the truth. His truth. And she needed to know it.

Charlotte pulled her mouth to the side and stretched her arm across the patterned cushion. It felt damp. Smelt it too. She pulled it back and wiped her hand down her thigh. Now her eyes shrivelled. 'Yet, I could never do what you did?'

With gritted teeth, Vinny pulled his hair back, tying it roughly with a band from around his wrist. *Trying to get some control*, Charlotte assumed.

'Well, obviously, you're a far better person than me then. You win. You're the best. I'm still not going. I'm still not giving up,' he retorted, his eyes inflating with every *you* and *I* before he finished with a tenacious shrug of the shoulders.

It was the shrug which did it, took her to that level which would need a bomb disposal expert to defuse. 'Good for you! Does that not make you better than me then? *You* win. *You're* the best.' She raised her glass and forced another mouthful, before thumping it on the table only for it to give an unsatisfying, empty *clunk!* As the notion grew to hit something tonight (something hard enough to make a very loud crash, something to transfer her fury into), she began to shuffle out in case it was the man sitting across from her.

Well, it wasn't going *exactly* as he had planned. 'Charlotte, wait!' A desperate hand stretched out to clutch her again, to possess what felt like his. But thinking better of it, he slowly lowered it to the base of his glass again. 'The last thing I want to do is stress you more or upset you. I need a place to work coming up to the trial. And no matter how you like to pretend otherwise, I think you need someone here until all this is over. When the trial is over, and if I haven't changed your mind about us, then I'll go. No questions asked.' *Over my dead body,* he thought but was willing to say he was born a woman if it bought him some time.

Stilling, she gazed across at him. Gone were the parallel lines and perpendicular arrangements of London. Instead, his work and laptop were scattered shambolically across the padded bench beside him, his face drawn and dull. It caused her resolve to waver a fraction. Half a fraction. A tenth maybe. Perhaps she would feel safer knowing he was close…just in case. But that was *it.* Nothing more, nothing less. 'Fine,' she groaned, 'but I don't need to be looked after Vinny. I've looked after myself long enough.'

'Agreed.' He said it instantly, raising his palms. 'You won't even know I'm here.'

Somehow, Charlotte very much doubted that since he was at the very top of her frets list and in clear view from her bloody window. 'Okay,' she shrugged like she wasn't bothered. The word *whatever* danced on her tongue, but she knew it would make her look even more petty and weaker in this battle of the wills. 'Stay then. But please – no expectations as I'm promising *nothin'.*'

Vinny nodded his head. It was a million times more than she was promising 10 minutes beforehand. But more than anything, it was a start.

Chapter Thirty-Nine

Audrey looked at the assortment in front of her. All the carefully wrapped and bagged batches reminded her of a partaking adult's fantasy pick and mix stall: crack cocaine, cannabis, heroin and a shitload of Spice. She knew the drill well enough by now. She had spent a good hour painstakingly picking apart the two juice cartons; she found *Tropicana* was her favourite as the edges didn't baggy or stretch and looked perfect when they were all glued back together.

She packed each carton like an OCD packs their suitcase: everything fitting perfectly together, neat and tidy. When the full batch was snuggly in, she glided her *Loctite* super glue (the strongest kind) along the perimeter, the tip of her tongue poking out in concentration. By the time she was finished, they would have easily passed quality control on the factory line: the silver seal unpunctured, the cellophane wrapped stripy straw still glued safely to the back, the edges perfectly aligned.

In her blue disposable gloves, she wiped every square millimetre with a series of *Dettol* wipes before sitting them on a single square of her *Blitz* kitchen roll on the worktop. She ran her eyes over each carton one more time, careful not to touch. Only when she was completely satisfied, did she carefully roll off each glove and discard them into the brown paper bag on the table (along with every other clue and piece of evidence of what she had just done).

She ran her dusty hands (covered in the powdery residue from the gloves) under the tap. Just the day before, Audrey had learnt on the BBC news channel (you know, the bit when they try to lighten the mood between the doom and gloom) that your hands are only fully clean when you soap and scrub for a full rendition of *Happy Birthday*. By the time she was finished, she had sung *Happy Birthday* 4 times and her hands were red raw.

Even the kitchen roll she dried her hands on joined the bag in the table. She lifted the tongs from the cutlery drawer and lifted the bag like it was a particularly smelly sock. With her free hand, she opened the back door and lifted the lid of the kettle drum BBQ. Dropping the bag on the grill, she reached to the shelve underneath and squirted the potent fluid over the bag until it looked soggy. She then struck a long match and stood back before the flames licked her eyebrows. When they settled down to a steady roar, she placed the lid on and went back inside.

'That's the last time,' she promised herself as she filled a glass of water to take to bed. Before tonight, there would never be a last time. She was trapped. He had her exactly where he needed her, and no-one, not even Ben, could save her from that.

When they first met, she felt as though Dolan had saved her. Saved her from her drunken dad and terrified mother who had long-since chosen to hang out the washing or walk to the corner shop for another pint of milk instead of protecting her. At only 16, he was her salvation. Plucked her away from the chaos. Set her up in her own little place: clean, modern, food in the fridge, electricity in the black. Financed and supported her through college where, much to her own surprise, she realized she was smart and had 5 glowing A levels to show for it. And she loved him, the way fragile teenage hearts love – completely. He was her protector, her lover, her everything. Or so she thought. Now she knew what he really was: a groomer, an exploiter, a monster. If only she could go back and have a word with her younger self and scream at her to escape. If only…

By the time he had her where he wanted her, she was happy to be part of it. Happy to help the man who had saved her. It was the least she could do. She didn't even mind that he had a wife and kids. In fact, she understood – that he had to stay with her until the kids were grown up and independent. His wife was such a bitch; he *had* to stay for their sakes. And what was the harm in helping him portion up the batches of cannabis? He was only supplying it to a few close friends…and it was a harmless drug after all, far less harmful than alcohol.

She had shared her visions to go to university to pursue her dream career in nursing; that would really show her dad how far she had come. Maybe he would even be proud? Still, he had persuaded her otherwise. 'Think of it – all those years of study for a shitty paid job where you'll be frazzled to a crisp. The pension is shit too. Anyway, everyone has a degree these days. You'd be as well joining something like the police or the prison service. The pensions are great and you're still helping people.' Talk about gullible – she joined the prison service the day after she left college.

But as the years went by, and his business grew, his requests became more…demanding. The first time she dared question his intentions, it was much to her own regret. He wanted her to get 'friendly' with a potential new supplier. She was a perk. It took 4 months for her jaw to knit together and she still felt the pain all these years later, particularly on cold days or when she laughed in a carefree fashion (which was rare). She regularly prostituted herself after that. There was no choice. She was in too deep.

And here she was, 10 years later, in the worst scenario of catch 22 there could be. Firstly, she was up to her neck in it. Supplying drugs, abusing her position of trust: they would lock her up and throw away the key (which seemed like an appealing option compared to what else was on the table). Secondly, she couldn't tell. For who was there to tell? The police (she was more than positive there was at least a couple of Audreys in the service). He would have her weighted down under a bolder at the bottom of the Clyde before she'd even made it home from giving a statement.

She could try to run away. But she'd done that before. And now that his home run business had grown to a multi-million-pound organization, he seemed to have eyes and ears everywhere. On everyone. Audrey only managed to look at the noticeboard at Glasgow Central before one of his thugs was at her side. Thankfully, he bought her story that she was only jumping on the train to the nearby town of Paisley for a bit of Christmas shopping.

'Make sure you tell me next time,' was the stark warning when she was summoned back home.

'God, sue me for trying to be romantic and get you that bloody leather coat you wanted,' she sulked, her heart clapping in her chest.

He softened then. 'Sorry, babe.'

She cried a bit when he hugged her. He thought it was for love. It was because her plan had failed.

And on top of everything, there was Ben. She'd been instructed to get to know him…well. And she had. But what she hadn't bargained for, was falling for him. Of all the people she was instructed to 'get to know', he was the only one she wanted to spend the rest of her life with. He never did let on about what he was doing, and he certainly didn't seem to suspect her. When she was asked for updates, she would do her best to protect him. 'He hasn't got a clue,' she would sneer. 'He's totally barking up the wrong tree. I've seen him snooping around the usual suspect's cells, sniffing for info. He has nothing.' It appeased the powers that be that he was harmless but put the pressure on her to continue to bring more shit into the prison.

She knew the net was closing in, especially after Amos' death. It had robbed her sleep and wracked her soul and she held herself fully responsible. All that on top of Charlotte. She liked Charlotte a lot. Her one and only friend, well, the only one she was allowed as it stayed within working hours. She didn't know how many times she had had to clamp her drunken mouth on the rare work's nights out she was permitted to attend. She did have to keep up appearances after all. Couldn't have her looking like a lone wolf as they needed her above suspicion. For some reason, Charlotte was the one person she wanted to tell. Knew she could tell without being judged and persecuted. But it would only bring Charlotte down with her.

She thought of Charlotte's face when she dropped her faux pas earlier that day. Part of Audrey's mind knew she had done it on purpose. Not as a threat as Charlotte had thought, but as a warning. A warning of what was coming. A way of trying to help her, to get her prepared. It backfired like everything else she'd tried. But like she tried to protect Ben, she had fed back that Charlotte was oblivious to everything, thought her brother's attack was a random act of violence. Was no more a danger than any other prison officer.

Sighing, she propped a creamy envelop in front of each of the cartons – one with Charlotte's name written beautifully across it in her bestest writing, the other with Ben's.

'Definitely the last time,' Audrey whispered as she turned off the lights, knowing, for the first time in years, she would sleep well.

Chapter Forty

'Fuck me!' Vinny cursed as he battered his elbow on the flimsy plastic panel for the fourth time. 'Showering in a coffin is probably easier than this,' he muttered, a piss stream of tepid water doing sod all to rinse the suds from his tall, athletic frame. After several more unsteady rotations, he knew it was the best he was going to get and grabbed for the towel which was only a few notches up from a threadbare dish cloth.

'Fucking hell,' he growled, grabbing another which looked like it had been set about by a bunch of angry moths. 'Oh, for the love of God!' Now his voice soared to a roar as the plastic panels reverberated, his green eye scrunched tightly by the sting of soap.

No matter how many times he ran the coarse excuse for a towel around his body, he didn't seem to dry, only move the water around the surface of his skin. So, he gave up on the notion and forced on the fresh shirt and trousers over his goose-bumped, damp body. When the clothes had unstuck enough to be tugged into place, he made himself a strong pot of coffee and opened the blinds.

The first thing he noticed, was that Charlotte's bedroom window emitted a warm radiance in the fading darkness and he felt disproportionately buoyant that she was awake, and by just knowing she was close, under the same purple sky as him. A piece of the knot which had been strangling his insides since she left gave a little.

The second thing he noticed was the unadulterated silence. He listened intently for a moment, just to make sure, then slid into his

Balenciaga shoes and shouldered open the frosted door to get closer to it. It only grew louder. With a wafting coffee in his hand, he ambled out to meet the dawn head on, keeping his shoes clean suddenly extraneous. The loch was so still it looked like it had iced to glass, a perfect mirror to the broken puffs of cloud and violet, peach hues of the stirring sun. The hills stood protectively in the background, green velvet draped in amethyst heather, sheltering the treasure in front of them, a wispy layer of mist lazing below each peak.

In that very moment, Vinny got it. Got what it was that Charlotte saw in the world, where she found her joy, and what stunned him most, he appeared to have found it too. His soul moved to somewhere it had never been before – insignificance. His insignificance compared to what lay before him, to what was permanent. It seemed a given, that he would always be a city man forever, feeding off the perpetual hum and obedient anarchy. But standing here, all he wanted was to waken up to this every day, at her side, forever. Nothing more. Nothing less. Complete and utter fulfilment. The realization took his breath away.

Sucking in the panorama, his eyes wandered back to the croft where the downstairs lights were now on. And there she was - standing on a chair trying to put up the curtains. She appeared to have succeeded until she drew the curtain open, sending the whole thing hurtling towards her head again.

Stepping off the chair, she glared at the floor, her hands on her hips, mumbling so angrily, Vinny could almost see the asterixis and exclamations form in a speech bubble aside her gathered lips. Chest ballooned, she looked up, only for it to deflate in a mighty puff when she saw Vinny stifling a laugh on the field above her. He ventured a small wave. She, with less apprehension, gave a two-fingered salute, causing him to free the laugh caught in his throat. But he was sure he could see the beginning of a frustrated smile soften her lips.

It was enough for him to risk a call, he decided, pulling the mobile from his pocket and dialling her.

'Morning, grumpy.'

'What do you want Vinny?' Already sounding on the wrong side of pissed-off, he watched her pick up the pole and toss it on a chair.

'A favour.' He clenched one eye shut, the one which was still lightly blood-shot.

'What?' Charlotte snapped, feeling it strange to have a phone call with someone she could see at the same time. Bizarrely, she couldn't decide if it made him feel nearer or further away.

'I'm picking up my hire car later, but can you give me a lift to work? Please? Pretty please?'

There was a moments silence as she battled not to match his light-heartedness as he attempted to edge another inch into her life. 'Well, I need to leave at seven then,' she barked, like she was somehow in charge.

He used his fingers in a more positive manner by hitching up a thumb. 'That's brilliant. Thank you.'

'Fine!'

They drove in a spikey silence, Charlotte keeping her eyes firmly on the road as if trying to convince herself he wasn't even in the car.

'Hm,' Vinny exhaled approvingly, breaking her trance and the road line back into separate white strips. 'I never knew you liked Prince.'

'Oh, was the *Purple Rain* t-shirt I wore most of the time in London not a big enough clue?'

He dared a glance. 'I thought it was you being all retro and arty.'

'Well,' she sniped, still unable to meet his gaze, 'I guess there's a lot you don't know about me.'

Vinny sighed quietly, averting his gaze out the window where the solitary silhouette of a bird hovered over its prey against a cloudless sky which had warmed to the colour of distant fire, the jagged forest treetops mere charcoal against its flare. Although controlled and disciplined, there was a certain ruthlessness as the bird dove down to the darkness.

Another pang of guilt hit, and Charlotte grimaced. Being rude certainly didn't sit well with her, no matter how justified the cause. Lightly stroking a finger over a brow, her following words were cordially forced. 'I don't like Prince…I *love* Prince. I think I'll be mourning him forever.'

Shuffling up slightly in his seat, Vinny grasped on to the olive branch with both hands. 'Yeah. He was an amazing musician. Did you ever get the chance to see him live?' His voice shuffled up too.

But her words still held a certain air of obligation. 'Seven times.'

Yet, as he studied her face, smug and passionate, he knew he'd found a way in.

'Seven times, eh? I met him once.' He turned away and, with his chin held high, waited for the wick to burn down to the dynamite.

This time, it was her head which quickly flicked to his then back to the road. She performed a re-take before accusing, 'No, you haven't!'

Vinny would have bet his law firm that her nose was really wrinkled now, but he kept his face straight and continued to trawl through the 17 emails which had been sent overnight.

'Yes, I did. It was on his *Hit and Run* tour in Camden. Our firm got backstage passes. They sorted out all the legalities for the event.'

A flare of incense ran from the toes she pumped sharply on the peddles as she jerked and tugged up to 5th gear, to her head which shook to let it escape. 'Shame.'

'What?' he asked innocently, clicking his home button as he gave up on the idea of being prepared before he hit the office. This was far more important not to mention entertaining.

Be cool, she warned herself as she shrugged lightly, checking her blind spot and flooring the pedal to overtake the leisurely Micra in front. Normally, Charlotte would have been quite satisfied to remain behind and complete the rest of her journey at a slower pace. Today, however, compelled a particular kind of rashness if it meant shortening the journey in any way possible. 'Shame it wasn't used on a fan who would have wet their knickers for the experience.'

'Oh!' He placed his hand on the dash as the car swerved back into the left-hand lane. 'I'm sorry my firm gave me a ticket to see a great show. I should have stood outside and given it to someone worthier.'

'Exactly.'

Vinny felt the familiar smirk back where it belonged, as well as the urge to push her buttons more, craving any sort of reaction other than silence. 'Well, I don't really see what all the fuss was about anyway. I mean, it was a great show, but definitely not my best,' he lied. It was his absolute best gig…ever.

Charlotte clicked her tongue on the roof of her mouth before sniggering, 'No Vinny, *you* wouldn't get it. That's why you should've given your ticket away - to make someone else's dream come true, to give someone their experience of a lifetime.'

He straightened the purple daisy in its holder, an almost inaudible mumble informing her, 'I would have given it to you.'

'Vinny!' she warned.

'Sorry,' he muttered. *Too soon*. But at least they were having a relatively normal conversation. He breathed slowly and tried to reassure himself that it was progress.

In the same breath, Charlotte gritted her teeth, knowing she was losing the battle. But he was a fool if he didn't know she had no intention of losing the war.

A buzz from Vinny's phone broke the deadlock. 'Rick,' he said, all remnants of humour evaporating in a second. 'Hi Rick,' he answered on loudspeaker.

'Where are you?' Rick asked, the background windy and echoing of the outdoors.

'I'm with Charlotte. She's dropping me off before she goes to work.'

'Good. I'm glad I've got you both.'

They looked uneasily at each other and Charlotte silently thanked God that Adam had been sneaky enough to house Vinny in the caravan next to her home.

'We have one Audrey Merrishaw in custody. Picked her up on the way into work this morning loaded with a fresh batch of goodies. Looks like we got to her just in time.'

'What do you mean?' Charlotte cried.

'I don't think she was planning on doing it again. *Ever*, if you catch my drift. We found two letters in her rucksack.' There was a brief pause as a noisy gust whistled over the speaker. 'Charlotte, one of them is for you.'

As soon as the words were out, Charlotte veered into the lay-by, jumped from the car and emptied the contents of her breakfast on to the roadside. Vinny held her hair back.

Chapter Forty-One

'That's weird,' Jim said as he turned back from the notice board, a full half of his moustache hooked an inch higher than the other. 'The Duchess never mentioned to you she wouldn't be in?'

As Jim continued to pull hard at the side of his moustache, Charlotte could see the beads of sweat pepper his brow. Perhaps it was because the others were playing Pontoon for 20p's. It was only last year he sought help for his addiction after racking up a crazy debt at the *Grosvenor Casino*. He'd handled the notion of divorce harder than most. There had been zero jokes and pranks for a while, and although he seemed back on form now, who knew what he was really thinking? *Bloody idiots should have known better*, she sighed inwardly, imagining it was like someone lighting a cig in front of someone with 17 nicotine patches stuck around their trunk. Then she watched as he took a sip of tea and swirled it around his mouth like it were Listerine. It took him a whole 15 seconds to swallow it. Quite a long time if you try it (which I bet you are).

'Fuckin' hell. We're no married, Jim! I was out with the boys last night. You know as much as me.' Ben bulged his eyes but kept them fixed on the two cards in his hand (which he continued to ogle, suddenly unable to add to 21).

'So?' Pete snapped, losing his patience for once. 'Stick or twist?'

'Eh…twist.' He slammed the cards face down on the table when he was dealt the King of Diamonds. 'Bastard!'

Charlotte said nothing, just tapped her foot along to, rather coincidentally she thought, *Suspicious Minds* as it played quietly over the canteen radio.

After what felt like the longest 9 hours in history, Charlotte raced to her car. As soon as the door was locked, she switched her phone to handsfree and called Vinny.

'Hi. Do you need a lift?' In complete contrast to that morning, there was a breathy keenness to her voice.

'No, it's fine. The car was dropped off earlier but thanks for asking.'

Flashing her lights to allow a car into her line of traffic which was queued bumper to bumper to get on the motorway, Charlotte flopped her head back on the rest. 'Vinny, what happened? I've felt ill all day.'

'It's good news. I'm just leaving now. Can I drop by and fill you in?'

'Yeah. You won't be long behind me, will you?' She checked her rear-view mirror again.

'No, I promise.'

And he kept his promise. Charlotte had just showered and was brushing her hair in the blemished mirror atop the kidney-shaped dressing table when she spotted what looked like a black tank pull up at the caravan. Bypassing his new rust-bucket residence, Vinny made his way right down the chipped path to the croft in slackened, stretched strides, his laptop bag slung lazily across his chest, his shoulders hunched.

Quickly grabbing her cardigan from the back of the bedroom door, Charlotte scuttled down the stairs and loitered in the doorway as his steps crunched closer, each chomp abating her fear a little more. Finally, he appeared, looking more exhausted than she'd ever seen before: his eyes heavy with shadows, his movements slow and sluggish. The instinct to hold him, to tell him how much she loved him too, became overwhelming. Yet she couldn't. *Wouldn't.*

'Hi,' she said, tying the belt of the cardigan tightly around her middle. 'Come in.'

A small, tired smile graced his face as he stooped below the door frame, his eyes growing as they skimmed the room. 'God, Charlotte. It's absolutely charming.'

Nothing matched – not one chair or swatch of fabric. No two lamps the same, no two picture frames. Yet it worked. It was in complete contrast to his Notting Hill home where everything was so angular and streamlined and coordinated that it caused stress if the sofa had strayed an inch in the wrong direction. His home, his *life* was cold. Somewhere along the line, Nadia's efforts to keep the place perfect (not with her own hands of course) took all the comfort from it. His efforts too if he were being truthful. The comfort *was* the technical wizardry, the convenience – the underfloor heating, the spa shower which blitzed you from 20 nozzles (he shuddered when he thought of that morning), the integrated media system which could control everything with the recognition of his voice, the hidden wardrobes and hypo-allergic air filtration system. But this place was so cosy, warmed the soul. Made you want to curl up under a blanket, light the fire and stay there forever without worrying if you accidently set a foot on and flattened the perfectly erect nap of the thick shag-pile rug before 9pm. He suddenly remembered what comfort really was.

'Thanks.' Her eyes fell as her hands smoothed along the back of the bald-patched, velour settee. 'You want a drink?'

Vinny suspected that it was only her fear which had let him over the threshold. But he'd take it. 'What've you got?' he asked as he hooked his coat and bag on the stand.

'Wine?' Charlotte fiddled with the dove at her chest and shrugged. 'Probably cheap and nasty but I like it.'

Although he knew there was no ill intent, a crushing fatigue caused him to scowl a little that she was still having the snob digs. 'Like you said Charlotte, I don't give a shit as long as it's wet.' An icy bite of cold seeped through his thin grey shirt and he gasped, 'Bleedin' hell, it's freezing in here. Do you have any firewood?'

'Yyyeeeaaah,' Charlotte's voice wrenched as, with her back to him (and her teeth clenched), she began unscrewing the top of the wine cap knowing he would normally only consume the corked variety. 'Just...out...side.'

Directly in front of the miniature doorway (which he nearly headed again on the way out) was an axe imbedded in a hefty log topping a heap of hefty logs and he raised an eyebrow. *Well, this is new*, he thought to himself, rolling up his sleeves. Planting his foot on the log, he heaved and prised until the axe was free. 'Bloody hell,' he panted, already feeling a lot warmer and thinking there must be an easier way to fuel the fire. He spread his legs and spread his hands to the neck and the base before hitching the axe over his shoulder. With a final wary look at the log, which warned, *Don't you dare move*, he brought the axe down with all his strength, breaking it cleanly in two. 'Ha!' A small laugh of victory escaped. But what really got to him was - it felt good. *Really* good. Even better than when he had to use a punchbag in the boxing club after a tough day. He lined up another log, then another. But just as he was really getting into the swing of it, the door rasped behind him.

'Vinny! Vinny! VINNY! What are you doing?' Charlotte cried although she was still reluctant to stop what looked like a scene from a *Diet Coke* ad.

Lowering the head of the axe, Vinny wiped his brow and pointed out the obvious. 'Getting firewood,' he puffed breathlessly.

'Vinny, that's for decoration! There's of bag of firewood there. It's already chopped.' A stern finger pointed to a bulging hessian sack at the foot of the door.

Suddenly feeling like a tosser again, he looked from one pile to another and Charlotte rolled her eyes and walked back inside.

Using the cuff of her cardigan to buff away any smears, she turned to give him the drink, the letter already in his hand. A tad awkwardly (with too many fingers and thumbs), they swapped, and Charlotte lowered beside him on the sofa, glad to feel his warmth once more (and he was *really* warm after all the chopping). The letter tapped rapidly against her thigh.

'So?' She looked up to him, not quite ready to read the contents yet.

He watched some residual droplets fall from her wet hair and streak down her face, wanting nothing more than to wipe them away. That, and the events of the day, caused Vinny to shake his head as he tried to jiggle his thoughts into order. 'She talked. Told us everything. Is willing to stand witness against him as long as we guarantee her witness protection.'

'Why? She's just as guilty as he is!' Her top lip warped, and the letter stilled in her hand.

Both his eyebrows shot up his forehead and stayed there. 'No, Charlotte. No, she isn't.'

'What do you mean?' Charlotte's, on the other hand, sunk like dead-weights.

'That bastard!' Vinny growled and leant forward, his fists clenching and unclenching like they were around Dolan's neck. 'He groomed her from when she was practically a kid. It's one of the worst cases of exploitation I've ever seen. She's been his slave for the last decade. Seen the hospital records to prove it.'

'Jesus Christ,' Charlotte gasped and stared out blankly towards the inky blackness of the loch.

Trying to drown out the echo of earlier, Vinny took down a mouthful of the harsh wine (which he thought tasted very similar to the *Tokaji Aszu* red-wine vinegar he used in his beef stifado) yet he could still hear the poor girl's sobs as her story unfurled. He closed his eyes as he spoke, trying not to see her tears either. 'Although she's the one who was bringing the stuff in, she was in too deep. She had no choice. I've no doubt he would have killed her.'

A few seconds passed before Charlotte groaned, 'My God.' Her face fell into her hands, the urge to scream overpowering all her other thoughts. To just run out to the jetty and scream. Scream at how her amazing, beautiful world had turned so ugly. Never leaving the croft again was becoming more tempting by the second. Yeah, hermitism suddenly seemed a very appealing life-style choice.

A hand poised to place on the back of her neck, Vinny hesitated, afraid she would reject it, shrug it off like he had a bad dose of the clap. But when he watched her shoulders sag further as she tried to make herself more ball-like, he didn't care if it was a step too far. What she felt, he felt. More than anything, he wanted to take away her pain (especially the part caused by him). *Fuck it,* he thought and carried through with the gesture, an ache somewhere in his gut dissipating as soon as he made contact with her skin. That milky skin which he had kissed and touched and stroked. He held his breath, but she never recoiled or shook him off. With her hands still glued to her face, her head rolled to his shoulder. Ever so slowly, he leaned back with his arm around her, but not the same as before; a certain level of stiffness remained as he tested the parameters of what level of contact was reasonable.

Seemingly hitting the right balance, they sat there for a while, just being close, each afraid of what it meant. Giving in or giving up? Rejection or acceptance? Now Vinny wanted to scream. But he spoke softly when he added, 'Charlotte, you should read the letter. It explains it all. It's a goodbye…and a sorry.'

'I know. In a minute,' she said, savouring his smell like her personal comfort blanket.

By the time she put down the letter, her eyes were blurry and her nose streaming. 'She was trying to warn me,' she sniffed, her woolly sleeve wiping away her tears as far as her neck.

'Yeah,' Vinny confirmed with a dry whisper.

Drawing another shaky breath, Charlotte folded the letter gently, careful to keep the same seems, and placed it back in its envelope. She slid it across the table but kept one finger attached as if Audrey might be able to feel it, might feel her regret that she'd gotten it so wrong. Wasn't it perhaps becoming a bit of a habit lately? 'Will she be okay?'

'She's safe now. Straight on a witness protection program.'

Charlotte nodded slowly and gazed at the familiar handwriting, soft and bubbly, just like Audrey. 'Vinny?'

'Yeah?' He eyed her warily, his stomach plummeting as he prepared for his marching orders, and it felt all the more painful after the silent permission to touch her. So close, so far.

'Is it really all over with Nadia?'

The curve-ball question silenced him for a moment. 'Absolutely.'

If everyone else is confessing, might as well too, she thought, feeling like she had nothing to lose. Keeping her eyes on the letter as her finger shuffled it from side to side, she whispered, 'Because I don't want you to go to the caravan tonight. I don't want to spend another second being away from you. But you hurt me. I need to know you won't do it again. And I'm scared.' She turned to him and shrugged, the energy to fight him gone.

There was too much bad. And she knew deep down, he was her good. At least with all the efforts he'd gone to, he wanted to be. 'I'm scared of you. Because, believe it or not Vinny Knight, I love you too.'

There was no hesitation this time as he reclaimed her. 'Charlotte,' he said softly, leaning forward and tipping her chin up to face him. 'I love you with all my heart. Always have. Always will. I don't want to be anywhere, except here with you.' His heart felt like it was melting in his chest as he slid his eyes over her face – her wide, glistening blue eyes, a dusting of fawn freckles, her plump lips. His.

'And we'll take it slow?'

'As slow as you need.'

'Good,' Charlotte said, standing abruptly and walking away, his hands still holding on to the air where she'd just been. As he watched her go, his stomach shrivelled to the size of a walnut. She trundled up the first few steps before turning back. 'Come on, then. I didn't mean that slow. Bring the wine.'

He was up the stairs before she was.

Chapter Forty-Two

Vinny watched her sleep as the early throngs of dawn thawed the room, her head on his chest, her arm slung across his stomach, her breath warm and soft against him. His whole world literally in his arms.

Everything was moving in the right direction with the case. Hopefully all plain sailing from now on. He'd mostly told her everything, except for his fears. That the fact Audrey was safe and willing to testify would mean Dolan would become more desperate. More likely to make rash decisions. And although no-one involved in the case knew they were together (except for Adam and perhaps Rick), he knew he would have to keep it that way. Vinny was sure there would be no interest in Charlotte, but if anyone started making the connections between Charlotte and Adam and him, then that would change the stakes in an instant. That was a far more tempting prospect. The last thing he wanted was to scare her, but he thought again and again about what happened to Adam and the starkest of warnings it brought. Although he was there to keep her safe, his presence might be the very thing which was putting her in danger.

Charlotte stirred and stretched against him, and he tenderly swept her hair from her face: gently enough not to waken her, deliberate enough to let her know he was awake. The toasty hand which clenched his hip was coupled by a drowsy yawn.

'Morning,' she said, squeaky and tired.

'Morning,' he returned, shuffling down and burying himself deeper against her.

Charlotte giggled croakily, letting him rub his face against her like a dog claiming the puppy which was theirs.

'Let's have a sicky today,' he suggested coming up for air from under several blankets which were topped with a fleecy pale blue throw and some sort of rose-pink blanket thing which Charlotte said was called a candlewick?

'I don't have to.' She stretched her arms free then quickly snapped them back under with a yelp. 'It's my day off.'

'Well, then,' he said leaning over to his phone and switching off the alarm, 'we have a lot of time to make up for, young lady.' He wiggled his brows before tugging the blankets and the fleece and the candlewick over their heads.

The daylight was bright and pure, and the space beside him was cold. After a few moments just listening, he began to feel uneasy of this silence: there was no background muffle of TV voices, no deep bass of a Prince hit, no clanging of flowery china tea cups or whistling kettles, no rocker grinding back and forth across the cold flags. 'Charlotte?' he yelled, and when the silence stretched, he hauled himself up quickly and threw on his crumpled custom-made trousers. He could almost hear his tailor Giles have a seizure at how he had just kicked them off on a pile on the floor. Not so long ago, so would he.

As Vinny spun in circles tugging on a resistant sock, he spotted her from the window which was perspiring with drips of condensation across the bottom – on the inside? Vinny smeared a finger across to check, the squeak letting him know - on the inside. Rubbing his fingers dry, he gazed at Charlotte who was perched at the end of the jetty: a sketchbook in her hand, a cute dark green bobble hat on her head. He planted his foot (the sock still only half-way on) and smiled.

His feet crunched in sizzles along the frosted wood in long, relaxed steps, a hot coffee in each hand, a blanket slung across his shoulder. She knew it was him, a smile taking hold without even looking up from the page.

'Hello,' she cheeped, turning the book from portrait to landscape.

'Hello, yourself,' he rumbled hoarsely. 'Here.' He saved the only unchipped mug for her.

'Oh, ta.' She put down the pad and let him wrap his legs and the blanket around her.

'What an amazing way to waken up,' he said, his words heavy with awe.

'I know. And, at this time of year, it's even more beautiful. Most people like the summer best or when the trees are swathed in a blanket of snow. But for me, it's the transitions between each which is most beautiful. Watching the summer die and the trees turn to burnt amber and deep reds and rose golds. The smell of smouldering oak and pinecones. The mist floating dreamily above the water. And then to watch it all resurrect with fresh new life in Spring – new blooms and perfumes. It feels... like hope,' she mused, taking a sip from the mug she held in green fingerless gloves which matched her hat.

God, he did not think it possible his heart could love any more. It hurt, physically hurt. A dull ache ground in his stomach when he thought of how much he loved her. 'I could stay here forever,' he thought quietly aloud.

'Maybe you will,' she whispered distractedly as an osprey swooped over the evergreen spruces on the other side of the loch, it's piercing cry echoing across to fill the expanse. The only sound to accompany it was the water lapping gently against the rocks which littered the pebbled shoreline.

He tightened his grip on her. 'I thought you said we needed to take things slow?'

Her head rocked on his shoulder. 'But…you've got me now…and after everything, I can't be arsed playing games. Life is too short. If you break my heart, you break my heart. I'll take the risk. And if it doesn't work out, at least I could say that I had experienced that kind of love…and have enough heartache to inspire a whole lifetime of work.'

Vinny laughed softly. 'Charlotte, if you let me, I promise to spend my life never breaking your heart. I'll…I'll make sure your holey slippers are lined up at the side of the bed in the morning and when your ugly green sock things are frayed bare, I'll make sure there is a new ugly green pair waiting for you. I'll never throw away any left-over kebabs again and I will shun all social media.' (Besides, he'd not been on it in days anyway because there was no signal and it felt liberating). 'I'll make you that coffee how you like it all frothy every morning but before then, I'll do that thing you like when I give you stubble rash inside your thi…'

'Vinny!'

'I will! Every day. I won't expect anything back in return either! Well…maybe once in a while it would be nice if you do that thing you do, you know, with your tongue and my…'

'Vinny! Stop!' Charlotte cried as her cheeks flamed at the very thought and a dull ache made her want to go back to bed with him immediately to do the things he'd just been talking about.

When he stopped laughing, he slid her to the side so he could see her face, all ruddy from the cold and embarrassment. 'If you give me the chance, I'll never leave you…or here for that matter.'

He watched the little lines pucker between her brows. 'But what would you do? For work, I mean, you know…if everything worked out and…you wanted to stay?'

Vinny thought it was very sweet how she factored an aspect of possibility into what he knew was certain. His bottom lip protruded as if in ponder. 'I'll set up office in the caravan,' he said, adding a single nod of *well, that's that sorted.*

'Yeah right!' Charlotte scoffed, turning her head forwards and wiggling her toes in her wellies.

'What?' He looked down, but she stared forwards. 'It has a meeting area with lovely stained beige velour swirly patterned seats. It has reasonable catering facilities, you know, a minifridge and a single gas-burning hob, not to mention, the perfectly functioning chemical toilette facilities. It has everything really.'

Nodding in agreement, Charlotte decided to play along. 'Maybe Mrs Dickson could be your legal secretary? You could set her up with a desk in the awning. She fancies you rotten.'

'No, she doesn't.' The words vibrated against her back.

'Eh, aye she does! When she told me you were here, she practically had to wipe the drool from her chin. She was rubbing her hands up and down her thighs like she had a burning in her loins or something!'

Vinny's chin dropped as he checked if she was serious. 'Ew! Charlotte Croft! You have a dirty mind! She's a perfectly charming granny, that's all!'

'Okay, okay. You wait n'see.'

Vinny squeezed his eyes shut. 'Please don't say any more Charlotte. I like Mrs Dickson and you are giving me disturbing mental images.'

'Tangerines in stockings?'

'Stop!'

Charlotte rubbed a sharp itch in her nose as if she'd snorted a feather. 'I bet she has a whip…'

'Charlotte! Enough!' Vinny cried, shielding his eyes now with a corner of the tartan blanket.

'Sorry! Sorry. But seriously. Could you set up…here?' Her last word ran up with some tentative hope.

Vinny nestled his bristles into her shoulder. 'Of course, I could. The firm has an office in Glasgow. I'm qualified to practise Scottish law too. Just like Adam. I could even get an office set up here, could work from…home.' His last word ran up as if it was a question.

'That would be amazing,' she oozed dreamily as a fishing boat chugged past spewing smoke from its rusted red funnel. A man in dirty yellow dungarees and a black beany hat unwound what looked like a giant ball of string. Every few seconds, another barnacled net cage attached to it plopped into the loch, blowing wide, ebbing ripples across the water.

Vinny rubbed his beard up and down the side of her cheek. 'And what about you? When are you resigning?'

Charlotte shrugged softly and blew the top of her mug which was till steaming ferociously in the nippy morning air. 'When the flat sells. I will have a big enough safety blanket then.'

'But that could take months. Resign now.'

Charlotte sat up quickly to face him. 'I can't. The studio isn't set up yet…,I don't have the right…'

He put his finger on her lips, trying hard not to be distracted by what she had done to him with them under the covers. 'Stop making excuses Charlotte and get it done. There will always be something which isn't quite right. But don't let it hold you back. That place is toxic, and it won't get any better.'

Charlotte pulled his finger away and frowned. 'But surely now Audrey's gone and Dolan's about to be sent down, it will slow down a bit?'

'Maybe. For a while. Then it will begin all over again with someone else. Another outfit. It can't be stopped.'

Despite feeling his warmth against her, Charlotte trembled. More than anything, she didn't want to be part of it anymore. This was her big chance to escape it and get everything she had ever wished for. The dream – with the bonus of him. It was all there, at the tip of her cold-nipped fingers. She had to take the leap.

'You're right.' Everything, though she wasn't quite sure how, had fallen into place. Had brought her to this perfect moment. She realized then that the only thing holding her back…was her.

Vinny looked at her in his arms and knew, with his whole heart, this was where he belonged. 'Come on. Show me what you plan to do with the place. We can even get started on setting it up today.'

'Really? Okay!'

Vinny laughed and held his coffee high as she began to wriggle out of his grip like a toddler spotting the swings at the park. As they unwrapped themselves, they were startled by the yelling and thrashing arms dashing down the hill towards them.

'Coo-wee! Mr Knight? Oh, thank goodness!' she yelled, scurrying along the jetty towards them, her spongy hair windswept from her face.

'Oh, God,' Vinny muttered to Charlotte as he folded up the blanket, a genuine look of pure fear on his face. He lifted his head, a wide smile now in its place. 'Yes, Mrs Dickson? Is everything okay?'

'Oh, yes,' she gasped, leaning against the old docking post to catch her breath, her wax jacket hanging off one shoulder. 'We…We were just very worried when you didn't come home last night. And when I checked this morning and you still weren't there, well…we thought something might have happened!'

'I'm perfectly fine. But thanks for your concern.' He heard Charlotte stifle a laugh with a cough as she packed up her pad and pastels.

'Would you like some breakfast? Erm…you too Charlotte, of course. I've got some lovely Stornoway black pudding and some of Mr

Dickson's famous home-made totty scones.'

'You know, Mrs Dickson, that sounds lovely. I have a raging appetite this morning. I've no idea why,' Vinny said, placing his hand on her shoulder and walking her back up the jetty.

'Oh, well then. That's settled,' she blustered, staring up at him, her hand fiddling with the rim of her turtleneck. It was beige today.

'I wouldn't have had you down as a totty-scone fan, Vinny,' Charlotte stirred as she followed behind, knowing fine well he didn't have a clue what they even were.

He kept Mrs Dickson moving forward but pinged his head back to Charlotte, his eyes wide and mockingly stern. 'You don't know everything about me Charlotte! I don't like totty scones. I *love* totty scones!

Chapter Forty-Three

This is it, you know! There will be no turning back. Charlotte tested her resolve one last time as she made her way to the office with the letter grasped tightly in her fingers. But only a smile resulted; her decision was the right one. It stayed plastered to her face when she by-passed the red fire hose reel suspended on the wall beside the staffroom, where Ben had been leaning when he offered her help. He hadn't been back to work since Audrey had gone into hiding. Maybe he was there with her, giving her the happy ending, that his absence wasn't just because his role at HMP Broadhurst was over. The poor girl deserved a bit of happiness. Since that option made Charlotte feel happiest, that was the one she decided to settle on.

Mr Miller was alone, marking out the rota for the night shift. She watched him scroll in bold red capitals – SUICIDE WATCH – CELL 207 – NICK REFUSED PAROLE.

The letter hiding at her back, Charlotte gave a slightly exaggerated clear of her throat. 'Sir, can I have a word?'

He didn't turn around as he underscored the message with squeaky, firm stripes. 'Charlotte. Of course. Please, come in.'

Unusually, his desk was clear today. It made her mouth even drier and caused her hands to fidget restlessly like she was in trouble with the head teacher, especially now that there were no files to hide behind.

As if sensing she was here for more than a pay rise, Mr Miller pulled his glasses down a tad, his eyes probing her face a bit more than usual. 'Is anything wrong?'

'No, well, not really.' She tried to swirl some moisture to her mouth and took a deep breath. 'I just wanted to give you this.' The envelope slithered across to him, the realization softening his eyes as Charlotte continued to tug hard at her earlobe.

'Oh, Charlotte!' He broke into a rare, broad smile, the one she'd only ever seen him wear on the retirement do's and staff-member's weddings. 'Never have I been happier to receive a resignation letter!'

Relief flooded through her, unpicking every tightly woven spasm and knot and she laughed. A quickly filling eye lightly scrunched closed as she asked, 'I wasn't that bad, surely?'

Picking up the letter, he examined his name, a different kind of resignation nudging his head slowly from side to side. 'No, you weren't that bad. You were that good. *Too* good.'

Almost as if the weight that had been lifted was a physical one, she straightened her back and added, 'Thank you, Mr Miller. I'd like to say that I'm sad to be going…but I will miss you. You've been such a support to me. I…I will always be grateful for that.'

Miller never was any good at receiving compliments, waving off the notion with the letter. A wry smile took hold. 'So!' he barked, throwing the letter in his top drawer. 'What will you do now?'

'Paint!' Charlotte barked the word too, swept up in his fervour. 'I've already had some interest from a few galleries in the area when they saw my portfolio.' On their day off, Vinny had made her visit them all to show her work. Four of them snapped her hand off. It was a start. A bloody good one.

'Sounds wonderful, Charlotte. I'm so happy for you!'

'Thanks boss.'

He inclined forward and lowered his voice like the microphone from the obsolete tannoy system on his desk was functional once more. 'I'll let you into a little secret. Just between you and me.' A mischievous tap on the side of his nose followed.

'What is it?'

From the twinkle glinting in his eyes, it was clear to see it was something good for a change. 'I won't be long behind you. Plan on retiring in the New Year. Finally got the pension pot to where I need it. Well, near enough. Near enough to leave this place behind.' Dimming, his eyes held no fondness, no affiliation when they whizzed around the room.

Another good piece of news? Is the tide finally turning? 'Oh, Mr Miller. That is brilliant news! What will you do?'

His eyes flared. 'Golf!'

Charlotte's giggle was buoyant as she drew up a single ball from the Newton's cradle. The metal sphere remained suspended for a moment until she released it, enjoying the satisfying, rhythmic clack of the balls as her life, and those she cared for, found their equilibrium again. 'Oh. Poor Mrs Miller!'

'Are you kidding? She'd hate it if I was at home getting under her feet! Might even get an allotment.' He stared off somewhere over Charlotte's shoulder, probably sowing the savoy cabbage and leek seeds. 'You just be happy Charlotte. You deserve it.'

'You too, sir. You too.'

After liberating each throbbing foot from a boot, Charlotte hung her coat on a wooden swirl on the Victorian coat stand and padded her way wearily through to the kitchen, the cool flagstones instantly waning the burn. *Hm,* she thought as she went, spotting the winged leaves of the walnut table in flight and four places set.

God, he rocked her world. Black slacks and tight black t-shirt, his hair free and wavy, she wondered if the feeling would ever die. From the way her stomach still flipped every time she saw him like it was the first, she seriously doubted it. 'Someone's been busy,' Charlotte drawled as she continued to leer, leaning against the door frame.

'Well,' he stooped down and opened a door on the range, removing a tray of garlic bread and placing it on the worktop, 'all my homework is complete. I have everything ready for the case. So, I can have some time off to look after you.' He threw her a cheeky wink as he tossed the dishcloth over his shoulder.

Definitely a forever thing, she knew as she wrapped her hands around his neck and kissed him. 'Won't you get fired? You do have a lot of time off,' she tittered, letting go to pilfer a piece.

'Hey! Hands off, grubber!' Vinny twisted the dishcloth and flicked it at her backside just as she took a molten bite, chewing and blowing at the same time. 'It's half my firm, Charlotte. My old man retired last year,' he chortled as he carried a basket of various coloured and sized bread rolls to the table. 'I take on cases as and when I please. I mostly just oversee things these days or take it on if it's a big one – like Tommy Dolan's.' His name was snarled.

'All right, big shot,' she teased, testing if it was safe to have another mouthful. Charlotte pointed to the table where the fancy *Jamie Oliver* placemats and matching cutlery were set. The new matching glasses were buffed sparkly too. 'Are we expecting company?'

'Well, I thought we could celebrate you resigning…and thank Mr and Mrs Dickson for their generosity.' That last part was rushed. 'You know, in how they sorted this place for you coming and how they are letting me use the caravan for work.' Vinny thought it would be a good idea until he could work out something more permanent like an extension. The croft was too small for them both to be working there, especially with his phone ringing every two seconds and the constant clicking of computer keys (never mind the constant temptation of being so close to her).

Charlotte thoroughly browsed the golden, crusty discs, careful in her choice of which one she would steal next. '*Very* nice of you!'

'Quiet Charlotte!' he warned, snatching the tray to safety from under her nose.

Pouting, Charlotte pulled her shirt out of her trousers. 'I phoned Adam earlier to tell him I had resigned. He sounded…strange.'

'How do you mean?' His eyes wrinkled as he continued chopping the spring onions like he was a contestant on Masterchef – The Professionals.

Charlotte held her breath. She loved all five of the fingers on his left hand equally. 'Well, I told him he was fit to travel now. Suggested he come up here, so I can look after him until he's 100%.'

'Right…' Vinny listened as he cupped the green gems and supplemented the salad.

'But he wasn't interested.' Charlotte commandeered an escapee oniony nugget and popped it in her mouth. 'Said he was happy at yours and that he was fine.'

'So?' He tossed like a professional too, flicking the bowl in the air without dropping as much as a rocket leaf.

Unbuttoning her cuffs, she scoffed, 'So, no disrespect Vinny, but he said your sister was a pain in the arse. I thought he'd bite my hand off to get away.'

Vinny held a knowing smile when he turned to her, the bowl now still in his hands.

'What?' Charlotte frowned.

'Charlotte, you're a pain in the arse. But that's what I love about you!' He pecked her on the lips as he passed.

'What? You mean…?' She spun in her socks to follow him as he placed the salad at the very centre of the table. After second thoughts and a few loops of the arrangement, he inched it a cm or two to the left.

Vinny held a glass up to the ceiling light with the pink fringed shade, his eyes squinting as he turned it. 'Yip. I've had my suspicions.' Seemingly passing the quality control test, he placed the glass on the bullseye of the coaster and rested his hands on his hips. 'When I spoke to Lucy, she said he was driving her crazy. But there was just something in the way she said it. And when I said she didn't have to be there anymore as he was on his feet, she insisted, like it was her duty. But I know Lucy – it was more.'

'Ooo. I hope so!' Now Charlotte began slowly unbuttoning the front of her shirt. 'Adam has been single for forever after that *cow* Sophie.'

'Fingers crossed,' he said huskily, buffering her against the wall as he fumbled to help her get undressed.

Mr and Mrs Dickson arrived armed with a clootie dumpling and a bottle of sherry just as the bubbling lasagne hit the table.

'So,' Vinny said, putting down his fork, 'tell me what this one was like as a youngster?'

'An angel!' Mrs Dickson began, clasping her hands together as if she was about to pray.

'A devil!' Mr Dickson contradicted with a flourishing laugh which caused his belly to wobble along with the stain on his shirt which might have been dried egg yolk. 'Aways pestering me to take her wae me on the fields. Wanted on the tractor, wanted to help me feed the coos and sheep. Aways hinging off ma back, yeh were. Your hair like some sort a Celtic wildling.' Charlotte was almost tempted to say *Pot, kettle, black*, considering his hair now resembled Doctor Emmitt Brown himself, Einstein even. And there was ear and nasal hair to match. 'And aways, *aways* in yer wellies.'

'Now, *that* version,' Vinny lifted a finger from his glass, 'I do believe, Mr Dickson. She is determined.'

'That she is,' he whispered indiscreetly to Vinny, his eyes remaining slit-like (because he still point-blank refused to wear the glasses he so desperately needed, opting to see and look like a mole instead).

Shushing his very accurate recollections, Charlotte began to pile the plates. 'You loved it! I even remember you calling me from the field to help you with the lambing.'

'If yeh insist!' He winked as he handed her his bread-swiped squeaky-clean plate.

Charlotte held it in her hand and gazed at the three different faces flickering softly in the candlelight from the ones she was used to here, but who she loved nonetheless. With the fire popping and sizzling behind them, their bellies and hearts full, Charlotte began to believe the croft was blessed in some way. It felt intrinsically loving and safe. Home.

'I love it here. So many happy memories of Mum and Dad, not to mention Supergran.'

'Aye, yer right there, Charlotte. Yer wee granny wis dynamite,' Mr Dickson recalled fondly, picking a piece of what she hoped was rocket (and not an extra passenger he'd picked up whizzing across the field in his quad bike earlier) from between his front teeth before trying to chew it down with the rest. It had only moved to the next tooth along when he explained, 'After your granda died when your da was jist a wee laddie, she wis determined not tae leave the place. Raised yer da single-handedly. And it was a tough life in them days. No benefits. Aye,' he laughed gruffly and folded his arms across his belly, 'yeh didnae mess wae Jean Croft.'

To Charlotte, just talking about them was keeping them alive in some way. The warmth of that thought coursed around her body as she placed the last plate on top of the pile and smiled. 'I remember once, when

Adam back-chatted her because he wouldn't come in for his dinner. She took off, marching up the lane, her arms swinging at her side and gave him such a look that he ran like his arse was on fire, right to the table. Didn't even stop to take off his boots...and you didn't dare wear your shoes inside!'

The warmth she felt soon oozed to those around the table and Vinny basked in the brilliance of her face as it re-lived the moment, a clear flashback of a not-so-long ago evening and Charlotte marching up the hill towards him ringing clear. Still not quite out of the habit of making parallels, he was in no doubt that Charlotte had a lot of her gran's blood pumping through her veins and spirit in her soul.

Mr Dickson summonsed them back from their amble down memory lane to look forward with a *ting, ting, ting* of his teaspoon against his sherry glass. 'I think we should toast yer return, Charlotte and this lovely young man ya've brought with you. A canny tell you how happy we are to have you here and this place back to life. Here's to the next generation of the Croft clan. Lang may yer lum reek!'

Her glass raised in the air, Charlotte suddenly felt the contents of her stomach threaten to come back out the way they had just gone in as she drove hard to keep her smile in place.

Chapter Forty-Four

'You all right?' A hand paused mid-loop as Vinny finished wiping down the table before he straightened, flipping the cloth to the clean side in his hands. 'You look like you've seen a ghost.'

'Hm?' Charlotte asked vaguely as she placed another wine glass back on the dresser. 'Oh, yeah. I'm fine,' she answered without him even having to repeat the question, her heartbeat thrumming in her ears. 'Just tired. It's been a long day.' The smile she returned was quick to fall.

"Hm, okay," he replied as he wandered back to the sink to have another go at scrubbing the welded cheese from the glass tray. 'Go put your feet up. I'll finish up.'

'Okay,' she said quietly, placing the damp dishcloth over his shoulder and following his instructions to the letter, a distracted glaze behind her eyes.

Elbow deep in suds, Vinny's eyes trailed her to the lounge as she shuffled away with the last clean wine glass still in her hand. Quickly drying off, he abandoned the tray for the long soak and joined her only to find she was staring off into space.

'Wine,' he said, tilting the bottle to fill the empty glass still loose in her hand.

Rocking back and forth, she watched the flames as if they had danced her into some kind of trance. 'No…thanks. Vinny, I'm just going to go to bed if that's okay. My head is pounding.'

'Sure. Let me get you some paracetamol.' He turned to the kitchen.

The rocker ground to a halt. 'No! No, honestly. I just need to sleep.'

'Oookay. You go up. I'll bring you up a glass of water.'

'Thank you,' she murmured as she passed.

No goodnight kiss tonight either?

Charlotte lay awake, her eyes travelling around the branches of cracks on the low, leak-stained ceiling. She was late. *Very* late. Even if Vinny *said* he was ready to move at any pace she wanted, this was g-force fast. *Shit!* she thought, envisioning the skid marks his tank would gouge into the field as he made his getaway. He lived life too much in the fast lane, was just too damn particular and purist – definitely not the type to cramp his style with a pooping, vomiting crying-machine. Maybe that's why he and Nadia split in the first place. Perhaps she wanted kids and it wasn't on the agenda for him? Perhaps she'd end up just like Granny Jean, bringing up baby alone. But the thought of losing him…Her mind couldn't bear to go there again. Resting her hand on what was either a nothing or everything, she whinged again. *And I've just resigned! Can I retract it?* she wondered as she listened to Vinny hum happily to some *Miles Davis*, the water slushing as he had another go at the lasagne dish.

The roads were still a suffocating shade of dark but at least it aided her clandestine detour to the nearest 24hr Tesco's before her next shift.

Glancing over her shoulder again as if she expected Vinny to be at her back at any moment demanding to know what she was up to, Charlotte harried down the aisles until she found the family planning section. *Family planning,* she scoffed at the irony of it. Because there was zero bloody planning here. *Oops Section!* was a far more suitable name, she decided as her eyes darted bamboozled from one brand to the other. They all claimed to be the best at giving clear results, but given her current state of mind, she opted for the one which said it in words instead of lines or crosses.

Smiling manically at the stern security guard who looked like he took his job way too seriously, she shakily scanned the eight kits in the self-service checkout before throwing each into a thankfully opaque bag. Much to her horror, it was him she needed to ask for the toilet key when the cashier at the cigarette counter (who looked like a regular at the local *Mecca*) informed her rather harshly, 'We canny keep them open aw night, hen. It's no a hotel.'

And it certainly wasn't as romantic and dreamy as she imagined either as she perched precariously on the pan, thinking there must be some easier way to find out rather than trying to pee on a stick. There followed a touch of stage fright and it felt there was nothing in her bladder but sand. 'Oh, come on!' she growled quietly, and after a few deep pushes of breath, a trickling stream began. One eye scrunched tight, she waved the stick around blindly, her tongue poking out the side of her mouth, hoping at least a few drops would hit the target.

Charlotte didn't leave the stick at the side for three minutes to develop without looking like the instructions told her to. She didn't pay attention to the advert on the back of the door asking to help stop *Period Poverty* and she didn't try to defy the *Smart One* toilet roll dispenser by pulling out two sections in a oner. The stick glued to her hand, she kept her knickers at her ankles, and watched the little grey window intently until after only a minute, the word *Pregnant* appeared. Charlotte began to pant and blow like she was in the last stages of labour. 'Oh, sweet holy Je-sus! Vinny's going to bloody kill me!' But that one word on a bit of plastic changed her world in an instant, the feeling far better than anything she could ever have painted in her mind.

With only her knickers up now, the phone began to buzz in her coat pocket. 'Hello!' she cried too cheerfully, the phone jammed between her shoulder and her neck as she pulled up her trousers and fastened the button. Maybe it was her imagination, but did it feel tighter already?

'Where the hell are you? You nearly gave me a heart attack!'

'Sorry. I've got loads of paperwork to catch up on and I couldn't sleep. Thought I'd get a head start before shift, so I can leave on time for a change. Get back to you quicker.' She winced an eye shut and whizzed up her zip, knowing it sounded flimsy at best.

'Oh, right.' There was a long pause. Obviously so did he. 'Can you maybe leave a note next time? I do worry you know.'

She forced her voice down to moderately manic. 'Sorry Vinny! I didn't mean to scare you.'

He laughed but it was uneasy. 'That's all right, baby.'

'Pardon me?' she yelped, her eyes shooting up from checking there were no squares of white stuck to her heel before she left the cubicle.

'That's…all right…baby?'

She slouched against the cubicle door (right beside a one-starred rating which declared in dark, angry capitals - *I WOULD NOT PEE HERE AGAIN!!!!*) and Charlotte puffed her cheeks now she understood Vinny hadn't developed a sixth sense on top of all his other superhuman attributes. 'Yeah, I should be back for 6.'

'All right. Have a good day. Be careful. I love you.'

A bit late now to be careful! 'I love you, too,' she beamed before hanging up, gazing at his smiling face on her home screen. A hand rested on her stomach. 'Your daddy's gonna kill me!'

Even so, there was a novel spring to her walk, a lightness, an unshakable air of bliss when she finished her last tour of the wing. It had started from the moment she left the toilet cubical and just seemed to blossom more with every footstep, with every passing second. And it wasn't just her walk which was different – it was everything: her smile, her glow, her purpose. Special, like a miracle was taking place inside her. Because, it was. Life's priorities instantly shuffled and rearranged until a few cells of nothing much yet were at the top of everything, triumphant. At that moment in time, she couldn't give a shit about Spice or Tommy Dolan or HMP Broadhurst. This was her few hours alone to own and revel in (before she had to tell Vinny of course). Now that was a whole other ball game.

And when she finally returned to the croft, the elation was muzzled by fear – the fear that she might lose him. And as she sat there counting the raindrops on the windscreen, her friends *if, but* and *maybe* took centre stage, conjuring up the spectrum of possibilities. The one which screamed loudest was that he just didn't want this. It didn't bear thinking about. Of course, he'd be angry with her. But still, he would at least understand in time what it felt like - falling head over heels in love for the second time. Or would he?

Only when his silhouette darkened the fairy tale window did she crank the door handle her fingers had been cramped around for the last few minutes.

'Hi,' Vinny said, an unfamiliar tentativeness in his eyes questioning her as he opened the door.

'Hi,' she returned, feeling suddenly faint. He took her coat and scrutinized her as she sat next to the fire, her face slumped on her balled fists, her knuckles white.

'Wine?'

'No, I'm fine. Thanks.' Her smile flashed and disappeared in the blink of an eye.

No wine? He folded his arms. 'Right! What the fuck is going on? Something is wrong!'

His forcefulness, although from his own fear, reduced her to silence. Gulping hard, she gazed up to him. 'Nothing.'

But the look in her eyes made his breath catch. 'Charlotte! You're scared! Something is scaring you. Has someone got to you?' he seethed, edging closer.

'No! It's not that…' she wailed impatiently, swivelling away to the fire.

'Then it is something!'

She swallowed hard again, suddenly wanting to cry. 'You're gonna kill me.'

'Why? What have you done?' he yelped, his blue/green eyes catching the flames like mirrors.

Charlotte shook her head nervously, wishing she had a brown paper bag to slow her breathing. 'Please…Please don't be angry.'

'Why would you think I'd be angry? I will get angry if you don't tell me what the fuck is happening!'

Although the fire was burning her leg, she couldn't move it. Charlotte covered her face with her hands and moaned, 'I'm pregnant,' preferring to imagine his reaction rather than witness it.

'What?' The word was almost inaudible.

'Pregnant. I'm pregnant.' Drawing her hands down her face, she risked a sideways glance.

'How?' he whispered in a way which could have been anger or shock or as it was in Charlotte's head, even worse.

'How do you think, Vinny?' her eyes rolled, the days fretting released in a snap. 'And *yes*, I was on the pill so…the only thing I can think of was I was sick a few times after Adam got hurt. And *no*, I didn't do it on purpose.' Snatching the bag from her feet, she emptied the eight tests onto the coffee table topped with dark green tiles. She stood, arms wide, palms bouncing to the artexed ceiling, talking to them instead of Vinny. 'They all

312

say it. All of them! I know it's too soon and wasn't planned and I'm sorry, and…and…well, it is yours by the way because me and Greg hadn't gone there in forever…I'm not expecting anything from you so…'

As his shadow ebbed towards her, she kept her head dipped to the latticework of white sticks.

'Charlotte,' he said evenly, his voice thick. Only when he turned her hips to face him did she look up. Although he remained speechless, she saw it in his face – the same joy she felt.

She burst into a squeaky hubbub of indiscriminate sounds as he pulled her into his arms, his embrace so tight she couldn't breathe.

And he pulled her down to him, right there in front of the fire, to show her just how much he loved her, although Charlotte couldn't relax. In fact, she was scared to move, lying on her back as stiff as an ironing board. 'Wait!' a hand keeping him painfully at length. 'What if you hit the baby?'

Vinny half laughed, half cried. He'd popped a few cherries in his time, but this was agony, her body frigid and unrelenting beneath his. 'Charlotte, I'm not that well-endowed!' he cried desperately after his fourth attempt to get inside her. 'It's perfectly natural. Now relax.'

The hand pushed harder against his hip. 'Yes, you are, and yes I know…but still.'

'Charlotte,' he almost begged as he looked deeply into her eyes. 'It'll be fine. I love you.'

God, those eyes, she sighed to herself feeling her resolve weaken and her hand give.

They made camp there, on collapsed sofa cushions, under scratchy wool blankets, a diet coke instead of champagne, but in flutes none-the-less.

'Oh, I cannot wait,' Vinny groaned looking down at her, sweeping his hand around her stomach. 'You're going to have a big fat belly and I'm going to love it and rub it and kiss it.'

'You won't be saying that when I have big saggy boobs and big aioli things!'

'Areolas.' Vinny laughed so hard, he choked, spitting a mouthful of coke back into an empty can. 'Aioli is garlic mayonnaise!'

Looking up at him propped on his elbow, Charlotte was still laughing as she tucked his sex-messed hair behind his ear. 'I thought you might leave. Didn't know if you even wanted kids. I was terrified to tell you.'

'One,' he pecked the tip of her nose, 'I'd never leave you, kids or not. Two,' he pecked her lips, 'I can think of nothing more amazing than becoming a parent with you. A little bit of me and you...in one little person.'

'Me too. And...I've always wanted to become a mum because... I miss her so much.' Charlotte turned to the fire and they were both silent for a moment. 'I just wish Mum and Dad were around to see it.'

Vinny watched the flames spark in her filling eyes, and now that he was going to be a dad, he began to understand the magnitude of her loss. 'Maybe they are. You said you really feel them here.'

'Yeah.' She sniffed and fluttered her eyes. 'Yeah, you're right.'

His tone quickly sobered as he propped himself a little higher. 'Charlotte, I don't want you to go back to that place.'

Her eyes flicked back to his. 'But I have to! I've got to work 4 weeks notice.'

'No.' He stroked the hair from her face. 'No, you don't. Go on the sick for the rest of the time.'

She tried to sit up, but he placed a hand on the space above her breasts. 'I'll be fine, Vinny. I don't like letting people down like that.'

'You're not letting anyone down.' He pinned a leg around both of hers. 'The world will still turn without you in HMP Broadhurst! It only

314

takes one silly bastard to knock into you, or for you to get hurt if someone needs to be restrained. That's our baby in there.' His hand smoothed over her tummy again. 'You're leaving anyway. Is it worth the risk?'

She knew he was right. 'No.' She rested a palm on his cheek. 'No, it's not.'

Chapter Forty-Five

Charlotte swiped the brush across the canvas as she explored the abstract. Although there were no figures, no trees, no obvious shapes even – there was pure happiness. She tilted her head and smiled.

From the fogged caravan window, Vinny watched her get lost in the moment, serene and beautiful. He found he was watching her more every day instead of getting his own work done. Watching her work was intoxicating: her hair coiled loosely into a plat, how she was becoming rounder, softer in the middle, how her neck became swan-like as she appraised her work. But more than that, he cherished her gift of taking nothing and creating the beautiful, the amazing. That, he realized, was why she never wanted more. She had it all in her already – her art, the outlet for sharing it. The ability to change coal to diamond.

He checked the email again. 3pm Thursday – *Chisholm Hunter*, Argyle Arcade, Glasgow. The ring was antique and intricate with small emeralds and diamonds and not ostentatious – he had an idea Charlotte wouldn't be one for a two-carat *Cartier* solitaire. Picking up the framed scan photo on his makeshift desk, he counted everything again: two tiny blobs, two tiny heartbeats, four tiny arms and four tiny feet – but only one tiny penis.

These days, he day-dreamed names and storage solutions. He'd go back home with a list after each day at the 'office'. Today, he thought of *Elle* and *Jack*. And he had drawn a sketch of a two-story side extension too (in keeping with the croft as Charlotte had insisted). It would hold an office for him on the ground floor, and two bedrooms on the first. Shaking his head, it hit him. Of course, they were never going to stop at two children. What was he thinking? He scrunched up the sketch and was about to start again when his phone buzzed.

'Adam,' he said warmly. 'How's it going mate?'

'Yeah, great Vinny.' The reply was sharp, and Adam spoke with a sense of urgency. 'Listen, are you by yourself?'

'Yeah. Why?' Vinny sat forward and frowned, threading the pen behind his ear.

'I've just had a phone call from Detective Atkinson. You met him. He dealt with the stabbing?'

'Yeah. Go on.' His eyes immediately zoned in on Charlotte.

'There's been a possible sighting of David Sullivan and…it was in Scotland.'

'Shit,' he whispered just as Charlotte rubbed her stomach again and his plummeted somewhere below the grubby carpet. It wasn't entirely unexpected; he had a funny feeling things would start to heat up in the weeks before the trial. But the stakes were so much higher now. Two fingers massaged his temple where he felt a hot poker stab at his skull. 'Where? When?'

'A services on the M74. Near Abingdon. He drove in the direction of Glasgow.'

Charlotte was munching again. She always seemed to be now she was pregnant. A pastry of some sort in one hand, she brushed tiny, upwards strokes in the other. That is, until she noticed the splodge of jam which had squirted out the bottom end of what he now realized was a jam doughnut. Dropping her brush, Vinny watched her curse what he thought looked like, *'Ah, bollocks!'* as the strawberry blob smeared down the length of her top with a swipe of her sleeve.

'Vinny?'

'I'm thinking.' *I'm not thinking. I can't think!* 'I…I need to phone Rick and let him know right away. I need to go Adam. Look after my sister.'

'I will. And Vinny? Make sure you look after mine.'

He never even got chance to hang up before Rick's call came through. A shaky finger whizzed between the options – *End call and accept? Hold call and accept?* Unable to process which was right, he pressed the first one. Thankfully, it worked. 'Rick? What the fuck is going on?' Now on his feet, Vinny threw his plastic mug in the sink with a clang and began to pace the threadbare strip of floorspace, the whole caravan quaking with every stomp.

'Vinny, it might not even be him. And even if it is, he's probably not interested in coming after you. He's probably just getting closer to home.'

'Well, I'm *not* taking that fucking chance, Rick! Charlotte, she…she's only just 3 months pregnant.' His arm shot towards her as he tried to make Rick understand. 'And I don't want her stressing. What protection can you provide without her knowing?'

'Give me half an hour, Vinny. I'm working on it now.'

A hand resting on the newly painted olive-green door, Vinny emptied his lungs with a lengthy exhale and tried to level the fear pulling at his face. After another deep breath, he pushed forward, the door creaking open to the sound of her singing…Prince of course.

'I never meant to cause you any sorrow…I never meant to cause you any pain.'

Unlike Prince, he knew exactly who he wanted to cause a lot of sorrow and an excruciating amount of pain, his mind already bursting with how he was going to commit the murder which would see him on the other side of the dock. Vinny threw his laptop on the sofa, needing to hold her.

A stool scraped up beside hers and Vinny wrapped his arms extra-tightly around her middle, nuzzling his nose into her hair. She smelt of spring, jam and turps (not necessarily in that order).

'Hey you,' she purred, closing her eyes as she leaned back into him. 'I've missed you.' Her eyes sprung wide. 'Christ! You're freezing, Vinny!' Charlotte rubbed her hands briskly across the arms knotted at her belly.

'Not half as much as I've missed you,' he whispered into her ear. 'That caravan is bloody Baltic!'

'I can tell! Take me to bed then and I'll get you all nice and warm. These bloody pregnancy hormones have got me all hot and bothered all right!' Charlotte began to brush her backside against his groin. 'Either that or it's just you as usual.'

Unusually, he did not move, his head remaining nestled into her back. 'Aw, I'd love to baby but I'm expecting a very important phone call…and the caravan will give me hypothermia if I wait in it for any longer.'

'Awwww! You're such a fun sponge!' she whined, pushing his hands away.

Nervous breakdown aside, Vinny let out a full-hearted belly laugh. 'A bloody what?'

'A fun sponge! A sponger of fun. *My* fun.' She laughed despite her frustration when he fought to cling to her like some sort of limpet.

'I'm sorry. Why don't you go up for a nap?' Giving up as she wriggled, he patted her already fuller backside, a very welcome addition as far as he was concerned. 'I'll join you when I can.'

'I'm going to have to. I can't keep my eyes open.' Heaving herself up, she'd already developed a cute pregnancy waddle (even though her bump looked no more than a moderate case of bloating) as she placed her palette on the sanded oak worktop Vinny had recently built. 'Vinny?' she spun her head back to him, her eyes dreamy and tired.

'Yeah?' Bloody hell, she was edible.

'Don't be long.' She threw him a look of urgency.

Listening to the creaking and twanging of mattress springs until they settled, he closed himself in the studio and waited. Although it felt like forever tapping his foot, jogging his knee, gazing out at the vista and expecting someone with a gun to come strolling up from the water, it was only 10 minutes before Rick called back.

'Yeah?' Vinny jumped to his feet.

'There is an old cattle shed about half a mile up the hill behind the croft. We have a unit there now, and they will stay there on rota as long as is needed. Can you get away for a minute? Get to the main road?'

He looked to the ceiling above him, to where she was waiting. 'Yeah, now. But I need to be quick.'

'Get to the slip road gate. One of the officers will give you a panic button. Keep it on you at all times, Vinny.'

'Okay. But what can you give me, so I can defend us here?'

'I'll make sure you have pepper spray.'

Vinny huffed audibly.

'Do you have knives?'

More like it. 'Yeah,' Vinny said, only recently bringing his own professional chef's kit back from London. *Nice and sharp.*

'Keep them handy. Keep one on you if you can. We can always work out a reason for it being there later.'

His hand was already poised on the wrought iron handle. 'Okay. Is that it?'

'I think so. If there is anything else you need in the meantime, just call.'

'Don't worry. I will.'

In his panic, Vinny galloped up the pebbled path as best he could in his purple monster feet slippers (which matched his fuzzy purple socks), an officer already waiting with a gloved hand outstretched to hand over his bag of goodies. Without as much as a nod, Vinny snatched the batch and ran back even quicker. Once he was back inside, it wasn't just a knife he planted. It was the woodcutting axe, the old baseball bat which must have been Adam's, the hoe and sheers Mr Dickson must have left behind. Only when everything was locked and barred and checked and re-checked, did he climb up to Charlotte.

Chapter Forty-Six

Although agonizingly long, the night passed without incident (well, apart from Vinny nearly having a heart attack when Mrs Dickson came to the door just before bedtime). 'Thought you two might like a cheese scone for supper,' she sang, a smudge of gloopy doe across her cheek, several white handprints on the thighs her brown slacks. Charlotte devoured it, warm and crumbly straight from the oven. Vinny, however, couldn't force down a single bite. Charlotte ate his too. 'Shame to see it go to waste,' she had shrugged, adding another thick layer of butter.

Any sleep snatched was broken and restless with Charlotte nudging his shin several times to stop the thrashing. In his stretched awake time, he rehearsed every scenario – if someone crept up the stairs to the room in the middle of the night, how he would prise the knife from under the mattress and cut their throat. If he heard the smash of a window or forcing of a door, he would press the button under his pillow and whisper to Charlotte to lock herself in the bathroom as he would take the baseball bat brandished in front of him down the stairs to the dark void below. With the refuge of dawn, he rose, his brain far more exhausted than his body.

His long legs and bare feet stretched out along the window seat, his hands stuffed in the front pouch of his hoodie, Vinny gazed out at the loch – so beautiful, so still, yet this morning, so sinister: the evergreens, smudged by the smoke of an icy fire, sanctuary and allies to a pair of murderous eyes? Needing to know something, anything, before he went mad, Vinny dialled Rick, keeping his voice low.

'Hi Vinny. How is everything?'

Rick's hoarseness indicated his night had been as rough as Vinny's (and like he had been drinking all the harder to remedy that).

A flash of red, the exact shade of Charlotte's hair, caught his eye. Keeping low, the pair of fox cubs darted quickly across the lawn, following the rutted path in the ice-bleached grass already cut by a larger set of paws, and disappeared into the undergrowth. Almost wishing he and Charlotte could do the same, he sniped, 'Funnily enough, Rick, not the best. I feel like we're a pair of sitting ducks here.'

There was a pause as Rick continued gulping down whatever it was he was drinking. Vinny just prayed it was water. 'I know, but you are safe. We've had eyes and ears on the croft all night.'

How the hell would you know? he thought cynically, biting his tongue to refrain from shouting at Rick to get his bloody act together. Sighing heavily, Vinny rubbed a hand across the creases and folds ironed on his face, noticing his beard was unusually long and straggly. 'I'd like to say that's reassuring…'

'Is there someone you can stay with until the trial is over?'

Vinny drew the thick cotton laces of the hood tighter. 'I can stay anywhere I bloody like but I've got a sneaky feeling it wouldn't make a difference. Besides, I want Charlotte to know *nothing*. She's only just past the pregnancy danger zone. That's not enough time, and if I land all this on her too…' A sweaty palm rested on his forehead.

'Okay, you're right. Look, just carry on as normal. Go out with Charlotte today. Do a bit of Christmas shopping, have a bit of lunch. You can't just sit there going stir-bloody-crazy. We'll be watching your place anyway.'

'Yeah,' Vinny sighed, pushing the straggly ropes of hair back from his eyes. 'Maybe you're right.'

'Come on,' he gazed down to her as they descended the escalator in *Frasers*, cute as a button in her favourite green bobble hat, her eyes twinkling under the ceiling of fairy lights, crimson curls spiralling down each side of her glowing cheeks. 'Let's go eat.'

'Yes!' she groaned, slipping an arm around his waist, an armful of bags looped onto the other. Throwing a severe glare and loud tut over her shoulder, Charlotte felt Vinny turn her forward to prevent a shopping-rage incident. She spoke quietly into his chest, shielding her words from the grumpy fucker whose bags were butting too close into them from the step above. 'It's my second favourite thing to do at the moment.'

'Oh, yeah? What's the first?' Vinny asked, lifting her hand in the air as they stepped off and the last tread disappeared beneath them.

'Painting.' She turned away to hide her smirk.

'Yeah, right,' he sniggered. 'You weren't saying that last night.' He heaved open the heavy door and Charlotte gulped as the chill stole her breath.

'Well,' she blustered, one eye closed by the icy blast as Vinny took the bags and pulled her coat collar up around her neck, 'it's my hormones. I've never known anything like it.'

Vinny drew her in to him by her waist, exaggerating his stature. 'Well, let's do your second favourite thing first, and your first favourite thing second?'

'Sounds perfect.'

After a lunch in which Charlotte did her very best to eat for three (endeavouring bravely to finish her starter, main *and* desert as well as Vinny's leftovers), he tried to tempt her around a few more shops, even suggested they make a night of it. Grab a show? Book a hotel? But when she complained that it was hoachin' (which he presumed meant busy) and that she was developing a bad case of chub (which she explained meant the inside tops of her growing thighs were rubbing raw, as in a combination of chubby and rub), Vinny reluctantly text Rick to let him know they were on their way back.

The late December afternoon had long lost its light when they reached the croft and Vinny felt the blindness render him helpless once more. As Charlotte went inside to make a cup of tea (she'd insisted they both switch some herbal concoction which tasted like piss), he unpacked the car, glaring around the darkness, listening for a more pronounced kind of rustling in the trees, looking for a glint of metal spark under the light of the cool, white moon. He loitered on the doorstep to be sure until Charlotte snapped, 'Vinny! Shut the door! Jeeze! It's minus 2.'

'Bloody hormones, right enough,' he chuckled dryly, closing and double locking the door behind him.

He lay in bed listening to Charlotte snore (although she insisted it was purring), murdering Sullivan over and over again in his head. Finally, after choking him till his eyes were popping out of his purple, swollen-lipped skull, Vinny unclamped Charlotte's leg from on top of his, and padded bare footed to the sitting room.

Although the flames had died to nothing more than a tawny glow, there was still enough warmth to keep him comfortable. He tried to resuscitate it with another log, but it was a step closer to dying than living. So, he sat in the darkness, checking every now and again that the knife was tucked down the side of the cushion of the sofa he sprawled on, just watching and waiting until the skies lifted to a glum battleship grey.

He'd only began to load the grate when his phone rang. It was Rick.

'Come on! Come on!' A log tucked under his arm, Vinny's heart took off in a sprint as he swiped several times across the screen before the call connected. 'Yeah?'

'Got him!' Rick's voice was gruff and victorious.

The log clattered to the stone flags. 'What happened?'

'He was staying in a bed and breakfast in Helensburgh. A routine patrol clocked the registration on the ANPR system. He had a knife on him, blood-stained too. We will cross match it with Adam's DNA. I'm hopeful there will be a match.'

'Thank God!' Vinny collapsed onto his backside, his legs crooked before him. 'Where is Helensburgh?'

'A town on the coast – just a few miles west of the loch.'

'Shit!' Vinny let the thought hit him as he scratched his beard, his bristles suddenly prickly. 'So, he was looking for us?'

'Looks that way. But it's over Vinny. Put it out of your mind and…have a lovely Christmas.'

It was immediate – the feeling like someone had lifted the bag from over his head, like he could breathe again. 'Rick…thanks, for everything.'

'No problems mate. I'll look forward to seeing you in court in the New Year!'

'I can't bloody wait.'

Vinny hung up and walked to the window. It was the first time he had really noticed the loch since the news of Sullivan's predatory movements, so he spent some extra time to catch up on what he had been missing. There was a hypnotising ripple across the water today, chopping and mixing the white curling clouds and clear, blue breaks above. The bordering peaks were snow-capped now, like they had been dredged with icing sugar. Permanent, they were like a crutch and he used them to prop himself back to prudence. Soon the idyllic scene worked its magic, making Vinny weighty and relaxed, allowing the natural state of his exhaustion to take hold. He clambered heavily up each stair, crawled back into bed and snuggled into her back.

'Where have you been?' she yelped in gasps as his cold hands found her under the sheets.

'Couldn't sleep. Too excited for Christmas,' he yawned and placed his hand on her stomach, shielding all 4 of them as best he could. His life.

'Oh, you're sweet,' she chortled before gasping, 'Vinny! How excited?'

'Sorry,' he lied. 'Was hoping maybe your hormones were needing an outlet to help send me back off to the land of nod?'

She rubbed her backside against him. 'Oh, all right then.'

Chapter Forty-Seven

'Vinny! Look!' Charlotte cried from the bedroom window.

'What!' he yelled, leaping panic-stricken and bollock-naked to her side, his hair never messier, one eye clenched tight.

An amused confusion constricted her eyes. 'What is it with you lately?' she sniggered shaking her head. '*Look!*' She pointed out of the icicled window, a thick blanket of snow swathing the fields, the sharp edges of the trees softened by a pillow of white. The top of the hills seemed to just run into the sky.

'Whoa! I can't remember the last time I saw snow, never mind nearly a foot of the stuff. Bloody hell!' The shock of the cold suddenly hit him as he jumped from one bare foot to the other, the floorboards squeaking and groaning in protest. 'It's fucking freezing! We need to get some central heating! And a carpet!'

'Rubbish. Where's your sense of adventure?' A cloud of white puffed from her mouth with each word. 'It'll make us appreciate the fire more.'

'Yeah, it's a real adventure, waiting to see if my balls fall back down from my stomach every morning!' His words were broken with sharp breaths and gasps, his moves spasmodic as he quickly tried to pull on his sweats.

Transfixed by the view, Charlotte remained still and staring. 'Now it really feels like Christmas. Sack it! I'm having a mince pie for breakfast!' she chirped happily before scuffing her slippers across the bare planks towards the kitchen.

Vinny laughed to himself as he watched her go, knowing fine well she was going to have the whole box. *Shit*, he thought as his brain fully wakened. Perhaps the roads would be too bad to get to Glasgow to pick up her ring? He was due to go later that day and it was the only thing to do before they bolted the doors for Christmas. The fridge was packed to the gills, the foot of the Norway spruce (which Charlotte insisted he dug up so it could be replanted again for next year) covered in an abundance of gifts, wrapped neatly and bowed, the laptop was closed and cold.

He found her on the old wooden kitchen stool which looked like it might have been salvaged from a Victorian classroom, gazing out of the window framed with a yellowed netting (even after Charlotte had steeped them twice in *Vanish Oxiclean* and wouldn't hear of them buying a new set), the warping wooden worktop she sat at littered with two empty foil cups beside another with a half-eaten mince pie in it. Suddenly, a vivid red breast hopped onto the windowsill and Charlotte gasped like the robin was an angel sent directly from heaven itself: a sign. That was something else he loved about her – she looked out for the signs, believed there was something more to it all. A rare breed these days, a stronger moral compass than most for sure. He'd lost count of how many white feathers she'd picked up and pocketed on their forest walks (not to mention the fact he could distinguish the faint murmur of an *Our Father* and *Hail Mary* every night before she went to sleep). 'Well, hello there, Mr Robin! How are we this morning?'

Filling a glass at the deep sink (the water still not quite as crystal as he would have liked), Vinny took a tiny sip before broaching the subject carefully. 'Charlotte, I need to go to the office today.'

'Why?' Her head swivelled to him as her back sagged.

A sense of guilt struck him as he watched his words immediately ruin her moment. But it would be worth it…he hoped. Vinny took the stool at her side and tucked a strand of hair behind her ear. 'The office closes for Christmas today. I need to catch-up with a few people. We're straight in court in the New Year.'

'But the roads are going to be atrocious, Vinny! No.' She shook her head and looked back out the window, the robin now gone. 'It's too risky.'

Having pre-empted her reaction, he pulled out his mobile, waving it around to catch some sort of a signal. When the page flashed up, he angled it to her from above them in the air. 'Look. I've just checked. The roads are open. I have a meeting at 3 then I'll be straight home. I promise.'

'Well...I don't like it Vinny! I don't like it one little bit!' she cried before snatching back the half-eaten mince pie he was trying to sneak from under her nose. It was guzzled quickly, his punishment for being so reckless. 'But... I suppose the fact you're driving a tank... makes me feel a *bit* better,' she garbled, stippling crumbs across the worktop with every pouty verb.

Before she'd even had chance to swallow it, he lunged forwards, grabbed the back of her neck and kissed her deeply.

'Ew! Vinny!' Charlotte protested, shrugging him off to keep the contents of her mouth her own.

'And once I'm back,' he paused to swipe a piece of sticky sauce stuck to the corner of his mouth, 'we close the door and won't come back out till next year.'

'Promise?'

'Promise,' he smiled, popping his finger in his mouth and sucking it clean.

To be on the safe side, Vinny sent the Dickson's a text to keep an eye on Charlotte. A few minutes later, he received their reply, predictive texting seemingly a foreign concept to the pair:

oF CouRsee B.e glAd 2..! ?

He presumed that was a yes.

Although happy enough that the risk had been dealt with, he wasn't letting his guard down regardless - the remnants of recent events too close and still hounding him to be vigilant. Vinny reached over and cranked up the heating, and although the roads were coated in compacted, dappled snow, he put his foot down, not wanting to waste a single second.

Charlotte pulled the fairy lights from their box, tutting when she realized it was going to take forever to detangle the spaghetti junction of knots. The tree and decorations had already been up for the last week, but she wanted an extra piece of sparkly Christmas magic for when Vinny got home. Tying her locks up in a loose bun and her tongue tickling her top lip as she concentrated, she began unpicking. *'I don't want a lot for Christmas…there is just one thing I need…'* she warbled to Mariah on her *Now That's What I Call Christmas* CD.

Quicker than expected, the maze of wires was unravelled and laid in a straightish line across the flagstones. She perched on a stool (knowing Vinny would freak if he saw her) and began pinning the thin cable along the window wall which faced the loch. Only halfway across and only halfway through *Band Aid*, the door rapped.

'Bloody hell,' she griped, lowering carefully from the stool and plodding for the door, her slippers slapping against her heels with every trudge. Mrs Dickson fell straight in with a flurry of fresh snow swirling violently at her back. Staring beyond her, Charlotte felt an angst grate in her chest just knowing Vinny was somewhere in the abyss. This was their safe place, their haven, and he wasn't there. *God, keep him safe*, she prayed silently to *The Sacred Heart* as she thrust the door to against the howling wind.

The short walk from her homestead had provided Mrs Dickson

with cotton wool eyebrows and a white moustache. *Very fitting for the season*, Charlotte thought as she tried not to laugh.

'Are you okay dear? You look a bit flushed,' Mrs Dickson asked, shedding the snow on to the doormat.

'Yes, I'm fine Mrs Dickson. Is everything all right?'

'Oh, yes dear. Just noticed Vinny wasn't here and just wanted to check all was well.' An eyebrow fell off.

'All is very well, Mrs Dickson. Vinny's got a meeting, but he shouldn't be too long.'

No matter how tempting it was to tell her to go, that she was busy trying to make a Christmas grotto for the man who she feared was used to far more sophisticated efforts than her own, she couldn't. In fact, Charlotte was in no doubt that Nadia would have employed an interior designer so that Vinny would come home to a picture-perfect Christmas wonderland like Santa's Lapland crib – her with not a bead of sweat or hair out of place or broken nail in sight (unlike Charlotte who had all three, not to mention a lump of crust in the corner of her eye and legs which could have been mistaken for a pair of cacti). Perhaps Nadia's Christmases were clinical and harsh – a black Christmas tree with built-in lights and only purple bobbles in keeping with the décor, she smiled smarmily to herself. Not this year, though – it would be real and warm and homely and magical.

But she couldn't turn Mrs Dickson away, even if it meant things weren't as perfect for him as she would have liked. Charlotte wiped her sleeve across her forehead and straightened her felt antlers. 'Would you like a cuppa?'

Mrs Dickson waved her hands, showering the floor with even more flakes which melted and merged into tiny puddles. 'Not at all dear. You get on. Just wanted to say, if you need anything, just give me a phone or text and I'll be right over.'

'Will do,' Charlotte smiled, already walking her to the door. 'Thank you for dropping by. We still good for Boxing Day?'

'Oh, yes dear. Mr Dickson has even looked out his *Wallace and Forbes* tartan troosers! He's not had them on for near 20 years. I'm in the middle of taking the waist out!' Mrs Dickson cried, mushrooming her hood over her curls. 'See you then.'

'See you then!' Charlotte called after her, but she'd already been consumed by the blizzard. She closed the door, blew out her cheeks and pressed play on the CD player.

When she finished pinning the last section, she stepped down carefully. Her hand traced along the length of the wire until she found the plug which she thrust into a cube socket already jammed into an over-burdened extension lead. Tucking it behind the dresser before Vinny flipped again, Charlotte dashed to the far end of the room, turned off the harsher ceiling light and turned to admire the soft twinkling of the dangling icicles, the roaring fire, the sparkly tree. 'There,' she breezed, her hands cupping the small of her back, her stomach protruding. 'Perfect.'

Right on cue, her phone pinged.

On my way baby. Love you. xxx

Brilliant, she thought to herself. Just time for a bath to sort her legs out.

Be safe! The snow is crazy here. Love you so much. Xxx

It was followed by three kissy emojis.

After hearing the message launch with a whoosh, she tapped the phone against her lips and admired her handiwork a while longer. That is, until the door knock interrupted her moment…*again*.

'Bloody hell, Mrs Dickson,' Charlotte murmured as she dashed to open it, her face fixing into a confused smile when she saw it wasn't her.

Chapter Forty-Eight

'Mr Miller?'

'Hello, Charlotte,' he yelled over the snowstorm, a hand shielding his eyes. There was a foil gift bag in his hand, the head of a golden teddy bear poking out like it had a bad case of dandruff.

It took a few seconds for her to recognize him in another setting, especially in his blue jeans and contacts. Then she remembered her manners. 'Come in. Come in!' she cried, opening the door wider.

He ducked under the threshold, shedding his coat as Charlotte shouldered the door closed. He grimaced apologetically as he handed it to her, more snow falling in bigger clumps to the floor.

Charlotte laughed lightly and hung it on the stand. 'Please, have a seat. Can I get you a drink?'

Both feet stamped heavily on the welcome mat, leaving cuboids of compressed snow from the long, straight treads of his boots before he stepped further into the room, his eyes sweeping appreciatively around the picture-perfect Christmas scene. 'No thank you, Charlotte. It's just a flying visit. Just wanted to drop these off. The staff at the nick chipped in and got you a leaving gift. Got a little something for the twins too.' He held out the bag with his usual warm chuckle.

Charlotte reached for it but felt the chill of his words cut her to the bone. 'But how…?' The bag remained mid-air, her smile dwindling as she watched him walk across the room, minus a stick or a limp for that matter.

'How did I know you were having twins?' He laughed again before making himself comfortable on her granny's rocker by the fire. 'Oh, you'd be surprised what I know Charlotte.'

If he'd have said it in the prison, she would have taken it light-heartedly. Yet here, where there was no files or cabinets or noticeboards, she knew there was no jest behind his sentiment. Adam did something similar when she went through her 'rebellious' stage. He told her to be in by 10. She insisted 11. 'That's fine. Do it your way Charlotte,' he'd shrugged and then he went on writing his paper on *Mens Rea and Intent*. There was no threat in his words either, but she was home for 9.30.

Easing the antlers from her head, the gripping panic caused a trickle of pee to warm her new size 12 *M & S* knickers. Although her feet couldn't move, her eyes fleeted to the door, to the window, to the kitchen. *Just run!*

Like he knew her every thought, Frank Miller pulled the gun from the back of his jeans and waved it loosely at her, his smile gone. 'Take a seat Charlotte and we can have a nice wee chat to fill the time till your Vinny is home.' He leaned over and patted the chair opposite him in such a friendly manner, the gesture was all the more disturbing.

Vinny nudged the wipers up to full, but the road ahead was swallowed into the whiteout, his eyes blinking against the bullet of fat snowflakes firing against him, the cars relying on the red lights in front to find their way, the road markings long since wishful thinking. Only a few miles from home, he noticed the urgent flashing blue lights of the emergency services zig-zagged across the road a few hundred metres in front of him.

The 4 x 4 slowed to a crawl and Vinny watched each car reach the barricade before being rejected and waved to turn around in the opposite direction. 'Oh, fucking hell,' he blazed as the window hummed open when he reached the officer. 'What's going on?'

'Jack-knifed lorry, sir,' the PC yelled over the roaring wind and snow, holding on to his hat, his eyes mere slits. 'Road completely blocked. You're going to have to turn back.'

Vinny's finger tapped restlessly against the steering wheel. 'I can't! My fiancée,' (he presumed it would be a yes), 'is at home only a few miles up the road. She's pregnant with twins.'

'Sorry sir,' he gulped against another gust. 'There is no way you can get through. You're going to have to turn around and drive the other way around the loch.'

There was no point in arguing as he considered whether it would be quicker to dump the car and walk. When he watched the officer lose his footing and grasp the wing mirror to save himself from sliding on to his arse (even in his chunky boots), he knew he had no choice. 'Ah, for fuck's sake!' Vinny spat as he jerked his steering wheel sharply left to join the cars queuing in the other direction.

A supernatural shade of pale, Charlotte sat across from Mr Miller, him looking like he was going to read her a *Jackanory* story. All that was missing was his pipe and slippers.

'Don't look so scared, Charlotte,' he said with such a smug expression of *I know something you don't know* that Charlotte knew he was enjoying himself.

'I'm not,' she lied, her heart battering too fast against her chest, saliva dehydrating to white in the crooks of her mouth. *Don't show your fear.* She quickly licked her lips. 'I see your leg has miraculously recovered.'

He winked, bending and straightening it a few times to show her just how limber it was. 'Had it fixed years ago but didn't want anyone questioning how I paid for it. When will Vinny be back? It's him I'm really here to see after all.'

Vinny. God.

'I don't know what you mean.'

'Please Charlotte! Do you think we don't know about you and Vinny? After that meeting! Been keeping an eye on you two ever since. Dolan's a clever man, see. And when you two got together, it was like he'd won the lottery. At first, he thought he could literally kill two birds with one stone. You, because you knew too much already and him…well, because he is the best prosecution lawyer in the UK. And then you set up nest.' He looked around said nest and nodded in approval. 'He wanted to sell it as a burglary gone wrong. Very easy. Until Sullivan got caught at the last hurdle.'

Sullivan? Sullivan was coming here…to get us? She felt a white sweat wash over her, just like the time she tried one of Adam's *DO NOT TOUCH CHARLOTTE OR ELSE!!!!!* labelled special brownies.

'But I like you Charlotte. I didn't want that for you, so I think it was a good thing really. I nagged and nagged Dolan to let you be at least. He was still swaying when one of our men got to overhear your joy that you had a bun in the oven. Not one, but two! Am a right you went for a wee coffee at the *Costa* on Byres Road afterwards? He said it was very touching, how you two huddled over the scan photo, all jolly. How gobsmacked you were that there were two blobs! What was it you said? How it was one of each? How you laughed that you would need two of everything? Including another set of nipples?'

Right, I get the bloody picture.

'That's when I had an idea. No-one needed to get hurt because Vinny wouldn't want a little hair harmed on your head. Would do anything to save you and the bairns. Would sway a case…'

Charlotte felt her heart kick and drop as it lost any sense of rhythm.

'So, Charlotte, when will Vinny be home?'

The phone lay hard and flat in her back pocket. If she could just slide her hand…'I don't know,' she shrugged and shuffled to an angle, trying to glide her hand naturally down her side. 'The weather is bad,' she said, sliding it back another inch.

'Just leave your hands where I can see them. Phone, please,' he ordered brightly like he was asking her for a cuppa like he used to do in the office.

Her chest inflated, Charlotte pulled it out and tossed it on the coffee table bridging the side of them where it lay halfway, a sign that she wasn't completely giving him control. Unphased, he sat back, just plain ignoring the gesture.

'So?' she said, her mind trying to piece together the situation and, most crucially, what was going to happen next. Charlotte had been trained for such circumstances. Hostage situations. But every skill, every negotiation technique she had been taught remained a mystery and she found she was going on with nothing more than instinct. But a protective mother's instinct, nonetheless, which warned her to keep calm and think. *Let him think he is in control until you are.*

Miller bent down and, lifting some logs from the brass bucket, stoked the fire. Like her ally, it appeared to spit and sizzle in protest. That small gesture felt completely invasive, along with every other which made him at home in *her* home. Like he was physically invading her, stroking her with every rock of the chair, caressing her with every examination of the crackle-glaze vase she had made on the shelf beside him. An infesting crawl itched over her skin.

'Not much to say really. I've worked with Dolan for many a year. Helped plump up that pension pot we were talking about.' His curiosity moved to the scan photo. That felt like his hands around her throat.

Charlotte pulled gently at the neck of her t-shirt to choke out the words. 'You mean worked *for*, another lackey.' Awaiting his reaction, she bit at another already ragged nail. It wasn't much, but she would not let him claim his glory status. She wasn't afraid to let him know exactly what he was.

He shrugged indifferently and nudged the scan image to an angle which suited him better. 'You say potato, I say potahto. Anyway, business was going smoothly until bloody Audrey pulled a blinder. Stupid lassie.' He shook his head.

Her nails dug into the heavy woven cotton of the chair. 'What do you mean?'

'Throwing Dolan under the bus. Standing against him in court. We can't have that Charlotte.' He smoothed a hand down the front of his Christmas sweater, the sleigh bell on top of an elf's hat tinkling merrily. Seems she wasn't the only one he was deceiving since he looked like he was on his way to a Christmas party.

Her eyes tapered. 'I don't get it. Why didn't she mention you? She spoke up about everyone else. And why did she bring in another batch when you knew the police were on to her?'

'Ha!'

Charlotte reeled backwards.

'She didn't *know* about me. Christ, no-one did. I had to laugh, none of you even cottoned on at the meeting when Dolan called – right under your noses! But her, she was only an errand girl. Nothing more. The less she knew about the big boys' work, the better. And, why not get in a few more batches while we could? Before we had to train someone else? She was…dispensable.'

'*Groom* someone else, you mean.' Charlotte dabbed a few bits of glitter from her leggings.

'Well, once *you'd* identified her, her cards were marked anyway, and since she knew nothing about me – win, win. Well, that is until she grassed up Dolan. Nobody saw that one coming. I mean, I don't know how Vinny pulled the whole witness protection thing! For her? And now we can't find her, and believe me we've tried, we need to explore other avenues…'

Charlotte remembered how wrong she had gotten Vinny when they'd first met, how she mistook his confidence and focus for arrogance and conceit - how she knew now a kinder, more caring soul she could never find. Shit - Frank Miller was the role reversal!

'W-Well, you can't stop it. She's already made a statement even if she doesn't take the stand.'

As if he were agreeing with her, he pointed his gun back and forth, forming a link tying them to the same side. 'And that's where our friend Vinny comes in, isn't it? I mean, I'm sure he can make some kind of mistake in court? Offer us a loophole in exchange?'

She tried to hide her gulp. 'In exchange for what?'

'*Your* safety. *Your* unborn babies' lives. A peaceful life here.' He swept the gun around the room before aiming it at her once more. 'No looking over your shoulders ever again. Because, believe me, if he doesn't come up with something, I cannot be responsible for what will happen. But I know Dolan…and it won't be good.'

Bastard, she thought, her teeth gritted so tight she began to understand how lockjaw must feel. It hurt when she prised them apart to snipe, 'Well, I think we'll take our chances. Vinny is a good man. He's not *bent* like you.'

Miller lunged forwards and struck her hard and quick across the face, blood from her nose and mouth splattering the fireplace stone, the sting crushing her eyes closed. Partly because she was stunned, mostly because she didn't want to give him the satisfaction, Charlotte didn't make a sound.

'Maybe I need to show him how serious we are then,' he said, rubbing his hand as if it hurt him more than her. 'It's my life on the line as well here, Charlotte! Now you know about me. I can't leave any loose ends, not after toiling for years in that fucking hell hole. I'm nearly free. You're not taking that from me Charlotte.'

She wiped the tears and blood from her chin, and looking at the deep scarlet smear across her sleeve asked, 'Why? Why are you involved in all this shit?' Was any part of him in there? The man who had been like a father-figure to her? The thought that there wasn't hurt more than her nose, which, after running her finger gingerly down it, felt kinked in the middle.

'I grew up with Dolan. We were neighbours, went to school together. He was a mate. He explained what he wanted. To turn a blind eye. To lead any suspicion in another direction. To tell him when it was safe to get the stuff in and when not, when the heat was on. I laughed it off for years, put it down to drunken banter. But things changed, the prison changed, and my knee was so bad… I would have done anything to stop the pain of it.' He sighed and decided to be straight for once. 'And…I was fed-up!' He began to wave the gun, much like her and spoons when she got going. 'Just scraping by. And for what? A fortnight in the Med once a year and a fucking four-bedded semi in Coatbridge! A lifetime's work for that?' Miller shook his head as he finished justifying himself. 'It was easier than I thought. We weren't killing anyone, Charlotte.'

Violins please? Her face hardened. '*You* killed Amos.'

He held up his hands, the gun picking up the warm glow of the fire and the twinkling lights behind her. 'Not guilty. That was unfortunate, I admit. Gary was a stupid wee shite for that one. In fact, Amos was the worst person it could have happened to! His son Perry *works* for Dolan in HMP Langford and we were supposed to keep an eye on his dad in return. Had to do a bit of damage limitation there but he doesn't suspect a thing.'

342

Nooooo! Surely not? Amos said Perry was good. Had only made one stupid mistake, like him. That he still had hope for him too. God, poor Amos. He'd turn in his grave if he knew. Just the thought of it stoked her fury, like his death was even more in vain.

As if in reply to her confusion, he explained, 'Between you and me, Perry was an unfortunate too.' He shook his head as if he had the ability to feel compassion. 'See Dolan kind of set him up. Grassed him up when he was delivering a shipment of his own bloody drugs! But he needed more people on the inside. And although Perry had been out the game for ages, his Mrs got him into a spot of bother, and he needed to make a quick buck. No such thing when you're working with Dolan though.'

Charlotte's accent didn't slip this time, not when she wanted him to feel every sharpened phoneme of her words. 'What about everyone else? That shite is crippling the place. You're taking away people's chances to turn their lives around, to become a better person. Isn't that the whole point of prison? A lot of them are just stupid bloody kids, made a stupid mistake. Your job is to help them turn things back around, to help them become a productive member of society. But *you...* you're practically sentencing them to death!'

'Oh, Charlotte.' His elbows perched on his knees, letting the gun dangle floppily from his hand.

Charlotte never moved her eyes from it, gauging every opportunity for her moment. But this wasn't it.

'You are a good kid. I used to be like you. Keen and not pissed-off with the lot of it. Do you realize how many lives I busted my ass for, to turn them round, wave them out the door to their new 'clean' life only to watch them walk back in two months later? If you stayed long enough, you'd realize there was no point.'

She tried to stem the flow from her nose with a fresh strip of sleeve. 'No, Frank. I don't believe that.'

'Then we'll agree to disagree. When I got to that stage, that's when I started working with Dolan. I had to get out. I couldn't stand it anymore. I still need to get my two through university. That would have seen me there another seven years at least. Now, I can put them through uni and not have to worry about the future. I deserve that.'

Charlotte sniggered. He deserved nothing, except to be locked up with those he had failed to protect. Those he'd let down. She lifted her chin to him, the blood still dripping down it and onto the iced dumpling covering her bump on her *Mummy's Christmas Pudding* t-shirt. 'Let's hope none of them go through an experimental drug phase then! I mean, you know how kids like to dabble. Would you just lock them up and throw away the key too?' Her nostrils bled and flared at the same time.

'Careful Charlotte,' he warned. 'I mean,' he paused to look at her like she was the mad one, 'do you *really* think ours is the only prison this happens in? That if we stopped, the problem would stop? That's just being naïve, Charlotte and you know it.'

Her face had begun to blaze as the pain ebbed through her cheekbones. 'I don't doubt you're right. But it doesn't make me think any higher of you, Frank. In fact, I don't think I've ever had a lower opinion of someone. I mean, you're always going to get your Dolan's.' She tried to hex him, but her eyes were too swollen. 'But you're a rarer breed. People *trusted* you Frank. Can't get much lower than that.' She ran her tongue lightly over her swollen lip, tasting the salty metallic tang of blood and prepared for the backlash.

Vinny pressed the green phone button on the dash – Charlotte's number at the top of his redial list. He sighed when it went straight to answer phone, the signal at the croft mediocre at the best of times.

'Hi baby. It's just me. There's been an accident and I've been diverted round the other side of the loch. Didn't want you worrying. Call me back when you get a signal. I should only be another, oh,' he checked the time on his *Breitling*, 'twenty minutes or so. Love you,' he smiled and hung up, eyeing the fancy ribbon-tied velvet box on the passenger seat.

Almost with a festive charm, the message tolled, and her heart ripped in two. Both sets of eyes fell to the phone. His face lighting up, Miller shook the gun towards the sofa, but she couldn't move such was the fear which paralyzed her. He helped her along, scrunching the hair at the back of her neck and yanking her to her feet. She cried this time, her hands clutching at the roots until he released his grip to push her where he wanted her. Much to her horror, he squeezed in beside her. Unable to look at him never mind have him touch her skin, she leant away and faced the flames, watching them spit a swarm of orange sparks as the logs took.

'Let's get a bit more comfortable Charlotte,' he said, panting from the effort or maybe it was the thrill? 'Unlock your phone and let's see what Vinny has to say then.'

Charlotte griped when her blood-covered thumb couldn't open the phone and her mind went blank when she tried to think of the passcode so long had it been since she had used it. *Why did Vinny get me this bloody thing!* It wouldn't have been a problem with her old phone where she only needed to press the star button for a few seconds. Miller laid his hand on her thigh and squeezed gently in a way she would only allow Vinny too. Not giving a shit about his gun, Charlotte swiped his hand away, typed in 1234 and they listened intently to Vinny's words and Charlotte thought of him, oblivious and beautiful – her everything. After the message played, Charlotte turned to him, the bile rising to her throat and charring her words. It was time to beg. '*Please*, Frank. Don't hurt him.'

He looked her square in her watery eyes and gave his solemn vow. 'I don't plan to Charlotte. You'll be the one getting hurt if he doesn't come up with a plan.'

That would have been a relief if it weren't for the lives she carried inside her. Charlotte decided then that she was going to kill him. It was as easy as deciding they were having duck this year for Christmas dinner instead of turkey.

Miller thrust the phone at her. 'Text him back. Say the signal is poor and that you're fine. Then the love you and kisses *blah! blah!* at the end.' He leaned in too close (so much so that she could smell the stale alcohol of last night), watching as she typed just what he had narrated. Charlotte felt the tip of the gun push into the bottom of her stomach when her hands fidgeted and paused.

Trembling now, she handed him back the phone and whined when he called her a, 'Good girl,' and put his hand around her shoulder, keeping the tip of the pistol hard against her bump. She had to warn Vinny. Get him to get help *before* he got home.

Vinny smiled when he saw the message flash up on the screen on the dash.

ALL GOOD HERE. NO SIGNAL. SNOW NOT HELPING! HOPE YOU GET THIS. COME BACK SAFE BABY. LOVE YOU. X

Then the thought struck him. *Odd*, he mused. Why the capitals? And Charlotte always signed off with three kisses and three kissing emojis now that her phone was technically advanced enough to do so. The pessimist in him of late made him question it. Was she okay? Puffing his cheeks, he checked the road ahead and overtook the line of dilly-dallying drivers in front of him.

The grandfather clock marked off every painful second to the trap. With each lost tick, her lip became weaker, her t-shirt stickier from the blood still streaming from her nose. Without moving her head, her eyes scaled the room, searching for anything, something. She pushed herself back, back an inch away from the gun. But as she did, a hand slipped down the side of the sofa, grazing something cold and metal and sharp - the most beautiful thing she had ever touched apart from Vinny and her bump. She eased her hand down further until she was able to coil her fingers round the handle.

Thick white flakes clumping on his face, Vinny jumped out to unlock the access, noticing fresh foot treads around the gatepost. *Too large for a lady. Mr Dickson? But they said they were staying in...would look after Charlotte.* Feeling like the snow had seeped to his bones, Vinny flew in the car, snuffed the lights and dulled the engine until he was coasting soundlessly down the bends and dips to the croft.

The car crunched to a stop before the last crook. Vinny stepped out, easing the door over without closing it. In hushed, tentative steps, he edged his way towards the front door, a new handmade wreath of willow and holly hung around the wrought iron knocker, an unfamiliar sleek *BMW M3* parked at the far end of the drive. Ragged pants clouded the air as he grazed his shoulders along the rough cast wall until he was at the brink of the wonky window. Only his nose edged over the blistered frame, but it was enough. Enough to see Frank Miller's back to him, Charlottes beautiful hair, her face obscured, a fancy gift bag on the table in front of them. He slouched under the porch light and set his hand against the wall to steady his shaking legs. His shoulders shuddered a relieved laugh as he muttered, 'Frank. Frank bloody Miller.'

He threw the door open, feeling like the luckiest man on the face of the planet. 'Hello! Great to see you Frank!'

His world stopped turning when he strode forward and saw Charlotte's blackening eyes, the blood, the gun pressed to her stomach. Her eyes wide in horror, she mouthed a silent, 'Sorry,' the blood trickling over her swollen lips.

Frank looked up and smiled. 'Lovely to see you, Vinny. Please have a seat.'

Chapter Forty-Nine

Both Vinny's eyes darkened to the same colour of granite. 'I'm only going to say this once, Miller. Take your gun away from her and put it on me. It's me you want after all.'

Miller swerved his eyes to the ceiling and tutted. 'Please, Vinny. Let's not be too dramatic. I'm a civil man, and if you do as I ask, no-one gets hurt. Now sit.'

Vinny ground his jaw and perched ever so slowly on the edge of the chair, looking like a panther ready to pounce. He turned towards Charlotte, dismissing Miller's presence. 'Are you all right?'

She swallowed and nodded quickly just as another red trickle ran from her nose and dripped to her lap.

He remained silent and insipid with rage. Molten metal. The exact colour of the crescent moon she been gazing at for the last quarter of an hour since his call, watching as its dimmer switch was cranked slowly from *off* to *on*. Charlotte had spent that time scheming and planning where on Miller's body she was going to plant the blade she still had her knuckles wrapped around.

'Right, you dirty piece of shit, what do you want?'

Miller laughed and stamped one of his good legs against the stone floor. 'Calm yourself, Vinny. I think you know what I want. We have a little problem who goes by the name of Audrey. You see, Audrey needs to stop being a problem for us Vinny. And you are the only man who can make that happen.'

'Fuck!' he roared and slapped a hand to his chest. 'And you think I can do that? How?'

'Come on, Vinny. You're a clever man. I'm sure you can factor in something that'll help Kate show Audrey's testimony is…flawed?' He perked his shoulders playfully like he was trying to tempt Vinny to join him for a lad's weekend in Prague.

Vinny sniggered a kind of laugh which made even her blood run cold. Charlotte's eyes pleaded, *Be nice. Please be nice. Don't bloody piss him off!*

'Oh, I've no doubt I could. But then what? Then you're free to come back here anytime and finish what you've started?' His knee was jogging quicker than she'd ever seen it and Charlotte clenched her eyes shut to accept Vinny was not going to kowtow to the piece of shit at her side.

Miller gave a mockingly sympathetic one-sided smile. 'Yeah. You're right…that probably will happen, but at least you'll have a head start, a chance. Or even better, maybe Mr Dolan will take a shining to you. May even get you working for him. I can assure you, the pay is good.'

Vinny sat back slowly and rubbed his chin for too long, as if really considering the offer. 'Hm…' He shrugged. 'I'd rather die, thanks all the same.' He said it in all seriousness and Charlotte finally gave in to a sob because he was so earnest, he probably would. She began to edge the knife up from the side of the cushion - slowly, slowly.

Miller leaned forward and returned the gesture. 'Fine. Have it your way. But you *will* do this for us because if you don't, then you leave me no choice but to take Charlotte with me now.'

Vinny slid his eyes to her, noticing hers amplify a signal then slip down to her left hand, the butt of a knife handle protruding from her clenched fist. When she looked back at him, he gave her a long blink of understanding.

He quickly licked his lips. 'All right.' He nodded then nodded again. 'We'll do it your way. Let's talk. But I'll only talk when you drop that gun from her stomach.'

'See!' Miller yelped, and Charlotte cringed as the hand on her shoulder tightened. 'Now you're making sense, Vinny.' He dropped the gun to his lap and pulled his arm from around her (which she helped along way with a disgusted shrug like she'd just put her arm in the spider's web again). 'But I hope you don't mind, I want to bring my friend in from outside. He must be getting cold.'

'Fine,' Vinny answered without as much as a blink. 'We need someone to make the tea.'

Miller pulled his phone from his back pocket and sent a text to his *friend*, giving Vinny a split second to signal with a flat palm for Charlotte to wait. She shuffled in understanding, wiping her nose with one hand, gripping the handle tighter with the other.

Vinny could feel it, the heavy cylinder in his pocket: the panic button. Before Miller had chance to push the send button on his text, Vinny had pushed his own button, removing his mobile which had shared the space and placing it on the table as if he was being helpful. But with the road closed, he had to buy them time.

'Good boy, Vinny. Good boy. Go let Mark in please,' he ordered, and Vinny was only happy to oblige, leaving the door the tiniest fraction ajar after the beast entered.

Mark was obviously the brawn of the duo, his knuckles a lot closer to grazing the flags. He stood himself uncomfortably close to Vinny's chair, his hands clasped in front of him. Charlotte glared at his knuckles – *KNOW HOPE* tattooed across them in swirly, cursive script. From the many ways she could have interpreted the message, she grabbed the shaft harder and smirked. If God had ever sent her a sign, that was it.

Vinny glowered at him and asked, 'Does he even speak human?'

Mark merely grunted as he pulled back his coat to reveal the gun strapped to his waste, making the likelihood of that even more remote.

Even Miller tittered. 'Don't poke the bear, Vinny.'

Still sniggering, Vinny drew his eyes away only to spot a set of fingers begin to crawl and curl around the edge of the front door, probing and spiderlike. *What the fuck?* It took everything not to let the arousal of it dilate his pupils and hasten his breath. Instead, he gave a little sniff and thumbed his nose. 'Let's get one thing clear Miller, I'll do it. But I need time to work on it. And,' he added, only then permitting his pupils to amplify, 'Charlotte stays here with me. I need time to dig deeper into Audrey's past to provide her with prompts which are going to make her evidence look untrustworthy but not in an obvious way. You can keep someone here if you like. But there is no way she leaves my side, or I won't do it.'

Miller pulled down his mouth and nodded slowly. 'Okay, that's progress I suppose. I think that might be doable.'

Vinny kept his eyes on Miller as his peripheral vision watched the baseball bat nose its way through the front door too, Rick's familiar lanky frame grasping the end of it. Ever so slowly, the door closed behind him. *How the hell did he get here so quick with the truck blocking the road? Where's everyone else?* Forced into a make or break situation, Vinny felt an upsurge of panic close his throat now his chance to eek things out till more back-up arrived was no longer an option. He fleeted his eyes to the gun resting on Miller's knee, a finger still hooked on the trigger. But at least it was pointing at him now.

'Good. Now…' Vinny declared, dropping his hand to the side of his leg nearest the fire where only Charlotte could see. Three fingers sprang rigid. Her breathing hitched, and he knew she understood. 'I want some guarantees.' One finger curled so only two were left. Charlotte edged the knife from the side of the sofa to the side of her leg and twiddled with the dove around her neck, a heavy reminder of what was right and just and good. No-one was ever going to cage her again, or those she loved. She'd rather die along with Vinny. 'We need guarantees. That after all this, we will be left in peace.' Only his index finger remained, and he could see Charlotte's knuckles whiten around the shaft of the knife, Rick's around the bat like he was taking the deciding strike in the *World Series*.

'Vinny, if you get Dolan off, I can guarantee, he will be in your debt. He is a man of his word. But if you fuck it up, Vinny…' His eyebrows perked as he warned, 'Then it's Charlotte's funeral.'

Several things happened at once. Vinny pulled the last of his fingers back to join his fist. It had the effect of a starter pistol. Everyone lunged. But he was quickest as he pounced at the gun on Miller's lap, propelling it and his arm in the air. There was a sickening wallop as Rick let swing and Mark's head whipped to the side, his body felling like a 300-year-old oak. But Miller wasn't for letting go, and in the skirmish, a bullet discharged into one of Charlotte's granny's prized artexed ceiling fans. With a primal roar, Charlotte swung the knife with military precision, and it plunged cleanly into what used to be Miller's bad leg. What would now be his new bad leg. He released the gun as his howl shook every fringed lamp and secondhand frame adorning the small room.

Vinny stared at the gun in his hand. Rick stared at the unmoving body at his feet. Charlotte stared at how white Miller had become and Miller stared at the oddness of having a very large kitchen knife speared erect in his leg. 'You…fucking…bitch!'

Now, instead of staring at the gun, Vinny was pointing it. 'Charlotte,' he said softly, holding out his hand for her but never moving his eyes from Miller. But she could not move, her hands clasping her mouth shut. But when he said her name again and reached for her, she sprung and coiled herself around his back.

He was joined by Rick, now armed with Mark's pistol.

Vinny kept his eyes forward. 'Am I fucking glad to see you! How did you know?'

'I was on duty. Heard about the lorry. Call it intuition, but I just wanted to do a drive by to be sure. The I heard your panic alarm had been depressed.'

At the sound of Rick's voice, Miller's eyes pulled up from his leg and grew even wider. 'Oh, Rick.' His hands gripped tighter around the knife, around the blood turning his blue jeans black. He grimaced in pain then snarled, 'You took your bloody…'

'Vinny!' Rick barked his interruption. 'Take Charlotte. Get out.'

'But where's the back-up and what if *he* wakens?'

'What?' Miller cried, his teeth bared in agony.

'*Now*, Vinny!' Rick's hand had never been steadier, him never more sober.

Vinny looked from one to the other, sensing the recognition. A lot more than from a quick meeting in an office, that was for sure. Sensing that this betrayal was working in his favour, he didn't dare question it. He felt Charlotte tremble, burying her face into his back and tying her hands at his stomach like a terrified spider monkey. *Must get her safe.* There'd be time for questions later. Keeping his eye on Miller, he began edging them towards the door. Still clinging to his back, Charlotte whimpered as they skimmed around the body on the floor, expecting it to reach out and grab her ankle at any moment like a bad American horror movie. All the while, Vinny swung his aim between the still-breathing mound and Miller until they were out the door.

He pulled Charlotte from his back to his side, the snow burning his skin and blinding his eyes. 'Come on, baby!' He tucked the gun into the back of his trousers, gazing towards the Dickson's farmstead. 'We need to run.'

Hand in hand, they took off, skidding and slipping but not stopping for breath until their feet caught grip on the salt-gritted path which led to their front door. They were far enough away to risk a backwards glance then. In the distance, Vinny could make out the blue-flashing train of a police convoy heading along the main road in their direction.

But there was no relief as his lungs burned and gasped for air. 'Come on. Let's get you inside.'

Just then, Mrs Dickson appeared at the door. 'Dears! What in the name of heavens has happened? Come on! Get inside and I'll make you up a nice cheese scone!'

The gun shot shattered across the snowy expanse before they even reached the doorstep.

Chapter Fifty

Three Months Later

Charlotte carefully rolled up the picture and slid it into the cardboard tube. Next was the letter to accompany it. She topped it with a red cap and eyeballed him.

'No Vinny!' she cried, gently tapping the tube against her other hand like a baseball bat. It was a mock threat. 'I veto it.'

'Why? What's the matter with Theo?' Vinny rocked back and forth in his new leather rocker opposite hers, a tongue swirling his cheek as he watched her get pissed at him. Oh, how he loved it when she got pissed at him.

'Jesus! Are you being serious? What's right with it? *Theodore*?!' Her blue irises became small islands in an ocean of white. 'Not a child of mine, I'm afraid.'

Didn't quite go with what they'd chosen for their baby girl – Eve (in a funny way, after Adam).

'All right then.' He couldn't help but chuckle before he landed the punchline. 'Michael.'

She threw her head back and let out a huge snorting laugh. 'Oh, now you are taking the piss! Michael Knight? As in Knight Rider?' Charlotte began to, 'Danananananananana,' the electro theme tune. She dropped her voice, all American and husky as she crept towards him. '*Knight*

Rider. A shadowy light into the dangerous world of a man who does not exist. Michael Knight: a young loner on a crusade to champ…'

'All right! All right! Smart arse. You watched far too much TV as a child.'

'Well,' she said as she waddled the last few steps and sat on his knee, 'Why don't we go the whole hog and call Eve *K.I.T.T* instead? Kit Industries Two Thousand, if I recall correctly?'

'Far too much TV.' Vinny shook his head as he gazed up at her, his hand swirling round what was most definitely now a firm, round bump. He thought back to when he first saw her at the airport, all fingers and thumbs, picking cases instead of packing them. Before then, he would never have believed in such a thing as fate. Yet now, 6 months down the line, he couldn't imagine any other reason why he was put on the Earth.

Charlotte ran her fingers along the lapel of Vinny's chunky knit cardigan, shot with gaping holes where the stitches had been dropped, a present from Mrs Dickson at Christmas. Come to think of it, she couldn't remember the last time she'd even seen a label or embroidered emblem. 'What about…Amos?' Her fingers still stroking, she slid her eyes to his.

'Amos? Amos Knight? Amos and Eve Knight. *Very* biblical.' He pursed his lips and nodded slowly. 'Yeah,' the word oozed from him. 'I think that could work.' The light mood darkened instantly when his phone pinged on the armrest. They looked at each other, the chair stilling. Vinny held the mobile in his hand, his Adam's apple bobbing up and down in anticipation. 'From Rick.'

He never did fill her in about what he knew. There was no need. And she'd been through enough without knowing how very differently things might have panned out that night. He freed a shiver. He'd save that one till the grandkids were out of university.

He turned the screen to Charlotte.

GUILTY

Given everything which had happened, Vinny was more than happy to let Adam take the lead on this case when he'd asked. *Give you two a break*, Adam had said. But Vinny knew it was because Adam was determined to exact his own revenge; he and Charlotte were more alike than either cared to admit. Physically, Adam was fighting fit. But mentally, he needed this. Needed this more than Vinny. Needed to face Dolan head on. And Vinny, he had every faith in him.

Charlotte just stared until the pixels blurred blank.

Vinny stroked her cheek. 'Shall we?'

She nodded slowly then smiled. 'We shall.'

It was only a 10-minute walk to the village post office. A lot easier said than done when you had ankles the same size as your calves.

'So how is the romance of the year going?' Vinny pulled her closer and kissed the top of her green woolly hat.

'God, I had to laugh. Adam said they were going for a weekend at *Centre Parcs! Centre bloody Parcs!* I hope he brings his inhaler!' Charlotte stooped down to pick up a pinecone, then continued, her arm winding back around his waist.

'He'll need it with Lucy. That girl makes the Duracell bunny look lethargic. Anyway, at least he's kept off the cigs. Every cloud and all that.'

'Every cloud,' she repeated as she held up the cone, watching the early Spring sunlight beam through the swollen spores.

'So, I had a word with Father McGuire from St Augustine's in the village. Said he could fit us in this Summer, when double trouble will be here to ruin the honeymoon.'

She snuggled closer to his side, just the thought of each of the things he'd just mentioned causing a fuzzy warmth to flow around her body. 'I heard honeymoons are over-rated anyway. Besides, what better place to honeymoon in the summer than here?' There was nowhere else in the world she wanted to be.

He couldn't agree more. Already the trees were budding, the blackbirds beavering to build their new nests, the daffodils had shot free from their buried bulbs. He couldn't wait to see it unfurl in all its glory. But he wouldn't even mind a weekend in a chintzy Blackpool B & B as long she was at his side.

'I think I might shave my beard for it, you know, the wedding.' He began scratching as if it was suddenly irritating him.

'Yeah, if you like. It's entirely your choice. But there'll be no wedding at all if you do.'

He chortled softly, knowing he had as much choice on the matter as Hobson himself. 'A handle-bar moustache then?' He looked both ways then led her across the quiet country road. 'They're really cool now.' *Prod! Prod! Prod!*

'I am *not* getting married with you looking like a blond Freddy Mercury!'

'*I want to break free...*'

'Vinny!'

'*I want to brrrreeeeeaaaaak frrrreeeeeeeee.*'

'Stop it, Vinny!'

He was still laughing when they reached the low roofed cottages on the outskirts of the village. They waved at Barry, their paperboy, as he passed on a bike which had seen better days. 'What will we have for lunch?'

'Oh, I fancy lasagne from *The Olive Grove*. Some chips too...and garlic bread...a little side salad maybe...'

'How many are you eating for?'

Flicking a V with her right hand and the middle finger on her left, she demonstrated, in true Charlotte Croft style, that she was eating for 3.

Shaking his head disparagingly, his finger lightly tipped the end of her frost-nipped nose. 'To be fair, you're going to need it. Mrs Dickson is cooking later. Stovies, I believe?'

'Oh, God. They're rank. I'm going to get a starter then.' She gazed up at that hairy chin she so loved (and which would be staying) and ran her hand down the front of his scarf. 'Maybe some soup…or fishcakes?'

They stopped at the white-washed store, the flaking red sign squeaking from its rusting hinges in the gentle loch breeze. Vinny inhaled deeply through his nose and looked down at her, the other half of him. 'Are you sure you want to do this?'

Closing her eyes, Charlotte rubbed the silver dove at her chest. This was a no brainer. 'Yes.' She tiptoed and brushed her lips to his. When her *Converse* were flat again, she took out the red-capped tube from the inside of her coat, her finger tracing over the recipient's details again:

Ben Stokes
108 Milton Street
Cambuslang
G20 3RT

.

'Positive.'

Epilogue

Tommy threw his bag on the top bunk, his new home for the foreseeable. 'Aye right. Fuckin' life,' he sighed, knowing it wouldn't be too long till the next appeal. In the meantime, all his men were hunting for Audrey – *the stupid bitch*. Shouldn't be too hard with all the mates he had on the force. He'd kill her himself, but only after he wooed her and gained her trust and only after she went to the police to say she'd lied. Plus, he had all his perks in the meantime. He looked around the claustrophobic room. It could have been a worse.

He clambered up to the top bunk, ditching the pillows to the floor and replacing them with his own – duck feather and down. His legs stretched out, long and lazy, and he stared at the ceiling. His delivery of cigarettes and new phone would be arriving any minute. *Aye*, he smiled to himself, *it could be worse.*

He was still smiling when the four bodies slid into the room, easing the cell door closed behind them. Ben (or Stuart as he was known at HMP Langworthy) strolled by on the landing, whistling a merry tune and turning a blind eye.

Perry gripped the shank in is hand. In two swift moves, he was on the top bunk, on top of Dolan, looking deeply into his fear-glazed eyes, his hand gagging Dolan's mouth whilst the others restrained his thrashing limbs.

When he recognized the grinning face leaning over him, Dolan's body relaxed, his face levelling as he mumbled a *Fuck off* through Perry's fingers. *A joke! A prank!* Perry always was a good laugh.

'Hi ya, mate. Long time, no see! How's business? What?' He pushed harder on Dolan's mouth and angled his ear closer to enjoy how the muffled words became spiked with ire. 'What was that, mate? Sorry, I can't hear you. Never mind. Let me fill you in on what I've been up to. Well, for one, I've kept things tickety-boo in here for you. That's right. Just like you asked. *Nothing you can do now but make the most of it, Perry. I'll look after Mel, Perry. Make sure your old man is taken care of on the inside, Perry. I'll make sure you're set when you get out, Perry.* And I have to say Dolan, you're a man of your word. Mel can't sing your praises enough – how you've set her up in a lovely little semi. A garden – front and back! All paid off. A nice little direct debit every month to take care of the bills and food and clothes for my little Sophia. Very generous of you, Dolan! Thank you.' The sincerity of his words made them even more unnerving.

Dolan stopped struggling now, holding on to Perry's every letter as he tried to decipher what the fuck was going on.

'But you see, Dolan. Here's the thing. A little bird told me that you're the reason I'm in here in the first place. You can imagine my surprise when some good Samaritan put a present on my bed. I thought, *it's not my birthday is it?* And when I popped the red cap from the tube, it contained a lovely *anonymous* letter and a lovely drawing of my dad. You should see it. It really is something.'

Dolan's eyes widened as what might have been 'No! No!' but 'Mmmmm! Mmmmm!' vibrated and tickle against Perry's palm.

'I know! I couldn't believe it myself, but you see, your Audrey gave quite a lot of information for her knew life. And your mate Miller too by all accounts. Well, before…' His fingers gun shaped, he shot them against his temple. 'Bang!'

Dolan suddenly burst into a desperate fit of struggle.

'You see, Audrey said…' Perry pushed harder on his mouth. 'Said you've done this thing quite a bit. Set people up to get them on the inside to do your work. Her included. Quite a list of names she's given to the police by all accounts. But I have to say bravo. Very clever. *Very* clever indeed. I thought you had my back, Dolan. Didn't think you were sticking a knife in it.' He tutted like he was scolding a naughty toddler.

The stifled moans heightened to desperate screams, snot flew from his nose, tears streamed from his eyes.

And Perry just stared, his head pivoting slightly to fully relish how Dolan's face reddened to a deep plum. 'So that leaves us in a bit of a situation, doesn't it Dolan? See the one thing you never thought would happen was that one day you would be in here with me. And me, I've had four fucking years to become king of this hole, ironically, because I was working for you. But you see, none of this lot give two flying fucks about you. They don't even know who you are, thanks to your insistence on confidentiality and how we *wouldn't want anything to happen to your nearest and dearest, would we Perry?*'

'And then, to cap it all off, I hear that it's your shit that killed my Dad? And now, oh this is priceless! I can't wait to tell you this part.' He laughed, his eyes wide and manic. 'A lawyer, I think you know him, Vinny Knight? Well, Mr Knight is coming to see me tomorrow. Said, in the light of Audrey's evidence, I will easily get my conviction quashed. He wants to represent me. Pro-bono. Very kind. Likes to see justice served. A bit like myself, really.'

'And this…' He took his time to rotate the comb which had been sharpened to a razor. 'This is for Amos. *My* father.' Perry's lip curled in appreciation of every quiver and puckered line of terror. He drank it up a little more before adding to the list with each frenzied stab to Dolan's chest. 'For Audrey. For every poor bastard's life you've destroyed. For the four years my daughter hasn't had a dad…'

In the wee small hours, he whistled quietly as he poured himself a coffee laced with cheap Scotch from his tartan flask. To accompany it, he lit a cigarette and cracked the window an inch to blow out a cloud of fumes. Suddenly, he lurched forward to turn up the radio on his dash:

And finally, notorious drugs lord Tommy Dolan has been found dead in his cell at HMP Langworthy. Dolan had recently been found guilty of the 1st degree murder of Jason Carter. Initial reports suggest Mr Dolan had been stabbed. No-one has been arrested in connection with the incident and the investigation continues.

With barely a perceptible twitch of the eye, he took another few long draws before dropping the cigarette into the coffee where it hissed and died. Looking around one last time (even though he knew no-one would come near, not when the heat was on), he got out the car. When he reached the red shutter of Unit 2, he typed the code he knew so well, especially since he had set up all the security himself.

A black *Ford Focus* still suspended over the pit, he clicked the green button to lower it with a dull, lazy hum. The car was quickly reversed and he jumped down to the void, winching up the false floor to reveal the access hatch. He typed in another code, a lid which wouldn't have been out of place on a submarine springing open with a champagne-cork *pop!* He eased it up and dropped down the ladder deftly because he knew the exact distance of every tread, knew the fourth one down was a bit wobbly.

He glared around the fluorescent-lit room, the buzz and clink steadying to an annoying, constant drone. Behind the grilles were the weapons. In the cupboards was what he wanted: the cash, as much as he could carry, some diamonds too in case he ever ran short. They were loaded into two large black holdalls. *No need to be greedy*, he reminded himself. *Greedy gets you caught.*

Both arms weighted down, he sped-walked to the car as fast as his legs would permit, closing the boot with a hefty *clunk!* After another glance around, he jogged back inside, a green can slushing at his side. Everything got a good soaking before he swiped the CCTV files on the computer. He added a few more glugs there for good measure.

When the stench of petrol was enough to make him gag, he turned to give the old place one last look. The end. No boss. No drugs. No collateral to buy with. No evidence he was ever there. The only way he'd ever get a good night's sleep again was to destroy the lot and make sure it would be nigh on impossible to start up again.

Just the very thought of that caused the weight which had burdened him for the last 20 years to lift in an instant. Broken promise after broken promise making his actions all the easier. 'I'll help you out, cuz,' Dolan had said. 'We look after our own,' Dolan had said. 'Sue doesn't need to know,' Dolan had said. *But Dolan was a cunt.* 20 years doing his dirty work to pay off a £1000 gambling debt? Half a life for a bad night at the poker table? But when you were in, you were in and this was his only chance to get out. Besides, he had nothing to lose, not now Sue had left him when it wasn't soil she found in the compost bag in the garden shed.

The whole set up was like a spider's web. All connected. All supporting Dolan's business. Yet some threads never encountering another. Audrey, he knew about. More worryingly, she knew about him. But she also knew he was stuck like her. Spider prey. They'd shared that wary look many a time. *I don't want to do this. I don't want to do this, and I'm scared.* God, she was only a bloody kid and he tried, *really* tried. Had even given her an address of an old mate who lived in a remote cottage in the Borders, a good sort who owed him a favour. But Dolan got to her before she'd even had chance to check the train timetable at Glasgow Central. Maybe that's why she never grassed him up. Maybe that's why she gave the names of the 6 prisoners who had been set up for business purposes, just like her. But he knew some of those prisoners, knew Perry. And he knew they would sing like a canary when they had their chance for freedom. Yet, he smiled as he screwed the lid back on the canister and threw it beside Dolan's chair, his gaffer-taped throne. Because, above all else, he was glad for Audrey. He only wished Amos was there to see it, to see justice for his boy.

But bloody Miller? All that time and he didn't know? Who else didn't he know about? No doubt, there were many more Miller's. Picturing the bullet between Miller's eyes, knowing it was Rick who'd put it there, his smile grew wider. Even after all these years, he was still haunted by Dolan's lowest ever blow. 'You help me out Rick, just every now and again, and I'll pay for that Proton Therapy your son needs abroad.' Latest he'd heard, Rick had taken early retirement (because of the PTSD) but with a full pension and commendation for his brave actions, nonetheless. Yeah, Rick deserved his revenge all right. Just like Audrey. Just like him.

Still, even if the prisoners didn't give him up, it would only be a matter of time before some smart-arsed, pube-bearded rookie on the fast track Graduate Recruitment Program joined the dots. He could already feel his silk thread tremble as the whole web began to unravel. Too many loose ends for him to tie up, that's for sure.

Jim lit another cig as he revved the engine and tugged the stick into gear. 'Good fucking riddance,' he spat as he threw the butt and watched a river of flames course into the garage. He turned up his *Elvis* playlist and waited to make sure it had taken. When he felt the flames begin to scorch his cheek, his boot eased off the clutch. 'Las Vegas, here I come, baby!'

Acknowledgements

Firstly, I want to give my forever gratitude to Julie DL for reminding me I too have wings. A huge thank you to my Bernie – for always being there and for being the best friend a girl could ask for. A massive thanks to the lovely Sue – perhaps a new career in editing beckons? Jackie P – you're a legend! Thank you for your time, support and kind words. As always, Wes, thank you for helping me ride the rapids…and for the marketing! Of course, can't forget the crazy crew: Granny Sal, Wee Jimmy, Tazer, Dez, Baby Lamb and Mossop - love you all so much. Miss you always. To my big, beautiful boy - thank you for making me smile every day. And last, but by no means least, thank you Jonny: for believing in me, and more importantly, for having the patience of a saint!

Author Page

JD Horner was born and bred in Glasgow but has lived in Greater Manchester with her husband for nearly 20 years. She taught in Salford for most of that time before leaving recently to concentrate on looking after her foster family. It was then she started writing - and she's been hooked ever since.

Facebook @JDHornerofficial

Twitter @jd_horner

Author Central: amazon.com/author/jdhorner

Printed in Poland
by Amazon Fulfillment
Poland Sp. z o.o., Wrocław